A WOMAN'S PLACE . . .

As much as Hannah loved her children, they could not fill that empty corner of her heart left by their father's indifference. "I can't force Reiver to love me. I must make the best of what I have."

Samuel withdrew his hand. "That's settling. No one should have to settle. Life should be lived to the fullest and savored like a sumptuous feast."

"Fine for you to say, Sam Shaw. You're a man. Women have to settle. They have no other choice."

"And what would you do if you did have a choice?"

Hannah cut her sewing thread with her teeth. "I'm a practical woman. It's futile to engage in daydreams."

"Hannah, Hannah . . ." he said softly. "You're not as practical as you think you are. I just have to look into your eyes to know that love does matter to you."

She said nothing because she feared he was right.

Diamond Books by Lindsay Chase

THE OATH
THE VOW

The VOW

LINDSAY CHASE

DIAMOND BOOKS, NEW YORK

This book is a Diamond original edition, and has never
been previously published.

THE VOW

A Diamond Book / published by arrangement with
the author

PRINTING HISTORY
Diamond edition / December 1992

ISBN: 1-55773-822-X

Diamond Books are published by The Berkley Publishing Group,
200 Madison Avenue, New York, New York 10016.
The name "DIAMOND" and its logo are trademarks
belonging to Charter Communications, Inc.

PRINTED IN THE UNITED STATES OF AMERICA

10   9   8   7   6   5   4   3   2   1

AUTHOR'S NOTE

Cheney Brothers of Manchester, Connecticut, was the oldest, family-owned silk manufacturing company in the United States. Founded by five brothers in 1840, the company survived until 1983.

Although the Cheney family's history provided me with valuable information about Connecticut's silk industry in the nineteenth century, *The Vow* is a work of fiction and not intended to be an account of the Cheney family.

For providing me with additional research materials, I would like to thank the staffs of the Lucy Robbins Welles Library and the Connecticut Historical Society, and Dr. John F. Sutherland, professor of history, Manchester Community College.

The VOW

CHAPTER
❧ 1 ❧

IF he succeeded, he would make a fortune. If he failed, everyone in Coldwater would say, "What else could you expect of Rummy Shaw's son?"

Reiver Shaw listened to his silkworms feeding, the sound as loud as the drumming of rain against a tin roof, and smiled to himself. He would succeed where so many others had failed. He had to.

Blackest night still pressed against the rearing shed's windows, the only illumination coming from several oil lamps hanging from the ceiling. Below stood row upon row of shallow trays, all filled with thousands of ravenous white silkworms, eating, eating, eating fresh leaves from the *Morus multicaulis*—the mulberry tree.

"Don't you ever get tired?" Reiver took care not to touch them as he fed the greedy little bastards even more from the basket he rested against his hip. "If you stopped eating, I could get some sleep."

But even as exhaustion made him giddy and light-headed, he knew he wouldn't stop until he had to. One day these ugly, squirming creatures were going to spin delicate golden threads of silk and make him the wealthiest man in Coldwater, Connecticut.

When his basket was empty, he went over to yet another and dumped its contents on a table and sifted carefully through the glossy green leaves, discarding those that weren't perfect and coarsely chopping the rest as if he were a master chef preparing a meal for a king.

The sound of a door slowly opening caused Reiver to look

up. Twenty-two-year-old James, his youngest brother, stood framed by the doorjamb, a lock of straight brown hair falling in a slant across his forehead, his heavy eyelids drooping. His grease-stained fingers held a broken gear as lovingly as he would a mistress, if he had one.

"Close the damn door," Reiver hissed. "A draft will upset them."

Annoyance flared briefly in James's eyes, then he shut the door with exaggerated care. "Don't worry, Reiver. I won't harm your precious worms."

"See that you don't," he said without looking up. He moved to another tray and spread out more leaves, making sure that he didn't miss a single worm.

"I have a stake in the success of Shaw Silks, too, you know," James said. "I keep the looms running, and Samuel has lent you money to keep Shaw Silks afloat on more than one occasion."

Samuel, the middle Shaw brother, was a successful artist who sold engravings of demure young ladies and pastoral scenes to lithographers for three hundred dollars apiece, an obscene sum in Reiver's opinion.

Reiver made no comment, but as much as he hated to admit it, he knew that James spoke the truth. Without Samuel's generosity and James's mechanical wizardry, Shaw Silks would sink into oblivion like so many other silk mills before this year of 1840 ended. But Reiver was so obsessed with the silk mill—his silk mill—that the thought of entrusting the care of his precious worms to anyone else rankled.

James said, "Go back to the house and get some sleep. I promise not to let the worms starve."

Reiver was about to growl some retort when another wave of light-headedness washed over him, causing the room to teeter ominously from side to side. He realized then that if he didn't do as James said, he risked collapsing into the trays and crushing the worms himself.

He sighed in capitulation. "I'll go, but I want you to wash your hands before you handle the leaves. And if they're not fresh, go out and pick some right off the bushes. The worms won't eat them if they're wilted."

James gave him an exasperated look. "Don't worry. They'll all still be alive when you come back."

"See that they are, or I'll have your hide." Reiver carefully opened the door, slid through the crack, and left.

The moment he stepped out into the cool morning air, he breathed deeply to clear his head. The eastern sky had already turned the pale gray of ashes with the coming dawn, enabling Reiver to notice that a heavy dew coated the grass.

He almost turned back to tell James to remember to dry the mulberry leaves before he fed them to the worms, then thought better of it. James knew that.

He strode away from the rearing shed, pausing only at the top of Mulberry Hill to survey the long rows of bushes flourishing there.

Reiver smiled. There were few places in the United States where the soil and climate were suited to growing mulberry trees, the silkworms' only food source, and Connecticut was one of them. There were even fewer men who envisioned a flourishing American silk industry that would produce cloth to rival the finest from France and Italy.

He looked beyond Mulberry Hill. "Someday I'll own this town."

The town he wanted to own still slept. Coldwater's central green stood deserted, with no boys chasing hoops or stray dogs across its length, and no farm wagons raising dust as they lumbered down the street on their way to market. The clapboard shops and houses, as sturdy and enduring as the Yankees who built and inhabited them, remained dark and hushed, with not so much as a light shining in an upstairs window. Even the bell in the tall white church spire breaking through the treetops waited to greet the day.

Stifling a yawn, Reiver turned and headed for home.

Hannah Whitby stared out over the endless sea of green tobacco shimmering like a mirage beneath the cloudless, hot blue sky of a Connecticut August. Her eyes stung with sweat and tears of frustration. She would never pick ten bushels of tobacco before early afternoon. Never. Later Uncle Ezra's new wife would shriek at her like a Gloucester fishwife and send her to bed without her supper as she had last night. Or she might let one of her sons beat Hannah.

Nate Fisher, the eldest, would enjoy that.

Hannah shuddered and tried to breathe deeply, fighting against the dizziness that had been plaguing her all morning, but the relentless whalebone stays permitted only a shallow breath. As much as she longed to loosen them, she couldn't un-button her gray homespun dress in the open where her uncle's stepsons might come upon her. She finally made herself a little more comfortable by rolling up her long sleeves, past caring that the merciless sun would soon bake her soft white arms as brown and leathery as a field hand's.

"That's what you are now, Hannah Whitby, a common field hand," she muttered, "not a Boston gentlewoman. Life's dealt you a hard blow, but you'll accept your fate, if you know what's good for you."

Determined to avoid a beating, she bent her aching back to the hated task and tried to work faster. Without warning, the sickness welled up inside her. Hannah staggered on shaking knees over to the low dry-stone wall running the length of the field and sat down, fighting to keep from fainting.

The clopping of hooves distracted her. She looked up and saw a sleek bay horse pulling a wagon down the wide dirt road that ran past the field.

When the driver halted beside her, Hannah saw that it was her uncle's neighbor, Reiver Shaw. Even though she had been living in Coldwater for only six months, since February of 1840, Hannah felt as though she knew all about this man. Uncle Ezra talked about Shaw often enough, ridiculing his grandiose plans to manufacture silk.

Shaw looked down at Hannah from his high seat. "Are you all right, miss?" he asked, his voice deep and resonant.

Hannah rose and regarded him from under the rim of her poke bonnet. Shaw wasn't at all good-looking, for his nose was too prominent and his jaw too long and wide. But his face had a warmth and vitality that was quite compelling, and his blue eyes sparkled with enthusiasm and determination. In his white shirt open at the neck, faded trousers, and scuffed black boots, he resembled a farmer more than a mill owner.

"I felt light-headed for a moment," she explained.

"It's no wonder. You must be mad to pick tobacco on a day like today. Why aren't you home, out of the noonday sun?"

"I am here because my uncle wants this tobacco picked," she

replied, reaching for her basket. "And I do as I am told," she added sarcastically.

Shaw scanned the field. "If he is so desperate to have his crop harvested, why isn't he out there as well, with his three stepsons? Those strapping boys are more suited to the work than"—his gaze flicked over her—"a slip of a girl."

Hannah felt her cheeks grow warm from Shaw's frank appraisal. She shrugged. "My uncle's word is law."

"I take it your uncle is Ezra Bickford?"

"Yes."

"Then you must be Hannah Whitby, from Boston."

"I am. And you must be Mr. Shaw, Uncle Ezra's neighbor."

He grinned, transferred the reins to his left hand, and tipped his wide-brimmed straw hat with his right, revealing hair as thick and light brown as Hannah's own. "Reiver Shaw, at your service, Miss Whitby." His smile died. "I heard about your parents. I'm sorry."

He sounded as though he meant it, and Hannah felt tears sting her eyes. Both her parents had been killed unexpectedly this winter when their carriage skidded off an icy road, rolled down a steep hill, and crashed into a tree. After the lawyers settled her father's many gambling debts, there was no inheritance to speak of for his treasured only daughter, consigning her to a life of hardship and misery with her only surviving relative.

She thanked Shaw for his sympathy, then added, "If you'll excuse me, I have nine more bushels of tobacco to pick."

Shaw swore under his breath, looped the reins around the wagon's brake, and jumped down. He climbed over the low stone wall effortlessly and strode over to Hannah. "I think you've picked enough tobacco for one day," he said. "I'm taking you home. Now."

Hannah regarded him as if the sun had addled his brains. He wasn't much taller than she, but his broad shoulders and stocky build told her that he was strong enough to tuck her under his arm and carry her off. "I can't go home until I finish picking tobacco," she said, stepping back apace.

Reiver Shaw placed his hands on his hips. "Look at you. You're as white as a sheet and the sweat's pouring off you. You stay out here and you'll die of heat exhaustion in five minutes."

"It'd be preferable to slavery," she muttered, turning away to return to her work.

Shaw took her arm and turned her around to face him. "What's that old skinflint doing to you?"

He works me in the fields until I'm exhausted, Hannah wanted to say. Then his wife makes me work in the house. She calls me lazy and threatens to beat me, and her sons threaten me with worse.

But all she said was, "It's none of your affair, Mr. Shaw. You'll only get us both into trouble if you interfere."

A stubborn glint appeared in the man's eyes. "I'm not afraid of Ezra Bickford."

"Well, I am!" Hannah regretted her impulsive words the moment she blurted them out. Desperate to convince him to leave her alone, she placed a hand on his arm. "I know you mean well, Mr. Shaw, but Uncle Ezra doesn't take kindly to outsiders interfering with his family. You'll do me a much greater kindness if you let me return to my work."

"I'm taking you home. And don't worry about your uncle. I'll deal with him."

Before Hannah could blink, Shaw placed his hand beneath her elbow and urged her forward. When she balked, he gave her a stern look. "I can't leave you here to die, Miss Whitby, whether you want to or not. Now, are you coming with me willingly, or shall I have to carry you?"

One glance at his implacable expression told Hannah that he meant it. She sighed and let him escort her to his waiting wagon.

Reiver prayed this chivalrous act wasn't going to cost him Ezra Bickford's good graces, but he never could resist a pair of wide blue eyes and graceful feminine figure. His brother Samuel always warned him that women would be his downfall.

He glanced across at the puzzling Hannah Whitby. She may have accepted her fate, but she wasn't resigned to it. She sat as far away from him as she could on the wagon seat, her back stiff and straight, her long fingers knotted tightly in her lap as if she were preparing herself for the ordeal to come. She looked straight ahead, so her bonnet's rim hid her face, but Reiver didn't need to look at her to recall its beguiling ivory beauty.

He drove in silence down the dusty, tree-lined road winding its way around Ezra Bickford's land. Reiver knew all his neighbor's property by heart, the several hundred acres of rich tobacco fields, woods, rolling hills, and the land adjacent to Racebrook.

He thought of that Racebrook land with a lust that almost became a physical ache in his groin. He would do anything to get that land.

He glanced over at Hannah again. "You must find Coldwater vastly different from Boston," he said, attempting to draw her into conversation.

"Yes."

That's all she said, leaving Reiver to listen to the clopping of hooves, the rattling of wheels, and the buzzing and thrumming of cicadas on a hot summer day.

Since he was a man who prided himself on his winning ways with women, he tried again. "I'm sure I would prefer being a doctor's daughter to a farmer's niece."

She looked at him, her blue eyes startled. "How did you know my father was a doctor?"

Reiver shrugged. "Coldwater is a small town. When your mother eloped with Dr. Horatio Whitby, it was gossip fodder for years."

"How do you know? That was nineteen years ago. You couldn't have been more than a boy at the time."

"I was only eight years old, but our housekeeper was much older, and she remembered it well." He didn't tell her that according to their housekeeper, most of the townsfolk disliked Hannah's mother because she put on airs and thought herself too good for the likes of Coldwater. "She never came back, did she?"

Hannah's shoulders relaxed a little. "We came for Aunt Ruth's funeral last year, but that was all. Mother never liked Coldwater. She thought it was . . ." Hannah's voice trailed off and she blushed.

"Too sleepy?" Reiver suggested. "Too dull?"

She smiled sheepishly as if he had caught her thinking forbidden thoughts. " 'Provincial' was the word she often used. She may have been born on a farm, but she preferred the liveliness and variety of city life, and I must confess, so do I."

Reiver knew that in Boston Hannah had lived in a fine, large house with an army of servants to cater to her every whim. Here, she was no better than a servant herself. He suspected she endured her altered circumstances by building a wall between herself and the town her mother had hated.

"And what about you, Mr. Shaw?" she asked. "Have you always lived here?"

He nodded. "My two brothers and I were born here and will no doubt die here."

"I've heard that one of your brothers is an artist."

"That's Samuel, my middle brother."

"Is he very good?"

"I suppose he is, but then I've always thought drawing and painting pictures was no occupation for a twenty-five-year-old man. But he often has money when the rest of us don't, so I can't criticize what he does, now, can I?"

Hannah smiled at that.

Reiver added, "My youngest brother, James, likes to build things and take them apart to see how they work. I'm sure he'll be a great inventor someday."

"Perhaps he'll invent machines for your silk mill."

Reiver's brows rose in surprise. So the reserved Miss Whitby hadn't totally removed herself from the goings-on in provincial Coldwater. "Perhaps he will."

The moment he turned the wagon down the drive leading to the Bickfords' house, he felt Hannah stiffen. By the time they halted before the old gambrel-style farmhouse built just after the Revolutionary War, Hannah's face had become a blank, expressionless mask, all the life and warmth drained out of it.

There, sitting beneath the cool shade of a stately oak tree, was Ezra Bickford, sipping apple cider that was undoubtedly as cold as the day was hot.

He was a short man in his early forties, and so gaunt that Reiver wondered if he starved himself just to save a few pennies; he also wondered if Bickford wore such old, well-mended clothes so he wouldn't have to spend the money on new ones.

"Afternoon, Shaw," Bickford said, his small dark eyes on Hannah. Even when he spoke, he doled out words by the teaspoon.

"Bickford." Reiver jumped down and rounded the front of the wagon to help Hannah down.

He grasped her around the narrow waist, waited while she balanced her hands on his shoulders, then swung her down. The moment Hannah's feet touched the ground, her uncle set down his tankard and came sauntering over.

"Why'd you bring the girl home?" Bickford asked in his soft, rasping voice.

"She almost fainted in the field," Reiver replied, treading carefully so as not to antagonize Bickford. "If she stayed there another minute, she'd die of heat prostration. You wouldn't want her death on your hands, would you?"

Bickford hesitated for a moment as if calculating how much money he'd lose if that happened. " 'Course not." He looked at Hannah and nodded toward the house. "Tell Naomi I said you could have some water and rest." He didn't say for how long.

"Thank you, Uncle Ezra," Hannah said politely, but not subserviently. She turned to Reiver. "And thank you for your assistance, Mr. Shaw. It was a pleasure meeting you."

"And it was a pleasure meeting you, Hannah," he replied with a smile. "Be sure to stay out of the sun."

She smiled fleetingly and left.

Bickford watched her disappear into the house, then turned to Reiver. "Don't know what I'm going to do with that girl. Too weak for farm work. Just like my sister."

"Some women are more delicate than others," Reiver said. "Your niece looks like she belongs in a ballroom, not a tobacco field."

Bickford's face registered no emotion. "The girl's got to earn her keep. Like the rest of us. Can't have her lazing around. Like her mother used to."

Reiver thought he detected a note of jealousy and resentment in the other man's flat tone, but he made no comment, just ran his hand down Nellie's glossy bay rump and said casually, "Have you thought any more about selling me the Racebrook land?"

"Thought about it."

"And?"

"Haven't decided."

Old bastard, Reiver thought. He'll keep me dangling for another six months. But all he said was, "You know where to find me when you do."

Bickford nodded, his dark eyes revealing nothing.

Because he knew Bickford was too miserly to offer him refreshment, Reiver decided to leave. He climbed into his wagon, gathered the reins, and wished the man a good day before urging Nellie into a trot and heading back home.

"Don't tarry now, girl! The men are waiting for their dinner."

At her aunt's harsh command, Hannah grabbed the steaming bowl of buttered summer squash in her left hand and balanced the platter of roast pork along her right forearm, praying the tinware wouldn't burn her fingers and go crashing to the floor. All she wanted was to get through another evening meal without mishap. She flew out of the kitchen, her aunt Naomi following with the breadbasket.

In the small dining room just off the kitchen, Uncle Ezra sat like some wizened potentate at the head of the long plain trestle table, his small suspicious eyes watching Hannah's every move as if just waiting for her to make a mistake. Zeb and Zeke sat together on one side and Nate on the other, next to Hannah. He made sure he always sat next to Hannah.

"It's about time," Nate said, scowling.

"She sure is slow, ain't she?" Zeb said.

Zeke added, "We'll have to teach her to move faster, right, Zeb?" He poked his brother in the ribs and Zeb whinnied at some private joke.

Unlike their mother, who was as small and sturdy as her husband, the Fisher boys were tall, hulking young men, with identical sly gray eyes always looking to take advantage, and black, unkempt hair as straight as an Indian's. Hannah had dubbed the trio "Naomi's gargoyles" because of their fearsome, stonelike faces.

She ignored them and set down the dishes gingerly, looking to Aunt Naomi for permission to sit. Her aunt sat down herself at the foot of the table, then nodded curtly for Hannah to take her seat. Once Hannah sat down, Uncle Ezra said grace and the boys dug in, hairy arms reaching and greedy forks spearing as if this were their last meal. Not once did their mother admonish them to mind their manners.

Hannah's stomach growled. She watched everyone else help themselves, and only when they piled their plates high did she dare take what was left, and there was precious little. After all, Aunt Naomi had told her, the men worked hard and should be given first choice at mealtimes, whereas women should eat abstemiously so they wouldn't get fat.

Aunt Naomi regarded her with resentful, rain-gray eyes. "Just look at her wolfing down her food. I thought you said you were sick."

"I was, Aunt Naomi," Hannah replied, keeping her eyes on her plate. "It was so hot in the field, I almost fainted."

"Aw, a little heat never hurt nobody," Zeb said.

Hannah felt the toe of Nate's boot lift her skirts and stroke the side of her foot. She managed to kick him away without the others suspecting what was going on, then glared at him.

He only leered back. "Hannah doesn't know what real heat is," he said, his taunting gray eyes dropping down to her breasts and lingering there.

Hannah's cheeks reddened, and she turned her attention back to her food before her aunt decided she was too sick to eat and divided her meager portion among the boys.

"She's just lazy, right, Ezra?" Naomi looked across the table at her husband.

"You're too hard on her," Ezra said. "The girl isn't used to living on a farm. Got to make allowances."

Hannah looked up in surprise. This was the first time she had ever heard her uncle defend her. It must have taken aback her aunt, too, for Naomi stared at him in shock. She recovered herself quickly enough.

"She's had six months to get used to it, but she's always ailing or she moves too slow."

Hannah said nothing, just ate and took her mind away to that secret place where they could never reach her. She knew her detached air irritated Aunt Naomi and her potato-brained boys more than any fiery outburst.

"You listening to me, girl?" Aunt Naomi snapped, reaching over to tweak Hannah's arm.

Hannah winced. "I always listen to you."

"No, she's not," Nate said, slipping his hand beneath the table so he could squeeze Hannah's knee. "She's got her head in the clouds again."

She didn't even flinch because she had been expecting his usual daily assault, but she was ready for him this time. Her hand shot beneath the table and she clawed at his vulnerable wrist with her fingernails.

Nate yelped in surprise and almost jumped out of his Windsor chair.

"What's the matter with you?" Ezra asked.

"Perhaps a bee stung him," Hannah offered, keeping her eyes demurely lowered while she gloated over her small triumph.

Nate glared at her, his sullen expression promising retribution. "Something bit me."

Aunt Naomi pursed her thin lips. "You've got to mend your slothful ways, girl, and mend them fast. Sloth is one of the seven deadly sins."

"I try my best," Hannah said.

"You'll try harder, if you know what's good for you. Your uncle and I took you in out of the goodness of our hearts, like the Bible tells us to, even though you're a burden. But we expect you to do your share."

I do more than my share! Hannah wanted to shout, but she held her tongue.

Aunt Naomi's eyes narrowed coldly. "And I don't want you spreading lies about us to the neighbors."

Hannah stared at her as if she had gone daft. "I don't know what you're talking about."

"I'm talking about Reiver Shaw."

"I didn't tell him anything. I barely spoke to the man."

"See that you don't, or you'll be sorry."

We mustn't let the neighbors know how we mistreat our kin, Hannah thought as she cleaned her plate.

The rest of the meal passed uneventfully, though Hannah could feel Nate's narrowed, watchful eyes boring into her, like a snake just waiting to strike.

Hannah flung open the window in the cramped attic room that had become her refuge, hoping to coax a breeze out of the still summer night. She sat there for a moment, ignoring her own bone weariness, to appreciate the beauty of the hazy full moon hanging high in the star-strewn sky, and the silence.

She savored every precious second of silence because it was so rare these days. No Aunt Naomi nagging. No Nate and his brothers taunting. Just silence.

Hannah rose and pulled away the thin batiste night shift where it stuck in patches to her damp body, then padded silently on bare feet to her hard, narrow bed, where she collapsed against the cool sheets. She was so exhausted, she fell into a deep sleep as soon as her head hit the pillow.

Moments—hours?—later, something tugged at her consciousness, screaming for her to wake. Rising from the depths of sleep, she sensed danger.

She felt something heavy kneading her breast, squeezing her nipple through the night shift's thin fabric, arousing an unfamiliar feeling of heat deep inside. Then she smelled the sour, acrid odor of a rutting pig, and her eyes flew open to find Nate sitting on the side of her bed.

For a moment Hannah was paralyzed by fear. All she could do was stare helplessly at his face, faintly illuminated by the moonlight coming in through the window. Lust gleamed in the depths of his eyes. He licked his lips as he grasped her other breast.

"You like this, don't you, Hannah?" he whispered, squeezing her harder. "Let's get this off you"—he reached for the hem of her shift—"and old Nate'll make you feel real good."

Hannah felt the trapped animal's surge of strength burst through every muscle and bone. She pushed his hand away and rolled across the bed before he could stop her, landing on her feet on the other side and quickly scrambling out of his reach.

"Get out of here before I scream this house down!" Her hammering heart felt as though it would burst out of her chest.

Nate chuckled softly as he rose and loomed before her, only the bed separating them. The dark hair matting his massive bare chest made him look more like a hairy beast than a man, for he wore only his trousers. "I wouldn't do that, if I was you," he whispered. " 'Cause Ezra gave me leave to be here."

"You're lying! Even he wouldn't—"

Nate lunged, reaching for Hannah across the narrow width of the bed, and she screamed, the terrified sound abrading and affronting the silence. She felt his clutching fingers miss her by inches as they swiped by, and her eyes darted around the attic, desperately seeking anything she could use as a weapon.

"That was real stupid," Nate growled.

Hannah's frightened gaze fell on the heavy pewter candlestick sitting on her nightstand, and she reached for it, her arm outstretched. Without warning, Nate sprung as lithely as a cat for a man his size, diving headfirst across the bed before Hannah could blink. When his feet touched the floor on the other side, he rose and made another grab for her.

Hannah felt a band of steel wrap itself around her waist and pull her away from the candlestick just as her fingers were about to close around it. She screamed again and clawed at his arm.

"Nate doesn't like being scratched." He grabbed Hannah's long braid and pulled. Hard.

The searing fire spreading along her scalp made her gasp and her eyes water as Nate pulled her body against his and forced her head back against his naked shoulder. She could feel his arousal insistent against her hip, smell the sickening sweat in her nostrils, clinging to her cheek where it pressed against his neck.

"Let me go!" She pushed ineffectually at his arm, not daring to scratch him again for fear he'd pull her hair out by the roots.

"You promise to be quiet?"

"Yes." She'd promise anything to stop the pain. Anything.

But when he flung her down on the bed and loomed above her, his clumsy hands fumbling with his trousers, terror got the better of her and she screamed.

"Damn you! I told you to be quiet!" To emphasize his point, he drew back his arm and drove his fist into her ribs.

Hannah gasped at the numbing pain that robbed her of breath. Instinctively she curled herself into a tight ball, hugging her knees to her chest to protect herself.

Sobbing, she closed her eyes and waited for Nate to hit her again, and worse. But the blow never came.

The attic door swung open with a soft creak. There, standing in his nightshirt and holding a candle aloft, was Uncle Ezra with Aunt Naomi peering over his shoulder.

"What's going on here?" Ezra's small dark eyes looked enormous by the flickering candlelight. "Heard screamin'."

Trembling and sobbing, Hannah sat up and swung her legs over the side of the bed, her arms still wrapped protectively around her aching ribs. "Nate tried to force himself on me," she said, her voice rising with hysteria. "When I tried to fight him, he—he—"

"She's lying!" Nate bellowed. "She invited me. Then she got scared and changed her mind. She started screaming and punching me."

"He's the one who's lying!" Hannah jumped to her feet, ignoring the pain. "Don't believe him, Uncle Ezra! Nate tried to force me. He hit me. He—"

"Quiet down, both of you," Ezra said, giving them a quelling look.

Hannah stood there trembling, the back of one hand pressed to her mouth to stifle her shuddering sobs.

Ezra looked at Nate. "That true?"

" 'Course not! She's just trying to get me in trouble. It's like I said. She invited me, then changed her mind." Nate cast a look of appeal to his mother. "You believe me, don't you, Ma?"

"You're my boy. Of course I do." Aunt Naomi stepped around her husband and glared at Hannah. "If my boy says that's what happened, then that's what happened. The girl's been trouble ever since she came to live with us, Ezra."

Hannah felt her tightly wound self-control finally unravel. "Why should I invite Nate or any of your sons to my room? I think they're all stupid and uncouth." She curled her lip contemptuously. "I'd rather sleep with hogs."

Hannah knew that she would live to regret her imprudent words, but the satisfaction of seeing Naomi's gaunt cheeks turn beet red burned hot and fierce in her heart.

Naomi whirled on her husband and sputtered, "Are you going to let her talk to me that way?"

"Be still," Ezra rasped, his inscrutable eyes still on Hannah. "Want to hear the girl's side of it."

Hannah took a deep breath. "As I said, I didn't invite Nate to my room. I was sleeping and awoke to find him sitting on the side of my bed"—she blushed—"touching me where I shouldn't. When I screamed and tried to fight him off, he pulled my hair and hit me." She looked Naomi straight in the eye. "If you think I'm lying, call the doctor. He'll know that Nate hit me when he sees the bruises on my ribs."

Ezra sighed and rubbed his jaw with his free hand. "One of you is lying. Can't tell which. Let's just forget it and go to bed. It's late. Lots of work to do tomorrow. Need our sleep."

"I want a key to the attic door," Hannah said. "I want to lock it in case Nate tries to force himself on me again."

Nate swaggered over to where his mother stood, still glaring at Hannah. "She don't need no key, Ma. No man'd want to break in here." His eyes skimmed over Hannah insolently. "For what?"

But Hannah knew Nate would be back. And the next time he would make sure they weren't interrupted.

Ezra stared at his wife's stiff back turned toward him in the bed they shared.

Naomi was going to make him pay for not taking Nate's side tonight. Whenever he displeased his wife, she turned her back to him and slept as near to the opposite edge of the bed as she could without falling out. The space between them was as cold as the Connecticut River in January.

Ezra sighed as he watched the white curtains billow ever so slightly in the faint night breeze. While he wouldn't admit this to Naomi, he believed Hannah's story. He didn't share his wife's illusions about her three boys. Privately, he agreed with Hannah. Nate, Zeb, and Zeke were stupid and uncouth, Nate worst of all.

Ezra had watched Nate ever since Hannah came to live with them. He had caught him leering at the girl often enough. He suspected Nate put his hands on her under the table at dinner and thought no one noticed. Ezra noticed, all right.

Hannah . . .

Ezra shook his head in the darkness. What was he going to do about this niece? She may have been a burden to him and a temptation for his stepsons, but she was still his late sister's only child, and he felt responsible for her. But she was a disruptive force in his household, and it was only a matter of time before Nate or one of the other boys lost his head and had his way with her.

Ezra had to do something about Hannah, and fast.

An idea came to him just before he fell asleep.

Reiver Shaw sipped his sweet cider beneath the cool shade of Bickford's oak tree and wondered what the old skinflint wanted. He still couldn't believe that Bickford had actually sent one of his stepsons to Reiver's house with a note inviting him to stop by the tobacco farm to discuss a matter of mutual concern.

The Racebrook land, Reiver thought. He's going to sell me the land.

He took another sip and forced himself to relax. He mustn't let the old skinflint get the upper hand. So he nonchalantly discussed the sweltering weather and asked about Ezra's tobacco crop.

When the tankards were half-empty, Ezra drew his sleeve across his mouth. "Bet you're wondering why I asked you to come calling today, Shaw."

"The thought had crossed my mind."

"Want to make a deal."

"What kind of deal?"

"For the Racebrook land."

Reiver set down his tankard and leaned back in his chair. "You ready to sell?" Finally.

"Yup."

"Well, name your price, and I'll see if I want to meet it."

"Prime land. Hate to part with it."

"Then why are you offering it to me?" he asked with a nonchalant shrug.

" 'Cause you can do something for me."

Reiver felt a shiver of suspicion crawl up his spine. "And what might that be?"

"Niece needs a husband."

Reiver stared speechlessly at Bickford. When he regained his voice, he said, "Me? You want me to marry Hannah?"

"Yup. For the Racebrook land. Can't give it to you. Sell it for fifty dollars an acre. And Hannah. Take it or leave it."

Reiver rubbed his chin thoughtfully. "Fifty dollars an acre isn't any bargain. That's how much you'd expect to get for it without Hannah." He smiled. "I need an incentive to marry her, Bickford. A powerful incentive."

"Forty an acre, then."

"Ten."

Bickford turned purple and his small, dark eyes bulged from their sockets. *"Ten!"* he sputtered. "You're crazy, Shaw! That's giving it away."

Reiver shrugged. "If you want me to marry a woman I don't want, you have to make it worth my while."

"Twenty, then."

"Fifteen."

"Twenty. Take it or leave it."

"Seventeen. And that's my last offer."

Bickford glared at him, his jaw working. Finally he said, "Deal. Seventeen an acre, and Hannah."

Reiver wanted that land so badly he felt light-headed. But was it worth marrying a woman he didn't know to get it?

"What does Hannah think of marrying a stranger?" he asked.

"Doesn't know yet."

"You think she'll agree to the match?"

"Doesn't matter. She'll do what she's told. She's eighteen. Time she wed." Bickford studied him out of those small, dark eyes. "Any objections to her?"

Reiver thought of her delicate ivory features and supple young body so sweetly rounded and inviting. It wouldn't be a chore to bed her even if he didn't love her.

Suddenly a thought occurred to him. "Has one of the boys had her already?"

Bickford shook his head. "Not yet. But boys are boys. If I don't get her out of the house, no telling what'll happen to her. You'd be doing her a favor."

And getting the land he wanted.

But still he hesitated. He thought of Cecelia Layton, the young sea captain's widow who had been his mistress for the past year. She was the woman he loved and had intended to marry as soon as he established his silk mill. How could he give her up?

With supreme male arrogance, he was confident that he wouldn't have to. Cecelia loved him and knew how important his silk mill was to him. She would understand why he had to betray her.

Reiver grinned, rose, and extended his hand. "You've got a

deal, Bickford. The Racebrook land for seventeen dollars an acre, and your niece's hand in marriage."

Bickford rose and shook Reiver's hand, a pained expression on his face. "Hate to lose that land, but I've got to do right by my niece."

"I'll treat her well."

But he'd never love her. That wasn't part of the deal.

CHAPTER

❧ 2 ❧

THE following morning after breakfast, when the boys left to pick tobacco and Aunt Naomi went to the cobbler to buy new shoes, Uncle Ezra interrupted Hannah's dusting and called her into the parlor, where he told her that she was going to marry Reiver Shaw.

Hannah stood there as if rooted to the spot. "You want me to what?"

"You heard me."

The dustrag slipped from her nerveless fingers and her knees buckled, forcing her to sink down onto the parlor's hard settee. Her whirling brain tried to reconcile an image of the stocky, forceful man who had rescued her from heat prostration with that of the man who would be her husband, with all the intimacies that state entailed, and failed.

"I can't marry him. I *won't!*"

Ezra's thin lips hardened into an implacable line. "You will. It's all arranged."

Hannah pressed her hands against her cold cheeks. "But—but I only met Mr. Shaw several days ago. I know nothing about him. I can't possibly marry a—a stranger."

"Happens all the time to girls your age. Don't need to know him. Marriage'll take care of that."

"There must be dozens of women in Coldwater who want to marry him. Why would he want to marry me?" She didn't delude herself for an instant that Shaw was smitten with her beauty. "I'm a poor orphan. I have no dowry."

"You do now."

Bewildered, Hannah stared at him.

"Shaw wants some land I own. That land's your dowry. Drove a hard bargain for it, he did."

Hannah breathed deeply to quell her growing panic and desperation as the room shrank, the walls closing in on her. She rose and crossed the parlor to where her uncle stood before the cold fireplace. Placing a supplicating hand on his scrawny arm, she said, "Please don't force me to do this. I promise I'll work harder. I won't annoy Aunt Naomi. I—"

"No use begging. My mind's made up."

"You promised my mother you'd take care of me. Is this how you honor your promises?"

Her uncle glowered at her and brushed her hand away as if she were some troublesome horsefly. "Didn't promise to take care of you forever."

Hannah knew it was pointless to argue or try to appeal to her uncle's finer sensibilities, for he had none. She turned before he could see her eyes fill with helpless tears. She brushed them away and turned to face him again, her head held high. "When am I to wed?" she asked.

He shrugged. "Whenever Shaw wants. Didn't set a date. He'll be here this afternoon to talk to you."

Hannah stood there woodenly, wishing the floor would open up and swallow her. She would have to live with Reiver Shaw for the rest of her life, share his bed, and bear his children. She shuddered.

Ezra's small dark eyes softened with rare compassion. "It's time you married. You're not happy here. You tempt Naomi's boys. Shaw's father was a no-account, but Reiver's decent. He'll treat you good." Then he walked to the parlor door, stopped, and turned. "You look peaked. Take some time to get used to the idea. Leave the cleaning for Naomi."

He hesitated for a moment as if waiting for Hannah to thank him for generously excusing her from her chores, but when she remained rigid and unforgiving, Ezra shrugged his thin shoulders and left her to ponder her fate.

Hannah couldn't wait until that afternoon to speak to her future husband. She put on her bonnet, tied the wide ribbons beneath her chin, and left the house at a brisk walk.

Fifteen minutes later she arrived at Mulberry Hill, which separated Shaw land from Uncle Ezra's. Hannah took a deep breath, lifted her long calico skirts, and started up the gentle slope along the horizontal rows of mulberry trees.

When she was halfway up, she noticed several women in plain black dresses and white aprons standing between the rows and picking leaves as easily as they might pick apples in the fall.

One of them noticed Hannah staring at her and smiled. "Good morning."

"Good morning," Hannah replied, not returning the smile. "Can you tell me where I might find Reiver Shaw?"

The woman laughed. "Mr. Shaw is where he always is, in the rearing shed with his worms."

Hannah frowned in puzzlement. "His worms?"

"Silkworms. Millions of 'em, eating these leaves we're picking." The woman shuddered. "Give me the shivers, those worms do."

"Where is this rearing shed?" Hannah asked.

"Just over the hill, near the mill."

Hannah thanked her and kept on walking.

When she reached the crest of the hill, she stopped for a moment to catch her breath and survey what would soon be her home unless she could convince Reiver Shaw to withdraw his offer of marriage.

At the far end of the sweeping green lawn stood a small white farmhouse half-concealed by several tall oak and maple trees shivering in the gentle morning breeze. To Hannah's right stood the mill on the banks of a swiftly running stream and a long, low building that must have been the rearing shed set nearby.

Hannah swallowed hard, squared her shoulders, and started for the shed. She was halfway there when the door suddenly opened and a lanky young man came out, closing the door gently after him.

He appeared more intent on some strange object he held than on where he was going, and almost walked right into Hannah. He caught himself in time and sprang back, startled.

"Excuse me, miss," he blurted, his cheeks coloring. "I never watch where I'm going."

Hannah knew this young man had to be one of the Shaw brothers, for he resembled Reiver faintly, like a blurred image viewed through a cloudy glass. He was handsomer than his older brother, with a less prominent nose and narrower jaw, and an endearing preoccupied air. Straight brown hair fell in a slant across his brow, and his demeanor was somewhat shy.

"I'm Hannah Whitby," she said, "and I'm looking for Reiver Shaw."

The young man recognized her name at once, for he colored again. "Pleased to meet you, Miss Whitby." He extended his hand, noticed it was dirty, and pulled it back with an apologetic smile. "Sorry. I never can seem to keep my hands clean."

Hannah smiled to put him at ease. "Then you must be James Shaw, the inventor."

His brows rose and he blushed again. "Inventor is too grand. Tinkerer is a more apt description of what I do." He glanced back at the rearing shed. "Would you like me to fetch my brother? That is, if I can pull him away from his worms."

"Please. It's very important that I speak with him."

James nodded and went back into the shed. A minute later he emerged, followed by his brother.

The moment Reiver Shaw's blue eyes held hers, Hannah became acutely aware of the man. When she had first met him in the tobacco field, he was like any other man she had happened to pass on the streets of Coldwater, a presence, but one kept at a distance. Now that he was to be her husband, that distance shrank alarmingly. Hannah wanted it back.

"Good morning, Miss Whitby," he said. "I didn't expect to see you until this afternoon."

So he knew why she had come.

Hannah tried to smile, but her face felt stiff and frozen. She managed to force out, "I'd like to speak with you, if I may."

James said to his brother, "Go ahead. I'll tend the worms." He smiled shyly at Hannah and went back into the shed.

Reiver glanced at her. "Let's walk down by the brook, shall we?"

She fell into step beside him, and they walked in awkward silence like the strangers they were.

Finally Hannah stopped and turned to face him. "My uncle Ezra told me that you've asked for my hand in marriage. May I ask why? You don't even know me, nor I you."

"I didn't ask for your hand in marriage," he said. "Your uncle offered it."

Stunned, Hannah rocked back on her heels. "Uncle Ezra approached you?"

Reiver Shaw nodded. "He told me that it was time you married, that he couldn't trust Naomi's boys to keep their hands off you. He thought I'd make you a suitable husband."

"And you accepted his offer?"

"I did."

Hannah gave him a sharp, assessing stare. "You must forgive my bluntness, Mr. Shaw, but you don't strike me as the kind of man who would enter into an arranged marriage without something to gain."

Her bluntness did surprise him, and he regarded her with respect in his eyes. "I won't insult your intelligence by claiming that I fell in love with you from the moment we met, Miss Whitby"—his gaze raked her up and down—"though you are a comely young woman. No, I accepted your uncle's offer because he agreed to give me something I've wanted very badly for a long time." He turned and gazed out beyond the brook. "Some land I've coveted."

The land that Uncle Ezra said was to be her dowry.

Hannah took a deep, tremulous breath. "Mr. Shaw, I don't want to marry you."

He turned back to face her, a smile of amusement tugging at the corners of his mouth. "May I ask why? I've been told I'm quite a catch."

She ignored his teasing tone. "I'm sure you are. But we are strangers who only met several days ago. You have no idea what I'm really like."

"Then why don't you tell me?"

Hannah took a deep breath. "Why, I'm headstrong, rebellious, argumentative—"

"A virtual virago," he added, suppressing a smile.

"Yes! And I could be a drunkard, for all you know."

He froze, his expression hardening. "I know you're not a drunkard, Miss Whitby."

"But that is my point; you don't know."

"And as for you being rebellious, you seem to obey your uncle Ezra well enough."

Hannah didn't know what to say to that observation.

He grew solemn. "Are you trying to discourage me because there is someone else? One of Naomi's boys, perhaps?"

Hannah thought of Nate and her lip curled in revulsion. "There is no one else."

"Ah, now I understand. You were hoping for a love match."

"Yes, Mr. Shaw, I was. As you know, my own parents' marriage was not arranged. They loved each other, and were very happy."

Shaw's face softened with sympathy, but his words were harsh and unyielding. "I'm afraid you won't be as fortunate. Your uncle offered me your hand in marriage, and I've accepted, whether or not you are a drunkard."

"How can you marry a woman you don't love, who doesn't love you in return?" Hannah cried in frustration.

"I want to manufacture silk, Miss Whitby," he said, looking back at his mill with obvious pride. "It's been my dream for years. I'll do anything to make that dream a reality."

Hannah felt her eyes fill with tears.

Shaw said gently, "You are still very young and may not realize that there are advantages to being married to me." When Hannah looked at him quizzically, he added, "I plan to be a wealthy man someday. As my wife, you would want for nothing."

"Except my husband's love."

His gaze fell. "I can't promise that, though perhaps in time . . ."

Even as she appreciated his honesty, a small part of her wished he would lie.

Shaw grasped her by the shoulders and forced her to face him. "I know you don't want to marry me, Hannah, and I'd much rather have a willing wife than an unwilling one. But I promise that if you make the best of it, you will have a good life with me."

She looked deeply into his eyes, took the man's measure, and knew he spoke the truth. Reiver Shaw wasn't cold like her uncle or crude like Naomi's boys. He was a fair man, honorable and good. She could do worse.

Hannah sighed in surrender, not feeling much like a virago at all. "I will do my best to be a good wife to you."

His grin was like the sun breaking through a heavy morning fog. Before Hannah could stop him, he grabbed her hand and pressed his lips into her palm with an ardor that surprised her. She pulled away, disconcerted by his touch. "I—I should be getting back. I have chores to do."

Shaw nodded. "I'll call on your uncle this afternoon to discuss our wedding."

"And when shall that be?"

"As soon as possible."

Whenever Reiver went to Hartford, he always paused to watch the flatboats float down the Connecticut River with their cargoes of lumber and brine-soaked beef and pork from the northern New England states. Once the railroads were established, the flatboats with their square sails would bow to the superiority of steam and a way of life would be lost forever.

Cecelia's home on Main Street was only a short ride from the bridge spanning the Connecticut River, and when Reiver arrived, he dismounted and tied his horse to the hitching post out front. He hesitated on the second step of the house that Cecelia had lived in ever since her sea captain husband had been lost in the Pacific three years ago. In the summer's slowly dwindling twilight, the sprawling house looked dark and empty.

Suddenly a light appeared in the downstairs parlor window, and Reiver watched as Cecelia, oblivious to his presence, lit an oil lamp. The light bathed her in golden warmth, reminding him of the night five years ago when he had first seen her.

He had come to her father's house hoping that the wealthy sea captain—one of Hartford's "River Gods" with a fleet of tall-masted ships sailing out of New London for the West Indies—would hire a poor boy from Coldwater. Just as he climbed the front stairs he caught a glimpse of the captain's lovely young daughter gracefully lighting an oil lamp. She symbolized all of Reiver's aspirations, and he fell in love with her right then and there.

Since Reiver had been too proud to use the backdoor that night, Cecelia's contemptuous father didn't hire him, and his daughter later married someone more suitable. But Reiver never forgot his desire for her. After Cecelia became a widow at the age of twenty-two, and Reiver became more prosperous, he wangled an introduction, and later they became lovers.

He watched as Cecelia replaced the lamp's glass chimney and moved away from the window with unselfconscious grace. Then he walked up the rest of the steps and knocked on the front door.

When Cecelia answered it, her huge brown eyes danced with a mixture of pleasure at seeing him and confusion that he had come so late in the day. Still, her radiant smile was like a balm on turbulent waters.

"Reiver!" she murmured in her soft, melodious voice that he had ached for days to hear. "I'm so glad to see you." She took his hat, then drew him into the shadowed foyer.

He closed the door behind him and swept her petite form into his arms, reaching hungrily for her mouth with his own. Cecelia stood on tiptoes for his kiss.

Reiver groaned against her mouth, letting the delicious heat radiate from his groin. When it nearly consumed him, he set her away from him, held her at arm's length, and studied her. "I've never seen a woman with such a tiny waist. That dress makes it look even smaller."

"Reiver Shaw, you're the only man I know who pays attention to what a lady wears."

He grinned. "Or doesn't wear."

Cecelia slapped his hand playfully. "Come into the parlor. We'll have some elderberry wine and you can tell me all the latest news about your mill."

Reiver loved Cecelia Layton not for her amatory prowess as his mistress, but because she ministered so tenderly to his spirit. No matter how much time passed between Reiver's visits, Cecelia never admonished him for neglecting her, never pressed to see him more often. When he was with her, he felt the worries of the world slide from his shoulders like an old skin and peace envelop him.

He sat down on the settee and she glided over to the sideboard to pour two glasses of elderberry wine. Then she handed him one and sat down beside him, her wide skirt brushing his knee.

She raised her glass. "To Shaw Silks."

He toasted the mill, took a sip, then set down his glass. He was about to hurt her cruelly, and if she never wanted to see him again, he wanted it over and done with.

Her face clouded as she divined his mood with her usual perceptiveness, and she placed her hand on his. "Reiver, what's wrong?"

He knew no painless way to tell her. "I'm getting married."

Cecelia grew very still and the color drained from her face, leaching all the sweetness and joy with it, until she was as pale as a death mask.

Reiver waited for her to scream, sob, claw his face to ribbons, or at least swoon, but all she did was stare wordlessly out of glazed brown eyes.

He squeezed her lifeless hand. "Say something. Please."

Cecelia's lips moved, but no sound came out. She finally croaked, "Do you love her?"

He hadn't expected that. He dangled his arms across his knees and bowed his head in shame. "No. I love you and I always will. I'm only marrying her for the land I need to expand the mill someday."

And while Cecelia listened Reiver told her about Ezra Bickford's offer and why he had agreed to marry Hannah Whitby.

He stared at the worn Turkish carpet, unable to look at the woman who deserved so much better for her love and loyalty. "I wish I had married you before this, but the mill has been struggling, and I wanted to be on more solid financial ground so I'd be worthy of you."

"Oh, Reiver, that wouldn't have made any difference to me."

"I know that now, but it's too late." He sighed dismally. "I wouldn't blame you if you told me to leave this house and never come back."

He heard Cecelia sigh, then felt her small gentle hands rest soothingly on his bent shoulders. She said, "I couldn't bear not seeing you again."

Reiver sat up and looked at her. "Did you hear what I said? I'm going to marry someone else."

"I heard you."

"And you want to go on seeing me?"

She nodded slowly. "If you'll still have me. You may fall in love with your wife and not want me."

"Not want you?" He shook his head. "I've wanted you from

the first moment I saw you in your father's house, and I'll always want you."

"I love you, Reiver," she whispered. "When you love someone, you want them to be happy. Shaw Silks is your dream. And if you need that land to make your dream come true . . ."

He buried his face in her silken chestnut hair that smelled faintly of sweet heliotrope. "I don't deserve you, Cecelia Layton. I don't deserve you."

"Let me be the judge of that."

"You're too understanding."

"And you're my life."

Later, after Reiver left, Cecelia lay in her dark bedchamber and stared at the ceiling. Her bed was still warm from her lover's body and the tousled sheets smelled strongly of their shared passion.

Reiver Shaw was not going to marry her after all. That realization was like winter ice encasing her heart.

Cecelia knew she should have told him that their liaison was over, but the thought of never seeing him again, of never having him share her bed, hurt more than her shattered pride. But then, she had no pride where Reiver was concerned. She would accept whatever crumbs of his life he deigned to share with her, and accept them gladly.

But his betrayal still hurt.

She buried her face in her pillow and sobbed until she had no tears left to shed.

Hannah refused to shed any tears on her wedding day. She had to marry Reiver Shaw whether she wanted to or not, and crying wasn't going to change anything.

Her wedding was a hasty, indifferent affair, of no importance to anyone but the bride. The Bickfords kept their niece working right up until the day they would lose her services, trying to eke as much as they could out of her. The groom was too busy with his silkworms to call on his intended bride. Only his handsome artist brother stopped by one day on his way to Hartford to introduce himself and wish Hannah well.

The ceremony itself on that cool, cloudy Monday morning seemed an afterthought more than an auspicious beginning.

Only Ezra's family, the Shaws, and several of their employees occupied the church's empty pews.

At least Reiver smiled reassuringly when Hannah met him at the altar, and whispered how pretty she looked in her best summer dress of pale lavender dimity, with matching chip bonnet. She thought he looked quite handsome in his bottle-green coat, tie, and tall silk hat. But Hannah felt only a sense of doom as Reiver slipped the narrow gold band on her finger and the Reverend Crane pronounced them man and wife.

When it was over, the Bickfords and Naomi's boys mumbled halfhearted good wishes before rushing back home. There had been no gifts from her Bickford relations, nor would they part with a penny to host the wedding breakfast. That was left to the Shaws.

"This is your home now," Reiver said, handing Hannah from the carriage. "Mrs. Hardy may be the housekeeper, but you're the mistress of the house and your word is law here."

Mistress of the house . . .

Looking at the white farmhouse—her new home—Hannah felt her spirits lift. She was mistress of this house. There was no Aunt Naomi to rail at her, no Nate to torment her. Being a wife conferred an exhilarating power.

She smiled at her husband for the first time today. "It looks very cozy."

Reiver smiled back. "With my brothers living with us, I'm afraid it will be that. Cozy and noisy."

The second carriage pulled up behind them, and the other Shaw brothers jumped down to join them.

"I never thought I'd see the day," Samuel said with a shake of his head as he pounded his brother on the back.

Hannah had always found the perfection of handsome men intimidating, and Samuel Shaw was no exception. His curly, dark brown hair fell just so, and thick black lashes a woman would envy framed eyes of such a pale blue they appeared ghostly. Hannah couldn't fault his thin, aristocratic nose, or his even white teeth. His shoulders weren't as broad as Reiver's, or his body as lanky as James's, and he moved with just the right amount of sensuous masculine grace. The only quality that rescued him from such relentless perfection was his utter lack of conceit.

Samuel turned and kissed Hannah on the cheek. "Welcome to the family, Hannah. Even though you haven't come to us under the best of circumstances, you're our sister now, and you'll be proud to be a Shaw one day."

His sincere words touched her deeply and her feeling of intimidation vanished.

James stepped forward shyly and added, "Welcome to the family."

"Before we go inside to meet Mrs. Hardy," Reiver said, "I've got to warn you. She's a crotchety old lady who speaks her mind no matter who takes offense."

"And she sometimes uses rather, er—impolite language," Samuel added.

"You have to excuse her," James said. "We all do."

Mrs. Hardy, who was in her late fifties, with a crown of silver hair and matching sharp silver-gray eyes, was awaiting their arrival with a lavish spread in the small downstairs dining room.

"It's about time," she muttered, those eyes scouring Hannah as if searching crystal for flaws. "I hope you've got a thick hide; otherwise you'll never last. Reiver will just have to take you back where you came from."

Hannah smiled. "I've got a very thick hide."

"Good. Now let's eat before everything gets cold."

If Hannah had any thoughts of lingering over her wedding breakfast, they were dispelled the moment her new husband finished wolfing down a slice of iced currant cake.

He rose. "As much as I'd like to tarry, there's work to be done. I have to get back to the worms."

Mrs. Hardy gave a ribald chuckle. "I thought you'd want to show your new bride your bedchamber."

"Martha . . ." Reiver chided her.

Hannah, however, welcomed the opportunity for some solitude. "Mrs. Hardy, why don't you show me the house? The sooner I assume my new duties, the better."

Reiver beamed at her. "I can see that I've wedded a woman who understands the value of hard work."

Hannah rose as well. She hoped that hard work would help her adjust to her new life as Mrs. Reiver Shaw.

• • •

By the middle of the afternoon, Mrs. Hardy had shown Hannah the household's routine, and the two women relaxed together over a cup of tea.

"How long have you been with the family?" Hannah asked, pouring herself a cup from the brown crockery pot.

"Seems like a lifetime," the housekeeper replied, pushing a plate of raisin cakes at Hannah. "I came from a neighboring farm to take care of the house when the boys' mother died. Their father was the town drunk, useless, but as handsome as sin." She winked at Hannah. "His name was Remy Shaw, but everyone called him Rummy because West Indian rum ran through his veins instead of blood."

Was this what Uncle Ezra meant when he referred to Reiver's father as a no-account?

Hannah shook her head. "That must have been hard on the boys."

"If it hadn't been for them, this family would've starved." Mrs. Hardy snorted in derision. "Rummy was always too drunk to see straight, never mind work. Oh, he always had plans. High-as-the-sky plans. But they were all smoke. A real dreamer he was. But his boys . . . now they're a horse of another color."

"I can see they're very fond of you."

The housekeeper chuckled at that. "If they don't listen to me, they don't get clean clothes and they don't get fed." She paused. "I want to see my boys married, with children of their own. It's too soon to tell about you, but I think you'll make Reiver a good wife. I don't know about Sam and James. Sam is too busy painting beautiful women to court one, and poor Jimmy is so shy, his tongue sticks to the roof of his mouth when one even looks at him."

"He does seem more comfortable with his machines."

Mrs. Hardy drained her cup and smacked her lips. "I'll tell you right now, it's not going to be easy being Reiver's wife. He doesn't like anyone telling him what to do. Never did. If you need to know how to handle him, you just come to old Martha here."

Hannah couldn't resist the invitation. She stared into her cup. "I want to be a good wife, but I'm not sure how. We're strangers."

The housekeeper put her elbows on the table and leaned forward, her silvery eyes shining. "That's easy. Give him whatever he wants in bed, and show an interest in his mill."

Hannah blushed and ignored the first bit of advice, asking, "Why does he want to manufacture silk?"

"Because he's got to prove to himself that he's not worthless like his father. He wants to make a fortune, and he thinks silk will do it. He says if American women could buy silks made in their own country, they would."

Hannah sipped her tea and recalled her own mother's extensive wardrobe of fine silk dresses and her father's good-natured complaints about their cost. Even the frugal Aunt Naomi had one best black silk dress reserved for special occasions and mourning.

Hannah dabbed her lips with her napkin and rose. "I think I shall see this silk mill for myself."

Mrs. Hardy beamed, delighted that Reiver's new bride was going to take her advice.

Hannah opened the rearing shed's door and paused in the doorway, blinking her eyes against the dimness.

"Close that door, damn you!" Reiver hissed.

Hannah just stood there, bewildered. Then her husband rushed toward her, grasped her arm painfully, and propelled her out of the shed. He closed the door gently and whirled on her, his face a furious mask.

"Never do that again!"

Hannah stepped back a pace. "Wh-what did I do?"

"You flung open the door, you little fool! A sudden draft can make them all sick."

"I—I didn't know." Hannah's cheeks burned.

Reiver's anger subsided like a passing summer storm, and he ran his hand over his broad jaw as if calming himself. "Of course you don't."

"I have heard everyone speak of your silkworms," she said, "so I thought I'd come to see them for myself."

He sighed. "And no one warned you to enter the rearing shed carefully?"

"No one did."

"Come inside then, but speak softly because noise disturbs them."

Hannah didn't even dare to breathe when she stepped into the shed, and she lifted her skirts so they wouldn't swish, for fear of disturbing the creatures. Two of the women she had seen picking mulberry leaves were now feeding the worms.

"They make so much noise," she whispered, surprised, staring at the pale cream-colored worms feeding in their shallow trays.

Reiver smiled. "Their table manners leave much to be desired."

"How do they make silk?"

He gave her an odd look as though surprised at her interest, but said, "In two more weeks they'll be full-grown and stop eating. Then they'll begin to spin their golden cocoons. Once the cocoons are formed, we kill the worm inside so it doesn't break out and ruin the silk. Then we soak them in warm water and unravel the silk threads."

"And then you spin it into silk for dresses?"

Reiver smiled and shook his head. "Shaw Silks just makes twists of silk thread right now, but someday . . ." His voice trailed off, and he got a faraway look in his eye.

"May I see the mill now?" Hannah asked.

He snapped out of his reverie. "Of course. Follow me."

They left the shed and walked down the path toward the mill, a solitary stone building sitting on the banks of the rushing brook.

Reiver said, "I don't expect you to take over the mill as well as the household, you know."

Hannah smiled at his teasing tone. "I don't intend to. I was curious." She looked down at her wedding band. "It's part of my life now."

"And it will be our children's legacy."

The mention of children sent Hannah's thoughts catapulting to the upcoming night ahead and she shivered slightly.

If her husband noticed her reaction to his words, he said nothing. They had reached the mill now, and he was holding open the door for her.

But even as he introduced her to the two girls winding twists of silk and explained the process, Hannah's thoughts refused to leave her upcoming wedding night and her husband's demands.

Not long after sunset, when the western horizon was still lined with a thin orange band, Hannah retired to the upstairs bedchamber she was to share with Reiver.

She had put on a nightshift that had once belonged to her mother, a bit of gossamer white batiste delicately embroidered with blue cornflowers along the yoke. Then she had extinguished the lamp and slipped into bed to listen for the sound of her husband's footsteps outside the door.

She heard them over the hammering of her own heart.

The door creaked softly and opened, Reiver more an ominous shadow than a flesh-and-blood man. He walked into the room, shut the door, and undressed in a soft rustle of clothing falling to the floor.

He said nothing.

Hannah closed her eyes and lay very still when she heard the bed creak and felt it sink heavily beneath his weight. She waited for him to soothe her maiden's fears, to murmur sweet reassurances, but all he did was draw closer to her and lift her night shift.

Hannah's eyes flew open and her cheeks grew hot with embarrassment as Reiver stroked and kneaded, his own breathing quickening, his skin hot and damp against hers.

Reiver's shadow loomed over her like a great black monster. When he entered her with one hard thrust, Hannah cried out at the unexpected invasion and tried to writhe away from him, but his strong hands pressing down her shoulders pinioned her to the bed.

It was over quickly, mercifully. Reiver groaned, shuddered, and rolled off her. Hannah pulled down her night shift to hide her nakedness and turned her back to him, letting tears of humiliation slide quietly down her cheeks.

Reiver could hear her muffled sniffles, so he knew she was crying, but all he could do was place an awkward hand on her shoulder. While he had enjoyed Hannah's sweet body, she wasn't Cecelia. She would never be Cecelia.

He closed his eyes and drifted off to sleep.

The following morning Hannah awoke before Reiver while it was still dark.

She washed and dressed quickly, resolving not to spare another thought to her wedding night, as there was nothing worth remembering except shame and pain. But she would survive, as she always had, and endure.

She went downstairs to light the stove for breakfast. It was going to be another long day.

CHAPTER

❧ 3 ❧

HANNAH looked out the dining-room window at the maple trees tossing in the late-October wind, whirling their bright orange and red leaves high into the air before scattering them across the lawn in a vivid carpet.

Rising from the breakfast table, she noticed the jagged tear in James's shirt. "James, your sleeve is torn," she said. "Why don't you change and I'll mend it this morning?"

James's face turned pink. "I must have caught it on the loom I was working on yesterday." He headed upstairs to find another shirt to wear.

Reiver drained his coffee cup and rose. "And I'll be on my way."

"Don't forget your coat," Hannah said. "It looks chilly outside."

He smiled. "Married just two months, and already she's telling us what to do, eh, Sam?"

Samuel grinned. "Our own little tyrant."

Used to the Shaw brothers' good-natured teasing by now, Hannah retorted, "Tyrant, indeed! If it weren't for me and Mrs. Hardy, the three of you would go around Coldwater dressed in rags."

Both men laughed.

Hannah rose and followed Reiver, wordlessly taking his brown homespun coat off its peg in the hall and handing it to him when he opened the back door. She shivered as a blast of crisp autumn air blew in and swirled around her skirts.

Reiver gave her a brief nod and walked across the lawn in his long stride.

Hannah stood there in the doorway, hugging herself against the morning chill and wishing he'd have kissed her on the cheek before he left, or at least turn and wave. But he didn't. He never did.

With a wistful sigh, she turned and shut the door, only to have James materialize before her. With an apologetic smile, he handed her the torn shirt and disappeared out the door.

When Hannah returned to the warm dining room and its homey aroma of bacon and coffee, she found Samuel still at the table, lingering over his coffee as he usually did after his brothers had gone to the mill. In a few minutes he would rise and go upstairs to his studio to paint or work on an engraving, but right now he was content to sit and talk with Hannah.

"Is something wrong?" he asked when Hannah resumed her place across from him. "You look troubled."

If Reiver's passion was the mill and James's its machinery, Samuel's passion was people. Not only was he interested in what they looked like—the curve of their cheek or the length of their nose—but also what they felt inside. His curiosity often led him to ask bold questions that had first embarrassed Hannah until she realized this was Samuel's way.

She feigned surprise and refilled her cup from the pewter coffeepot. "Nothing is troubling me."

His pale eyes clouded with skepticism. "Far be it from me to contradict a lady, but I think you are quite troubled, Hannah."

She shook her head vehemently. "Nothing is wrong."

Samuel glanced at James's torn shirt that Hannah had draped across the back of a Windsor chair. "James and I have been burdening you with our washing and mending."

Hannah smiled. "You have not." The smile faded, and her voice grew wistful. "It makes me feel useful."

Without hesitation Samuel said, "How have you and my brother been getting on?"

She rose quickly. "You must excuse me. I—I have to clear the table. Millicent will be here any minute to do the laundry." And she began collecting the soiled tin plates that clinked in her trembling hands.

He made no move to stop her. All he said was, "Please don't run off."

Hannah paused, set down her pile of dishes, then seated herself. Even though she felt disloyal talking about her husband to his brother, she couldn't keep her feelings bottled inside any longer.

"He treats me with"—she chose her words carefully—"courtesy and respect. Indeed, you all are kindness itself to me. But—" She shrugged helplessly. "Reiver is so—so distant. I realize ours is an arranged marriage and that I can't expect him to warm to me right away. But he always keeps me at arm's length. And I thought I was adept at building walls." After she confessed, she blurted, "I know you must think me a foolish, romantic schoolgirl."

"I don't think that at all," he said softly. "I find you intelligent and wise beyond your years."

Hannah looked out the window at the falling leaves. "I couldn't bear to have a life like Uncle Ezra and Aunt Naomi's." She turned to Samuel. "Do you know that in all the time I was there, I never once saw my uncle touch his wife's hand, or kiss her on the cheek, or look at her with any genuine warmth?"

"Knowing the pair of them as I do, that doesn't surprise me." He grew serious. "Reiver isn't like that, Hannah. It may take time, but he'll come around."

"I hope so." She looked at him uneasily. "You won't tell him what I said, will you?"

"Of course not."

She felt relieved. She could trust Samuel.

Samuel knew why Reiver was so distant with his wife.

When Millicent, the hired girl, arrived and Hannah joined her to tackle the mountain of Monday laundry waiting to be boiled in huge kettles on the stove, Samuel went upstairs to his studio to work on a new engraving, for winter was coming and with the mulberry trees bare and the silkworms' life cycle over, the family would depend on his earnings until spring.

This sunny, spacious room was as much his domain as the mill was his brothers'. Here, with the sharp smell of turpentine strong in his nostrils and an engraving plate heavy in his hand, Samuel Shaw gave his visions shape and substance.

But today even the golden autumn light flooding his studio through the overhead skylight failed to motivate him. He couldn't stop thinking of Hannah's forlorn face mirroring the hurt and rejection she felt inside.

Samuel rolled down his shirt sleeves, grabbed his coat, and went in search of Reiver.

He found him where he knew he would, in the mill with its humming reeling looms and feminine chatter, supervising one of the girls soaking and unwinding the silk threads from the last of the cocoons.

Today Samuel didn't return the girl's appreciative stare or her bold, flirtatious smile. He walked up to his brother and said, "Reiver, I've got to talk with you."

Reiver scowled in annoyance. "Can't you see that I'm busy?"

"This is important."

Reiver gave him a look that plainly told him nothing was more important than what he was doing.

"It's about Hannah," Samuel said, watching his brother's face closely for any sign of concern.

Reiver hesitated. "Let's go outside."

Once outside, they followed the brook until they were out of earshot of the mill.

Samuel stopped and confronted him. "You're still seeing Cecelia Layton, aren't you?"

Reiver placed his hands on his hips. "What business is it of yours?"

"You're married now."

A sardonic smile twisted Reiver's mouth. "Don't go all pious on me, Sam. You're a man of the world. You've had your share of mistresses."

"But I'm not married. That's the difference between us."

"Just because a man is married doesn't mean he has to give up his mistress."

"If you want her so badly, why didn't you marry her instead of Hannah?" Samuel snapped.

Reiver turned and gazed out over his land that had once belonged to Ezra Bickford. "You know why."

"Stupid me, how could I forget? Your precious Racebrook land."

His brother stepped back a pace and regarded him strangely.

"What's gotten into you, Sam? Why are you so concerned about Hannah?"

"I'm fond of her."

"You know why I married her. I didn't hear you raise any objections when I told you and James what I intended to do."

Samuel fought to keep his anger in check. "Now that she is your wife, at least show the poor girl some affection. Beyond bedding her," he added.

A dull flush crept up Reiver's face and he lowered his head like a bull about to charge. "Has my wife been talking about our private life to you behind my back?"

"She didn't need to. I'm not blind." Samuel jammed his hands into his pockets and stared out at the horizon of colored trees. "Do you remember how Ma and Pa were with each other? How he would hug her when he didn't think we boys were looking? Do you remember how Pa would listen—really listen—when Ma spoke, and how her eyes would follow him wherever he went?"

Reiver's lip curled in a sneer. "All I remember about Pa is that he was always drunk. If Ma's eyes followed him, it was to make sure he didn't pilfer the money we boys brought home."

"They loved each other in spite of Pa's weakness," Samuel insisted. "You just never saw it."

"How could she love him? He was a drunk who never worked two days together in his life! He lived off the money we boys earned, or have you forgotten?"

"I'm not here to argue about Pa. I'm talking about Hannah." Samuel paused. "She's falling in love with you."

That caught Reiver by surprise. "Did she say that to you?"

"She's got too much pride for that. I doubt if she even realizes it herself. But I know women well enough to recognize the signs."

Reiver said, "You spend too much time with women, little brother. You're getting as soft as they are."

That old childhood insult failed to sting Samuel, but he had to resist the strong urge to smash his fist into Reiver's face.

When he saw that he couldn't get a rise out of his brother, Reiver turned to return to the mill.

Samuel caught his arm. "You have to give Hannah a chance. And she'll never have it if Cecelia's still a part of your life."

Reiver shook his hand off. "You spend too much time thinking and talking, Sam. I don't want to fight with you. I've never told you how to run your life, so don't start trying to run mine. And if you tell Hannah about Cecelia, you'll regret it."

With that threat poised like drawn daggers between them, Reiver stalked off toward the mill, his broad back stiff with anger.

"Blind, thickheaded fool," Samuel muttered to himself. He leaned into the wind and headed back to the house. He had an idea.

He found Hannah in the parlor, seated in a wing chair by the window, intent on mending James's shirt.

She inspected her fine, almost invisible stitches and smiled in satisfaction. "There! It's finished."

Samuel looked around the room to make sure Mrs. Hardy or Millicent wouldn't interrupt them, then said, "Hannah, would you pose for me?"

Her hand flew to her chest in surprise. "Me?"

"Yes. I'd like to sketch your portrait, or make an engraving. You may give it to Reiver as a Christmas gift, if you'd like."

"Your family celebrates Christmas? Mine did, too, but most New Englanders don't."

"My mother was from New York and insisted we celebrate the holiday just as she did when she was little."

"Do you think Reiver would like such a portrait of me?" Her voice trembled with uncertainty.

"I'm sure he would. And we would want it to be a surprise, so we wouldn't tell him."

"When would we start?"

"Tomorrow morning, as soon as he goes to the mill."

Hannah's expression grew wistful. "My mother sat for her portrait just before she died. It was never finished."

"Well, I guarantee you that this one will be. And in time for Christmas."

Then he left her with her eyes shining like a child with a secret and returned to his studio.

In Samuel's studio, Hannah sat in her usual place by the windows, where the even southern light illuminated her.

She felt chilly in spite of the roaring fire in the fireplace, her thick, flannel petticoat and the warm wool shawl around her shoulders. But it was November after all, and cold weather spread its chill throughout New England.

She risked a glance out the window despite Samuel's admonition to sit still. The day was pewter gray and cheerless, with the trees stripped bare of their leaves, their brown skeletal branches clawing at a sky that threatened sleet or snow later that day.

"You're doing splendidly, Hannah," Samuel said. "One more sitting, and I shall have all the sketches I need to do an engraving."

When Hannah had first begun to sit for him several weeks ago, she found it most disconcerting to have Samuel's pale, ghostly eyes stare at her while he worked. His scrutiny was so penetrating that she felt as though he must know her more intimately than her own husband.

"What were you thinking of?" Samuel asked. "Your expression changed so suddenly."

His keen artist's eyes saw too much.

"The truth be known, I haven't been feeling too well lately," she replied.

Samuel stopped sketching. "You do work yourself too hard, Hannah. You should let Millicent do most of it."

But work helped her to forget her remote husband and her own loneliness in the midst of the boisterous Shaw family.

Without warning Hannah felt as light-headed as that fateful summer day in the tobacco field. The studio wheeled to one side and the world went black.

She heard someone calling her name from a great distance, and when she opened her eyes, she found herself cradled in Samuel's arms, his pale, worried face floating above hers.

"Wh-what happened?" She struggled to rise.

"Lie still for a moment. You fainted."

Hannah did as she was told, and the world swung back into focus.

Samuel assisted her to her feet and steadied her with a secure arm around her waist. "Why don't you lie down on your bed and I'll get Mrs. Hardy?"

Hannah nodded and let him escort her to her bedchamber, where she lay down and waited for the housekeeper.

Mrs. Hardy bustled in a minute later, her silvery eyes dark with concern. "Land sakes, Hannah . . ." When she noticed Samuel lingering in the doorway, she shooed him away and closed the door.

The housekeeper sat on the edge of the bed and rested her hand on Hannah's forehead. "Now tell me what happened."

"I fainted," Hannah replied.

The housekeeper's eyes narrowed suspiciously, and she asked Hannah several personal, embarrassing questions in her usual blunt manner.

When she had her answers, Mrs. Hardy chuckled and slapped her thigh. "Leave it to my Reiver. The only thing wrong with you is that you're breeding. In the family way. Going to have a baby nine months to the day, I'll bet."

Hannah felt the same stunned disbelief she had experienced when Uncle Ezra told her she was to marry Reiver Shaw. "I—I can't be."

"You're a married woman. You most certainly can. Surely your mama told you that."

"There must be some mistake."

Mrs. Hardy shrugged. "All the signs are there."

She was going to have a child. Her thoughts screamed mute denial.

"Babies may scream and mess and break your heart, but they keep the human race going," Mrs. Hardy said. "And if it's a boy and the Shaw heir, just think how proud your husband will be!"

Hannah said, "I'd like to be alone now, if you don't mind."

The housekeeper nodded. "I suspect you need some time to get used to the idea."

She patted Hannah's hand and left, closing the door behind her. Hannah heard muffled voices behind the door as the housekeeper said something to Samuel, then silence and retreating footsteps.

A baby . . .

Hannah rolled onto her side and drew up her knees, curling into a tight ball of denial. Somehow it didn't seem fair that Reiver's fumblings beneath her nightshift could do this to her. But they had. Once again, fate had played a cruel trick on her. Hannah squeezed her eyes shut and let the tears flow.

When she could cry no more, she rose, straightened her

skirts, and went to the washbasin to bathe her red, puffy eyes in cold water.

Now that the tears had washed away her initial shock, she was ready to assess the situation calmly and rationally. She rested her hand against her still-flat belly, thought of Reiver's child growing within her, and felt a surge of hope.

How could a man not love the mother of his child?

She hoped Mrs. Hardy hadn't told Samuel the real reason why she had fainted. She wanted Reiver to be the first Shaw to know.

Hannah told him later that night, just as they were getting ready to retire.

She was sitting on the edge of the bed, just finishing plaiting her hair into one long braid for the night, when Reiver came in and headed for the oil lamp, which he always extinguished before undressing himself and joining her in bed.

"Don't turn out the light yet," Hannah said, her heart pounding. "I have something to tell you."

Reiver's hand fell away and he looked at her, puzzled. "What is it?"

Hannah swallowed hard and focused her attention on the thin blue ribbon at the end of her braid. "You're going to be a father."

Silence. Stillness.

She risked a glance at her husband. He stood there, his wide jaw slack, his face as white as the first snowfall.

When he found his voice, he managed to croak, "You're . . . ?"

Hannah nodded, her cheeks flaming.

"Oh, my God! Hannah, that's wonderful." He reached her in two strides and knelt at her feet, his head bowed as he took her hands and brought them to his lips as if paying homage to a queen.

Again, Hannah felt this new life conferring a strange and wonderful power on her.

"You're pleased?"

"Pleased . . . I'm the happiest man in the world." He rose, but to her dismay he didn't take her in his arms and hug her to him like the cherished wife she wanted to be. "This child shall be

the first Shaw of my generation, and if it's a son . . ." His eyes
sparkled in anticipation.

"I hope it will be."

Reiver stepped back, his customary reserve returning.
"Under the circumstances, I think it best that I sleep in the spare
room. I wouldn't want to hurt you or the baby."

So Hannah would be spared her husband's advances until the
baby's birth, sometime in the spring, if Mrs. Hardy's calculations were correct.

"I think that would be best," she agreed.

To her surprise, he leaned down and brushed his lips stiffly
across her own. "Thank you, Hannah." Then he blew out the
lamp and left her to the darkness and her own thoughts.

Reiver's own thoughts both soared and plummeted as he
walked down the dark, narrow hall and settled himself in the
spare room's cold, hard bed.

He was going to be a father. He felt happy, excited, proud,
and thankful all at once. Then he thought of Cecelia, and his joy
soured.

Reiver pulled the blankets more snugly around him and listened to the November wind keening through the eaves and rattling the windows as if demanding entrance.

He would have to tell her at the first opportunity.

Several weeks later Reiver took the sleigh into Hartford to
break the news to Cecelia.

Six inches of snow had fallen several days before, but now
the roads were packed down and the fifteen-mile trip passable.
Seated in the sleigh with a thick rug over his lap and a hot brick
warming his feet, Reiver looked out over pristine, snow-
covered fields and houses with threads of pale gray smoke rising lazily from their chimneys. His thoughts were not on the
brown-and-white winter landscape, but on his conversation
with Samuel just before leaving early that morning.

Helping to hitch Nellie, Samuel said, "Both James and I
couldn't be happier for you and Hannah. She'll make a fine
mother."

"I'm sure she will," Reiver agreed.

"Have you told Cecelia?"

Reiver looked at his brother, whose face was red and pinched with cold. "Not yet. That's why I'm going into Hartford."

"If she has any sense, she'll have nothing more to do with you."

Those words haunted Reiver for the rest of the long drive.

When he arrived at Cecelia's house, which looked as though it had been dusted with sugar, he knocked at the front door, and within minutes Cecelia appeared, surprised and delighted. Today her glossy chestnut ringlets were brushed smooth and pulled back into a simple chignon of the type Hannah favored.

"Get out of the cold this instant, Reiver Shaw," she said, shivering, pulling him into the warm parlor.

Then she was in his arms, providing a special warmth of her own.

He wanted to wait and tell her about the baby after he had given her the peace offering hidden deep in his coat pocket, after he had made long, leisurely love to her upstairs. But he couldn't.

So before Cecelia could take his coat, he looked at her unflinchingly. "You should know that Hannah is going to bear my child."

"Hush," she said, hiding her surprise by putting her fingertips against his lips. "That part of your life has nothing to do with me. It doesn't exist when you're here."

Reiver had never heard such sweet words. Samuel was wrong. Cecelia wasn't going to end it after all.

She pulled off his coat. "Come upstairs."

He reached back into his coat pocket and took out a small box. "Not until I give you this."

Her brown eyes danced. "What is it?"

"An early Christmas gift. Open it and see."

Cecelia gasped when she opened the box and saw the ear bobs glowing dully with dark wine-red garnets and white seed pearls. "Oh, Reiver, they're beautiful."

"They were my mother's most precious possessions, the only jewelry she ever owned. I wanted you to have them."

He wanted his mistress to have them, not his wife. The significance of his gesture was not lost on either of them.

Cecelia slipped them in her earlobes, then took Reiver's hand. "Come upstairs. Now."

"Where is your maid?"

"Visiting her mother. She won't be back for hours."

He grinned and followed her upstairs.

Once they were in Cecelia's bedroom, Reiver flung the heavy drapes aside to let in winter's cold watery light, for he wanted to see every curve and hollow of her supple ivory body as he made love to her, needed to watch her rising passion darken her brown eyes to onyx and see her rosy lips part in abandon. When he turned, he found Cecelia standing at the foot of her bed, one delicate hand curved around the turned maple post, only her bright eyes betraying her impatience.

He crossed the room and started undoing the tiny buttons running down the back of her gown, his excitement rising as he worked. When he was through, he slid his hands beneath the unsuspecting Cecelia's arms and grasped her breasts, pulling her against him so she could feel his arousal through her petticoats.

"Reiver!" she gasped, and shuddered when he thrust his tongue into her ear, mimicking other intimate invasions to come.

"Sweet Cecelia," he whispered, squeezing her breasts harder, frustrated because he couldn't feel her nipples beneath the thick corset cover. When he released her, she was trembling and so weak-kneed that she had to grasp the bedpost for support.

Almost delirious with desire, Reiver stripped himself quickly, his skin too hot to notice the room's slight chill, for the fire had long since died in the grate. Cecelia shrugged out of her gown, but he became impatient with her slowness, so he ripped off her petticoats and unhooked the offending corset for her.

This time he wanted her to ache sweetly from his lovemaking so his passion would linger in her memory long after his departure.

When they were both naked, he tangled his hands in her soft mahogany ringlets and brought his mouth down hard on hers, his questing tongue possessing her and demanding absolute surrender. Cecelia complied with a soft whimper, pressing herself greedily along his length, her eager fingers clutching his smooth muscular shoulders.

He moved away, his hands cupping her breasts, teasing the erect nipples with the callused balls of his thumbs. As he squeezed and tugged he reveled in the way Cecelia arched her back in blatant invitation while she tried to stifle her moans and failed.

"Dear God, Reiver, have mercy!"

"Not this time, my love." He replaced his hands with his mouth, sucking and nipping with wild abandon until Cecelia shrieked and almost swooned with pleasure. Reiver laughed in triumph as he swept her into his arms and carried her over to the bed, where he flung her down on the smooth scented sheets and dived in after her, imprisoning her body with his own.

Their mutual passion ignited beyond bearing, the lovers devoured each other with feverish hands and mouths, their rising groans shattering the room's stillness. When Reiver finally took her, he turned Cecelia over on her knees despite her feeble protestations. Watching her voluptuous curved flanks bounce and rock with his every thrust and her hands clench helplessly at the rumpled sheets, he felt on the verge of exploding.

His head tipped back and he howled his own release just as Cecelia screamed his name and shuddered along his length.

Later, when they had slaked their desire with each other's body, they lay with their limbs entwined beneath a cloud of warm, deep quilts. Reiver wished she would at least congratulate him on the possibility of fatherhood, but she didn't and wouldn't. Cecelia had put his other life with Hannah out of her mind. To her, it no longer existed, and he had to respect her need to deny it.

Reiver propped himself up on one elbow and drank in Cecelia's delicate loveliness, her heart-shaped face and rosebud mouth. "It's getting late. I have to go."

"Must you?" she murmured, running her small hands over his muscular chest.

"I suppose I could stay a little longer."

And he did.

On Christmas morning, while the rest of the family was at church services, Hannah took one last look at her gift to Reiver—the framed engraved portrait of herself that Samuel had done—before wrapping it.

She stared at it in wonder. Surely the beautiful woman regarding the world through grave eyes was not she. When she had protested to the artist that he had misrepresented her, Samuel smiled enigmatically and said, "But that is how I think you will look one day."

Hannah ran her fingertips along the smooth wooden frame. Is this how Samuel saw her, as a beautiful woman with such a worldly, knowing air far beyond Hannah's limited experience of life? She didn't feel particularly worldly or knowing.

A sudden bout of the nausea that had been plaguing her all morning—indeed for the past month—sent Hannah running for the washbasin. When she finished retching, she rinsed her mouth and lay down for a while, then returned to wrapping her husband's gift.

No sooner did she take it downstairs than she heard the front door open and the rest of the family came trooping in, stamping their feet noisily to shake the snow from their boots and mumble, "Brrr!" and "Damn, it's cold outside!"

"How was Reverend Crane's sermon?" Hannah asked.

"So boring I fell asleep," Reiver replied.

Samuel laughed. "You have to learn to sleep with your eyes open, as I do, then no one would glare at you so disapprovingly."

Mrs. Hardy said, "We saw your aunt and uncle in church."

"Did they ask after me?" Hannah said.

Reiver replied, "They bustled off before we could speak to them."

"Just as well," Hannah said.

James removed his hat and unwound his scarf. "Are you feeling better, Hannah?"

"Much better," she replied, collecting coats. "I was sorry to miss the service."

"If the Good Lord can't forgive you under the circumstances . . ." Mrs. Hardy brushed some snow from her silver hair. "Now, let's sit down to Christmas dinner, shall we?"

After a sumptuous feast of roast goose, the family gathered in the parlor to exchange gifts.

Hannah was delighted to see that James and Samuel were pleased with the wool stockings she had knit for them, and she in turn loved the leather-bound edition of *Ivanhoe* that they both had given her. But she nervously watched Reiver open her gift to him.

When he looked at the framed engraving, a peculiar expression flitted across his features and was gone in an instant, leading Hannah to believe she had imagined it.

He held up the portrait for all to see. "Look what my brother has done for me . . . a lovely portrait of my wife." He bowed his head. "She has already given me the grandest gift a man can hope for."

Then Reiver handed Hannah a package and kissed her lightly on the top of her head. "This cannot compare with the gift you've given me, but I hope you'll like it."

When Hannah tore the paper off, she found a serviceable gray wool shawl. "It's just what I need to ward off a chill on these cold days," she said, slipping it around her shoulders.

Later Reiver followed Samuel out to the barn. At first the darkness blinded him, but as his eyes became used to the dimness redolent of fresh hay and horseflesh, he saw his brother in the back, saddling his horse. The horse threw up his head and whickered softly, warning Samuel of someone's approach.

Reiver stood before the stall, feet slightly apart, head lowered like a charging bull. "What in damnation did you think you were doing?"

Samuel fitted the saddle on his mount's back. "What am I supposed to have done now?"

"Don't play the innocent with me!" Reiver scoffed, the barn's cold air turning his furious breath into clouds. "That portrait you did of Hannah . . . it doesn't look anything like her."

Samuel stopped and turned. "It's quite an insult to tell an artist he can't capture a subject's likeness."

"Well, you didn't. You made her look too—too—"

"Sensuous?" Samuel tightened the saddle cinch. "I draw what I see in a person. I can't help it if we don't see the same qualities in Hannah."

"Don't mock me, Sam."

His brother stared at him coldly. "You're making something out of nothing in your usual thickheaded way. I offered to do Hannah's portrait as a Christmas gift to you, and I captured what I saw. I'm sorry if you don't like it." He took his horse's reins and led him out of the stall. "Now, if you'll excuse me, I'm going visiting."

Reiver watched his brother mount his horse in the barnyard

and ride off, graceful and erect in the saddle. Women swooned over Samuel's looks and his attentiveness. Could he be trying to woo Hannah?

"He's my brother," Reiver said, dismissing that thought at once.

He turned and walked back to the house.

Spring came early the following year, and Hannah felt in harmony with the season of rebirth, always so welcome after a harsh New England winter. Just as the maple and ash trees sprouted tight green buds, Hannah blossomed with her unborn child.

Round and cumbersome now, she spent her days napping and dreaming of a little boy sledding down Mulberry Hill, or she sat by the window and watched the world turn greener as April slid into May. It wouldn't be long now, the midwife had assured her.

The day came sooner than she expected.

A nagging backache had plagued Hannah all afternoon, and by early evening the dull pains had crawled around to gnaw at her belly like a starving beast.

She heaved herself out of her wing chair and lumbered across the parlor to where Reiver sat, his brow furrowed and head bowed over the account books.

She placed a trembling hand on his shoulder. "You had better send for the midwife."

He took one look at Hannah's face and turned gray. "Dear God, are you sure?" When she nodded, he jumped to his feet, almost sending his chair toppling in his haste to assist her.

If another pain hadn't gripped her, Hannah would have found Reiver's concern touching. But all she could think about was her upcoming labor and the primitive female fear that she might not survive it.

"Mrs. Hardy!" Reiver bellowed as he slipped his arm around Hannah and guided her toward the stairs. When the housekeeper appeared in the doorway, he snapped, "It's time. Don't just stand there. Find Sam and tell him to go for the midwife. My son is about to be born."

"Don't get excited," Mrs. Hardy said. "He won't come for hours yet."

Hours later Reiver's child still had not yet arrived.

Banished from his wife's lying-in chamber by women determined to do women's work without masculine interference, Reiver paced back and forth outside the door until Hannah's groans drove him back downstairs to where Samuel and James were keeping a vigil.

Reiver circled the parlor, running his hands through his hair. "I wish there was something I could do."

Samuel poured half a glass of apple brandy and pushed it across the table in his brother's direction. "There's nothing you can do. Hannah has to do this alone."

Reiver grabbed the glass and downed it in two swallows, savoring the burn as it slid down his throat. He stared at his brothers. "What if she dies?"

Then you can marry your precious Cecelia, said the look in Samuel's accusing eyes.

Reiver's gaze fell away in shame.

"Hannah won't die," James said, tinkering with a piece of machinery. He rose. "I'm going for a walk. Call me when the baby's born." And he left.

Reiver spent the next few hours pacing the parlor while Samuel sketched the brandy bottle sitting on the sideboard. Both men stopped whenever Hannah's screams of agony filtered down.

Reiver regarded Samuel with desperation in his eyes. "This has been going on too long. I'm going upstairs, and they had damn well better let me in."

Suddenly the door flew open and James stood there, white-faced and panting, a lantern in hand. "Reiver! A cat got into the rearing shed. The worms . . ." Words failed him and he gestured helplessly.

Reiver swore loudly enough to shake the walls. He bolted for the door, his wife and child forgotten as he and James went running through the darkness, the wildly swinging lantern casting eerie arcs of light on the grass.

When he stormed into the rearing shed, the ominous silence seemed to scream disaster and made Reiver want to retch. Overturned trays, mulberry leaves, and dead worms were scattered all over the floor. The surviving worms squirmed in pathetic confusion.

He whirled on James. "Where in the hell is that miserable, useless Freddie Bates?"

"H—here, Mr. Shaw," came a wee frightened voice from the doorway.

He looked around James to see Freddie, a tired-looking little boy of ten, standing there, quaking in abject terror.

Reiver was on the boy in two strides, cuffing him before he could dart out of range, sending him sprawling. "Damn you, you little idiot! What do you think I pay you five cents a week for, to sleep on the job?"

Freddie sat up. "N-no, sir."

"I hired you to keep an eye out for cats and rats so they don't attack the worms. So what do you have to say for yourself?"

The boy scrambled to his feet and dusted off the seat of his trousers. "I—I'm sorry, sir. I guess I fell asleep and a cat got in. I didn't do it on purpose."

Reiver took a menacing step forward. "When I find that cat, I'm going to put you and it in a sack filled with stones and drop the miserable pair of you into the brook!"

That was too much for Freddie. He turned and ran for his life.

James said, "Weren't you a little hard on the boy?"

Reiver whirled around. "Hard on him? Skinning him alive would be hard on him." He looked around at the devastation and swore again. "A whole crop of cocoons is gone. Lost. Ruined. And all because one goddamn stupid little boy fell asleep."

"Maybe we can salvage something," James said softly.

Reiver scoffed at that. "Those that weren't killed are probably too shocked to spin."

"Let's try, anyway."

So James and Reiver got to work, Hannah and the baby forgotten.

Her ordeal was over, and she had survived.

Hannah looked down at her infant son feeding greedily at her breast, and the long hours of agonizing pain that had racked her body vanished from her memory as though they had never occurred. She felt a surge of love so powerful that it jolted her physically. He was so tiny, with ten perfectly formed, miniature fingers and toes.

"Giving birth is hell, isn't it?" Mrs. Hardy said. "But now you've earned a rest. When you wake up, Reiver will be here."

But when Hannah finally did awaken, she saw Samuel sitting beside her bed, his eyes bleary and jaw shadowed with stubble.

He squeezed her hand. "How are you feeling?"

She smiled wanly. "Much better, now that it's over."

He looked down at the baby lying in the wooden cradle that James had built for him just two weeks ago. "Thank you for giving me such a handsome nephew. What are you going to name him?"

"Reiver and I have agreed on Benjamin," she replied. She frowned. "What time is it?"

"It's almost morning."

She looked past him at the door. "Where is Reiver?"

"He and James are still in the rearing shed," he said. "A cat got in and—"

"You needn't make excuses for him, Samuel," Hannah said bitterly. "Those worms mean more to him than me or his son."

"Not that I want to defend my brother, but this accident was a calamity. He and James have been working all night trying to salvage what's left of the worms." He managed a reassuring smile. "He'll be here soon. And he'll be delighted with his son, I promise."

After Samuel left, Hannah looked down at her peacefully sleeping son. Suddenly she realized that her husband no longer mattered to her as much as her child. She was bound to her husband legally, but she was bound to her son by blood. She would give all her love to Benjamin, and he would return that love a hundredfold.

Her son was her future, her family, her power.

There came a knock on the door, and it opened to reveal Reiver, looking both haggard and sheepish.

"I'm sorry your worms were destroyed," Hannah said, thinking those were the words he wanted to hear above all others.

But his eyes were on the cradle as he crossed the room.

Hannah reached down and picked up the sleeping bundle, holding him as if he were made of glass. "Isn't he beautiful?"

Reiver ran one finger down the baby's soft cheek and stared down at him as if he had never seen one before. "My son."

No, Hannah thought. *Mine.*

CHAPTER
❧ 4 ❧

"BENJAMIN Shaw, you are the smartest little boy in the whole world," Hannah said, beaming down at her fourteen-month-old son as he sat on the nursery floor and carefully piled the little wooden blocks atop each other. "You've just built a house, yes, you have."

Benjamin's cherubic face split into a wide grin at his mother's effusive praise just before he swung his hand and demolished his creation with one quick swipe, sending the blocks clattering and scattering all over the floor. Then he giggled and clapped his hands.

"Oh, we're so pleased with ourselves, aren't we?" With an indulgent sigh, Hannah knelt to retrieve the blocks and set them before her son to pile up and knock down again.

She rose and the dizziness hit her like an unexpected slap in the face. Groping for support, she found the back of a chair and clung to it, waiting for the nausea to pass.

When the room stopped spinning, she smiled at her son, who was eyeing her strange behavior solemnly. "Well, Benjamin, soon you will have a little baby brother or sister to play with."

She knew it wasn't the stifling July heat that was making her light-headed. She had missed two monthly cycles, and since Benjamin had been weaned, the tenderness in her breasts had nothing to do with nursing.

No, she didn't need Dr. Bradley to tell her that she was going to have another baby. Joy as bright as the summer sunshine filled her. She couldn't wait to tell Samuel.

The moment Hannah realized her mental slip, she blushed

and looked down at her son as if he could read her thoughts. "I meant your father."

Scooping up the baby in her arms, she said, "And I'm going to tell him right now."

After Hannah left Benjamin in the kitchen with Mrs. Hardy, she hurried across the lawn toward the mill.

She hadn't meant to think of Samuel first. His name had just popped into her head. It meant nothing. Nothing at all.

Hannah reached the mill and went inside, still a little awed by the huge square stone building with its windows set high to collect as much daylight as possible to illuminate the work area below. It was so obviously Reiver's domain, a mysterious world of noisy water-powered looms spinning silk onto bobbins.

She searched the room for her husband, and finally found him standing in a corner, a paper in his hand, deep in animated conversation with James. Although she couldn't hear him over the din of the machines, she knew from his scowl that he was furious about something.

She walked over to them. "Reiver, may I speak to you for a moment?"

He didn't even glance up from the paper. "Not now, Hannah."

"But it's very important."

"It will just have to wait." Ignoring her, he stabbed at the paper he held and said to James, "Can't you see that this gear configuration will never work?"

Hannah turned and quietly left, trying to ignore the mill girls' sidelong pitying glances for their employer's slighted wife. Outside, she blinked rapidly, telling herself that her eyes were watering because of the painful, blinding sunlight. She walked back to the homestead.

No sooner did she reach the backdoor than she noticed that Samuel had tied his new horse, Titan, in the shade of a nearby oak tree and was industriously brushing the chestnut's coat to a burnished shine. Because of the hazy afternoon heat, Samuel went shirtless.

Hannah should have gone inside, but found she couldn't tear her eyes away from Samuel. While his bare shoulders and back were not as broad or muscular as Reiver's, they rippled beneath his pale skin as he extended his arm to the crest of Titan's neck, then drew the brush down in a firm sweeping line. His narrow hips shifted his balance with every movement.

Hannah was just about to go inside when the horse betrayed her by lifting his head, perking up his ears, and whinnying softly in welcome. Samuel turned, saw her, and smiled.

She had no choice but to join him. "He's beautiful," she said, extending her hand so Titan could nuzzle her palm with his velvety muzzle. If she kept her attention focused on Titan, she wouldn't have to look at Samuel's bare chest, as shiny with sweat as his horse's hide.

"Isn't he?" Samuel scratched Titan between the ears, causing him to close his eyes and sigh in equine contentment. "He's as fast as the wind and as gentle as a baby."

"Speaking of babies," Hannah said, blushing, "Reiver and I are going to be parents again." She kept her eyes focused on the horse's cheek.

Even though she wasn't looking at Samuel, Hannah could sense a change in him at once, a withdrawal, as if she had disappointed him somehow. Then it was gone in an instant.

"That's wonderful," he said, transferring the brush to his right hand and moving away to brush Titan's sleek hindquarters. "Congratulations. I'm sure my brother must be excited and pleased."

"I haven't told him yet."

Samuel stopped brushing and raised his brows in surprise. "Reiver doesn't know?"

Hannah faced him. Even in the cool dark shade, his pale blue eyes collected the light, making them look more vibrant. "I tried just now," she said.

"Don't tell me. He said he was too busy to talk to you." He paused. "I can tell you're disappointed."

"I try not to be. I know Reiver is working hard to make the mill a success."

Samuel's handsome features darkened. "He could still spare you a minute of his time, especially to hear wonderful news like this."

Hannah lifted one shoulder in an unconcerned shrug. "I'll tell him tonight, before dinner, when he's had a chance to rest and isn't so preoccupied with the mill."

"I think it's time I had a little talk with my brother."

She placed a restraining hand on his arm. It felt pleasantly hot and damp, the hairs rough to the touch. "Please don't. You'll only make Reiver angry."

When Samuel glanced down at her hand still resting on his arm, Hannah became self-conscious and quickly withdrew it.

"My brother may know a great deal about running a silk mill," Samuel said, "but he has much to learn about being a considerate husband. Still, if you don't wish me to speak to him . . ."

"It would be best."

"Then I won't." He studied her. "How are you feeling? You look very pale today."

"I felt a little dizzy this morning while playing with Benjamin, but it passed."

He frowned. "You're running yourself ragged. Perhaps you should get more rest and let the girls do the household chores."

The distinct aroma of horseflesh and male sweat tickled Hannah's nose. "You needn't worry, Samuel. I'm fine, really."

He took a step closer. "I worry about you."

Titan swung his head around and stared at his master. Hannah stared at Samuel as well, all too aware that the atmosphere between them had suddenly thickened, becoming as charged with promise as a summer thunderstorm. Part of her wanted to run from it. Another part of her wanted to embrace it.

She reached out and combed her fingers through Titan's coarse mane. "You needn't worry. The dizziness will pass. I'd endure any physical discomfort to have another child." She couldn't stop the words from tumbling out of her mouth. "Benjamin is such a joy that I can't wait to have another, hopefully a little girl this time."

"I hope you get exactly what you want, Hannah."

Why did she have the uncomfortable feeling that he wasn't referring to her unborn child?

"I'm sure we will. Now, if you'll excuse me, I have to get back to the house."

She fled before Samuel could say another word.

Once back in the house, Hannah busied herself in the buttery chopping dried rosemary and lemon verbena, but her thoughts kept dwelling on Samuel standing in the shade, grooming his horse.

She inhaled the rich spicy aroma and smiled to herself. He listened to her. He shared her happiness about the baby. He expressed his concern for her well-being.

Hannah finished chopping the herbs and refilled the spice box. Tonight when she told Reiver her wonderful news, he would be just as excited and solicitous as his brother.

Later that evening Hannah hesitated in the doorway of their bedchamber. "Reiver, may I speak to you for a moment?"

He buttoned a clean shirt. "Only for a minute. I'm on my way out."

Hannah hid her disappointment. "Oh? You won't be having dinner with the family this evening?"

He shook his head and slipped into his best waistcoat. "I'm dining with the Athelsons. Important business." He looked at her. "What did you want to tell me?"

"You're going to be a father again."

Reiver's hand stopped at the third waistcoat button. "Another child?" When Hannah blushed and nodded, he grinned, strode over to her and kissed her on the cheek. "That's wonderful news. Another son for the Shaw silk empire."

She didn't say she hoped it was a daughter. She waited for him to realize that this was the exciting news she couldn't wait to tell him at the mill today and to feel remorse for brushing her off so pointedly, but all he did was return to the cheval glass and finish buttoning his waistcoat.

"Does the rest of the family know?" he asked.

"I wanted to tell you first."

"I'm sure they'll be as excited as I am." Reiver put on his black frock coat and straightened it so that it hung properly. Then he walked over to Hannah, took her hands, and kissed them. "I'll probably be late, so don't wait up for me. And I'll go back to sleeping in the other room until the baby comes."

Then he disappeared down the hall.

That summer of 1842 passed too slowly for Hannah, and she was relieved when September flew by more quickly. Already five months pregnant, she had to wear looser dresses to accommodate her swelling middle.

One cool October morning she was churning butter when Samuel came into the buttery, his eyes sparkling with excitement.

"I've just sold five more engravings," he announced, "and I want to celebrate."

Hannah stopped her work and smiled. "Celebrate in the middle of the week? Samuel Shaw, how sinful. Reverend Crane would never approve."

"I'm in the mood for sin," he said, grinning. "Would you care to join me?"

She recognized his teasing for what it was and retorted, "I'll have you know that women in my condition avoid sin at all costs."

He wiggled his eyebrows and twirled an imaginary mustache like a stage villain in some lurid melodrama. "Would the unsuspecting damsel agree to a carriage ride into the hills south of town?"

Hannah laughed. "I'd love to, but I have my chores."

"Forget them. You've been working too hard. And if Reiver can leave the mill to go into Hartford today, then you can go for a short carriage ride."

She cast a longing glance out the window. "It is a beautiful day for it."

He crooked his arm and extended it to her. "Turn your churn over to Mrs. Hardy, grab a shawl, and let's go."

Minutes later Hannah was seated next to Samuel in the carriage, on the road leading south from Coldwater. Wrapping her gray wool shawl more closely about her, she found the cool autumn air invigorating.

"You seem especially happy today," she said.

"I am. Not only have I sold five engravings, I've been commissioned by a wealthy farmer named Broome to paint a portrait of his daughter, Patience." He glanced at her with a mischievous twinkle in his eye. "I've heard the young lady is quite comely, so I'm sure it won't be much of a chore."

"How fortunate for you." Just at that moment Hannah realized that she had never ever heard Samuel mention another woman romantically. Surely a man so handsome, charming, and attractive to women had a lady love somewhere. The thought made her decidedly uncomfortable and she couldn't understand why. "Where did you meet this Miss Broome of yours?"

Suddenly Samuel's lighthearted mood vanished. "She's not my Miss Broome. In fact I've never even met her. Her father contacted me about the portrait."

"I see." Hannah plucked at the edge of her shawl. "With winter coming, I'm sure Reiver will appreciate your contribution to the family coffers."

"He always does. At least he'll be able to buy raw silk from China."

They drove in silence up the dusty dirt road, passing few other carriages on their way up to the hills. Samuel didn't stop until they arrived at a spot at the crest of a hill where they could pull over the carriage and enjoy the panorama.

A breeze tugged at the long, wide ribbons of Hannah's bonnet, brushing them against Samuel's chin. He looked down at her and smiled. "Is it too chilly for you up here?"

"Not at all." In fact she felt quite warm, perhaps because her arm touched Samuel's and she could feel his heat through the sleeve of his coat.

She took a deep breath to savor the autumn air and felt a pain so sharp that she gasped and doubled over in agony.

"Hannah, what's wrong?"

She wrapped her arms around her abdomen and looked at him helplessly. "I—I don't know."

"Are you in pain?"

She swallowed hard and nodded as another pain knifed through her.

He slipped his arm around her shoulders. "Is it the baby?"

"Oh, dear God, Samuel! I'm going to lose my baby!" Hannah screamed her denial and clutched at the lapels of his coat, feeling as though her insides were being ripped out. "Please! Get me home."

"Hang on!" Samuel untied the reins and brought them down on the horse's rump with a sharp smack, causing the animal to throw back its head in alarm, but it managed to turn the carriage and start down the road at a brisk trot.

Samuel drove like a madman, keeping one eye on Hannah,

curled into a tight ball on the seat as if she could physically retain the baby in her womb. Where the road was straight and relatively smooth, he urged the horse into a canter to make better time, and slowed the animal down to negotiate any ruts and rocks.

The moment they pulled up in front of the homestead, Samuel was out of the carriage before it had come to a full stop. He grabbed the bridle to stop the horse from trampling him before racing around to the other side and extending his arms up to Hannah, who rose, swayed, and collapsed.

Hannah opened her eyes to find herself in her own bedchamber, in her own bed, the curtains drawn to keep the room as dark as her thoughts.

Impressions exploded on her consciousness . . . excruciating pain, urgent voices, soothing hands. But most of all, her body that had been changing to nurture and protect the helpless child growing within her now felt empty with an aching hollowness.

A gentle hand came out of nowhere to brush damp strands of hair away from her face. "Hannah?"

She turned her head. There was Samuel where she knew he'd be, sitting at her bedside as he had just after Benjamin was born, his pale eyes bright and sad, his handsome face grave, yet radiating strength.

"I lost the baby, didn't I?" she said, her voice breaking.

"I'm so sorry."

"I suppose it was God's will."

"I find it difficult to believe that any god would want you to suffer so much."

Without thinking, Hannah sought his hand with her own, lacing her fingers between his and holding on tightly. "Was it a boy or a girl?"

He hesitated as if debating whether to tell her. "A boy."

She laughed, a bitter, hysterical sound, and tightened her hold. "Another son for the Shaw silk empire."

He pulled her into his arms and held her head against his shoulder so she could cry.

Later that day, when Reiver returned from Hartford and was told that his wife had lost their baby, he went to her room. Even as he held her hand, telling her of the other children they would have one day, Hannah couldn't help thinking that he hadn't been at her side when she needed him most.

By the time autumn eased into winter and the first snow fell, Hannah had recovered. She couldn't indulge in mourning her lost child for too long, for her own feelings of loss had to be subordinated to Benjamin's welfare and to family responsibilities.

One raw, bleak November day, Hannah went upstairs to Samuel's studio to bring him luncheon on a tray and found him studying his preliminary sketches of Patience Broome.

"She's very beautiful," Hannah said. Why did that admission diminish her own feelings of attractiveness?

Samuel flung down the sketches. "That's all I've captured, her beauty, nothing else." He rubbed his jaw. "Or perhaps that's all there is to her."

When Hannah thought of the engraving he had made of her and how it revealed more than she wanted to see, she realized it was not his lack of skill that was at fault.

He looked at her. "Enough of Patience Broome. How are you?"

Hannah shrugged. "There are times when I wonder what he would have been like, whether he would have had light brown hair or dark, blue eyes or brown, and a laugh like Benjamin's." Her eyes glazed as she looked inward. "But then I count my blessings and it passes."

"I can't pretend to know what it feels like to lose a child, but I do know that time does heal all wounds."

"When my parents died, I thought I'd never stop grieving for them. But I did. Eventually." Hannah fell silent for a moment, her gaze sliding down to the sketches of Patience Broome scattered on Samuel's sketching table. This time she felt strong dislike.

Her expression must have reflected her emotions, for Samuel said, "Are my sketches really that bad?"

She snapped out of her reverie. "I beg your pardon?"

"The way you were staring at my sketches just now makes me want to tear them up and throw them away."

Hannah's cheeks grew hot with embarrassment. "They're

wonderful, Samuel. I was merely thinking of some particularly distasteful chores I have to do this afternoon, that's all."

He looked relieved.

She smiled. "I really have to get back to the kitchen. Reiver and James will be home for their midday meal any minute now."

After she left the studio, she didn't return to the kitchen right away. She went to her bedchamber, closed the door, and leaned against it, trying to understand why she had such strong feelings of animosity toward a pretty young woman she had never met.

Then the answer dawned on her. She was jealous.

Her hand flew to her mouth. For her to be jealous of Patience Broome, she had to have deep feelings for Samuel.

Hannah shook her head. That was impossible. Samuel was her husband's brother. She couldn't be in love with him. She couldn't.

She put such thoughts out of her mind and returned to the kitchen.

Reiver stood at the base of Mulberry Hill and watched part of his dream die.

All winter he had looked forward to the spring of 1843, when the new mulberry trees would send up their shoots, but now that April had arrived and the trees weren't thriving, he was filled with a feeling of dread.

James pulled up a plant and examined the roots. "It's the blight," he said. "The trees are rotting in the ground."

Reiver whipped off his hat, threw it on the ground, and let out a string of profanities that shocked even James. "So much for trying to raise our own silk," he muttered bitterly.

"We can still manufacture it," James said. "We'll just have to import more raw silk from the Orient like everyone else."

"I had my heart set on raising my own."

James brushed his hair out of his eyes. "Everyone told us we couldn't raise silk in this country. I guess they were right."

Reiver pulled up a plant, swore at it, and flung it down. "Plow them up and burn the lot of them."

"At least we tried, Reiver," James called after him.

"Trying doesn't count," Reiver retorted over his shoulder. "Success is all that matters."

He strode to the homestead, his anger and bitterness rising like bile in his throat and leaving the sour taste of defeat on his tongue. Wait until the good citizens of Coldwater learned that Rummy Shaw's son had failed in his attempt to provide his own raw silk for the mill. He'd be a laughingstock again.

When he entered the parlor, he found Hannah seated in the wing chair by the cold fireplace. Although she had suffered another miscarriage just two weeks ago in her second month of pregnancy, she had recovered as quickly as if it had never happened.

She stood up the moment she saw his face. "Reiver, what's wrong?"

He ran his fingers through his hair. "A blight has killed all our mulberry trees."

Hannah's blue eyes widened until they became enormous in her thin face. "Oh, no! Does that mean . . . ?"

"This crop of worms will all die without mulberry leaves to feed on." Reiver braced his arms against the mantel and leaned heavily against it, trying to control his rage.

Hannah placed a hesitant hand on his arm. "I'm so sorry, Reiver. I know how much it meant to you to raise your own silk."

He stared into the fireplace. "Ruined. Everything's ruined."

Her hand fell away. "You can still import raw silk, can't you?"

He nodded.

"And you'll still be able to manufacture thread."

"Yes, I can still do that."

"Then you've experienced a temporary setback, not ruination."

Reiver moved away from the fireplace. "You'll have to excuse me, Hannah. I've got to go help James dig up what's left of those trees and burn them."

And he had to find a way to see Cecelia. He needed her more than ever to comfort him and soothe his shattered dreams.

Hannah watched him leave, then returned to her chair. While she knew the loss of the mulberry trees was a catastrophe, she had more pressing matters on her mind.

She could deny it no longer. She was falling in love with Samuel.

How else could she explain the warm flush of pleasure she experienced whenever he spoke to her, the way she caught herself listening for his quick footsteps or his resonant voice? How else could she explain why Samuel occupied her thoughts, never her own husband, and her guilt at imagining him making love to her whenever Reiver did?

After her second miscarriage, Samuel shared her deep sorrow as he had that first time last fall, helping her to regain her strength and easing her bleak despair so she could look forward to the future again. He willingly provided the comfort that Reiver never could.

Hannah closed her eyes and pressed her forehead to the heel of her hand to ease her torment. She could never reveal her true feelings to him. That would only result in disaster.

CHAPTER
❧ 5 ❧

THE outstretched arms of the ancient oak tree in the backyard provided the only respite from the hot July sun, so Hannah and Samuel placed their chairs deep within the cool cave of shade. She sewed while he sketched Hannah's second son, David, treasured all the more after her two heartbreaking miscarriages.

Hannah set down her sewing and scanned Mulberry Hill's long slope, now barren of the mulberry trees that had once been Reiver's hope and pride.

"It's so sad," she said, glancing down at Davey, sleeping soundly on a blanket at her feet. "Reiver was so confident that silk could be produced in this country. And now . . ." She shrugged.

"After five years of marriage, you should know that my brother's not the kind of man to let a mere act of God or nature stand in his way," Samuel replied, his intent gaze darting from the sleeping child's cherubic face to his sketch pad.

Hannah smiled. "Indeed I do."

With the price of mulberry trees plummeting so low that desperate nurserymen were selling them for firewood and last year's blight delivering a devastating coup de grace to the few remaining trees, Reiver had abandoned his dream of producing silk and was now concentrating on manufacturing thread from imported Chinese raw silk. If there was one thing Hannah had learned about her husband since their marriage, it was that Reiver Shaw was a practical man and undaunted in his obsessions.

Five years . . .

So much had changed. The rearing shed where Reiver tended his worms with such single-minded intensity had been torn down after standing empty for so long. Last year, in 1844, Hannah managed to carry another son to full term, though she remained haunted by her previous miscarriages. While she tried to keep her feelings for Samuel a secret, she feared he was falling in love with her.

Hannah picked up Reiver's lawn shirt and resumed sewing, focusing on stitching a small tear in the cuff so she wouldn't be distracted by Samuel's perfect profile and his calm, focused energy.

"If Elias Howe has his way, all women will do their sewing on his sewing machine," Samuel said, "though I doubt that any machine could duplicate your stitches. They're so fine, they're almost invisible."

Hannah stared down at her husband's shirt. For all the times she had darned its tears, Reiver had never once complimented her on the fineness of her stitches. "Wouldn't such a machine put thousands of seamstresses out of work?" she asked.

"That's one point of view. But Reiver thinks it could also help them do more work faster. And if seamstresses use more thread, Shaw Silks will have to produce more to keep up with the demand. More demand means more profits."

"Reiver never mentioned that to me."

Samuel said nothing, just set down his stick of charcoal and held his paper at arm's length to study David's likeness, but Hannah could feel the tension in him as palpably as the sluggish summer breeze stirring the leaves overhead.

"Are you happy here, Hannah?" he asked.

She looked down at the cherubic David, who started and suckled in his sleep, and she smiled. "I have two beautiful, healthy children, and I'm content."

"And are you just as content with my brother?"

"He's my husband."

Samuel placed his hand on her arm, forcing her to stop sewing and face him. "He may be your husband, but I know you don't love him."

Hannah glanced at the house nervously, searching the windows. "Please don't. Someone will see you and make false assumptions."

He removed his hand with great reluctance. "No one will see me. Mrs. Hardy took Benjamin to feed the ducks, and James went to Hartford to see about using belts to run his machines. Reiver won't be back from Northampton until early evening. We can speak freely, Hannah, and it's time we did."

As he leaned back in his chair, with one long leg stretched out and the other ankle crossed at the knee, Samuel's casual demeanor would have fooled the most suspicious observer, who would assume brother- and sister-in-law were having the most innocent of conversations as they enjoyed each other's company on a lazy summer afternoon.

Trembling inside, Hannah forced herself to look away. "Perhaps we should not speak at all, lest we say something we'll both regret."

"I must," he replied, keeping his voice low so as not to wake the sleeping child. "I've kept silent for so long, I feel fit to burst."

"Samuel—"

"No. You must hear me out."

Seeing the fire of determination in his ghostly eyes, Hannah sat still and listened.

"When my brother first married you," Samuel began, "I accepted you as his wife. I welcomed you into the family as I would a sister." His brow furrowed. "Over the years I've watched you trip over yourself in your haste to please Reiver, and I've watched him treat you with nothing more than exquisite courtesy." He paused. "Even giving him two sons hasn't won you a place in his heart, has it?"

She reared back in her chair, stung. "Reiver loves Ben and Davey!"

Samuel's gaze didn't waver. "I'm not disputing that. But does he love their mama?"

Hannah turned away. "I'm twenty-three and a matron with two children, not some schoolgirl of sixteen waiting for a Lochinvar to carry her off. Love doesn't matter."

He rested his hand lightly on her arm again, his touch as warm and vital as Reiver's was impersonal. "You can't fool me, Hannah. I just have to look into your eyes to know that love does matter to you."

He was right, of course. His damnable artist's all-seeing eye always read her mind and saw deep into her soul. As much as Hannah loved her children, they could not fill that empty corner of her heart left by their father's indifference.

She bowed her head in defeat. "I can't force Reiver to love me. I must make the best of what the Good Lord has given me."

Samuel withdrew his hand. "That's settling. No one should have to settle. Life should be lived to the fullest and savored like a sumptuous feast."

"Fine for you to say, Sam Shaw. You're a man. Women have to settle. They have no other choice."

"And what would you do if you did have a choice?"

Hannah cut her thread with her teeth. "I'm a practical woman. It's futile to engage in daydreams."

"Hannah, Hannah . . ." he said softly. "You're not as practical as you think you are. Inside, you want a Lochinvar to sweep you off your feet."

She said nothing because she feared he was right.

He added, "You're practical because it helps you to survive my brother's indifference. You don't have to remember that he wasn't by your side when Benjamin and Davey were born, or when you lost those two other children. You think that by filling every waking minute with raising your children and keeping house you can make up for what your marriage lacks. But you can't."

Samuel set down his pad, rose, and leaned his graceful frame against the tree trunk. Several gold coins of sunlight spilling through the trembling leaves above crowned his tousled hair.

He looked away, frowning. "I never was one to keep my feelings to myself." He turned, his eyes daring her to look away. "I love you."

Hannah's heart stopped and she balled her hands into fists. "You mustn't say that, Sam. You mustn't!"

"Why not? It's the truth."

"But I'm your brother's wife."

"Not in the ways that matter."

Panic forced her to her feet. She had to pick up Davey and flee to safety before Samuel inferred the truth that would destroy them all.

"Don't run from me, Hannah," he said, without making a move to stop her. "Please hear me out."

The torment in his voice drew her back, and she sank down into her chair.

"I didn't mean to fall in love with you," he began. "It just happened slowly, over time. In the beginning I sought to make up for Reiver's neglect by offering you friendship, nothing more. But as time went on and I came to know you . . ." He shrugged. "Against my better judgment I found myself falling in love with you."

Hannah shook her head in dismay. "Oh, Samuel . . ."

"Look at me, Hannah." Again, he didn't move, but compelled her to do his bidding with his voice. "I would have kept silent if I thought you didn't return my feelings. Lord knows the last thing I want to do is open a Pandora's box and destroy the family." He paused. "But I know that you love me, even if you won't admit it."

She looked deeply into his eyes and tried to lie for all their sakes. "I don't love you. You're imagining it."

Samuel smiled wryly. "Don't try to be noble, Hannah. I've seen the way you look at me, the way your face lights up when I come into a room."

Hannah's cheeks burned. Then she panicked. "Have the others . . . ?"

"Noticed? I doubt it. Reiver is too sure of himself to think that his own brother would risk his wrath by coveting his wife, and James thinks only of his steam machines. And if Mrs. Hardy suspects, she isn't saying. Our secret is safe. For now."

For now . . .

Feeling like a cornered animal, Hannah rose, her long skirts brushing the sleeping baby, but not waking him. She knotted her long fingers together to keep her overtaxed self-control from shattering. "Let sleeping dogs lie, Samuel! No good will ever come of dredging up matters that are best left unsaid."

He moved away from the tree, and for one horrible, thrilling moment Hannah feared he was going to take her into his arms. But he stopped just in time. "You're right."

She relaxed as the danger retreated into its hidden lair.

He said, "Do you know that this morning I was planning to ask you if you would run away with me to Europe?"

Hannah's eyes widened.

"I could support us quite comfortably with the sale of my engravings, but I decided that I couldn't bring myself to demand such a choice." He glanced down at Davey, now stirring, and smiled ruefully. "I know you would never leave your children for any man, especially to live in sin."

"Even if I could leave my children, you could never betray your own brother. You're too honorable."

Samuel's troubled eyes darkened. "Don't be too sure of that."

Davey spared her from replying by opening his sleepy blue eyes, struggling to sit up, then extending his chubby arms to his mother as if demanding that she choose him.

The choice was no choice at all. Hannah knelt down, picked up her grinning son, and hugged him, breathing deeply of his warm, clean scent. "There, there, my little sleepyhead. Mama's here." She will always be here.

From a distance a small, high-pitched voice called, "Mama! Uncle Samuel!" and Hannah looked up to see four-year-old Ben come racing across the lawn toward them, with Mrs. Hardy struggling to keep up. Tall for his age, Ben resembled Hannah's own father more than the Shaws, with golden hair and a winning grin.

I wanted him to be my child, Hannah thought, but he is so like his father, curious and bold. But Davey is mine, gentle and sensitive.

When Ben reached them, he said, "The old mallard tried to peck my hand, but I ran away from him."

"Did he quack and chase you?" Samuel asked, swinging the boy into his arms.

"Yes, but I ran faster," Ben said proudly.

Puffing hard, Mrs. Hardy joined them. "That little rascal is too fast for these old legs."

Ben laughed and his uncle set him down. "I ran away from Mrs. Hardy, too."

Hannah gave him a stern look. "That was very naughty of you, Benjamin Shaw. You mustn't run away from Mrs. Hardy ever again."

"Yes, Mama." But by the defiant twinkle in her son's eye, Hannah feared he was merely appeasing her, as his father was wont to do.

"What are you drawing, Uncle Samuel?" Ben demanded, reaching for the sketchpad.

"Davey sleeping," Samuel replied, showing him the drawing.

The slow clopping of hoofbeats and rolling of wagon wheels in the drive distracted them for a moment, and all turned to see the peddler's wagon pull up in front of the house.

"The peddler! The peddler!" Ben squealed with excitement, the drawing forgotten. He tugged at Hannah's skirts. "Can we see what he has today, Mama?"

Hannah smiled, for she looked forward to the peddler's monthly visits as much as her son did. "Let's see, shall we?"

But she suspected that this time, looking through the peddler's collection of pots, pans, needles, and ribbons would not erase Samuel's passionate declaration from her mind.

Later, after the peddler had departed a few dollars richer and Hannah was alone in her bedchamber, dusting the furniture and watching the late-afternoon sky turn an ominous pewter gray with an approaching summer storm, she found herself haunted by Samuel's confession.

Hannah opened a window to let a cool breeze into the stuffy room. What had he said, that he hadn't wanted to open a Pandora's box? Well, he had. In a few seconds he had shattered the pretense of Hannah's existence.

She leaned against the windowsill and closed her eyes. How she wished he had never told her he loved her. Now that she knew, how could she spend day after day pretending that she was satisfied with her empty marriage?

She straightened. "You will do it for your children. No one will ever know about your feelings for Samuel." She glanced at the bed. "Especially Reiver."

Hannah listened to the first distant rumblings of thunder and wished her husband would return home soon.

When a train of the newly opened railroad line from Springfield, Massachusetts, pulled into Hartford an hour later, Reiver did not catch the stagecoach leaving for Coldwater, but instead went to Cecelia's house, eager to tell her about his trip to Northampton, where he had spent the last several days learning from another manufacturer the intricacies of dyeing silk.

He knew something was amiss the moment he walked into Cecelia's foyer and she did not break into a welcoming smile or fling herself into his arms.

He set down his valise and took off his hat. "What's wrong?" Noticing her white cheeks, red, swollen eyes, and downcast expression, he took a step forward, intending to enfold her in his arms, but stopped when she stepped back. "Cecelia, why have you been crying?"

She dabbed at her watery eyes with a handkerchief and sniffed. "Come into the parlor, Reiver. I have something to tell you."

"That sounds ominous." He followed her into the neat parlor and stopped, watching her take a position near the fireplace. "Why are you suddenly treating me like a leper? You were delighted enough to see me two weeks ago." He thought of their wild, breathless, bed-shaking lovemaking. "Ecstatic, in fact."

She took a deep, shuddering breath, causing her chestnut ringlets to tremble. "Amos Tuttle has asked me to marry him. And I've accepted."

He stared at her in disbelief. "I must be going deaf. What did you say?"

Cecelia squared her shoulders like a brave soldier facing battle. "I said, I'm marrying Amos Tuttle."

"Tuttle? The banker's son? Why, he's just a whey-faced boy!" Reiver smiled and strode toward her, intending to take her in his arms. "You can't mean it."

Determination hardened Cecelia's soft brown eyes. "I most certainly do. Amos Tuttle has asked me to marry him, and I've accepted his proposal."

Reiver stopped in his tracks and spread his hands helplessly. "Cecelia . . . you can't. We love each other."

She whirled away in an angry rustle of taffeta. "I'm twenty-seven years old, Reiver. I'm not getting any younger, and I have to think of my future. I can't live forever on what my father and husband left me. The Tuttles are wealthy and well respected here in Hartford."

"Where did you meet him?"

"His father was a friend of my late husband's. And while

Amos may be two years younger than I, his parents approve of the match."

Reiver clenched his teeth. "Were you lovers behind my back?"

A blush stained Cecelia's ivory cheeks. "Of course not! He thinks I'm a respectable widow."

"You are respectable, Cecelia," he said softly. "But I wish you wouldn't marry him."

"How can you even ask such a sacrifice of me? You're married, with two children. Why must you deny me a chance at happiness?"

"Because you'll only know happiness with me. You've always told me that my love was enough for you."

"Not anymore. I want a husband and children of my own now." Her bitter voice rang through the room. "Will you leave your wife for me? Will you father my children?"

"You know I can't."

"You mean you won't because of your precious silk mill."

"I thought you understood how important my mill is to me."

"I've decided I no longer wish to take second place to it."

Reiver ran his hand through his hair in frustration. "I can't leave Hannah."

Fresh tears filled his mistress's eyes. "Then there is nothing more to say, is there, except good-bye?"

The pain tore at his heart. Reiver went to her, catching her hand before she could pull away. "Is this what you really want? To marry someone else and never see me again?"

Determination warred with yearning on her tormented face. "No," she said with a sigh, "I don't want to lose you. But as much as I love you, I am going to marry Amos Tuttle."

"But you don't love him!"

"You married your wife without loving her. Why can't I do the same?"

Reiver grasped her by the shoulders. "Don't do this, Cecelia. I'm begging you, for both our sakes."

She stood there, stiff and unyielding. "Good-bye, Reiver."

If only he could coax her upstairs into bed . . .

Cecelia read his intentions, for she knocked his hands away and stepped back. "Don't you dare try to seduce me, Reiver Shaw."

His pride stung, Reiver gave her one last long, level look, then turned on his heel and headed for the door. When he reached it, he stopped and turned. "Then go ahead and marry him."

He left without looking back, though he heard Cecelia's sob of anguish just before a rolling clap of thunder rocked the house.

Cold rain poured out of the darkening evening sky like water gushing from a pump, dripping off Reiver's narrow hat brim and soaking him to the skin the moment he stepped out of the stagecoach and started down the drive.

He had lost the one woman he had ever truly loved.

He trudged down the muddy drive, rain—or were they tears?—stinging his eyes and blinding him. His soul felt as if it had been scraped raw and salt rubbed into the open wound. Reiver swallowed hard. He wanted to sink down into the mud and never get up.

Through the wall of water he saw the warm, welcoming glow of lights up ahead, and as he drew closer he discerned Hannah standing on the porch waiting for him, the lamp in her hand illuminating her worried expression.

She motioned to him. "Hurry, or you'll catch your death."

But he didn't hurry. Death would be preferable to the pain.

Hannah gave him an odd look. "Welcome home. Did you have a good trip?"

Beneath the shelter of the porch roof at last, he removed his wet hat. "Very pleasant." He surprised himself by kissing her hard and swiftly on the mouth, hungry for the feel of a woman's soft lips against his.

Startled, Hannah drew back and stared at him, her lips parted. She hid her confusion by turning and opening the front door. "You're soaked. I'll heat supper while you change. James and Samuel are eager to hear all about your trip."

"They'll have to wait," he replied, following her into the house and setting down his valise. He exchanged greetings with his brothers seated before the cold fireplace. "I'll tell you boys all about my trip later. I'm exhausted and going straight to bed."

But James wasn't about to let him. He sprang from his chair, his face shining with excitement. "We've got to convert the looms to belt drives, Reiver. We'll have less breakdowns and—"

"Hold it," Reiver said, holding up one hand. "You can tell me all about the Jewells and their invention later, James. I'm going to bed." And he wanted his wife with him. He turned to Hannah. "Will you find some dry clothes for me to wear?" It was as good an excuse as any to get her alone.

She nodded and headed up the stairs with Reiver following.

"The boys are in bed," Hannah said over her shoulder. "Ben wanted to wait up for you, but I told him you might be very late."

Reiver couldn't take his eyes off Hannah's gently swaying hips. "I'll see the boys tomorrow morning."

Once in their bedroom, Hannah set down her lamp and went right over to the chest. She glanced back at him. "You're shivering."

He closed the door and locked it. "Then warm me, Hannah."

She hesitated, her blue eyes wide with confusion, for in their entire marriage he had never once asked her to love him.

He removed his jacket and unbuttoned his shirt, just to make his intentions plain, and smiled when Hannah turned down the bed. When she went to blow out the lamp, he said, "Leave it on this time," and found his pulse quickening when a knowing blush suffused her cheeks.

She turned her back to him and undressed, peeling away the many layers of feminine clothing, revealing the graceful curve of her naked back and hips that had lost their boyish narrowness to childbirth. Naked himself and fully aroused, Reiver went to her, slipping his arms around her waist and pulling her against him so he could nuzzle the sensitive spot that always smelled of warm, sweet spices just below her ear. He felt her involuntary shudder, though he suspected it was more distaste than feminine arousal.

Cecelia! he cried in silent desperation, sliding his hands up beneath Hannah's breasts so he could peer down at the enticing mounded flesh rising and falling with her every rapid breath.

Stiff and unyielding as a virgin, Hannah said, "Reiver, please, you mustn't—" but he cut off her protest in midsentence by raking his teeth against her sensitive earlobe.

"Get into bed." Tonight of all nights, he needed to both conquer and satisfy to soothe the soul-searing pain of Cecelia's rejection.

Hannah complied dutifully, as always, but pulled the sheet up to her chin and stared at the ceiling in glassy-eyed resignation.

Reiver stood beside the bed, his hands on his hips. "Look at me, Hannah."

She closed her eyes and shook her head.

"I can't understand why you won't look. I'm not so ugly that I'll turn you to stone, you know."

The gentle teasing in his voice so startled Hannah that she turned her head, her eyes flew open of their own volition, and she saw her husband naked for the first time. She tried to look away, but couldn't despite her embarrassment. His powerful, stocky body was beautifully formed, from his broad, muscular shoulders and chest down to his narrow waist and flat stomach. His desire for her was all too evident.

She blushed and looked away again. "You're not ugly at all."

He reached over and flipped her sheet away. "Neither are you." His hungry blue gaze roved over her. "And since it gives me great pleasure to look at you as well, we'll keep the lamp on this time."

She swallowed hard. "You never wanted to before."

"Well, I do now."

As Reiver slid into bed beside her Hannah stiffened, preparing herself for their usual hasty coupling. Tonight, however, he drew her into his arms and kissed her mouth slowly and deeply. When his hand began stroking and fondling her bare breast, Hannah's bewilderment turned to astonishment at the heat pulsing through her body. She melted inside, her breathing becoming shallow and ragged as Reiver's mouth closed over a taut nipple and his hand slid down her thigh.

She closed her eyes and wished it were Samuel giving her such pleasure.

Reiver kept touching her everywhere, using his flicking tongue and teasing fingertips to ruthlessly explore every inch of her with a tormenting slowness that enslaved her to sensations she had never experienced.

At what point had she turned into this wanton creature writhing and moaning, greedy for more? She didn't know, for time had stood still. All she knew was dizzying, heart-stopping, endless pleasure.

Reiver finally possessed her, moving above her and within her with consummate skill, building the fires higher and higher. When Hannah finally climaxed for the first time, the only way she survived its intensity was to scream.

Later, Hannah looked down in wonder at Reiver's tousled head nestled against her shoulder, his breath warm against her breast. Something had changed between them, something major and inexplicable. Never had he loved her like this. Never had she felt so close to him. She closed her eyes, remembering every shocking, tormenting caress, and felt her body clench in response. She had never dreamed her marital duties had this hidden, dangerous, exhilarating side.

She opened her eyes and absently ran her fingers down Reiver's muscular arm. Now that she had experienced such ecstasy once, she wanted to experience it again. And again. She regretted that it could never be with Samuel.

Downstairs, Samuel stood at the window, his mood as black and volatile as the evening sky.

"It's still pouring," he said to James, who was crudely sketching some piece of machinery at the dining-room table.

James glanced up. "What's keeping Reiver? His supper will spoil."

He's bedding her, Samuel thought. He doesn't give a damn about his supper because he's bedding her.

The moment Reiver had walked in the door, his expression bleak and haunted, Samuel knew some monumental catastrophe had befallen his brother, and he suspected it had everything to do with Cecelia.

Tomorrow he was going to find out exactly what had sent the faithless Reiver rushing to warm his wife's bed.

When the following morning dawned bright and clear, Samuel left the house early and went for a walk down by the brook so he wouldn't see Hannah at breakfast. He returned just as Reiver left the house for the mill.

Samuel joined him. "Something happened between you and Cecelia yesterday."

Reiver's eyes darkened with pain. "She's broken it off. She's marrying Amos Tuttle."

Samuel stared at him. "Cecelia's getting married? To the banker's son? He's quite a catch."

Reiver grunted and kept on walking, forcing the stunned Samuel to hurry after him.

Samuel said, "Can you really blame her? You're a married man. She'd have no future with you."

Reiver stopped and whirled around, his head lowered like a bull about to charge. "I love her, damn it! How could she do this to me?"

"If you weren't so hurt, I'd feel sorry for you."

"She said she loved me. She said she understood why I had to marry Hannah." Reiver stopped at the top of Mulberry Hill. "She knew I'd always take care of her. And what does she do? Leaves me for some whey-faced banker who's tied to his daddy's apron strings."

Samuel shook his head. "Reiver, you may run a successful business, but you know nothing about women."

"Oh, I don't, do I? Well, my wise little brother, I know that women want to be loved and cared for. I was doing both."

"Most of them also want the respectability of marriage and their children untainted by the stigma of bastardy."

Reiver's broad shoulders sagged in surrender. "You're right. I couldn't expect Cecelia to go on being my mistress forever."

"Magnanimous of you to admit it. And what about Hannah?" Samuel held his breath and waited.

"I'm going to try to be a better husband to her. She'll never take Cecelia's place, but I'm going to try to love her."

The fool makes it sound as though it's such a chore, Samuel thought.

Reiver grinned and clapped him on the back. "I got a good start last night."

Samuel forced himself to smile. "You rogue."

"Well, I've wasted enough time talking to you. I had better get to work."

Samuel watched him stride toward the mill, then he turned and went back to the house.

He found Hannah alone, smiling and humming to herself as she cleared the breakfast dishes. He watched her, unobserved, seeing a contentment on her face that had never been there before.

She looked up and saw him. "Samuel . . . I didn't hear you come in."

"Are we alone?"

"Yes. Mrs. Hardy is upstairs with the boys, and James went out to the barn." She wiped her hands nervously on her apron. "Samuel, about what you said to me yesterday . . ."

He held up his hand to still her. "While I meant every word, it's best forgotten for all our sakes."

Hannah nodded. "I don't know why, but Reiver has changed."

His mistress has sent him packing, that's why, Samuel thought. But he said, "Perhaps he's finally realized that he's a fortunate man to have you for his wife."

She blushed shyly. "Perhaps."

"I'm very happy for you, Hannah." He hated to lie, but he had no other choice.

"It's going to be better from now on," she said. The brilliant light of optimism banished the doubt from her eyes. "I'm sure of it."

It pained Samuel to see her so trusting, so confident, for he knew his brother, and he was sure Reiver's fidelity would never last.

Later, after forming bread dough into loaves and setting them aside to rise, Hannah wiped the flour from her hands, removed her apron, and went outside to find her husband and tell him of her plan.

She found Reiver in the mill yard helping to unload two wagons stacked with baskets of cocoons that had traveled from China by clipper ship to the coastal town of New London and overland to Coldwater.

Hannah watched him work, his shirt sleeves rolled up out of the way and his furrowed brow beaded with the sweat of exertion on a hot summer morning. She remembered last night, and the strength of those arms around her.

He jumped down from the wagon, drew out his knife, and ripped open one of the baskets, the covering of which was stamped with strange black markings that Hannah knew were

Chinese writing. Reiver plunged his hands into the cocoons, straightened, and bellowed an epithet that made all the men freeze and stare.

"Broken!" Red-faced, he cursed again and held up the cocoon for all to see. "Those bastards have cheated us again!

"Let's get these baskets open and see how many more are broken," Reiver said to his men. He turned and noticed Hannah.

The anger faded from his blue eyes, and he smiled. He stopped working and walked toward her.

"I'm sorry to interrupt your work," she said.

He looked back at the baskets in disgust. "You're a most welcome interruption."

He's never said that to me before, Hannah thought. She said, "Isn't there anything you can do about this . . . this thievery?"

Reiver shook his head. "Short of going to China and watching them select the cocoons myself, there is nothing I can do except complain to the middleman and take my business to another company."

"They're cheating us, and it's just not right!"

Her indignation on his behalf must have surprised him, for he placed a soothing hand on her arm. "I'm just as furious as you are, Hannah, but I'm afraid this is just a cost of doing business with the Chinese. Since I can't raise my own silk, I have to import it." He raised one brow. "But I'm sure you didn't come down here to discuss Chinese silk with me."

She knotted her fingers together. "I—I'd like your permission to buy some books for the women to read in the skein room."

His face clouded. "But I don't want to encourage laziness. I want them to work."

"Reading wouldn't encourage laziness. It will make their work go faster and improve their minds. I thought they could take turns reading aloud and taking the books home at night."

"Why do you wish to do this?"

She looked away shyly. "Because the mill is important to you, and I want to help."

"But you do help me by taking care of my home and children."

"And I will continue to do so. But the mill is our family business, after all, and I feel that I should know something about it."

When he hesitated, she added, "Running the mill itself is men's work, I know, but at least I could concern myself with our workers' welfare just as I do for my own children."

Reiver rubbed his wide jaw thoughtfully, then nodded. "All right. You may buy books for the women in the skein room. We'll try this plan of yours for three months. But if their productivity falls, no more books."

"Agreed. Thank you, Reiver." Hannah stood on tiptoes and kissed him swiftly on the cheek, delighting in the way his eyes darkened expectantly before she turned away and returned to the house.

The following day, when Samuel left for Hartford, Hannah gave him a list of books she wanted, and the moment he returned with them she went to the skein room to put her plan into action. Constance, Henrietta, and Sadie were wary at first, but once Hannah began reading, they relaxed and their fingers flew. That evening Constance and Sadie took books home.

By the end of the week Hannah deemed her project a success.

As the summer passed and Reiver made no comment about the success or failure of Hannah's plan, she grew increasingly apprehensive. But he had given her three months, so she would just have to wait until the fall.

The leaves blazed red, yellow, and orange on the cool October evening that Hannah would learn the fate of her daily readings with the mill women.

Holding Davey in her arms, she touched her lips to his downy head before putting him to bed and murmured, "You and Ben are going to have another little brother or sister soon."

After bearing two children, she knew the telltale signs all too well. Watching Davey's eyelids droop as he fought sleep, Hannah smiled to herself. While she loved her two sons with all her heart, this child was going to be special because it had been conceived in mutual desire. And she hoped that this time it would be a girl.

Once Davey drifted off to sleep, Hannah went downstairs to tell Reiver her own news.

She found him in the parlor, reading the newspaper. Suddenly he sat up straight and his expression contorted in pain and anger. He swore and flung down the newspaper before bolting out of his chair and stalking off to the window, where he stood running his hand through his hair and muttering.

"Reiver, what's wrong?" Hannah crossed the room to his side. "Did something you read upset you?"

He looked at her, his expression bleak as he fought to control his emotions. "No, Hannah, nothing's wrong. I just received another shipment of inferior cocoons from China, that's all, and I'm steamed about it."

Hannah moistened her dry lips. "Reiver, I have something to tell you."

He smiled. "And I have something to tell you. The women can go on reading. If anything, their productivity has improved over the last three months, so I see no reason to stop."

Hannah flung her arms around her husband's neck and hugged him. "Oh, Reiver, that's wonderful!" But she drew away in puzzlement when he stiffened in her arms. To hide her confusion over his rebuff, she added, "I have news of my own." She took a deep breath. "I'm going to have another baby."

He stood there in silence for a moment, then he tilted her chin with his fingers and kissed her swiftly on the mouth. When he released her, he smiled wanly. "So I'm to be a father again. Thank you, Hannah." But the joy he had displayed those other two times just wasn't there.

Crushed, Hannah stepped away from him. "Aren't you happy about this baby?"

"Of course I am. I've just had a particularly hard, frustrating day, that's all. Now if you'll excuse me, there's something I have to attend to down at the mill." And he walked out of the parlor, grabbing his coat before disappearing out the door.

Hannah stared after him, her eyes filling with tears. She hadn't expected him to be so unenthusiastic, so cold. And she didn't believe an inferior shipment of silk was the cause. Reiver's mood had been pleasant that evening.

She looked over at the *Hartford Standard* crumpled on the floor where Reiver had thrown it. Something he had read upset him. She was sure of it.

Hannah picked up the newspaper and scanned the headlines of the page Reiver had been reading. A steam boiler had exploded . . . the banker Amos Tuttle wed the widow Cecelia Layton . . . the Connecticut River was lower than usual due to the dry autumn. Hannah frowned in puzzlement. Nothing written here should have upset her husband so.

She folded the newspaper neatly and placed her hand reassuringly on her abdomen. "Don't worry, little one. He'll come to accept you in time."

CHAPTER

❧ 6 ❧

"MAMA, is Abigail an idiot?" Benjamin said, kneeling on the floor and peering into his baby sister's cradle.

"Benjamin Shaw! What a horrible thing to say!" Hannah lifted her eight-month-old daughter and held her against her shoulder as if she could physically protect her child from hurtful words. "Who called Abigail that?"

Benjamin shrugged. "I don't remember. I just heard it somewhere."

"Was it Mrs. Hardy? Or that gossiping Millicent? Come, come. I'm waiting for an answer, young man."

He rose and scuffed the floor with the toe of his shoe. "I said I don't remember!"

"Fine. Then you'll go to your room and stay there until your memory returns."

For one moment defiance flared in Ben's eyes, then he muttered, "Yes, Mama," and left the nursery to accept his punishment. Hannah knew from past experience that he would remain in his room for the rest of the day and evening, and even then he might not capitulate unless his father scolded him. Ben idolized his father, whose disapproval hurt more than a whipping.

Once alone, Hannah hugged Abigail, her cheek pressed against the downy blond head. "You're not an idiot, my darling. You're my sweet, precious little girl."

But though her mother's heart denied it with a lioness's protective ferocity, Hannah's rational mind suspected that her daughter wasn't quite right.

Abigail always had been slow. In the womb, she hadn't kicked as often or as hard as the boys, and she took an excruciating three days being born, almost taking Hannah's life. As the weeks passed and she grew, she took longer to raise her head and roll onto her stomach.

Hannah shifted Abigail in her arms and looked down at the grave, chubby face, and her heart sank when the baby made no sign of recognition, just stared up at her mother as if she were a stranger. Without warning, recognition finally dawned like the rising sun and Abigail smiled, filling her mother with false hope.

Hannah smiled back and tickled her daughter's chin. "Why, hello there, little Abigail." Her smile died. "You're not an idiot, and when I find out who dared call you that . . ."

She shouldn't compare Abigail with the boys. After all, she was a little girl, and little girls were different, quieter and less fussy. Hannah knew that Abigail possessed all her mental faculties, and she would catch up to her brothers all in good time.

Hannah carried Abigail downstairs and found Mrs. Hardy in the buttery, giving Davey some gingerbread.

Mrs. Hardy's silver gaze went to Abigail, and she frowned slightly before looking up at Hannah. "Where's Ben? I'm waiting to take him and Davey for a walk."

"Ben's being punished," Hannah replied. "Mrs. Hardy, will you step into the parlor while Davey finishes his gingerbread? There's something I have to say to you."

"I can see I'm in for a talking-to," the housekeeper muttered.

Once in the parlor, out of Davey's hearing, Hannah said, "I've sent Ben to his room because he asked me if Abigail was an idiot, and wouldn't tell me where he heard the word. Do you know who would dare make up such a horrible lie about my little girl?"

"You have to accept it, Hannah. This poor mite just isn't like the other children."

Hannah reared back. "That doesn't mean my little girl is an idiot!" She pressed her lips to Abigail's forehead. "She's just a little slower than the boys, that's all. She'll catch up one day."

Mrs. Hardy's doubtful expression spoke volumes.

Hannah said, "You've all been discussing Abigail behind my back, haven't you?"

A guilty red flush stained the housekeeper's neck. "I won't lie to you. We've talked among ourselves. We've all noticed that Abigail isn't as"—she groped for the right word—"lively as the boys were at her age. Reiver didn't want us to upset you."

Suddenly fatigued, Hannah dropped down into the rocking chair. Abigail, oblivious to the undercurrent swirling about her, had fallen asleep in her mother's arms. Ben and Davey had always been quick to sense tension and quicker to wail in protest, but not Abigail. Despair rose like bile in Hannah's throat.

Four-year-old Davey, his chin still decorated with gingerbread crumbs, appeared in the parlor doorway. "I'm finished, Mrs. Hardy," he announced. "I want to play with Ben now." Davey stuck to his older brother like a shadow.

"You can't play with Ben today," Hannah said. "He's being punished and will have to stay in his room."

Davey blinked hard, his eyes filling with tears.

"Take him for a walk," Hannah said dully. "I'm tired and I want to be alone with my little girl."

Mrs. Hardy nodded, brushed crumbs from Davey's chin with her apron, then took his hand and left for their walk.

Just before the door closed behind them, Hannah heard her son ask, "But why is Ben being punished?" Then the voices died and she was alone.

Hannah rocked back and forth, back and forth, letting the soft creak of the runners and the quietness of the house soothe her. She looked down at Abigail, so serene in repose, and her heart clenched in fear.

What did life hold for her innocent, imperfect daughter? Would she recognize her own name? Would she be able to read and make her letters? And when she grew into a young lady, would some respectable young man fall in love with her and ask her to marry him? Or would people ridicule her and call her an idiot?

Idiot . . .

Why had God done this to her child? Why? Hannah closed her eyes, squeezing hot, bitter tears onto her cheeks. But she brushed them away as soon as they fell.

"God may have abandoned you, my precious little girl," she whispered, "but I won't. I'll always be here to protect you."

Always.

• • •

Reiver walked home to the faint pounding of hammers.

Instead of going directly to the house for his noon meal, he turned left and went to see how construction was progressing on his new house.

We should be able to move in by the end of summer, he thought in satisfaction, for the framing of the large Greek Revival–style house had just been completed. At last he would have a residence large enough to house his growing family comfortably, and one that would reflect the modest success of his silk mill. Samuel and James would remain in the homestead, however.

He looked back over his shoulder at the cluster of buildings where once the rearing shed had stood. Now he had three sheds for reeling where once he had one, and a separate building for the wet, smelly work of dyeing. Someday rows of buildings would stand there.

Reiver saluted the carpenters, then headed home.

When he walked through the door, a thin, high-pitched wail scored his nerves like a cat's claws. Reiver shuddered in revulsion. This one—he couldn't bear to think of it as his daughter—even cried differently. "Hannah?" he called, rolling up his sleeves as he strode into the buttery to wash his hands.

Seconds later she appeared in the doorway, her pale face tear-stained and drawn, and her blue eyes desperate. Her arms cradled the wailing baby, and she murmured, "Don't cry, sweeting," over and over.

Reiver suppressed his rising resentment and dried his hands. He turned to Hannah. "You look exhausted. Why don't you give the baby to Millicent for a while and join me for luncheon?"

"Do you know what Ben said about Abigail?" she asked.

"Hannah—"

"He called his baby sister an idiot." She pressed the baby's head to her cheek, quieting Abigail instantly. "I'm sure he was just repeating something he overheard."

Reiver turned away to hide his guilty expression.

Hannah said, "Who would dare say such a cruel, hurtful thing? I'd hate to think Samuel or James—"

"Don't dwell on it." He turned to face her. "Bring her upstairs to Millicent. I want to speak to you alone, in the parlor."

Hannah left the buttery without protest and returned to the parlor a minute later, her arms empty and her expression bleak.

"Please sit down," Reiver said, and when she did so, he knelt at her feet and grasped her cold, stiff hands in his. "Hannah, there is something wrong with this child."

Her face crumpled and she squeezed his hands. "But she's not an idiot, Reiver. She's not."

He thought of his midday meal growing cold and the three new girls demanding his supervision at their looms, and his impatience grew. He rose and released her. "You've got to be strong, Hannah. You've got to accept the fact that Abigail may be simpleminded for the rest of her life."

"No!"

"Hannah—"

"I want Dr. Bradley to examine her. Perhaps he can do something."

"Bradley tries to heal bodily ills. There's nothing he can do for an affliction of the mind. Nothing any of us can do."

Hannah bolted to her feet. "There's got to be something—"

"Enough!" Reiver grasped her arms. "Do I have to remind you that you have a duty to me and our two other children?"

"But Abigail—"

"And what of the mill girls? You haven't set foot in the mill since this child was born. And don't think that Constance and Henrietta haven't noticed."

"My daughter demands my complete attention right now."

"So do your sons and my brothers!" He gave her a little shake. "Don't defy me on this, Hannah! I'll not have you placing her welfare ahead of anyone else's."

Her eyes widened in stunned comprehension. "You hate her because she's not perfect, just as you hated your own father for not being perfect."

He grew very still. "Who told you about my father?"

"It doesn't matter. I know you hated him because he was the town drunkard and an object of scorn."

His hands fell away and he stepped back. "And with good reason. He was a lazy, no-account drunkard who made our lives a living hell. It has nothing whatsoever to do with the way I feel about Abigail."

"Reiver—"

"No matter what you may think, I don't hate her. I am merely being realistic, and if that sounds unfeeling to you, so be it. As the head of this family, I have to decide what's best for everyone, and I will not see our sons neglected by their mother!"

"The boys will do just fine. It's Abigail who needs more of my love and attention."

Reiver scowled. "You are my wife and you will obey me for the good of the family."

"Must I obey you even when you are wrong?"

Her unexpected retort caught him by surprise. Then he said, "Especially when you think I'm wrong."

Hannah hung her head, but her hands were balled into mutinous fists at her sides.

"I've made my wishes known," he said, rolling down his shirt sleeves. "Now I'm hungry and I'd like to eat."

Without another word, Hannah returned to the buttery to fetch Reiver his noon meal. He ate the cold food in even colder silence.

In the nursery, Hannah looked down at Abigail sleeping so sweetly and wished they could run away.

Then, wafting through the open window came Davey's carefree voice exhorting poor Mrs. Hardy to run faster, and Hannah felt her love and loyalty part like the Red Sea, one half staying with Abigail and the other encompassing the rest of her family.

She sighed. Reiver was right. But while she could forgive him for that, she would never forgive him for not loving their imperfect daughter.

She knelt down and stroked Abigail's smooth cheek. "Don't worry, my sweet little girl. I will always have enough love for the both of us."

The following morning a new shipment of raw silk arrived, and Reiver asked Hannah if she would help Constance Ferry sort cocoons and reel the silk fibers.

As the two women sorted, Hannah asked, "Do you like working here, Constance?"

Constance didn't even glance up from her work. "Yes, ma'am. I earn more than I ever could in another factory. Oh, I'll quit when I get married someday." She blushed a guilty shade of pink and lowered her voice. "But don't tell Mr. Shaw."

Hannah smiled. "It will be our secret."

Hours later, when the cocoons were sorted, Hannah said, "Now what do we do?"

"We boil 'em," Constance replied, rising and taking a basket of cocoons to another room, where a large tank filled with scalding water stood near the reeling machine. "Be careful of your hands. The water has to be hot to loosen the silk fibers."

Hannah watched the other woman toss the cocoons in, let them soak for a moment, then quickly dip her fingers gingerly into the hot water and brush away the outer web before finding the end of the true cocoon. When Constance had the filament ends of six cocoons, she began reeling the silk.

Hannah said, "Let me help with the next batch."

The moment her fingers touched the hot water, she wished she had never volunteered, but once her hands got used to the temperature, she managed to find the filaments so Constance could reel the silk.

Later, when Hannah was through, she left with sore red hands and a new appreciation for the mill girls' hard work.

Reiver hadn't seen Cecelia for two years, ever since the day in 1845 she told him she was marrying Tuttle. Tonight they were among the Shaws' four dinner guests, for Reiver needed a loan from Tuttle's bank to expand the silk mills. But from the way Cecelia studiously avoided Reiver's gaze, he could tell she knew the second reason for the invitation.

Her adoring husband kept her well, judging by her elegant, lace-trimmed gown in a flattering shade of rose. The necklace at her throat flashed with genuine sapphires, not humble garnets and seed pearls.

"Nice house you've got here, Shaw," Tuttle said, his bland, boyish face flushed with envy. In a manner reminiscent of Ezra Bickford, he mentally assessed the value of every stick of furniture in the parlor. "It's new, isn't it?"

Reiver nodded. "We just moved in two months ago." He smiled at Hannah, seated next to Cecelia on the settee. "With our growing family, we need the room."

He compared his wife with his former mistress. While Hannah wore her light brown hair as she always did, parted in the center and swept over her ears into a chignon, Cecelia favored fashionable beribboned ringlets that gave her a sweet dainty air. Her graceful movements contrasted sharply with Hannah's broad, abrupt gestures. Cecelia's vivacious personality drew a man's attention like a sailor to a siren, while Hannah didn't merit a second look.

Cecelia said, "And how many children do you have, Mrs. Shaw?"

"Three," Hannah replied. "Two boys and a girl. And you?"

"A son, fifteen months old."

The thought that Cecelia must have conceived a child on her wedding night filled Reiver with primitive jealousy, and he sipped his imported sherry to conceal his irritation.

Hannah turned to their two other guests, portly George Burrows, who had just opened a paper mill on the north side of town, and his colorless wife, Louise. "I know your children are almost grown."

Reiver only half listened as Burrows boasted about his eight sons, for his thoughts were on Cecelia, who was pretending to be absorbed in the conversation. But he could tell by the tense set of her alabaster shoulders that she was just as aware of him. He wondered how he could contrive to get her alone tonight.

Before he could come up with a plan, Mrs. Hardy appeared in the doorway and announced that dinner was ready. Reiver proffered his arm to his wife, and they led their guests across the hall to the dining room.

"Mrs. Tuttle," Reiver said, holding the chair to his right for Cecelia.

She thanked him charmingly, and only Reiver noticed her hand tremble as she gathered her skirts and sat down.

Once everyone was seated and Mrs. Hardy served the cold strawberry soup, conversation resumed, presenting Reiver with the challenge of simultaneously participating in the talk and feasting on Cecelia's beauty. By placing Tuttle at his wife's right, Reiver couldn't avoid looking at Cecelia whenever he spoke to her dull husband. A clever ploy, he thought.

"Coldwater seems to be expanding by leaps and bounds," Tuttle said.

Reiver said, "In addition to my silk mill and Burrows's paper factory, we've seen a soap factory, a foundry, and a cotton mill go up in just the last six months." Out of the corner of his eye he saw Cecelia dart him a glance beneath her long, dark lashes.

Tuttle nodded in satisfaction. "We're on the threshold of a new era, the manufacturing age. Tuttle Senior—that's what I always call my father—thinks that farming is fast becoming a thing of the past in Connecticut."

And he droned on and on until the arrival of the fish course stopped him long enough for Hannah to say, "But surely you don't spend every waking hour concerned with commerce, Mr. Tuttle."

Ah, but he does, Reiver thought, risking another glance at Cecelia. In an unguarded moment, she revealed the glassy-eyed look of a wife who has heard the same boring speech once too often.

Beneath the table, Reiver extended his foot, slipping his toe beneath Cecelia's petticoats until it touched her foot. The intimate caress brought a blush to her cheeks, and she glanced guiltily around the table. When she saw that everyone was listening to her husband expound on his father's theories of the virtues of hard work, she shot Reiver a malevolent warning glance and jerked her foot away. He suppressed a smile, his point made.

After dinner Hannah and the ladies retired to the parlor, leaving the gentlemen to their cigars and apple brandy.

Burrows unbuttoned his straining waistcoat, sipped his brandy, and looked around the dining room in frank admiration. "You've done well, Shaw. Someday I hope my paper mill will do as much for me."

"And I intend to do even better," Reiver said, "with a little help from Tuttle's bank."

Tuttle said, "I must admit that Tuttle Senior and I had our reservations when you came to us for a loan, Shaw. After the mulberry-tree disaster, I thought the silk industry was finished in this country."

Reiver shook his head. "Many silk mills did go bankrupt, but the smart owners learned from that mistake and know that the future lies in manufacturing silk, not trying to raise mulberry trees and silkworms. America's climate isn't right for either, as I myself discovered several years ago. Now I import cocoons from the Orient and manufacture sewing thread."

Tuttle's small dark eyes assessed Reiver with new respect. "What does the future hold for Shaw Silks?"

Reiver sipped his apple brandy. "Innovation. My brother James is an inventor and has been working on a machine to salvage waste materials from broken cocoons. And looms to make our thread strong enough for use in Howe's sewing machine." He smiled confidently. "Your loan would be put to good use, Tuttle."

The banker lit his cigar and took several deep drags. "I'm impressed, Shaw, and I know Tuttle Senior will be, too. Come to the bank tomorrow and we'll discuss it with him."

"You won't regret it." Reiver drained his glass and rose. "If you gentlemen would care to see the mill, I'm sure the ladies will be able to get along without us a little while longer."

Both men chuckled, then rose to join him for a tour of the mill.

Later, when his guests were ready to leave, Reiver made sure that he was at Cecelia's side to drape her wrap over her shoulders. She thanked him smoothly, but he could tell from the faint blush that he still disconcerted her.

He wondered what her reaction would be when he called on her tomorrow.

A white-faced Cecelia received him the following day in her expensively furnished parlor.

For the benefit of the maid who had announced him, Reiver said, "Forgive me for the intrusion, Mrs. Tuttle, but my wife asked me to bring you several jars of her apple jelly while I was in Hartford today."

"Why, thank you, Mr. Shaw. How considerate of you." Then she ordered the maid to take the jelly to the kitchen.

When the maid closed the door behind her, Reiver and Cecelia were finally alone.

She stepped away from him. "Dear Lord, are you out of your mind coming here? What if Amos finds out?"

"He already knows. When I saw him at the bank, I told him that I intended to call on you—to deliver my wife's jellies, of course."

Cecelia's brown eyes widened in panic. "You shouldn't be

here. You must leave at once." She started for the door, but Reiver restrained her.

"I have no intention of leaving, until I've said what I came to say."

"Reiver, please!"

He felt her tremble beneath his hand. "Stop acting like I'm going to take you right here, and sit down."

Cecelia hesitated, and when Reiver's hand fell away, she turned and seated herself in a nearby chair, her back stiff and straight, her hands folded.

He looked down at her. "Are you happy?"

"I'm very happy. I have a kind, generous husband who adores me, and a lovely little boy. Why shouldn't I be happy?"

"Because you don't love your husband. Admit it."

"That's not true! I do love Amos."

"You always were a poor liar. You may think you've convinced yourself that you love him, but you don't." He reached out and lifted her chin. "I can see it in your eyes. You're desperately unhappy."

She jerked her head away and rose. "Stop it! No good will come of this."

"I still love you. God knows I've tried to stop, but I can't. Two years have passed, and I can't stop wanting you."

Cecelia stiffened, as if gathering courage. "Then you'll just have to stop. This is wrong, Reiver. Need I remind you that you have a lovely, charming wife? She doesn't deserve this."

"But I've never loved her."

"That doesn't justify your—your obsession with me."

He raised one brow. "I hardly think it's one-sided."

She shook her head repeatedly. "You're wrong."

He was at her side in two strides and grasped her cold hands so she couldn't draw away. "Prove it. Show me that you don't want me, that you don't need me."

"Reiver—"

"Let me kiss you, and then tell me how you feel."

"No, I—"

"Afraid I'm right?"

When a sigh of surrender passed her lips, Reiver took her face gently in his hands and searched the depths of her eyes until he found the desire hidden behind the fear. He lowered his mouth to hers.

The kiss told him all he needed to know.

When they parted, both panting and breathless, Cecelia looked dazed and bewildered.

"Where can we meet?" Reiver whispered.

She clung to him. "I don't know. Somewhere safe. I know a friend who might let us use her house." She told Reiver the address.

"Make the arrangements with her and meet me there tomorrow at one o'clock."

She nodded helplessly, still clinging.

He kissed her harder this time. "Until tomorrow."

After Reiver left, Cecelia stood at the parlor window and watched until his carriage disappeared. "Damn you, Reiver Shaw," she whispered. "And damn me for my weakness."

Yet even the thought of the fires of hell couldn't stop her from anticipating tomorrow.

At dinner that evening Hannah noticed that Reiver ate, but said nothing unless spoken to, his blue eyes glazed with a far-away look and his expression inscrutable.

Something's troubling him, she thought.

She glanced at Samuel and James to see if they noticed, but both were too involved in a discussion of the proposed Providence-Hartford-Fishkill railroad to pay attention to their eldest brother's strange mood.

Hannah looked at him. "How was your trip to Hartford today? Did Mrs. Tuttle like the preserves I sent?"

Reiver devoted his attention to sopping up the gravy on his plate with a piece of bread. "I don't know. I left them with her husband at his bank." He glanced up and smiled. "But I'm sure she did."

"I like Mrs. Tuttle," Hannah said. "She is so charming and kind."

"She is." Reiver looked down the table toward James. "Have you tested our thread on the sewing machine yet?"

James nodded. "Unfortunately it breaks. It's just not strong enough to withstand such a machine."

"Then what do you propose to do to make our thread stronger?"

"I'm going to invent a loom that will double-twist the thread as it's reeled," James replied. "That should strengthen it."

Reiver nodded absently, then rose and excused himself.

When he was out of the room, Hannah turned to Samuel and James in bewilderment. "He doesn't seem himself tonight."

Samuel stared at the door, a curious expression in his pale eyes. "Perhaps something happened in Hartford today."

James added, "Reiver's always direct. It's not like him to be so moody."

Hannah smiled brightly. "I'm sure he'll tell me what's troubling him."

She learned just that later when Samuel and James left for the farmhouse and she went upstairs to retire for the evening.

Hannah found Reiver standing before his chest, the drawers open and a pile of clothing in his arms. He froze when he saw her and looked as guilty as a thief caught in the act.

"What are you doing?" she asked.

"I'm moving to the other bedroom."

Hannah felt as if he had struck her. "The other bedroom? Why?" Damn her voice for trembling so! "I thought you enjoyed . . ." Her words trailed off.

He continued to add shirts to the pile in his arms. "I do."

"Then why?"

He stopped and looked at her. "I don't know of any way to tell you except straight out." He paused, as if weighing each word. "I don't want to risk having another child like Abigail."

For a moment Hannah thought she had gone deaf. "What did you say?"

"You heard me."

She wanted to pull the shirts from his arms and stuff them back into the drawers, as if that could make him stay. But her pride kept her hands clenched at her sides. If he didn't want to share her bed any longer, she wouldn't beg.

Reiver said, "Don't look so crestfallen. You know you never enjoyed . . . that aspect of marriage."

"Not at first," she admitted. "But you know it ceased to be a duty years ago." Now she hungered for his touch with an avidity that frightened her.

"Be that as it may, how can we indulge ourselves if it means bringing another simple child into the world? Isn't Abigail enough of a burden for you?"

"Abigail isn't a burden, damn you! I love her as much as the boys. Besides, you don't know that another child would be the same."

"I don't intend to take that chance!"

Hannah almost reminded him of all the times he had withdrawn from her just before releasing his seed, and all the times children hadn't resulted from their union, but she held her tongue.

Her hurt silence must have moved him, for he stepped forward to touch her cheek. "It's not that I will never share your bed again, Hannah. I just don't believe in tempting fate too often."

She fought back tears. "If this is what you wish . . ."

"I said that I don't want another child like Abigail, and I mean it." He turned and left, closing the connecting door behind him.

Hannah stared at the closed door for a long time. With a resigned sigh, she undressed for bed. She threw back the quilt, placed Reiver's pillow on a nearby chair, then set her own pillow in the center at the head of the bed. After blowing out the lamp, she slid beneath the sheets and closed her eyes, but sleep wouldn't come.

She didn't know why Reiver had become so remote, dancing elusively just out of reach at the very moment when she thought the mill and their children had brought them closer together. But Hannah knew better than to argue or challenge him.

She closed her eyes. Reiver would come back to her in his on sweet time.

The following day Cecelia met him at her obliging friend's house just as he knew she would.

"I almost didn't come," she said, lifting her heavy black veil once they were alone in an upstairs bedroom.

He grinned, enfolding her in his arms. "Don't torture me with empty threats, Cecelia. You know you want to be with me." She was so soft and her chestnut ringlets smelled of sweet heliotrope as he buried his face in their silkiness.

She closed her eyes and leaned against him. "This must be the last time. It's far too dangerous."

His fingers made short work of her gown's infuriating buttons. "Why do you say that, to make a pretense of resistance? You know you'll come whenever I want you."

She gasped as he squeezed her breasts, all thoughts of her husband and son disappearing in a blaze of passion.

CHAPTER

❧ 7 ❧

THE following spring the traveling peddler gave Hannah an unlikely idea that might be a boon to Shaw Silks.

That cool April afternoon of 1848, while Hannah stood with Mrs. Hardy before Septimus Shively's overflowing cart, listening to him extol the virtues of various butter presses, clothes sprinklers, and brushes in his singsong voice, her thoughts kept wandering to Reiver and his persistent denial of their hapless daughter. But then something the peddler said brought her back into the present.

"Ladies, I have a new line of pretty china that I'm sure will appeal to women of taste and refinement such as yourselves." With a flourish, he proffered a plate rimmed with delicate yellow roses. "It's called Parisian ware and sells for only a nickle apiece, platters a little more."

Hannah took the plate, squinted at the design, and ran her finger along the rim. "How can you sell French china so cheaply?"

The peddler stiffened. "Did I *say* this pretty china was from France, my good woman? I made no such claim. Septimus Shively never misrepresents a product, no sirree."

"Then why is it called Parisian ware if it doesn't come from France, you fool?" Mrs. Hardy asked.

"It's merely a descriptive title. The china is just *like* French china, so the manufacturer calls it 'Parisian ware.'"

Mrs. Hardy put down a hot-water belly warmer and gave the peddler a baleful stare. "Why, you hairy old goat! You're trying to hoodwink us!"

"My good woman! Septimus Shively is as honest as the day is long. He never misrepresents a product, no sirree." Then he shrugged. "But if a customer should misunderstand and *assume* that this fine Parisian ware is from France . . . well, I can't help what people think, now can I?"

Hannah smiled and handed back the plate. "Do many of your customers make such a mistaken assumption?"

Septimus Shively smiled back. "A surprising number do, yes sirree." The peddler quickly pocketed payment for their other purchases. "The maker of these dishes couldn't give them away before. Then he fancified them into 'Parisian ware,' and suddenly everyone wants to buy them, and I keep running out."

"All because he changed the name?" Mrs. Hardy asked incredulously.

"Yes sirree. Unbelievable, isn't it?"

Then Septimus Shively climbed into his cart, waved goodbye, and started off in a clanging of pots and pans to the next house on his route, leaving the two women to marvel at their fellowman's gullibility.

Later, as Hannah sat sewing and chuckling over the peddler's Parisian ware, she glanced down at the label on her thread that said simply, "Silk Thread—Shaw Silk Manufacturing Company." The idea came to her like a flash of lightning in a dark summer sky.

She rose and went to find Reiver.

He was in the machine shop with James, leaning over an array of greasy gears spread out on the long wooden table. "I don't think this is going to work, James," he said with a shake of his head.

"I disagree," James replied. Then he looked up, saw Hannah, and greeted her with a warm smile. "Hannah. What brings you into the shop?"

"I need to speak to Reiver."

Her husband didn't look up at her. "Can't it wait? James and I are very busy."

"It's important."

"So important that it couldn't wait until tonight?"

She stood her ground, unwilling to allow him to dismiss her like some bothersome child. "I think it is."

He straightened and crossed his arms over his chest, his blue eyes bored and impatient. "Well?"

Hannah plunged right in. "I have an idea that may sell more thread."

Reiver gave her a patronizing smile. "And what is this wonderful idea of yours?"

Hannah took a deep breath. "I think you should call our thread by an Italian name."

His eyes widened incredulously, then he burst out laughing. "An Italian name? Whatever for? Our thread isn't from Italy. It's made in Connecticut by the Shaw Silk Manufacturing Company, and that's the name it will always have." He bent over the table again, dismissing her.

Cheeks flaming, Hannah didn't move. "Before you're so quick to discount my idea, Reiver Shaw, let me tell you about Septimus Shively's Parisian ware."

"Hannah, I told you that James and I are busy."

James wiped the grease off his hands. "This can wait. Let's hear Hannah out."

Reiver capitulated with an annoyed sigh, and Hannah related the story that the peddler had told her. ". . . and isn't Italian silk known throughout the world as the best?" she finished.

"For now," Reiver said.

"So why don't we call our thread 'Genoa Silk Thread' or 'Milanese Silk Thread'? After all, it's just as good as Italian silk, isn't it?"

"It's better," Reiver said. "But the thread isn't made in Italy, and to call it an Italian name is deceptive. I'm proud of our silk and I won't be a party to such deception."

"But it isn't deceptive. The label would still say that it's manufactured by Shaw Silks of Coldwater, Connecticut, and if people assume that it's better somehow because of an Italian name, that's their own fault, not ours."

James grinned. "What she says makes sense."

Reiver rubbed his wide jaw. "I'm not so sure. I'll have to think about it."

"Couldn't you at least try it?" Hannah pleaded.

"I said I'll think about it."

Judging from Reiver's flat, uninterested tone, Hannah suspected that he would ultimately find some reason to discard her idea, so she left the machine shop feeling more estranged from her husband than ever, and headed for Samuel's studio.

• • •

Hannah stood at the window, looking up at the main house while Samuel engraved at his worktable.

"He won't do it," she said. "It's a good idea, but because I thought of it and he didn't, he won't do it."

"My brother may surprise you," Samuel said. "He is stubborn and proud, but he always puts aside his personal feelings for the good of the company. If giving the thread an Italian name will benefit Shaw Silks, Reiver wouldn't care if one of Naomi's gargoyles came up with the idea."

Hannah smiled at that.

Samuel rose and crossed the room. "It's a joy to see you smiling again. You haven't smiled in such a long time."

Aware of him standing behind her, so close that if she stepped back she'd bump into him, Hannah kept staring out the window. "You've noticed."

"I always notice everything about you," he said softly, "but I usually refrain from saying anything for both our sakes." He hesitated. "But if you should ever need to talk, I'm always here."

Hannah turned to face him, ready to decline his offer until she looked into his ghostly eyes and saw the warmth and sympathy there. Suddenly she had to share her loneliness or burst.

"Reiver has moved out of our bedchamber. He says it's because he doesn't want another simple child like Abigail."

Wordlessly Samuel drew her into his arms. Hannah considered moving out of danger, for lately even the most innocent contact—the touch of his hand on her arm, his cheek pressed against hers in greeting—aroused such shameful thoughts. This time, though, she let him hold her.

"My brother can also be a heartless son of a bitch," he said.

Hannah closed her eyes and rested her head against his shoulder. "It hurts me so to see how cold he is toward Abigail. You and James are so kind to her, so patient. Yet her own father can't even look at her without cringing."

Samuel rested his cheek against the top of her head. "He sees his children as reflections of himself, and he can't accept Abigail because she is imperfect."

Hannah stepped back. "It's not her fault that the Good Lord made her that way."

"Your indignation on Abigail's behalf is commendable, but aren't you furious with Reiver for denying you? You're a passionate woman." His tone deepened with rough intimacy as his cool, burning gaze scanned her face. "I can't imagine you sleeping alone forever."

"Don't say such—such intimate things, Samuel. You know how it upsets me."

"I know, but I can't seem to help myself, especially when I see you suffering."

She made a dismissive motion with her hand. "The pleasures of the marriage bed are greatly overrated. I'm sure I'll survive sleeping alone."

A muscle twitched in Samuel's jaw and he grew very still. "What in God's name has my brother done to you?"

"Nothing! Nothing at all. Just forget I said anything."

Hannah turned and walked toward the door, but the feel of Samuel's hands dropping lightly onto her shoulders stopped her as effectively as a brick wall.

"How can I forget?"

She turned back to him. "I came to you because I needed someone to talk to, someone to comfort me. I didn't come here for a—a dalliance!"

More's the pity. "I know that."

"I don't want to come between you and Reiver."

Ah, but you already have. "You won't," he lied to banish the guilt tightening her face.

She relaxed. "Good, because if that ever happened, I would never forgive myself."

"I don't want to frighten you away," he said gently. "I never want to make you feel that you can't come to me for companionship or comfort."

She smiled. "I value your friendship, and would hate to lose it."

He reached for her hand and brought it to his lips. "You never will."

She withdrew her hand and headed for the door.

He called after her, "Let me know what Reiver decides to do about your idea."

"I will."

He waited until her light footsteps died away on the stairs, and waited for the emptiness to follow. Then he went to the window. Seconds later Hannah emerged and walked up the hill to her own house, the greedy April breeze tugging at her skirts.

"I know why he's not sleeping with you, Hannah," he said heavily, "and it's not because of Abigail."

He didn't want to be around when she finally learned the truth. Or maybe he did.

When Hannah reached the top of the hill, she turned and looked back at the homestead, trying to ignore the pull of her heart.

I value your friendship, she had said to him. Who was she fooling? She didn't want Samuel to be her friend, she wanted him to be her lover.

"Oh, Samuel," she muttered to herself, "how can I go on resisting my feelings for you?"

But she had to. So she would go on pretending that all she wanted from him was simple friendship, that her heart didn't ache with longing every time she saw him. Perhaps if she told herself those lies often enough, she would even come to believe them herself.

Two days later Reiver told Hannah he would try her idea.

"We're going to call our thread 'Milanese Silk Thread.' If the name helps us to sell more, it will remain."

Hannah could hardly contain her excitement. "When will you know if it's a success?"

"By the end of summer, I suspect."

But as early as the end of June, the tremendous increase in orders for Milanese Silk Thread proclaimed Hannah's idea a success.

Reiver smiled as he studied the pile of orders that had just come in that morning. At this rate he would need to add more looms and hire more girls, but that was a welcome dilemma.

Now he felt like a fool for discounting Hannah's idea at first, but at the time it seemed so preposterous. After all, what did she know about the silk business? Her sphere was the home, as it should be.

Still, he was magnanimous enough to admit when he made a mistake, and he would tell Hannah so at the first opportunity.

Through the open door of his study, Reiver heard the front door open and a hoarse voice shout, "Shaw? Come out and face me like a man, you coward!"

He rose and stepped into the hallway. He took several steps forward, then stopped and stared at an Amos Tuttle he barely recognized.

The banker's son had aged ten years, his boyish face drawn and haggard, his soft mouth nothing more than a thin, hard slash. The moment Reiver looked into the boy's devastated eyes and saw the hatred blazing out, he knew why Tuttle had come.

"Bastard!" Tuttle reached beneath his coat and pulled out one of Colt's revolvers.

Before Reiver could even think to dive for the floor, Tuttle aimed and fired.

Hannah was upstairs putting away yesterday's laundry when the explosion startled her. She froze for a heartbeat, eyes wide like a frightened doe as the sound reverberated through her skull and died.

Screaming Reiver's name, she dropped the laundry, hiked up her skirts, and ran.

She was halfway down the stairs when she saw Reiver sprawled facedown on the floor. "Reiver!" she screamed, catapulting down the rest of the stairs so fast her legs almost got tangled in her petticoats.

She stopped at the foot of the stairs when she saw Amos Tuttle standing in the hall, a pistol hanging at his side, the air acrid with the smell of burned gunpowder.

"Why?" she cried, kneeling by her husband's body. "Why did you kill my husband?"

Dull, dead eyes bored into hers. "Because the bastard was nailing my wife."

"Liar!" Hannah rolled Reiver over, blanching at the dark red stain spreading over his white shirt just above his trouser's waistband like an obscene blossoming flower. Her fingers frantically ripped a square of cloth from the hem of her petticoat, and she stuffed it against Reiver's side to stanch the flow of blood.

She felt his neck and sobbed with relief when she found the barest throbbing of a pulse. "Thank God!"

Help. She had to get help. Samuel. James. *Anybody.*

Hannah scrambled to her feet and flew down the hall past Amos Tuttle and out into blinding sunlight. She sobbed in relief when she saw Samuel and James running up the hill, and stumbled toward them.

"Hannah, what happened?" Samuel demanded, reaching to stop her headlong flight. "We heard a gunshot."

"Amos Tuttle shot Reiver!" she cried. Her chest hurt. She couldn't breathe. *"Hurry!"*

James swore and ran, with Samuel and Hannah following close at his heels.

They raced into the hallway. Reiver still lay where he had fallen, and Tuttle sat on the stairs, legs akimbo and arms dangling from his knees. When he raised his head and looked at them, his smooth cheeks were slick with tears and he looked like a lost little boy.

With an incoherent growl, James launched himself at Tuttle and dragged him to his feet by his shirtfront.

"Don't waste time on him," Samuel snapped, kneeling to tend to Reiver. "Go find the doctor!"

James flung Tuttle against the wall. "If my brother dies, so do you." He ran down the hall and out the door.

Tuttle slid down the wall, whimpering like a child.

Samuel said, "Hannah, get that bastard out of my sight before I shoot him myself."

With shock came a certain detachment that allowed Hannah to take Tuttle's arm calmly and lead him to the parlor, where she made him sit down on the settee.

Just as she turned to leave he grasped her hand. "You must understand. Your husband has been committing adultery with my wife. That's why I had to shoot him. I had to make him pay. I had to."

Hannah snatched her hand away. "How dare you blacken my husband's good name with your filthy lies! Reiver would never do such a thing."

"Then you don't know your husband as well as you think you do. He's been doing it for years."

"I'm sick of listening to you. My husband needs me."

He cradled his head in his hands and his shoulders shook.

"How could she betray me like this?" he moaned. "My beautiful Cecelia . . ."

Hannah left the parlor, followed by the sound of Tuttle's sobbing.

"Your husband is a lucky man, Mrs. Shaw," Dr. Bradley said sometime later. "The bullet didn't do much damage, and with rest and diligent nursing, he should recover."

Hannah sagged against Samuel. "Thank God!"

Dr. Bradley patted her arm. "I'll leave instructions for his care with Mrs. Hardy."

"May I see him now?"

The doctor nodded.

Hannah took a deep breath to steel herself. Later she would face Amos Tuttle's accusation fully, but now she couldn't afford the luxury. Praying for strength, she walked into Reiver's room.

He was lying in bed, his face almost as white as the single sheet drawn up to his chest that was rising and falling gently.

Hannah went to his bedside and gently placed her hand against his cheek. It felt smooth and warm. Reiver stirred at her touch, but didn't open his eyes.

Hannah sat down in the chair by the bed and held her husband's hand, thoughts clamoring for attention through the numbness of shock. What would she tell the boys? What was she going to say to Reiver when he regained consciousness? What would happen to Amos Tuttle now?

Was her husband an adulterer?

Not Reiver.

She didn't leave his side until darkness fell and Samuel came for her.

"Hannah," he whispered, "supper's ready."

She didn't take her eyes off Reiver. "I'm not hungry."

"But you've been sitting here all day. You must be exhausted."

"He's my husband. My place is by his side."

Samuel knelt beside her chair and looked up at her. "The boys have been asking for you. I told them that a crazy man shot their father, but I assured them that he's going to be all right."

Hannah closed her eyes and leaned back in her chair. "Didn't

Benjamin want to know why someone would want to kill his father? He's very intelligent."

"He's also just a little boy. Right now he and Davey are frightened and need their mama." He rose. "Go to them, Hannah. I'll stay with my brother."

Hannah rose, smoothed her untidy chignon into some semblance of order, and went to her children.

Later, when she returned, she found Samuel with his brow furrowed and his handsome face reflecting some inner turmoil.

"How are the boys?" he asked softly.

"They were afraid for their father, but I told them they must be strong and brave for me, and they calmed down." Hannah knotted her fingers together. "Was Tuttle arrested?"

Samuel shook his head. "James was just about to turn him in when Tuttle Senior arrived on our doorstep. He begged us not to press charges against his only son. He even offered to forgive Reiver's loan."

Hannah glanced at her husband. "Though I want to see Tuttle pay for what he did, Reiver will probably agree to such terms if the mill will benefit."

Samuel stared down at his hands resting on his knees. "Hannah, about Tuttle's accusations—"

"They're false, of course. When Reiver is well enough, he'll tell me so himself."

"I'm sure he will tell the truth."

And Samuel left.

Reiver awoke to excruciating pain and Hannah's familiar worried face floating above him.

"Don't try to talk," she whispered, her eyes filled with a concern he surely didn't merit. "Dr. Bradley said you'll get better, but you have to rest."

So he wasn't going to die after all. He thanked God for making Tuttle such a bad shot.

He rewarded Hannah with a faint smile, then closed his eyes and sought refuge from the pain in blissful darkness.

"You just couldn't keep your hands off her, could you?" Samuel looked down at Reiver sitting up in bed, his left side swathed in bandages, and shook his head in disgust.

"I'm an invalid," Reiver retorted. "Don't you have the decency to wait until I've fully recovered to skin me alive?"

"Oh, I think you're strong enough to hear what I have to say."

Two weeks had passed since Amos Tuttle shot Reiver, and he was now well enough to sit up in bed for a few hours each day. Dr. Bradley said he could take a few steps tomorrow, so Samuel didn't feel the least bit guilty in confronting his brother with a few unpleasant truths.

"Everyone in Coldwater is laughing at you just like they laughed at Pa. 'Rummy had a weakness for the bottle,' they're saying, 'and his boy has a weakness for married women. Like father, like son.' "

Reiver turned crimson. "That's a low blow. You say that again and I'm going to get out of this bed and smash your face in. I'm not like Pa in any way."

You really can't see it, Samuel thought.

He jammed his fists into his pockets. "Was she worth it? You almost died, and now everyone in Coldwater and half of Hartford knows about your adulterous fling."

Anger hardened Reiver's pale, drawn features. "Don't make it sound so tawdry. I love Cecelia. I always have."

"And that justifies it?" Samuel flung up his hands. "Didn't you stop to think about all the people who would be hurt if you were discovered? What about your wife and your own children, not to mention Cecelia and that hopeless, lovesick husband of hers? Of all the thoughtless, selfish—"

"Lower your voice before someone hears you."

"It doesn't matter. Everyone *knows*!"

Reiver leaned forward. "What's happened to Cecelia? Has Tuttle cast her out?"

"I'm delighted to see that your first concern is your wife, as always."

"You don't understand. You never did. I do care about Hannah." He hesitated. "She hasn't said one word to me about Tuttle's accusation. Has she said anything to you?"

"Nothing. I think she's trying to ignore the incident by working herself to death. She's at the mill—"

"The mill? What is she doing there?"

"Who do you think has been running it in your absence, you

dolt? She opens it every morning, sees that the girls have plenty of work, and locks it up at night. When she's not doing that, she's either nursing your worthless hide or running the household like a general."

"Hannah's strong. She will come through this unscathed. It's Cecelia who stands to lose everything."

"Then why didn't you think of that before you started up with her again?"

"Because I can't help myself." Reiver winced in pain and leaned back against the pillows. "I have to know what's happened to her, Samuel. Will you find out for me?"

"I wish I could pity you, but I don't." Samuel reached into his back pocket and flung a letter at Reiver. "I went to Tuttle Senior yesterday to discuss your terms for forgiving the loan. Just as I was leaving, Cecelia stopped me in the hall and asked me to give you this. She said that it would explain everything."

"How did she look?" Reiver asked eagerly, pouncing on the letter. "If Tuttle has hurt her, I'll—"

"You needn't worry. She looked tired, sad, and red-eyed, as if she'd been crying for weeks, but fine otherwise."

"When I'm better, I'll go to see her for myself."

Samuel groaned in frustration. "Do you want Tuttle to kill you for sure this time? Leave the poor man's wife alone!"

Reiver ignored him and read the letter:

My beloved,

Please forgive me. If I had known that Amos intended to harm you, I would have stopped him somehow. Thank God you will recover. If Amos had succeeded, I would not want to go on living.

I suspect one of my servants noted my frequent absences and betrayed us. Amos followed me one day when I went to meet you. When I returned home, he confronted me and threatened to take my son away unless I told him the truth. Please forgive me, but I had no choice.

Now I must write the hardest words I have ever had to say. We must never see each other again. Amos swears he has forgiven me and will forget my infidelity because he still loves me, but I must forswear you and move to New

York City with him. His father has arranged for him to work in a bank there. I have agreed to go with my husband.

It is for the best. You must forget me as I must forget you.

Keep well,
Cecelia

Reiver turned white and the letter fluttered from his hand. "What is it?" Samuel snapped.

"She and Tuttle have reconciled and they're moving away. She never wants to see me again." Reiver rubbed his eyes. "I can't believe she agreed to it."

Samuel raised one brow. "Under the circumstances, what else could she do? She's chosen to salvage what's left of her marriage, and I commend her."

Reiver said nothing, but the bleak devastation in his eyes spoke what was in his heart.

Samuel rose. "I find it difficult to feel too sorry for you, brother. You brought this disaster on yourself and deserve everything you're going to get."

"I don't want your sympathy," Reiver replied, his voice thick and trembling. "I want you to leave me alone now. I need to rest."

"Oh, you'd better get all the rest you can. You still have to explain yourself to Hannah, and I wouldn't be in your shoes for all the silk in China."

A week later Reiver realized he could no longer postpone the inevitable.

That morning, after he finished the breakfast that Hannah had brought to him on a tray, he rose, dressed, and went downstairs, where he found Mrs. Hardy sitting in the parlor, watching Abigail play quietly.

"Where's Hannah?" Reiver asked.

Mrs. Hardy looked up. "She's where she's been every morning since you were shot, at the mill."

Now he remembered. "Will you tell her I need to see her? I'll watch Abigail."

The housekeeper nodded and walked off, returning with Hannah five minutes later.

Hannah entered the parlor, concern written on her face. "Isn't it too soon for you to be dressed and about?"

"Yesterday Dr. Bradley told me that I've made a remarkable recovery, and may go about my business." Reiver glanced down at Abigail seated on the floor, staring at her blocks as if choosing one were a momentous decision. "Would you have Mrs. Hardy take Abigail outside to play? I have to talk to you."

God, how he dreaded this! His palms felt damp and his mouth dry.

Mrs. Hardy scooped up Abigail and left while Hannah eyed her husband warily.

Reiver closed the parlor door against curious ears and turned to face his wife. He took a deep breath and blurted, "Tuttle told the truth."

Hannah's eyes widened and she froze. She couldn't lie to herself any longer. All color drained from her face, leaving her as pale as death, and she shook like an autumn leaf in the wind.

Reiver stepped forward to catch her. "Hannah—"

"Don't touch me!" She backed away and collapsed onto the settee, where she sat dazed and trembling. Finally her eyes focused on him. "Mrs. Tuttle was your—your mistress? Her husband found out, and that's why he shot you?"

Reiver couldn't bear the pain in her ragged voice, and his gaze slid to the floor. "Yes."

"How long?"

"Hannah—"

"I said, *how long*!"

Her vehemence threw him off balance. He hadn't expected such a reaction from his dutiful, compliant wife. "While she was still a widow. A year before you and I married."

"And after we were married?"

"I still . . . saw her."

"Did you love her?"

I still do. "Yes."

"Then why didn't you marry her instead of me?" A bitter smile twisted her mouth. "How stupid of me to forget. You married me for my uncle's Racebrook land, nothing more. It's unfortunate that Mrs. Tuttle didn't have something of comparable value, then I would have been spared."

Reiver shot her an annoyed look. "What does it matter? It's over. We all have to put it behind us and get on with our lives."

Hannah bolted to her feet, her hands balled into fists at her sides. "Oh, I see. I am just supposed to forget that you've broken our marriage vows and betrayed me with another woman? I'm supposed to pretend I don't hear the pitying whispers behind my back wherever I go? I'm supposed to ignore Benjamin's tears when he comes home from school?"

For the first time white-hot shame slammed through Reiver. "My son comes home crying? Why?"

"Why do you think? Because the other children call his father vile names that they hear from their own parents." Tears welled up in Hannah's eyes. "But he never says a word because he knows it will upset me. And he does idolize his father so."

He hung his head. "I didn't realize—"

"Didn't realize? Dear God in heaven, are you so—so arrogant to think you're the only man in the world? That your actions wouldn't affect anyone else? Well, they have." She shook her head in disgust. "And we're supposed to pretend that nothing happened?"

"Unless you are prepared to take a gun and finish what Tuttle started, or walk out on me, Hannah, that is exactly what we must do."

"Oh, don't tempt me, Reiver Shaw!"

Once again, her unexpected vehemence disconcerted him. "I'm sorry for hurting you and the boys, but I almost paid with my life." He extended his hand. "Now I'm asking you to forgive me."

She wiped away her tears. "I don't know if I can."

His hand fell to his side. "Perhaps it's time I moved back into your bedchamber."

Hannah recoiled. "And risk siring another idiot like Abigail?"

She gathered her skirts and ran from the parlor. Reiver made no attempt to stop her.

Hannah left the house and kept walking. She planned to walk until she fell off the face of the earth, but when she reached the tobacco field where she had first met Reiver, she stopped.

She settled herself atop the hard dry-stone wall. The tall,

broad-leafed plants rippled like a green sea in the faint June breeze, fragrant with dusty red earth and rain to come.

"Damn you, Reiver Shaw!" She screamed so loud, she startled a flock of crows that scattered into the overcast sky like a blast of buckshot, their raucous screeches mocking her. *Haw haw, haw haw.*

Hannah cried, great choking sobs that shook her so hard, she had to grasp the warm, flat stones to keep her from toppling off the wall. Even fresh tears couldn't wash away the pain.

The soft, slow clopping of hooves coming down the road sent her fumbling for her handkerchief to dry her eyes and blow her nose. Once she composed herself, she looked over her right shoulder and saw that the horseman was Samuel.

He stopped his chestnut mount a few feet away and looked down at her. "So he told you."

She nodded, her eyes watering helplessly.

"Oh, Hannah . . ." Samuel dismounted in one fluid motion and strode over to her, kicking up dust. "I'm so sorry." He climbed the stone wall and sat down close to her, but did not attempt to touch her.

She said, "You've known about Mrs. Tuttle all along, haven't you?"

He gazed out over the field rather than look into her tormented eyes. "Yes. She's been my brother's mistress for years."

"Why didn't you, of all people, tell me? I thought you were my friend. I thought that I could trust you."

Samuel flinched at the scathing reproach in her voice. "What good would it have done? You would have been hurt unnecessarily, and I couldn't bear that."

"It wouldn't have been worse than the agony I feel now." She closed her eyes and fought back tears. "I've tried so hard to make the best of my lot and be a loving, loyal wife to Reiver. I've slept with him, borne his children, tried to share his passion for the mill. And what is the thanks I get? He betrays me with another woman."

Samuel clasped her cold hand in his warm, solid one, offering comfort.

Hannah looked at him. "You should have seen him in the parlor when he told me. He acted as though he had done nothing more reprehensible than—than steal a pie from the kitchen windowsill. 'We all have to put it behind us and get on with our lives,' he said to me. It doesn't matter that he's shamed his family and made us the laughingstock of Coldwater."

"He may not show it, but Reiver deeply regrets what he did."

Anger hardened Hannah's tears to glass. "I don't think he regrets it at all. Reiver's a selfish man. He thinks only of himself."

Samuel caressed her white knuckles with his fingertips. "So what are you going to do now? Leave?"

She sighed. "Where would I go, back to my aunt and uncle? I'm sure they'd welcome me with open arms. And I have to think of my children." Hannah withdrew her hand and rubbed her arms as if they were cold. "No, I'll stay, but any feelings I had for Reiver are dead."

"They'll return. Give yourself time."

She shook her head vehemently. "No. He's hurt me too deeply. Mr. Tuttle may have forgiven his wife, but I'll never forgive my husband."

The first drops of rain fell, rustling the tobacco leaves.

Samuel looked up at the darkening sky, which seemed to mirror his emotions. "We should get back before we're soaked."

She looked at him defiantly. "I don't ever want to go back."

"You have to."

"Ah, yes. Duty," she said bitterly.

Samuel slid off the wall and retrieved his horse that was grazing placidly at the side of the road. He swung into the saddle and extended his hand to Hannah.

She didn't move, their gazes locked. Finally she climbed down and Samuel lifted her up to sit in front of him. The feel of his hard right arm firmly holding her around the waist and the solid wall of his body against her back did more than soothe and comfort her.

Samuel made his horse walk slowly down the dusty dirt road darkly spotted with intermittent raindrops. Hannah leaned back, letting the rain wash away dried tears, her cheek touching Samuel's.

She looked at him, savoring the long clean lines of cheekbone and jaw. "Do you remember that day years ago when you asked me to run away with you?"

He smiled wistfully and nodded.

"I wish I had."

He jerked the reins, causing his startled horse to fling back its head with a snort of protest and dance in place. Samuel looked at Hannah, his pale gaze bald with yearning, his lithe body taut with tension. "Don't do this to me."

Hannah turned and pressed her lips to his. They were as warm and inviting as they looked, and after a moment's resistance, so responsive.

Samuel finally tore himself away, anger replacing the yearning in his eyes. "Was that to get even with Reiver?"

"A little. But more for myself, to stop this terrible hurt inside."

"Good. Because I won't be a substitute for any man."

He hugged her and sighed dismally, his breath warm against her ear. "Hannah, Hannah . . . you make it so easy for me to forget I'm Reiver's brother."

"And you make it so easy for me to forget I'm still his wife."

They rode the rest of the way in silence, each refusing to acknowledge that they flirted with disaster.

Several weeks passed before the sting of Reiver's betrayal lessened in Hannah's heart. She found that assuming more duties in the mill helped to clear her mind and keep her from dwelling on her husband's affair with the lovely Cecelia Tuttle.

When bottles of indigo, cochineal, and other assorted dyestuffs arrived one morning, she made note of their delivery and brought them to the dye house herself rather than wait for Reiver to do it.

The moment Hannah entered the dye house, a large, spacious building lined with tall windows to let in as much light as possible, she wrinkled her nose at the acrid odor of dye emanating from the copper tanks, or barcs.

She stood in the doorway and looked for Giuseppe Torelli, the dye master that Reiver had gone to great lengths and expense to bring over from Italy, and she saw him by one of the barcs, examining five skeins of freshly died silk hanging from a long dyeing stick.

"Mr. Torelli," she called.

He looked up, smiled and nodded, and handed the dye stick to one of his sons.

"Good morning, signora," he greeted her in broken English, with a courtly bow.

"Another shipment of dyestuffs," Hannah said, handing him her collection of bottles.

"*Grazie*. Thank you." He took them over to a wide table, where he set them down and began taking a pinch of this and a spoonful of that and blending the dyes with the skill of a wizard mixing some magic potion while Hannah watched in amazement.

She shook her head. "How do you know how much to use?"

Giuseppe Torelli tapped one indigo-stained forefinger to his forehead.

Hannah's eyes widened. "From memory?"

He nodded.

Enrico, his youngest son, passing by with several soft muslin bags of boiled silk now ready for dyeing, smiled and said proudly, "My father's formulas are carefully guarded secrets. Only he knows how much dye to mix for each color."

Hannah stared at him. "Enrico, you don't know? No one else knows this except your father?"

Enrico nodded, smiled, and blithely went about his work, leaving Hannah to wonder what would happen to Shaw Silks if their dye master were to die tomorrow.

Later that evening Hannah cornered Reiver in his study. "I learned something very alarming today," she said.

He kept his eyes trained on his ledger, for relations between them were still strained. "What is it?"

"Did you know that Giuseppe blends the dyes from memory, that no one else knows the formulas and they're not written down?"

Reiver gave her a condescending look. "Of course I do. A dye master's formulas are closely guarded secrets. They don't write them down, otherwise they could be stolen and sold to a rival silk house. When I hired Torelli, he brought his secrets with him."

"But what do we do if something happens to him?"

"Find another dye master."

Hannah's voice rose in exasperation. "Wouldn't it be so much simpler to have his formulas written down and locked away somewhere, especially the one for black dye?"

Black was the most difficult color of all to achieve and always in demand because black thread was needed to sew mourning clothes. Giuseppe Torelli's black was always rich and consistent, his scarlets and crimsons from cochineal more vibrant than any Hannah had ever seen.

Reiver leaned back in his chair. "I don't know if Torelli will want his secrets written down. These Italian dye masters are pretty tight-lipped."

"There must be something you can do to persuade him."

Reiver looked thoughtful. "You have a point. If something were to happen to Giuseppe—"

"The quality of our threads would suffer, not to mention all the time you'd lose finding a new dye master."

The following day Reiver struck a bargain with Torelli: he would teach his secret formulas to his son Enrico, and if either of them left Shaw Silks for a competitor, they agreed to pay Reiver all costs he incurred finding a new dye master.

Hannah suspected the Torellis would be faithful Shaw employees for a long, long time.

CHAPTER
❧ 8 ❧

ONE cool morning in June, Hannah took her tin pail and headed for the blueberry patch on the west end of Shaw property, for she had promised Benjamin and Davey blueberry cobbler when they returned home from school.

Life was slowly returning to normal. The flame of the Shaw scandal burned a little less brightly in Coldwater these days. Conversations ceased less frequently when Hannah walked down Main Street, and fewer surreptitious, speculative looks came her way. Benjamin's taunting at school dwindled and died.

But Hannah's wound was deeper and slower to heal. Mercifully Reiver kept his distance and made no demands. He went to the mill before six o'clock in the morning and didn't return until eight o'clock at night, when his conversations with Hannah were polite, but still strained. At night they retired to separate bedchambers.

She reached the blueberry bushes and picked to the slumberous accompaniment of bees humming, unable to resist tasting a handful of the sweet fruit herself. The *ping-ping-ping* of the first berries hitting the bottom of the pail sounded as soothing as falling rain. Her pail was one quarter full when she noticed a man leaving the road and walking toward her.

It was Nate.

The years had thickened and coarsened his stocky body and drawn his fleshy face into slack jowls. He lumbered closer, like a bear sighting its dinner, and with every step he took toward Hannah, she resisted the urge to take one step back.

Instead she smiled politely when he reached her. "Good morning, Nate. I'm sorry to hear your stepfather is so ill."

Nate's white shirt was grimy and reeking of sweat. More than his odor, the maliciousness glittering in his eyes made Hannah's stomach queasy.

"Sorry, are you? That's a lie. You're one of the high-and-mighty Shaws. You look down your nose at the likes of us."

Hannah plucked a cluster of berries and threw them into her pail. "That's not true. We went to your wedding last year, and I've asked Aunt Naomi to the house many times. She's always sent her regrets."

"If you're so high and mighty, Mrs. Shaw," he jeered, "why has your husband been"—he thrust his hips back and forth—"with the banker's wife?"

Hannah's face burned, her fingers tightening on the pail's handle. "Do you know why I'd never have you in my house, Nate Fisher? Because you're so common and crude."

He turned crimson, then his dirty hand shot out and grasped her wrist. "Why don't we see just how crude I am under these here bushes?"

"You lay a finger on me, and my husband—"

"Your husband will do what? He doesn't care about you. All he cares about is nailing his doxy." Nate's scornful gaze roved over Hannah, and he flung her away. "What man would want a cold, stiff piece like you, anyway? You're not even good enough for breedin', with your idiot girl. If it's pleasure a man's after, he'd get more taking a sheep to his bed."

Hannah was too outraged to be shocked. Without thinking, she lifted her bucket and dumped it on Nate's head, then gathered her skirts and ran for her life. She heard his muffled bellow of surprise and rage, but she didn't risk looking back.

She kept running.

Finally, when she realized that the only footsteps pounding the hard earth were her own, Hannah slowed down, her corset stays squeezing the breath out of her. She stopped and turned. Nate had disappeared.

Hannah crossed her arms and shivered in the warm sunlight. No matter how much the boys wanted blueberry cobbler, she would not return to the berry patch today. She turned and walked toward the house, but Nate's taunting words rubbed old wounds raw.

Hot tears stung Hannah's eyes, and her step slowed. No man had ever desired her for herself. Nate wanted only her body. Reiver had married her for the river land, and he came to her bed for physical release or to sire children, not because he wanted her.

But men desired Cecelia with her porcelain prettiness and chestnut ringlets. Reiver wanted her enough to risk scandal, and her husband wanted her enough to cause one. But would anyone fight to possess Hannah?

She reached the homestead, nothing more than a blur, and leaned back against the rough bark of the oak tree's wide trunk. She was still standing there moments later when Samuel came striding out of the house toward her.

"Hannah, what's wrong? I saw you running across the field like the devil was after you." He was painting today, not engraving, for a dab of blue smudged one high cheekbone and dark brown spots freckled the backs of his hands and forearms where he had rolled up his shirt sleeves.

"I'm just feeling sorry for myself." She wiped away her tears and managed a brave smile, but when she thought of Nate's vicious, hurtful words rending her fragile confidence to shreds . . .

Samuel frowned, his pale eyes always seeing too much. "What has my brother done to you this time?"

"Not Reiver. Nate."

"Naomi's gargoyle?"

"He came over while I was picking blueberries, and he said—he said—"

"Come inside and tell me."

Hannah followed him into the hushed, empty house and upstairs to his studio. Welcoming sunlight flooded the room. The vigorous smell of turpentine, the assortment of brushes and engraving tools scattered on his worktable proclaimed this room Samuel's domain.

He smiled. "Now, what did the gargoyle say?"

Hannah suddenly became tongue-tied and shy. "I don't know if I should tell you. It wasn't very flattering. Quite humiliating, in fact."

"Then you must tell me," he said gently, "so that I can refute his lies."

So Hannah went to the window, took a deep breath, and told Samuel everything.

Everything.

When she finished, she turned around to face him. She expected him to express indignation on her behalf, and sympathy, for he was her friend and champion. But Samuel appeared curiously unmoved, his handsome face shuttered.

"Naomi's gargoyle is wrong, and I would like to prove it to you." He crossed the studio to the door and grasped the key, only his trembling fingers revealing the crack in his outward calm. "If you want to leave, Hannah, you must leave now, otherwise I'm going to lock you in and make love to you."

His declaration stunned her. She couldn't breathe. Excuses rushed to her lips unbidden. *I am married. I have three children. This is wrong. We mustn't. Someone will catch us.*

Yet the words remained unspoken. Reiver's infidelity had left her feeling so hollow inside, so unworthy of love. And she realized with blinding clarity that she also wanted Samuel for reasons that had nothing to do with filling that void.

"Will you stay?" Samuel's low, soft, beguiling voice promised untold riches if she did.

"Lock the door."

He closed his eyes and sighed, a mixture of wonder and relief. When he turned the key in the lock, the click reverberated through Hannah's mind like a gunshot.

Samuel walked toward her. For the first time Hannah allowed herself to assess him as a lover, and she found him stirring indeed. Her fingers ached to stroke the springy softness of his dark, curly hair, and the thought of his sensuous mouth roving over her naked body left her knees weak and shaking. She wanted to push his shirt open and feel the smooth, silky skin and hard muscles of his shoulders and chest beneath her fingertips. She wanted him. Oh, yes.

He grinned and drew her away from the window before some passerby could see them together. "My, my, what wicked, wanton thoughts you have."

She blushed like a schoolgirl. "That's not fair. You can read my mind."

Samuel cupped her face in his hands, lightly stroking her cheeks with his thumbs. "No, only your beautiful eyes." Then his fingers went to her chignon, pulling the offending pins from it and letting her glossy hair tumble down her back in sweet abandon.

When he kissed her, Hannah felt as though she had never been kissed before, an unrestrained, openmouthed, hot-tongued possession that left her dizzy and drowning.

They kissed until kissing no longer aroused them. They needed more. Samuel's palm closed over Hannah's left breast, caressing it through thin calico and thinner lawn, then teasing the nipple with his thumb until she gasped through clenched teeth.

He brushed his lips along the delicate shell of her outer ear, whispering, "Let me see your breasts."

Hannah's shaking fingers undid the buttons down the front of her dress, and when it spread gaping and inviting, he parted it further and slid it off her shoulders and down her arms, where it gathered at her elbows, imprisoning them against her sides. Her chemise came down next over her breasts.

Samuel stared. "Ah, but you are beautiful."

At his sweet, husky words, Hannah felt a clench of white-hot heat unfurl deep inside. Reiver never spoke when he took her, never complimented her.

Still staring, Samuel took several steps back to his worktable, picked up a large, dry paintbrush, and returned to her, his eyes sparkling mischievously. At Hannah's puzzled look, he murmured, "I have the urge to paint you."

He dipped the brush's soft tip in the moisture gathering in the hollow of her throat, then slowly drew it down her chest in a seductive, voluptuous tickle.

"Samuel, you mustn't." She shuddered. "This is—this is—"

"Indescribable? And it's only beginning." He drew the brush down her right breast and traced the areola around and around before quickly flicking the soft bristles back and forth across one straining nipple then the other, teasing them.

Hannah's knees buckled and she swayed. Samuel steadied her, and resumed stripping her with the attention and dedication of one performing a sacred ritual. He knew just what to unhook and untie. Soon Hannah's dress, corset, petticoats, and undergarments lay on the studio floor in a crumpled heap and she was standing naked before a man not her husband. Her lover.

My lover. How wicked that sounds.

She watched him undress with masculine grace, and blushed when his trousers and drawers slipped down over his narrow hips. She stared, for Samuel was larger than his brother.

He took her hand and led her over to the old settee standing against one wall. "It's not as grand as I'd like, but it will have to do."

Hannah lay down and prepared herself to accept Samuel's weight, but he surprised her by kneeling on the floor and continuing his arousing caressing with hands, lips, and flicking tongue. He concentrated on her breasts, tugging and sucking until she groaned and writhed in abandon. When his palm cupped her most intimate flesh and his fingers explored her relentlessly, Hannah almost arched off the settee.

"Dear God, Samuel!"

He came to her then, parting her thighs and possessing her with one swift thrust. He felt so hot and hard, filling her to bursting. Hannah moved with him, compelled to reach for the ecstasy that often eluded her in her husband's arms. When it came, rising, rising, exploding like a Roman candle, Hannah finally awoke inside.

Then Samuel gave her another gift.

After his own shuddering climax that caused the settee to hop up and down, Samuel kissed her tenderly and murmured, "You are not a cold piece, Hannah Shaw, and you've given me more pleasure than a man deserves."

Afterward, Samuel knew Hannah would be racked with guilt.

He saw it in the furrow etched between her brows as she cast darting sidelong glances toward the door, in the hurried way her nervous fingers smoothed her disheveled hair and arranged it back into its familiar chignon at the nape of her neck, in the way her gaze avoided him.

He helped her dress with the efficiency of a ladies' maid, though he couldn't resist kissing inviting patches of flesh before concealing them.

"I—I have to go," she said, rubbing her wrists as if they'd

been locked in a pillory for hours. "I've stayed too long and Mrs. Hardy will wonder where I am."

He caught her hand just as she was about to flee. "I want to make love to you again, Hannah. All day, every day."

Panic and fear flooded those huge blue eyes. "We mustn't! I—I'm a married woman. I have children. Someone will catch us."

"No one will find out, if we're careful. I'm alone here for most of the morning. James is always at the mill, tinkering with those damned machines, and the women don't come to clean until later." He smiled. "You don't think this was a mistake, do you? A momentary lapse in sanity? Because it's not, my sweet little Puritan. At least for me. And I don't think it was for you, either."

"No, it wasn't. But I have duties. Responsibilities that must come before personal desires."

"Forget about duties and responsibilities. Live for the moment, because it will never come again."

She gave him a curious look. "And what about you? Don't you feel some shame for what we've just done?"

"For coveting my brother's wife? No, because Reiver doesn't deserve you. I want you so badly that I'm willing to risk everything to have you."

Her brow furrowed. "But what if we're caught?"

"Then we'll beg Reiver's forgiveness just as he begged your forgiveness for his affair with Cecelia."

His blunt reminder that Reiver had first wronged her brought Hannah up short. "Two wrongs don't make a right."

"No, but when I see you become the beautiful, sensual woman in the portrait I engraved when you first married, I know it's right."

Her hand flew to her abdomen and her eyes darkened in panic. "What if I conceive a child?"

"I'll show you how not to. All it takes is a piece of sponge, vinegar, and a little care."

She stared at him. Such forbidden, mysterious knowledge belonged to a Samuel she didn't know.

He caught her hand and kissed her palm to allay her fears. "Come tomorrow. Please. Take the risk. You have nothing to fear, I promise."

Hannah drew her hand away and headed for the door. "I—I don't think that would be wise, Samuel."

And she fled.

Everyone will know, Hannah thought on her way back to the house. They just have to take one look at my guilty face and they'll know I've been unfaithful to Reiver.

All Mrs. Hardy noticed was that Hannah didn't have the berries for the boys' blueberry cobbler and went out in a huff to pick them herself. Later that evening a⸍ dinner, Reiver and James were too preoccupied with designing new looms to notice the "A" for adulteress Hannah had branded into her own forehead.

That night, when Hannah was alone in the heavy summer darkness, her thoughts invariably turned to Samuel, the only one to understand her lonely, wounded heart. Restless and unable to sleep, she rose and went to the window facing the homestead. Velvet darkness enveloped the house, except for one illuminated window in the upstairs studio. She saw Samuel's familiar shadow limned by golden light, and felt his hot, hungry gaze on her bedchamber window.

She had to keep away from him. She had to.

Samuel stood before his studio window, staring moodily out at the morning drizzle graying the landscape. He resisted the urge to fling his engraving plate right through the glass.

Eleven days had passed since he had seduced Hannah, and still she hadn't come to him. Oh, he saw her every day. He could hardly avoid her. But, to his surprise and chagrin, she acted as though nothing untoward had happened.

He ran his hands through his hair in frustration. How could she pretend that their union meant nothing to her? It meant everything to him.

Then he heard it, the pattering of light footsteps up the steep stairs.

He held his breath until he felt light-headed, not daring to hope.

The door opened a crack, then swung wide.

The breath he had been holding came out in a soft swoosh. "Hannah."

She hesitated in the doorway, her ivory cheeks flushed with

either shame or excitement. Fine beads of moisture from the drizzle outside clung to her smooth, straight hair like stars and dampened her blue calico dress so that it smelled faintly of dye.

"I wanted to stay away," she said, resigned at last, "but I find that I can't." Her hand dipped into the deep pocket of her dress and she pulled out a clear stoppered bottle and small sponge. "I suspect I shall be needing these."

Vinegar and a sponge. A tangible, but unspoken admission of surrender and premeditation, of sweet, illicit complicity. It had taken eleven days, but he had won. She was his at last.

Reiver threw down another broken cocoon in disgust and stepped on it, grinding it with his boot. "How many does this make?" he snapped at Constance Ferry as if she were personally responsible for the catastrophe.

Constance sat at her table surrounded by the white mountain of cocoons that she was sorting. "At least a hundred in the last basket alone, Mr. Shaw," she replied.

"Damn it, that's too many! I don't pay good money for broken cocoons!"

Constance's long face puckered. " 'Tain't my fault, Mr. Shaw. They come that way."

Reiver stormed off, oblivious to the young woman's distress as he bellowed for James.

In the reeling room the half-dozen looms hummed industriously, a sound Reiver usually found relaxing. Today their monotonous droning set his teeth on edge.

"James! Where in the hell are you?" He ignored the workers' questioning looks as he went striding into the machine room and almost collided with James.

"What's wrong?" James wiped his greasy hands on a towel.

Reiver glared at him. "Why haven't you invented a machine that can use those damned broken cocoons? I'm damned sick and tired of throwing them away. It's waste, pure and simple."

"I'm trying my best, but inventing something takes time."

Reiver lowered his head like a charging bull. "We don't have time. We lose money every time we have to throw away a broken cocoon."

James bristled, his eyes darkening in anger, for he was not

used to being the brunt of Reiver's temper. "What are you hollering at me for? It's not my fault. I'm working as fast as I can."

"Then work faster."

A red flush crept up James's cheeks. "You know, Reiver, I don't think the cocoons are setting you off. You're mad about something else and taking it out on anyone foolish enough to cross your path."

"I've never heard anything so stupid in all my born days."

James shrugged. "You think about it. I'm getting back to work." His lanky figure drifted away.

Reiver had to get out of the mill before he exploded at all the incompetents around him. He whirled on his heel and stomped off.

Once he was outside, the soft September breeze fanning his cheeks cooled his steaming temper. His angry stride slowed and he considered what James had said.

Reiver jammed his hands into his pockets. James was right; broken cocoons were not responsible for his incendiary temper.

He missed Cecelia. He ached whenever he thought of her. He still wanted her.

Cecelia.

Reiver approached his brothers' house just as Hannah emerged through the back door, several shirts draped over the crook of her left arm. In the crystal richness of an autumn morning, he mistakenly attributed her flushed cheeks to the invigorating air, and her sparkling eyes to some remembered sally of her children's before they went off to school that morning. Today she wore a demure dress of soft blue wool, its white collar edged with a narrow border of black lace, a token bit of mourning for her uncle Ezra, who had died just this summer of a bad liver.

Hannah closed the door behind her, and when she turned and noticed him, she froze. The light in her eyes dimmed as it usually did whenever she looked at her husband these days. Hannah smoothed the shirts with a nervous hand and walked down the path toward him.

"Samuel had some shirts for me to mend," she said, as if compelled to explain her presence in the homestead.

"It's time my brother married and let his own wife mend his shirts."

"I don't mind."

She walked back toward the house, and Reiver joined her. As usual when they were together, an uncomfortable, unforgiving silence rose between them like a stone wall.

Reiver said, "It's hard to believe summer's over."

"Yes."

He waited. When she said nothing else, he added a few more platitudes about the weather, then stopped and placed his hand on her arm. "Is this what we're going to do, spend the rest of our lives discussing the weather?"

Hannah hugged the shirts tight against her waist. "We can always discuss the children. Abigail can say her name now—at least the 'Abby' part of it."

He recognized her irritating statement for the challenge that it was. "I'm pleased. No, don't look at me as if I'm lying. I am pleased for her. But I don't wish to discuss the children. I want to discuss their parents."

"Then we should go inside."

Once inside the foyer, Reiver checked to make sure they were alone, then ushered Hannah into the parlor and closed the doors behind them.

She stood there, still clutching Samuel's shirts, still smoothing them nervously in a gesture that was beginning to annoy him.

"I've suffered enough, Hannah," Reiver said quietly. "You've had all summer to accept what happened and—"

"I'll never accept what happened."

Reiver's temper flared. "Well, whether you can accept it or not, you are still my wife, with a wife's responsibilities."

Hannah turned paste white. "You are speaking of my responsibilities in the marriage bed."

"I'm moving back into your room tonight."

"Even if I don't want you there?"

"I'm sure you'll put your personal desires aside and do your wifely duty." He smiled wryly. "I promise you that I will be quick, and you won't have to suffer my intimacies longer than necessary."

"You would force me?"

Reiver shook her out of sheer frustration. "Damn it, I will not let you make me feel like some rutting pig, do you hear me?"

When he saw her stricken look, he released her and fought to control himself. "You will obey me, Hannah. The longer we delay this, the rift between us will only grow wider."

His decision made, he whirled on his heel and strode away before he noticed his wife's shudder of revulsion.

When she was sure she was alone, Hannah pressed Samuel's shirts to her face and breathed in the faint scents of paint, turpentine, and maleness. How was she ever going to endure Reiver touching her now, after knowing such sweet delight in his brother's arms? She trembled, wondering if Reiver would be able to tell that another man had possessed her. Surely every curve, the texture of her skin, the very depths of her, would feel different and strange to him now. Surely her own body would betray her in some subtle way.

She set the shirts in her lap and smoothed them absently as if she could coax out the answer to her dilemma. There was none, save the one she wanted to ignore.

The straw basket filled to the brim with rosy apples was heavy, but when Hannah thought of baking apple pies and how the calm, satisfying ritual would cleanse her mind—at least for a little while—she ignored the aching muscle in her forearm and marched resolutely along the path.

Then she saw Samuel.

He stood on the hill rising to her left, his feet spread slightly apart in a commanding and expectant stance, hands on hips, pale eyes alight with a mixture of triumph, desire, and reproach. A strong breeze sprang up out of nowhere, snapping his white shirt as if it were laundry on a clothesline and flattening it erotically against his chest and ribs.

Hannah envied the wind. She stopped, unable to smile and wave nonchalantly, helpless to drag her eyes away from his, even though they softened, giving her permission to flee.

She couldn't.

Samuel walked down the hill, slowly at first, then faster as his impatience grew. When he reached her, he extended his hand. "That basket looks heavy."

The moment she relinquished it to him, she regretted it, for now she had nothing to do with her nervous hands.

"Shall I walk back to the house with you?" he said. Without

waiting for her answer, he began walking, and Hannah fell in step beside him.

They strolled without speaking, presenting the most innocent picture of a man carrying a basket of apples for a woman.

Finally Samuel said, "I've missed you." When Hannah made no comment, he added, "The last eight days have seemed like an eternity to me. I can't sleep, I can't work." He chuckled, a dry, bitter sound. "Now I know what hell is like."

She knew as well.

"Why haven't you come?" he asked gently. "Couldn't you get away?"

"It's not that." Hannah took a deep, shuddering breath. "Reiver has moved back into my bedchamber."

Samuel stopped in his tracks and looked at her, a rare burst of jealousy distorting his features. "That explains much."

She couldn't reassure him by revealing how she had lain in her bed that first night, stiff with terror that Reiver would divine her secret the moment he touched her. She couldn't tell him how she willed her mind into his bed while her husband used her body with the merciful quickness he had promised. Some things were best left unspoken, especially between lovers.

Hannah jammed her fists into her apron's deep pockets and stared at the mills not far away. "I loathe his touch, but what right do I have to refuse him? I'm no better than he is."

"But you are."

Hannah looked at him out of tormented eyes. "We can't go on being lovers, Samuel, not while Reiver occupies my bed. I can't jump from one man to the other, I just can't. It would make me feel like a—"

"Don't you dare call yourself that!" He set the apples down and reached for her, but Hannah bent over and grasped the basket's handle with both hands, holding it between them as if she were offering him the fruit.

"You mustn't touch me, Samuel! Someone may see." Hannah's gaze darted around nervously, then she froze. In the distance a man walked out of the throwing shed and looked in their direction before disappearing into the dye house. Hannah sighed in relief, but she was visibly shaken.

Samuel pried the basket from her stiff fingers. "Come back to the homestead with me. We'll talk."

She knotted her fingers together. "I—I have to get back to the house and bake pies."

"Don't act as though you must carry this burden alone. I'm just as responsible as you are, so share your misgivings with me," he said, his voice soothing but insistent.

"Someone will see us."

"You're worrying needlessly. We'll stay down in the parlor, and if anyone should come by looking for you, we'll say that you stopped by to give me and James some of these delicious apples."

"I—I can't."

"Why not? Are you afraid that once I get you into the house, you won't be able to resist me, and we'll wind up in my studio?"

"I've managed to resist you for eight days, haven't I?" Both of them knew that wasn't much of an accomplishment.

"Then you shouldn't be afraid to come with me."

Hannah didn't reply, but when they came to the fork in the path, she hesitated for only a fraction of a second before turning right and heading for the homestead.

Once inside, Samuel set down the basket and turned to Hannah, but made no attempt to touch her, though he wanted to do that and more. "You're safe here. We're alone. No one will see us."

He failed to reassure her. Visibly agitated, she crossed the parlor to the window and looked out as if expecting Reiver or Mrs. Hardy to peer in. "I'm afraid I'm ill-suited to deception."

"That's because you're so honest, Hannah."

"I'm not. I'm an adulteress, no better than Cecelia Tuttle." She sighed. "Now that I'm in the same situation, I can understand why she and Reiver did what they did, but I still can't forgive him. I suppose that makes me the worst kind of hypocrite."

"You're nothing of the sort. You're the kindest, most generous, most loving woman I've ever known, but your guilt is like some great cat-o'-nine-tails ripping away more of your courage with every stroke. You must overcome it."

She grasped the windowsill until her knuckles turned white. "We must stop seeing each other, Samuel."

"Do you mean that? Can you look me in the eye and tell me that you don't want me?"

She turned. "It's not that. It's just that I live in fear of being caught and bringing disaster down on both our heads. I shudder to think what Reiver would do to you if—"

"That will never happen."

"But it almost did."

He stared at her. "You never told me. When?"

"Nine days ago. He caught me leaving here after we had just made love." Mad, passionate loving that had left her skin warm and rosy for the world to see. "Fortunately I was carrying your shirts and made the excuse that I had just stopped by to retrieve them for mending."

"Did he believe you?"

"Yes." Hannah closed her eyes and swallowed hard. "But I was so afraid he would see the guilt written on my face and know that I was lying."

"I know all this secrecy and deception is torture for you, but you must not let your imagination anticipate the worst."

"Don't you see?" Hannah cried in despair. "It's only a matter of time before Reiver learns the truth. Or Mrs. Hardy. Or James. They'll wonder why I spend so much time in the homestead. Or they'll notice the way I look at you across the dinner table. They're not blind or stupid, Samuel!"

He went to her and rested his hands lightly on her shoulders. "Then we'll go away together. Paris . . . London . . . Rome. Somewhere we can be free, where my brother will never find us."

"And my children?" she reminded him bitterly.

"We'll take the boys and Abigail with us."

Hannah noticed his pointed inclusion of her daughter in their plans. "Then Reiver will surely hunt us down until he finds us, if only to claim his sons."

Samuel dropped his hands and shrugged helplessly. "Then what are we to do? And don't tell me that you will no longer come to me, my sweet Hannah, because I don't believe that you can stay away any more than I can."

"I must." But when she looked into his eyes, all her fine resolve to resist him crumbled, because he had enslaved her mind as well as her body. With a cry of surrender, she threw herself into his arms, and as his lips came down hard on hers she knew she would risk and endure anything, even her husband's unwanted intimacies, to experience Samuel's love just one more time.

"No one will ever know," Samuel promised through lips pressed against her cheek, her jaw, her chin. "We'll be safe."

But even as Hannah came alive beneath his questing mouth and hands, she wondered for how long.

The following morning Hannah just finished breakfast when Reiver appeared in the kitchen, an irritated scowl on his face. "Back so soon?" she asked, for Reiver had just left for the mill a half hour ago.

"Mary Green is sick today," he said, "and I need someone to show my newest employee how to prepare the silk for boiling."

"I'd be happy to help." Hannah dried her hands, took off her apron, and followed Reiver back to the mill.

When they entered the skein room, Hannah was shocked to see a fearful, nervous little girl of about nine or ten sitting at the table, chewing the end of one braid and staring longingly out the window.

She whirled on her husband, blue eyes flashing fire. "You've hired a child to work here?"

"This is Sally Bierce," he said, ignoring her simmering rage. "Sally, Mrs. Shaw will show you what to do."

Hannah forced herself to smile and place a reassuring hand on the child's shoulder. "Hello, Sally, how are you?"

Sally smiled shyly. "I'm fine, Mrs. Shaw."

Hannah looked at Reiver. "May I speak to you for a moment?"

He nodded curtly and indicated his office.

The moment they were alone, Hannah said, "How despicable! That little girl should be in school, not working in a mill for twelve hours a day."

A muscle twitched in Reiver's broad jaw. "She'll be working for only nine hours a day, and not on Saturdays."

"For God's sake, Reiver, she's just a child! She should be outside playing with her friends."

He lowered his head defiantly. "Her father is sick and can't work. Her mother came to me and begged me to take the child on. At least the twenty-five cents a day I'm paying her will keep her family from starving."

Hannah just shook her head helplessly. "There must be some other way."

"There is no other way. And don't look at me as if I'm some kind of slave master. I'm not letting her do any of the hard work." Reiver placed his hands on his hips. "What does she need school for, anyway? She'll just marry and have children."

Hannah bit back the retort that was on the tip of her tongue. "You won't reconsider?"

"My hiring Sally is a humanitarian act. If she didn't work here, she'd work somewhere else for someone not as considerate."

Realizing that it was pointless to argue, Hannah whirled on her heel and returned to the skein room, where she showed Sally how to divide the silk into skeins and place them in the muslin bags for boiling.

But as the morning wore on and the child's head dropped with weariness and boredom, Hannah vowed that if she were running Shaw Silks, she would never hire children.

CHAPTER
❧ 9 ❧

THE hot, crowded ballroom bustled with people who had drifted upstairs from the parlor in search of music and movement. The sprightly scraping of a fiddle rose above the low rumble of conversation as several couples skipped and hopped around the room in an energetic polka, skirts swirling, faces flushed, and feet stomping.

Reiver stood in the doorway searching for Hannah, but she wasn't among the dancers or the gossiping women lined up along the wall in chairs and fanning themselves, though the windows opened wide to the cool spring night.

He turned, peering over and around the sea of bobbing heads in the upstairs corridor beyond, but Hannah's was not among them. Just as Reiver eased himself back into the crowd to search for her, Geoffrey Page, owner of a successful print shop in Hartford, stopped him by blocking his path with his own short, squat body.

"Enjoying yourself, Page?" Reiver asked, his eyes still scanning the throng.

"I always do at your shindigs," he replied. "You're not stingy with the vittles, and a man can relax and enjoy himself."

Reiver smiled, still searching for Hannah, needing to ask her if she had seen the new thread samples he had brought home.

"I understand you're off to Washington the day after tomorrow," Page said.

Reiver nodded. "I'm going to try to convince our esteemed Congress to raise the import tariff on foreign silks." Where *was* she?

"Do you think you'll succeed?"

"It's hard to say. But if they want silk manufacturing to succeed in this country, they're going to have to pass legislation to make us more competitive; otherwise we'll never progress beyond thread and ribbons."

Page nodded vigorously. "As a fellow merchant, I quite agree. Our government should help its own people, not foreigners. Washington needs a good dose of Yankee common sense."

"I hope to give it to them."

At the other end of the hallway, near the head of the stairs, a radiant Hannah glided into view, smiling and chatting with her guests as she wove her way between them to the ballroom. While not as enchanting as Cecelia, she did her husband credit in a blue striped gown with fanciful knots of flowers in her hair.

Reiver excused himself.

Halfway down the hall, he raised his hand and waved in an attempt to catch Hannah's eye, but she was conversing with a man who, though his back was to Reiver, looked oddly familiar. Reiver's eyes never left her as he inched closer, so he saw the look that transformed her in the space of a heartbeat.

Reiver halted. He blinked several times as one coming out of darkness into blinding sunlight. When he focused on Hannah again, the look had vanished.

But he recognized lust in a woman's eyes, no matter how fleeting.

And what of the man?

Turn around so I can see who is cuckolding me, damn you!

As if answering Reiver's unspoken command, the man half turned, revealing his patrician profile.

It was Samuel.

The last guests departed at two o'clock in the morning.

Reiver watched the carriage disappear down the drive, but his tumultuous thoughts were on Hannah standing at his side.

His wife and his brother . . . were they lovers?

Doubt and suspicion had gnawed at his insides like the rending fangs of a tiger ever since he had caught that look in Hannah's eyes earlier that evening. After the initial shock of betrayal had worn off, Reiver's mind roiled with questions screaming for answers.

He would start with his wife. If she were guilty, she would surely betray herself.

Hannah closed the front door and leaned back against it with a contented smile. The people and laughter might be gone, but their collective conviviality lingered in the quiet, empty house.

Hannah looked at Reiver standing before the hall mirror and savagely yanking off his embroidered cravat as if it were strangling him. His blue eyes sparkled with social triumph, and he looked almost handsome in his somber black frock coat and high white collar. It was at times like this that she wished she could love him.

She stifled a yawn. "I'm going upstairs to bed. Will you extinguish the lamps?" She started past him, but Reiver placed a restraining hand on her arm, his face both grave and determined.

"Wait," he said. "There's something I have to say to you."

She fought down panic. There's no way he can know about Samuel. Hannah settled her mask into place with practiced ease. "It's late, and I'm very tired."

"This won't take but a minute."

She waited, praying that her guilty conscience wouldn't betray her.

Reiver's eyes searched hers as if taking her measure for the first time. Finally he took her hand and brushed it with his lips. "Thank you, Hannah. You outdid yourself. All of our guests will be talking about this evening for a long time."

The low intimacy of his tone startled her, for she heard it so rarely. She withdrew her hand, flustered. "No thanks are necessary. I want your friends and business associates to always feel at home here."

"I know they do." He smiled. "Why don't you go to bed? I'll join you as soon as I'm through down here."

Puzzled by her husband's sudden attentiveness, Hannah took the oil lamp from the hall table and hurried upstairs. When she reached the landing and looked back, he still stood there, watching her, a strange expression on his face.

Upstairs, Hannah stood before her mirror and pulled out her hairpins, studying her reflection by lamplight for any physical manifestations of the hardened adulteress. To her relief, she saw only an unhappy young woman.

She was brushing out her chignon when Reiver came to stand behind her. "Do you need help undressing?"

She nodded, not trusting her voice to reply.

Reiver unhooked the back of her gown, his fingers adept from long practice, but his sharp gaze pinned her reflection to the glass. "I think Samuel has finally fallen in love."

Her heart leaped into her throat. She couldn't breathe. She must not faint. "Oh? With whom?"

His finger stopped, for he had expected quite a different reaction from her. "Patience Broome."

A lovely, laughing vision of spun-gold hair and decidedly impatient green eyes flitted through Hannah's memory. "She's the youngest daughter of a gentleman farmer, isn't she?"

Reiver nodded, his fingers moving again, but his suspicious stare unwavering. "She's pretty, sweet-tempered, and her father has enough money to buy Hartford. Samuel could do worse."

Hannah gathered her hair over her left shoulder and tied the end with a ribbon.

"Samuel seemed very attentive to her tonight," Reiver added, "and I've never known him to single out any woman for special attention. The rogue has always preferred variety." When Hannah made no comment, he said, "I'm surprised we don't have an irate father on our doorstep every week demanding that Samuel marry his daughter."

"Reiver Shaw, what a terrible thing to say about your own brother! You make him sound like some tom cat on the prowl."

He shrugged and grinned. "Well, it's the truth. Samuel always has been quite the ladies' man. There was an onion farmer's daughter from Wethersfield that he once fancied. I thought for sure he'd marry her, but he never did. She was probably too prudish for his tastes."

Reiver finished unhooking Hannah's gown, and she stepped out of it, glad that she still wore her petticoats to hide her shaking knees. "Perhaps he is ready to marry and settle down."

"He'll leave a string of broken hearts behind him."

A string of broken hearts . . . Hannah felt an irrational stab of jealousy toward these faceless women, though she concealed it by stepping out of her stiff petticoats and making a great pretense of putting them away.

"I wouldn't be too sure about Patience Broome." Two could

play at his little game. "I noticed Samuel lingering with the blacksmith's daughter after church last Sunday."

Reiver frowned, but not at the thought of his brother's interest in the blacksmith's daughter. "How would you feel if Samuel did marry?"

My heart would break. "I would be happy for him and welcome his bride as my sister-in-law."

"Would you, now."

"Of course. Do you think I would resent another woman coming into the family?" Before Reiver could reply, Hannah forced herself to smile sheepishly. "Well, since I look upon Samuel and James as the brothers I never had, perhaps I would display a sisterly resentment toward the women they married."

That seemed to satisfy him, for the taut lines of strain around his mouth vanished.

Reiver placed his hands on her shoulders and brushed her bare nape with his lips. "Enough talk about Samuel's marital prospects."

Hannah froze.

He slipped his hands beneath her bare arms, grasped her breasts, and pulled her back against him so he could whisper in her ear. "I want you to make love to me tonight, Hannah. And I'm going to tell you just how you can please me."

She listened, red-faced, to his bold demands, but when Reiver stripped off his clothes and took her to bed, she did exactly what he wanted as her penance for loving Samuel.

Two days later Hannah and her children stood on the porch to see Reiver off to Washington.

He placed his hand on Benjamin's shoulder. "You're the man of the house while I'm away, so be sure to take care of your mother and little brother."

"And your little sister," Hannah added as Abigail shyly peered at her father from the safety of her mother's skirts.

Davey glared at his older brother. "I'm not little anymore! Ben doesn't have to take care of me."

Suppressing a smile, Reiver dropped down on one knee so he was at eye level with his two fractious sons. "Well, then both of you can take care of your mother for me." He glanced up at Hannah. "And your sister."

Hannah stroked her daughter's downy head. An afterthought. That's all she ever is to him, an afterthought.

Davey grinned in triumph, but Benjamin muttered, "No matter how big you get, I'll always be older."

"But Papa said I could—"

"I'll not stand for any more fighting!" Reiver's stern tone silenced them. "If your mother tells me that you've misbehaved while I was gone . . ." He let his threat hang in the air.

"How long will you be away?" Hannah asked. She thought of Samuel, waiting. Suddenly an image of Patience Broome, winding a long lock of spun-gold hair around her finger as if it were a prospective suitor, spoiled her daydream.

Reiver rose. "Two weeks, perhaps three. After I finish in Washington, I may stop in New York City for a few days."

Patience, with her impatient green eyes, and Samuel . . .

"I thought I'd investigate the possibility of opening a sales office there," Reiver went on, his eyes scanning Hartford Road. Then he turned to Hannah. "Well, the stage should be coming any minute, so I had better go."

He said his good-byes quickly, even managing a pat on Abigail's head. Benjamin grabbed his father's bags, one in each hand, causing Davey to try to wrest one away.

"What did I just say to you two about fighting?" At their father's bellow, the boys halted their determined tussling. "Benjamin, you take one bag, and let Davey carry the other."

Satisfied, the two boys each lugged their prizes toward the road, though Benjamin got there first.

Reiver stared after them and shook his head. "They remind me of me and my brothers at that age. Always fighting about something."

"But you outgrew your childhood rivalries," Hannah said, "and I'm sure Benjamin and Davey will, too."

"There are some rivalries brothers never outgrow."

Was he talking about himself and Samuel? Hannah held her breath.

Then he bade her good-bye again before following his sons down to the road.

Long after Reiver had gone, in the homestead's quiet parlor, Samuel reached for Hannah. "I thought he'd never leave."

She evaded his embrace. Samuel stopped and his arms fell to his sides. "What's wrong?"

Hannah hid her trembling hands in her apron's deep pockets. "I—I can't stay. I only came to tell you that we can't . . . be together anymore. It's far too dangerous."

She would have fled if Samuel hadn't grasped her arm. "Don't run away," he said softly. "Tell me what I've done to make you angry with me."

Her eyes widened in surprise. "I'm not angry."

"Annoyed, then."

"I'm not—"

"Don't deny it. You're upset with me about something, otherwise you wouldn't be keeping me at arm's length with these irrational fears of discovery." A ghost of a smile touched his sensuous mouth. "If you weren't, you'd be in my arms right now."

She stared at the top button on Samuel's shirt to avoid looking into his eyes. "I've heard that Patience Broome is in the market for a husband."

"What does that have to do with us?" Then he understood. "Surely you don't think that I—" Samuel captured her chin between thumb and forefinger. "Hannah, look at me." When she did so, he said, "I do not intend to become Patience Broome's husband."

"She's very pretty."

"So are you." Samuel's hand fell away and he gave her an exasperated look. "Who told you that I was courting Miss Broome?"

"Reiver. He said you were most attentive to her the night of the gala."

"Goddamn him! I spoke to every woman that night, as I usually do, but it doesn't mean I desire any of them." Samuel drew her into his arms. "You're the only woman I want."

Even as Samuel's impassioned declaration banished Hannah's jealousy and doubts in a giddy rush, a more disturbing thought lit the fire of panic in her breast. She pulled away. "Samuel, I'm certain Reiver knows about us."

"Why do you think that?"

"Because after the gala was over, when we were undressing for bed, he acted strangely and said some very odd things."

He frowned. "Odd in what way?"

"First he told me that you had been attentive to Patience Broome, and watched me carefully to gauge my reaction. Then he went on and on about your being such a ladies' man." She paused as if something quite startling had suddenly occurred to her. "My clever husband . . . all along he was goading me, trying to make me jealous, to make me doubt you."

"And did he?"

"By the time he was through, I wanted to tear out every blond hair on Patience Broome's head."

The vehemence in Hannah's voice made Samuel's laugh die in his chest. He coughed. "The thought of being fought for is very flattering, but there's no need."

Hannah folded her arms. "And—and there's something else. When we . . . went to bed, Reiver made me . . ." She shrugged helplessly and said in an embarrassed rush, "I could tell that he was just waiting for me to refuse him, and if I did, something terrible would happen."

Pain and rage darkened Samuel's eyes. "I could kill him for that."

"You mustn't say that. I am still his wife. He was within his rights as my husband."

Samuel stroked her cheek. "I ask you to endure too much for me."

"I do it gladly." Her eyes drifted to the door as if she could see disaster lurking just beyond it, and she shivered. "But I am so afraid."

He took her cold, stiff hands in his and rubbed the warmth back into them. "Then we'll just have to banish those fears, won't we."

But this time he couldn't. Up in the studio, while she and Samuel coupled fiercely, Hannah half listened for the telltale creak of a downstairs door opening and surreptitious footsteps on the stairs. Afterward, she didn't linger, but rose and dressed quickly, fleeing from her bewildered lover like a thief in the night.

Hannah stood before one of the tall, narrow windows in James's machine shop and watched Samuel take Abigail over to Titan for their afternoon ride. When the chestnut lowered his massive head to investigate this small human, the child didn't recoil in terror as she had the first time Samuel introduced her to his horse. Now Abigail patted Titan's nose and smiled.

James stopped sawing and came over to Hannah's side. "When's my brother due back?"

"Sometime this week," Hannah replied, her eyes never leaving Samuel as he picked up Abigail and set her carefully on the saddle's pommel.

"I wonder if he had much success in Washington."

"I expect we'll learn the answer to that when he returns." Hannah hadn't received so much as a note from her husband in the week and a half since he'd been gone.

Samuel swung into the saddle behind Abigail. With the reins in his left hand and his right arm secure around his little niece's waist, he urged Titan into a slow, sedate walk. Hannah could see her daughter's wide grin from across the yard.

She shook her head. "I wish Reiver were as patient with her."

Shame colored James's gaunt cheeks. "I wish I could say something in my brother's defense, Hannah, but I can't. I understand machines better than I do Reiver."

"She repulses him. You can see the revulsion on his face every time he looks at her." She watched the normally spirited horse walk at a turtle's pace through the yard as if it carried a cache of crystal. "If she were perfect, I know he'd love her as much as he loves the boys, but that's small consolation."

James was spared replying when Mary Geer came running into the room. "Mr. James, my loom just broke down again. That's the third time this week."

"Be right there, Mary." He excused himself, picked up his toolbox, and left.

Hannah followed, walking out in the yard to wait for Samuel and Abigail to return. Moments later Titan came clopping into view, his two riders beaming.

"Mama!" Abigail said when Samuel reined in his horse. "Abby run."

Hannah reached up for her. "You did? Mama is so proud of you."

Samuel grinned and swung down from the saddle, his dark hair tousled and cheeks flushed from their exhilarating run. "You should be. I cantered Titan, and Abigail wasn't frightened at all, were you?" He shook his head, and when she imitated him, Samuel said, "Did you see that, Hannah? She said no. Abigail said no!"

Hannah knelt down and hugged her daughter, tears stinging her eyes. If only her husband could delight in his daughter's small triumphs the way her lover did . . .

The sound of someone calling "Mama!" distracted Hannah for a moment, and she looked to see her two sons running toward them, Benjamin leading the way.

They went up to Titan and petted him, Davey standing on tiptoes to reach as high as Benjamin.

"How was school today?" Samuel asked.

Benjamin glanced at his brother. "I was good, but Davey had to sit in the corner."

"David Shaw!" Hannah scowled at him. "Why did Mr. Ellis have to punish you?"

"It wasn't my fault," Davey muttered. "Henry Lake kept poking me in the arm, and when I hit him back, Mr. Ellis put me in the corner. It wasn't fair, Mama. Henry started it."

Poor, wronged Davey, always the victim. "See that it doesn't happen again, or you'll answer to your father."

Benjamin said, "Can we take Abigail and go play now?"

"Yes, just don't let her out of your sight."

"We won't." Benjamin took Abigail's hand in his and led his docile sister off. When he saw that his brother hung back, he turned. "Are you coming?"

Davey hesitated as if debating whether to forgive his older brother, then capitulated and went running after them.

Hannah stroked Titan's glossy neck absently and watched her three children march off, Abigail between her two protectors.

She shook her head. "Benjamin does so love to best Davey every chance he gets."

"Just like his father with me and James," Samuel said.

"But once he does it, he wants to be friends with Davey again."

Samuel took the reins and led his horse off. "He may enjoy tormenting Davey, but he's always so gentle and patient with Abigail."

Hannah walked with him. "That's why I trust them with her.

I know they'd never let anything happen to my precious little girl."

An hour later Hannah was peeling potatoes in the kitchen with Mrs. Hardy when the door slammed and Benjamin catapulted into the room, his eyes terrified and chest heaving.

"Mama, Mama!" he sobbed. "We—we've lost Abigail. We can't f-find her anywhere."

"Settle down." Hannah calmly wiped her hands in her apron and grasped her distraught son's shoulders to steady him. "Take a deep breath and tell me what happened."

Benjamin gulped air. "W-we found a rabbit hole, so D-Davey and I tried to make the rabbit come out, and the next time I looked up, Abigail was gone!"

Mrs. Hardy shook her silver head. "Aw, the poor mite just wandered off somewhere, or maybe she's hiding in the barn. She likes the dark and quiet."

The boy turned to her, tears streaming down his face. "But that's the first place we looked, Mrs. Hardy, and she's not there."

Hannah fought back the mind-numbing panic. "Hush, Benjamin, don't cry. I'm going to tell Uncle Samuel and Uncle James, and we're all going to look for Abigail. I'm sure we'll find her safe and sound." She managed a brave, reassuring smile and tousled his hair. "You'll see."

She prayed that she was right.

Half an hour later her optimism vanished.

"Abigail?" Hannah stood in the homestead's parlor and called out her daughter's name over and over. "Where are you? Please don't hide from Mama."

Only the silence answered.

With a growing sense of dread, Hannah systematically went through every room, searching behind chairs, under beds, and inside chests—anywhere a small child could possibly crawl in and hide. Nothing.

"Abigail, where are you?" she muttered to herself after she had searched the house from top to bottom to no avail. She was out the parlor door and halfway down the path when she saw the others headed her way.

They've found her, she thought, feeling light-headed with relief. They've called off the search because they've found her.

Hannah gathered her skirts and ran. Abigail Shaw, don't you dare cause your poor mother such worry ever again.

One look at the collection of grim, stunned faces stopped her.

James and several of the weeping mill girls who had been leading the procession stepped aside, parting the way for Samuel.

Abigail was cradled in his arms, her head lolling back and her eyes closed as if she were sleeping.

Hannah reached out and touched her daughter's cheek. Why did it feel so wet and cold? Why was Samuel crying? "Wake up, sweetheart. You're safe now. Mama's here."

Samuel said, "She fell into Racebrook." His voice broke on a sob. "We were too late to save her."

Hannah shook Abigail's shoulder. "Open your eyes, sweetheart. Smile for Mama."

"I'm so sorry," he said.

Hannah screamed and screamed until the merciful blackness silenced her.

"Where in God's name is Reiver?"

Hannah, dressed from head to toe in deepest black bombazine mourning for her only daughter, stood before the small casket in the parlor and dabbed at her red, raw eyes with her crumpled handkerchief.

Samuel, also dressed in unrelieved black, stood at her elbow. "We can't find him. I telegraphed his Washington hotel this morning and was told that he had checked out several days ago."

"Then he must be somewhere in New York City," Hannah said, looking down at Abigail's serene face. "He said he might go there after he left Washington."

"Did he mention where he'd be staying?"

"No." With an exclamation of frustration, Hannah turned. "Damn him, Samuel! His daughter is—is dead and he's nowhere to be found!"

Samuel placed a comforting hand on her arm. He suspected that Hannah's anger with her absent husband was all that was sustaining her in her grief.

Hannah sniffed. "We've delayed the funeral for as long as we can. We'll just have to hold it without him. Not that Reiver will miss attending it," she added bitterly. "He never loved Abigail."

Samuel couldn't refute her because he knew she spoke the truth.

He said, "How are the boys? I know Ben is devastated by what happened. He blames himself for not watching his sister more carefully."

Hannah's drawn, white face softened. "I told him that it wasn't his fault, that I didn't blame him or Davey for what happened." She sighed and rubbed her aching forehead. "I did at first, you know, when I was half-insane with grief. But I don't now."

"You've always been fair."

Hannah took a deep breath. "Will you try to locate Reiver once more? Would you send telegrams to some New York City hotels on the chance that he's staying in one of them?"

"I'll do my best to find him."

The moment Reiver returned home three days later and saw the black wreath on the front door, his heart constricted in his chest.

Who had died? Benjamin? One of his brothers? Hannah?

Dropping his bags in the drive, he ran the rest of the way, bounding up the steps and flying through the front door like a hurricane. Listless swathes of black crepe framed the foyer's mirror, and both the faded, cloying scent of flowers and an unnatural quiet hung on the air.

"Hannah?" he bellowed, too terrified to respect the silence. "Mrs. Hardy? *Anyone*, damn it!"

Movement on the stairs caught his eye, and he looked up to find Hannah standing on the landing. Her white, grief-stricken face appeared calm and composed, but her wild blue eyes smoldered.

He strode across the foyer and stood at the foot of the stairs. "Why is there a funeral wreath on the front door?"

She gathered her long black skirts in her right hand and walked stiffly down the stairs, brushing past him. "Obviously because someone in the family has died."

"Jesus Christ, Hannah!"

"Abigail," she replied, her voice measured and controlled. "Not Benjamin, or Davey. Just Abigail."

Reiver bowed his head in shameful relief that it hadn't been one of his sons. "How?"

Hannah folded her hands primly in front of her. "She drowned in Racebrook. The funeral was yesterday. We tried to find you in both Washington and New York, but we couldn't." She took a deep breath. "Considering the way you felt about your daughter, perhaps that was for the best."

Reiver's head shot up. "That's not fair. I never wanted her to die. She was still my daughter."

Hannah stood there in stony silence, refusing to look at him. Finally she said, "Where were you?"

"In New York City, looking into opening a sales office for Shaw Silks."

"And were you successful in Washington?"

"No, but this is hardly the time to discuss it."

She nodded wearily. "If you'll excuse me, I'm going upstairs to lie down."

He caught her arm to detain her. "I'm sorry about Abigail, and that I wasn't here."

"You needn't be. Samuel, James, and Mrs. Hardy were a great source of comfort."

His hand fell away. Hannah trudged back up the stairs as if she were a tired old woman.

Reiver walked into his study, locked the door, and poured himself a generous glass of apple brandy. He savored it slowly, searching his heart for sorrow that just wasn't there.

He went to the window and looked up at the cloudless, hot blue sky. The brandy's heady kick brought to mind what had happened to him in New York City the day before yesterday.

That day he had no trouble finding the fashionable Washington Square house he sought, one built of red brick with steep, break-your-neck steps and a doorway trimmed in white. He hesitated only for a second before ringing the bell. When a butler answered, Reiver handed him the note he had composed in his hotel room just an hour before, then got into his hired carriage and ordered the driver to wait at the end of the street.

He waited. And waited.

Just when Reiver was about to admit defeat and signal the driver to move on, the carriage door swung open.

He leaned forward and extended his hand. "I was afraid you wouldn't come."

Cecelia gave him her hand, and he noticed that her fingers were trembling as much as his. "I shouldn't have."

"Then why did you?"

He hadn't seen her in so long. When he thought of what he ached to do to her to make up for lost time, he felt as though he would explode.

She seated herself across from him and settled her wide skirts gracefully around her in a rustle of stiff crinoline. "When I read your note and realized that you were right outside . . ." She shrugged helplessly. "You always were my weakness, Reiver Shaw."

He closed the carriage door and told the driver to drive anywhere, then he sat back and let his starving eyes feast on Cecelia.

"You're still as beautiful as ever," he said, staring at the chestnut richness of her hair, her soft brown eyes, her petite figure with its tiny waist.

"And you're just as brash and devilish as I remember." She smoothed her skirt with a nervous gesture. "Has Shaw Silks become the biggest silk mill in America yet?"

"I didn't come here to discuss Shaw Silks."

She raised her brows. "That doesn't sound like the Reiver Shaw I used to know."

"You've changed as well. I don't remember you being so sad."

"You are mistaken." Cecelia's smile was forced. "Amos is ever the generous, attentive husband, and the Good Lord has even blessed me with another child—a daughter."

He thought of Abigail. "She should be mine."

Cecelia made a move to rise. "This is madness. I promised myself that I would resist you. I never should have come."

He placed his hand on her arm. "You came because you're unhappy."

"Why do you keep saying that? I am quite the happiest woman on earth."

"Are you trying to convince me, or yourself?"

She balled her hands into exasperated fists. "I am quite content."

"Cecelia, if you truly were, you wouldn't be sitting here, your eyes begging me to take you."

He couldn't tell who moved first. Perhaps they both did. Suddenly Cecelia's arms were entwined about his neck and he was stroking her breast while his tongue plundered her willing mouth that tasted as heady as apple brandy.

Now, back home, he savored the brandy in remembrance and stared up at the hot blue sky. The day his daughter died, he had been making Cecelia his mistress and planning more trips to New York. He couldn't help himself. He loved her. It was going to take more than distance and her whey-faced husband to keep them apart.

He rubbed the place where Amos had shot him and took another deep swallow of brandy. This time no one would find out.

CHAPTER
❧10❧

"MARY, why are you crying?"

Hannah stopped on her way to the mill's small library when she noticed the tears streaming down Mary Geer's plump face.

"It's my brother Jake, Mrs. Shaw," Mary replied, keeping her eyes on the looms' spinning bobbins even as she cried.

"What's happened to him? Is he ill?"

"No, ma'am. He's run off to California." She sniffed. "To find gold."

Ever since gold had been discovered at Sutter's Mill last year, the trickle of people heading out to California dreaming of striking it rich had turned into a virtual flood. Every person Hannah spoke to knew someone who had joined the "forty-niners"—the blacksmith's son, Benjamin's teacher, the miller on the other side of town. Even Nate's brother Zeb had deserted tobacco farming at the prospect of such wealth, breaking Aunt Naomi's heart.

Mary added, "We're all so worried about my brother. He's taking a ship around South America. I've heard the storms down there are worse than hurricanes." She took a deep shuddering breath. "And even if he gets to San Francisco, what if he finds gold and some claim jumper kills him for it?"

Hannah patted her shoulder. "Don't worry, Mary. I'm sure Jake will be fine. He's young and resourceful," was all she could think of to say.

After delivering new books to the library, Hannah left the mill, relieved that her sons were too young to succumb to gold fever. She pulled her black shawl more closely about her against the chilly October morning and walked resolutely, stopping only to pick a spray of bright orange bittersweet growing in wild profusion against a split-rail fence. When she arrived at the cemetery, she lay the bittersweet down on Abigail's grave.

I still miss you, she thought, tears sliding down her cheeks. You weren't perfect, but you were a child of my body and blood, and I love you.

She thought of Reiver and how she could never forgive him for repudiating Abigail. He hadn't shed a single tear for his child; perhaps if he had, Hannah wouldn't have felt so alone and bereft.

But I'm not alone, she amended. I have Samuel. And Reiver doesn't know.

For the first time her betrayal of Reiver gladdened rather than shamed her, the thought of it bringing an overwhelming desire to pay him back, to hurt him as much as he had hurt her by rejecting their daughter.

Smiling, Hannah touched Abigail's tombstone in farewell and left.

Hannah stared out of the parlor window at the first snowstorm of the season, watching the raw, blustery November wind drive the large flakes through the air like a flock of wooly sheep. In the hall Reiver put on his coat, then wound his blue knit scarf several times around his neck.

Hannah watched him tug on his leather gloves. "Are you sure you want to go to Hartford today? This snowstorm could get worse."

"James needs those parts right away, and if someone doesn't go after them, three looms will be down. We can't afford that." He settled his broad-brimmed hat on firmly. "If I get snowed in and the stage doesn't run, I'll stay in Hartford overnight." He smiled. "You needn't worry about me."

Hannah went into the hall to see him off. "I won't."

Reiver kissed her perfunctorily on the cheek, then lifted his scarf over his mouth and nose until only his eyes showed. He opened the front door, letting in an icy blast of air that swirled around Hannah's wide skirts and made her shiver. She waved good-bye, then closed the door quickly and returned to the warm parlor, where she stood at the window and watched

Reiver trudge down to Hartford Road until the slanting snow blurred his dark, shapeless form into nothingness.

She waited until the stage pulled up, then drove away.

She stood at the window and kept waiting. Minutes later a dark form materialized out of the swirling snow, hatted head bowed and shoulders leaning into the wind, his open mouth emitting clouds of gray vapor.

Hannah smiled and hurried to the front door. This time when she opened it, she didn't feel the cold at all, just the sweet warmth of anticipation.

"Hurry," she said to Samuel. He climbed the front steps, stomping his feet to shake the snow clinging to his boots.

The moment the door closed behind him, they flew into each other's arms.

Hannah pressed her warm lips to Samuel's cold, stiff mouth, then sought to heat it with her tongue. His arms tightened about her in response and she could feel his arousal through his heavy layers of clothing.

When they finally parted, she warmed his cold face with her hands. "He's gone. He won't be back until late this afternoon, unless he decides to stay in Hartford for the night."

"And Mrs. Hardy is still tending her sick friend?" His eyes roamed over her face.

Hannah nodded. "The boys are at school, and James is down at the mill."

Samuel grinned. "We're alone and we have the house all to ourselves. Perfect."

She entwined her arms around his neck and kissed him fervently again. "Perfect."

They hurried upstairs, both impatient to undress and enjoy another sweet, illicit union, for they hadn't been able to meet secretly for weeks.

When Hannah entered the bedroom she shared with Reiver, Samuel balked on the threshold, his jubilant mood sobering. "Why this room?"

"Because I need to make love to you in my husband's bed," she replied. "I need to repay him for not loving Abigail, and for betraying me with Cecelia Tuttle."

Samuel removed his hat and peeled off his gloves. "But Reiver will never know that we used his bed."

"I'll know."

He raised his brows. "Just when I think I know you, you surprise me."

"Why? Because I'm capable of wanting revenge?"

"It's just that I've never seen such a . . . calculating side to you before."

"I'm not a saint, Samuel," she said defiantly, plucking the pins from her hair and shaking out her chignon.

He watched her thick brown tresses fall down past her shoulders like a glossy spun-silk waterfall. "Oh, I know that, especially when you're in my bed."

She stared at him intently, as if measuring his mettle. "Will you do this for me, Samuel?"

He stepped across the threshold.

Later, when they lay naked beneath the covers, Samuel warmed himself against Hannah's smooth, pliant body and kissed the pulse in her neck. The familiar surge of excitement made his blood sing, though the idea of loving his brother's wife in his brother's bed filled him with a strange sense of unease.

He cast his reservations aside. Hannah needed him to do this. He had seen the desperate pleading in her eyes when she led him to this room. She had to repay Reiver in her mind to satisfy some inner demons, even if he never knew. Samuel would do anything to lay her demons to rest.

And Reiver would never know.

Shivering uncontrollably, Reiver swore under his breath and shuffled through the snow. Over an hour ago and two miles back, the stage had glided off the slippery road into the gutter and broken a rear wheel, panicking the passengers and effectively canceling his plans to get to Hartford today.

Now he could see the dim outline of his house silhouetted against the flat gray sky, its white clapboards almost annihilated by the thick, shifting curtain of falling snow. He smiled when he thought of dry stockings, a roaring fire in the parlor, and a cup of hot apple brandy to warm his insides.

Wouldn't Hannah be surprised to see him walk through the door. . . .

But when he entered the foyer, no Hannah came to greet him.

He listened. No light footsteps, no telltale swishing skirts heralded her arrival.

She must be in the kitchen, he thought, quickly shedding his hat, gloves, scarf, and coat and hanging them on the coatrack by the door. Then he removed his wet boots.

"Hannah?" he called.

Upstairs, Hannah froze and stilled Samuel's exploring hand. "What was that?" When he frowned in puzzlement, she whispered, "I thought I heard someone call my name."

Samuel listened, then smiled. "It's only the wind. Reiver's halfway to Hartford by now."

Downstairs, when Reiver didn't find Hannah in the kitchen, he went upstairs, his stockinged feet making no sound on the carpeted stairs.

In the upstairs hall, he was just about to call Hannah's name again when he heard soft voices.

Reiver crept down the hall toward his bedchamber, the floorboards silent beneath each careful, calculated step. The sounds continued, deep, masculine groans this time. The door was ajar, so Reiver peeked inside the bedchamber and wished he hadn't.

Hannah lay in bed with another man, his dark head outlined against her bare white breast.

Reiver stood there, unable to believe his own eyes.

His wife and his own brother were lovers, just as he suspected.

Suddenly Reiver burned with blinding, white-hot rage. He flung open the door so hard that it ricocheted against the wall with a resounding crash.

Hannah's eyes flew open and she stared at the doorway in disbelief. No, it couldn't be. . . .

"Reiver!" This was a Reiver that she had never seen before, a stranger with the livid face of doom and murder in his eyes.

"Bastard!" He was on them in three strides, his clawing hands whipping the coverlet away, then dragging Samuel off her and flinging him out of the bed. "I ought to kill the both of you!"

Samuel scrambled to regain his balance, then faced his brother fearlessly, unmindful of his own nakedness and vulnerability. "You touch her and *I'll* kill *you*!"

Without warning, Reiver swung at Samuel, sending his fist

into his brother's jaw with a sickening crack. Samuel's head snapped back as he recoiled from the blow, crumpling to the floor, where he lay limp and motionless.

"Dear God! Samuel!" Hannah screamed, bounding out of bed. She nearly reached his prostrate form when she felt her shoulder gripped in painful, punishing fingers, and Reiver flung her back onto the bed.

She lay there trembling on her back, waiting to feel Reiver's hands on her throat, but he merely let his scornful gaze rove up and down her body as if she were no better than a whore.

"Get dressed," he snapped, "and get my brother on his feet. If you're not down in my study in five minutes, I'll throw the both of you out just as you are."

Then he strode out of the room.

Hannah went to Samuel, kneeling beside him and lifting his head off the hard floor, crooning his name over and over again as she begged him to wake up. Finally he groaned and struggled to sit up, his pale eyes glazed with pain and blood trickling from the corner of his mouth.

"Are you all right?" she whispered, her eyes bright with tears. "Did he hurt you badly?"

He shook his head. "What about you?" The words were forced and slurred, as if talking pained him.

"Terrified." Hannah trembled with the fear and shame of discovery. "What's going to happen to us now? I've never seen Reiver so—so furious." She closed her eyes against fresh tears. "I never should have asked you to meet me here. I've ruined everything. I'll never forgive myself. I—"

"Hush." Samuel stroked her cheek. "You're not to blame. The fault is mine."

"What's going to happen to us?"

"I honestly don't know. Perhaps he'll cast us out and we can go to Europe together. Perhaps he'll forgive and forget, just as he expected you to forgive his transgression with Cecelia. But I won't let him hurt you, Hannah. You know that."

"Dear God, I feel as though the end of the world is coming and there's nothing I can do about it."

He brushed his bruised mouth lightly across hers and winced. "No, Hannah. It's not the end of the world for us. You'll see."

● ● ●

Reiver stood at his study window, his hands clasped tightly behind his back, when Hannah and Samuel came into the room. Hannah appeared suitably guilt-ridden and subdued, her eyes downcast, but Samuel held his brother's gaze with infuriating defiance.

Reiver glared at them. "How could you? My wife and my own brother . . ."

Hannah's head snapped up and the subdued wife disappeared. "How dare you stand there looking so self-righteous, Reiver Shaw! Need I remind you of Cecelia Tuttle?"

"Is that why you've betrayed me with my own brother, to get back at me for Cecelia? Such petty vindictiveness is beneath you, Hannah. At least I thought it was."

She reached for Samuel's hand. "I turned to Samuel because I felt lonely and unloved."

"And you're the one who made her feel that way," Samuel said.

Reiver's arms fell to his sides. "So I'm to blame for what you two have done, is that it?"

"No one is to blame," Hannah said.

"Does that assuage your guilt, Hannah?"

Her gaze slid away, and a blush stained her cheeks. "No." She looked over at Samuel and drew strength from him. "I wish this had never happened, Reiver, but it has and there's nothing any of us can do about it."

He raised his brows. "Oh, but there is."

Fear crept into Hannah's eyes. "What do you mean?"

"You certainly don't expect me to look the other way, to go on as if nothing has happened."

She stiffened. "You expected me to act as though you had never had an affair with Cecelia Tuttle."

"It's not the same, Hannah. The world is willing to overlook a married man's desires, but a mother must be above reproach."

Samuel's expression hardened. "Why, you damned, sanctimonious hypocrite!"

Hannah knotted her fingers together. "Our marriage is a sham, Reiver, and has been since the day I had to marry you. Samuel and I intend to go away together, and we're taking the children with us."

"Oh, no, Hannah," Reiver said. "You'll be going alone. I'll not give up my sons."

"I'm their mother!" Her voice rose in panic. "You wouldn't separate children from their mother."

"They're also my sons, and the heirs to Shaw Silks."

Samuel wiped fresh blood from his mouth with the back of his hand. "That's all you've ever cared about, your precious silk mills."

Reiver's eyes narrowed. "Hannah may choose to stay. But I want you out."

"Out? What do you mean?"

"You're no longer welcome here. You're going to leave and never come back. I don't care where in the world you go, just as long as I never see your face again."

Samuel looked as though he had been struck by lightning. "You can't be serious. This is my home."

"Not anymore. You're forgetting that Father left me this land and the homestead because I'm the oldest. You and James have been living here through my generosity." Reiver's jaw clenched. "But you've betrayed me. And I don't reward betrayal."

Samuel turned white. "And what of all the times I gave you money to keep your precious silk mill afloat?"

Reiver shrugged. "You'll always have my profound gratitude."

"Who in the hell do you think you are, trying to banish me like some angry monarch?" Samuel said, eyes flashing. "I'm staying right here in Coldwater, whether you like it or not."

"Then you can take Hannah with you, and explain to this town's good citizens why you're living in sin with your sister-in-law."

Hannah stared at him, aghast. "You wouldn't!"

"I will, if Samuel doesn't agree to my terms."

"Please, Reiver." Hannah went to him and placed a beseeching hand on his arm. "Don't do this. I'll do anything you ask. I—"

"Don't waste your breath pleading with him, Hannah," Samuel said. "My brother always gets what he wants, and he never changes his mind once it's made up."

"You know me too well." Reiver paused. "You have one

week. I trust that will give you enough time to pack your bags and get out. Consider yourself lucky that I'm letting you off so easy."

Hannah didn't hear Samuel's reply. She focused her attention on the soft, silent snow falling outside the window, blanketing the land like a fluffy down comforter. She wanted its purity to embrace her, enfold her, drift over her, bury her.

Voices faded. The room slid away. Snow smothered the pain.

Hannah opened her eyes to find Reiver looking down at her with an unexpected air of concern.

Gradually her senses awoke and she realized that she was lying on the parlor sofa with several pillows beneath her head and a cold cloth draped across her forehead.

"You fainted," he said. He knelt beside her, lifted her head, and held a glass to her lips, tending her as impersonally as a physician. "Drink this. It will make you feel better."

Hannah took several sips of apple brandy, choked as it seared her throat, and coughed.

Reiver stood. "You needn't look for Samuel. He's gone back to the homestead."

Hannah closed her eyes, trying to seek the snow's comforting oblivion once again, but Reiver's hand on her shoulder, shaking her, kept the snow outside.

"Do you feel strong enough to talk?" he asked. He sounded calmer now. "We have much to discuss."

Hannah took a deep breath and sat up. When the world stopped spinning, she faced her husband and wished desperately that Samuel were sitting beside her, giving her strength. Then she wouldn't feel so awkward and alone.

Reiver sat in the chair across from her and leaned forward, resting his elbows on his knees. "How long has this been going on?"

"Since after Amos Tuttle shot you." She clasped her hands tightly. "I was suffering the humiliation of having everyone in Coldwater know that my husband had been keeping company with another man's wife." Her voice grew stronger and sharper as her strength returned. "Then I had to struggle with your refusal to love your own daughter no matter how hard I tried to bring you closer. Samuel was always so kind and understanding, and—and before either of us realized what was happening—" She shrugged helplessly.

"For more than two years you and my brother have been lovers in my own house?"

"Not here. In the homestead. It was perfect for our . . . trysts. No one was ever around. No one ever suspected."

A muscle twitched in Reiver's jaw. "There will be no more trysts at the homestead or anywhere else before Samuel leaves, do you understand me?"

"You needn't worry."

Reiver raked his fingers through his hair and stared at the floor. "I know that I share the blame for what happened."

Surprised by his admission, Hannah rose and went to the fireplace to warm her cold hands. "We're all at fault." She looked at him. "Why won't you let me and the boys go away with Samuel? You and I don't love each other. You married me for my uncle's land, not because you loved me. What is the point of our staying together?"

"I'm not keeping you here, Hannah. You're free to go with Samuel, if you wish. But my sons will stay here with me."

"You know I couldn't leave them."

He rose. "Then it seems you've made the choice to stay."

"Won't you let Samuel stay? This is his home, too."

"No, Hannah. My brother betrayed a sacred trust. And if I allowed him to stay, who knows what would happen between the two of you again?"

"Nothing! I give you my word."

He shook his head sadly. "I can't take that chance."

"People will wonder why Samuel is leaving Coldwater. Do you want another scandal?"

"There won't be one. The curious will be told that he has wanderlust."

"But James will surely wonder. Do you plan to tell him about Samuel and me?"

"Of course not. I do have my pride."

She went over to a window and looked out at the snow. Her soul felt as bleak and empty as the shifting white landscape. "You've thought of everything, haven't you?"

"I usually do. That's why I'm so successful." He turned and left her staring at the snow.

Once in his study, Reiver put his feet up on his desk and leaned his chair back on two legs, balancing precariously. Hannah had surprised him. He never would have expected such wanton behavior from the mother of his children. Though he wouldn't admit it, her infidelity had hurt his pride as much as Amos Tuttle's bullet had injured his body.

Reiver rose and went to the window, watching the snow drift against the house. He rubbed the stiffness out of the back of his neck, trying to shake the unsettling feeling that even after nine years of marriage, he didn't really know his wife at all.

"Where will you go?"

Hannah stood in the doorway of Samuel's bedchamber, watching him pack several clean, folded shirts in the large brass-bound trunk standing in the middle of the room.

"I've decided to go to California," he replied, "with the rest of the dreamers and fools."

"Samuel, no!" She stepped into the room, forgetting her promise to Reiver. "Go to Europe. At least there are museums there, and other artists. And you'll be safe. California is so—so uncivilized."

He winced because it still hurt to talk and grasped her hands tightly. "Don't you see? I can't go to Europe because you and I were supposed to go there together. Without you there, I'd miss you even more."

Tears stung Hannah's eyes. "Then why not go to Boston? Or New York?"

"Because I'd still be too close to you." He dropped her hands and took a step back. "I hope the other end of the country will be far enough, but somehow I doubt it."

She went over to his bed, where piles of neatly folded clothes awaited packing, and ran her hand down one of the shirts. "Will you prospect for gold?"

"I don't know yet. But I do intend to make plenty of sketches and record the life out there. Who knows? Perhaps I'll sell engravings to the newspapers back east."

She turned to face him. "Reiver will change his mind, you'll see. One day he'll want you to come home."

Samuel's smile died. "Don't delude yourself. My brother is a stubborn and unforgiving man. When he said he never wanted to see my face again, he meant for as long as he lives."

"But you're his brother."

"I also betrayed him."

Hannah sighed. "I'm surprised he hasn't cast me out along with you."

"And sully the good name of Shaw once again? No, despite his claims to the contrary, Reiver cares what other people think of him. Our father was the object of ridicule because he was the town drunk. Do you think Reiver wants to be known as town cuckold? Not after what happened when Tuttle shot him." Samuel added his hairbrushes to the trunk. "I also think he's feeling hypocritical about Cecelia."

"In what way?"

"Well, he's been unfaithful to you, so he can hardly spurn you for being unfaithful to him, now can he?"

"I didn't become your lover to get back at Reiver."

"I know that," he said softly, "but Reiver thinks otherwise."

Hannah just shook her head. "Has James guessed why you're leaving?"

"No. I told him I've developed a yearning to see the world, and he's accepted it. My innocent brother tends to believe what people tell him."

Hannah grasped the bedpost. "I'd hate to have him think ill of me."

Samuel stopped packing and looked at her. "No one who knows you could possibly think ill of you."

Her lip quivered as she fought back tears. "I'm going to miss you so much."

He closed the distance between them in three strides and swept her into his arms, crushing her to him. She didn't care who might walk in on them. She wound her arms around his neck, letting her body commit the feel of every muscle and bone of him to memory, storing up enough to last her a lifetime. When she opened her mouth for his kiss, she surrendered to the rising passion, even though she knew it could never come to fruition.

"I love you, Samuel," she whispered through her tears. She took his beloved face in her hands and looked into his eyes, their merriment replaced by a profound sadness that broke her heart.

"And I do love you, Hannah Shaw."

"Then take me with you."

He shook his head sadly. "As much as I want to, I know you won't go."

"You're right. I could never live without my children." She drew away and covered her trembling mouth with one hand. "But how am I going to live without you?"

"Day by day, as will I. Your strength will help you."

"Will you at least write to me? Let me know how you are?"

"I don't think that would be wise. I'll write to Benjamin instead. Surely my brother won't have any objection to that."

"Surely not." With superhuman effort, Hannah pulled herself together. "I—I should go now. If Reiver finds me here, there's no telling what he'll do."

"Wait. There's something I want to give you." He went over to his chest of drawers, took out a piece of paper, and handed it to her.

It was a sketch of Abigail.

"I made it just before she—"

"It's beautiful. She's laughing, just as I'll always remember her."

She ran from the room without so much as a backward glance.

Three days later Hannah saw Samuel for the last time when family and servants gathered in the parlor to bid him farewell and wish him luck in the California goldfields. She tried to draw on that strength he had always claimed she possessed, but inside, she was nothing but an arid wasteland.

When it came her turn to say good-bye, she pressed her cheek to Samuel's, then hurried from the parlor.

Davey said, "Papa, why is Mama crying?"

"She's just sad because Uncle Samuel is leaving," Reiver replied.

Never to see him again.

One cold morning in December, three weeks after Samuel's departure, Hannah thought she felt him beside her, solid and warm, but when she awakened alone and shivering, she realized she had only imagined her lover curled against her.

She closed her eyes and fought down the bitter disappointment before flinging back the covers and rising.

Without warning, her insides clenched and waves of nausea sent her running for the basin. When she finished retching, she laughed for the first time in weeks.

She was going to have a baby.

Samuel's child. Or Reiver's.

No, she had always used her sponge and vinegar when sleeping with Reiver, so it had to be Samuel's. She smiled. He had left her with part of himself after all.

Brushing her hair and dressing, she felt her despondent mood lifting. When she went downstairs to the warm, fragrant kitchen, where Mrs. Hardy and Millicent were chatting like squirrels and preparing breakfast, her benevolent mood even extended to Reiver sitting at the table and finishing a stack of griddle cakes.

He looked at her warily, for she had been decidedly cold to him ever since he banished Samuel. "Good morning," she said brightly. "Mrs. Hardy, is there enough hot water for tea?"

The housekeeper bobbed her silver head. "I've just made a fresh pot, but once that's gone, it's every man for himself."

Hannah poured herself a cup and sat down across from her husband, who now looked frankly puzzled.

"You look happy this morning."

"I am." She sipped her tea, gazed out the frost-covered window, and watched the rising sun spread its fire across the shadowed blue crust of snow.

"May I ask why?"

She shrugged. "No particular reason."

Mrs. Hardy ladled batter onto the griddle, where it sizzled and steamed, filling the kitchen with its enticing aroma. "I miss that Samuel. But I guess we'll have to get along without him and face the future."

Reiver's blue eyes held Hannah's. "Is that why you're happy this morning? You're facing the future?"

"Yes." I'm creating a new life that will be part of me and part of Samuel.

"It's for the best," Reiver said quietly.

Yes, Hannah thought, you'll forget Samuel as if he never existed. But I will never forget him.

Reiver drained his cup, rose, and went to give Hannah a kiss on the cheek, but she ducked her head at the last minute and his lips brushed her hair. She wasn't quite ready to forgive him.

Anger flared in his eyes, then disappeared. "I'm going to open the mill," he said, and left.

Later that morning, after most of her household tasks were done, Hannah bundled herself up and went down to the homestead. James now lived there alone, but she was hoping to find some lingering trace of Samuel, so she went upstairs to his studio.

When she walked through the door, she stopped in shock. The room had been picked as clean as a turkey carcass. His worktable, which had been strewn with sketches and engraving tools, was gone. Pristine stretched canvases were no longer propped haphazardly against the wall. The old settee where they had first made love had disappeared, doubtlessly sold to one of the grateful mill girls for a pittance.

All traces of Samuel had been eradicated as if he had never existed.

Tears sprang to Hannah's eyes. "How I do hate you, Reiver Shaw!"

And then she smelled it, a mere whisper of turpentine, a remembrance of Samuel that nothing, not even Reiver, could destroy. Memories flooded through Hannah's mind as sharply etched as one of Samuel's engravings, and she laughed.

But her triumph was short-lived.

She was on her way back to the main house, picking her way carefully up the path the men had cleared through the snow, when a sharp, searing pain cramped her insides, stopping her cold.

Her baby!

Hannah staggered forward as another grinding pain sent her gasping. Then she felt the rush of her child's lifeblood leaving her body, and she screamed in denial. She managed to stagger a few steps closer to the house before collapsing, leaving a trail like red roses in the snow.

● ● ●

Hannah awakened to the keening of her own heart. A few hours. She had only a few hours to love it.

"The doctor says you'll be fine."

She turned and found Reiver sitting beside her bed, his brow furrowed and his face grave.

"Fine?" Her laugh sounded half-mad to her own ears.

Reiver stared down at his tightly folded hands. "Was the baby mine or Samuel's?"

"I hope it was Samuel's."

"But you're not sure."

"No," she uttered through clenched teeth.

Satisfied, he rose. "The doctor says you must rest now." When he reached the door, he turned. "For what it's worth, I am sorry, Hannah."

"Then bring Samuel back to me."

"Rest now. We'll talk later, when you're stronger."

He waited two weeks before telling her that she had lost far more than Samuel's child.

CHAPTER
☙ 11 ❧

HE couldn't put it off any longer.

Reiver found Hannah in the warm kitchen, assiduously rolling out the top crust for a dried-apple pie, her smooth hair hidden beneath a neat white cap.

He hesitated in the doorway. "You shouldn't be working so hard. You should rest."

She touched her forehead with the back of one hand, leaving a smudge of flour, then returned to her rolling without so much as a glance at her husband. "I can't afford to loll around in bed all day. I have work to do."

Work kept her from missing Samuel so much. Work soothed the heartache. Work kept her sane.

"Let someone else do it." He walked over to the table so she couldn't ignore him. "Hannah, you're killing yourself. You're as white as quicklime."

She dragged the rolling pin across the dough, tearing it. "I've lost a baby. How do you expect me to look?"

"Would you come into the study for a moment?" he said. "There's something I have to tell you." And how he dreaded it.

Her mouth hardened into an exasperated slash. "Can't you see that I'm in the middle of my baking?"

Be patient with her. "Your baking can wait," he said gently. "What I have to tell you is more important."

Eyes flashing, Hannah yanked off her apron and wiped her hands. Then she preceded Reiver into his study.

She turned around. "What is it you have to tell me?"

"You'd better sit down."

"Reiver, I—"

"Damn it, Hannah, sit down!"

She sank into the nearest chair.

Reiver leaned against his desk and gripped the edge. "I don't know any other way to tell you this, except straight out." He took a deep breath. "The doctor said you can't have any more children."

What little blood there was left in her cheeks drained away, leaving her as white as sun-bleached bones, her eyes wide and glazed with shock. Her jaw worked, but no words passed her lips.

Reiver knelt before her chair and grasped her cold hands. "I'm so sorry."

She stared at him as if he were a stranger speaking a foreign language. "I don't understand."

He touched her cheek. "You can't have any more children."

"No!" Hannah knocked his hand away and bolted from her chair. "It's not true! It can't be!" Dazed, she took several steps toward the door. She couldn't endure it, losing Samuel's child only to be told she could never have another. Surely God couldn't be so cruel. She whirled on Reiver. "The doctor is lying."

He swung to his feet. "I wish he were."

She howled in agony, raking her nails down her own cheeks in madness and despair. Reiver swore, maneuvered behind her, and pulled her close against him, pinning her arms helplessly to her sides. Hannah screamed and struggled.

"Hush," he crooned, even as she flung her head back to butt his jaw. "Easy, Hannah, easy." In spite of the pain that made his eyes tear, he kept up wordless, soothing mutterings until her struggles ceased and she finally went limp with exhaustion.

Reiver swung her into his arms and carried her upstairs.

He laid her on the bed, then mixed a sleeping draft the doctor had left. He turned back to find Hannah shivering and hugging her knees to her chest, her hair loose and streaming out wildly across the pillow. Her eyes were open wide, but glazed and unseeing; her lips moved soundlessly in a conversation only she could hear.

"Drink this," he said, managing to hold the glass to her lips. "It will help you to sleep."

After Hannah drank, Reiver moistened a cloth and gently

cleansed the angry red scratches scoring her cheeks like an Indian's war paint. "You needn't worry that they'll leave scars," he told Hannah. "Mrs. Hardy will put her special salve on them and they'll disappear."

Suddenly Hannah's vacant stare sharpened and focused on Reiver with such malevolence that he instinctively recoiled. "You did this to me!"

"No, you scratched yourself, remember?"

She fought against the powerful sleeping draft. "You didn't want me to have another child of Samuel's, so you and the doctor did something to me so I couldn't."

Reiver reared back. "You think that I . . . ?"

Her eyelids fluttered, then closed.

Reiver rose, breathing hard, feeling as though she had just accused him of murder. *How can she possibly think that I would do such a thing to her?*

The answer hit him like a physical blow. She had lost her mind. Reeling, Reiver staggered from the room.

Hannah heard faraway voices.

". . . Samuel gone, then she lost our child. And now I fear the shock of learning that she can't have any more has driven her mad."

Mad? Was this gray corner of her mind where the soothing snow quietly fell madness? She retreated, letting the snow envelop and warm her, but a second voice intruded.

"Your wife can't afford the luxury. Her husband and children need her. No, Mrs. Shaw has had a terrible shock, but she'll soon be herself. Give her time."

Would she? Samuel was gone. She had lost their baby. And now she could never have another to fill the loneliness inside. God was punishing her swiftly and surely.

Hannah let the snow drift higher and higher around her until the voices grew fainter, and fainter, then died, smothered by the snow.

Reiver sat at his desk and watched the snow fall listlessly outside his window. He tried to concentrate on his accounts, but he couldn't stop thinking of Hannah.

Their lives had changed so much in the two weeks since she

retreated into a world where no one else could follow. Mrs. Hardy now distracted Reiver from important mill business with petty, annoying household matters that had once been Hannah's province. The boys fought constantly, as if their fractiousness could startle their mother from her waking sleep. And Reiver, who had always taken his wife for granted, found to his surprise that he missed her.

He rubbed his eyes with the heels of his hands and sighed. He hated feeling so helpless.

A knock sounded at the door, and it opened to reveal Mrs. Hardy, her solemn silver eyes matching her expression.

"No change, Mrs. Hardy?" Reiver asked.

"None. She just sits there by the fire and doesn't hear a word I say. I wash and dress her as if she were a rag doll. At least the scratches have healed, so she won't be ugly." The housekeeper coughed. "Is she going to stay that way for the rest of her life?"

"We can only pray that she doesn't."

"She needs Samuel."

Reiver searched her wrinkled face for any sign that she knew Samuel and Hannah had once been lovers, but saw only innocence.

Mrs. Hardy added, "Samuel always could make her laugh. Maybe he could bring her back to us."

"My brother must have reached South America by now. There's no way a letter could reach him until he arrives in California. Hopefully Hannah will be well by then." His voice sounded unconvincing to his own ears.

Mrs. Hardy's hand dipped into an apron pocket. "We may not be able to write to Samuel, but he's able to write to us." She handed Reiver a letter. "This came in the post today."

A letter in Samuel's sprawling handwriting, addressed not to Hannah or Reiver, but to Benjamin.

Clever of them, Reiver thought.

He opened and read it. Satisfied that the contents were innocent enough, he said, "When Benjamin comes home from school, he can read this to his mama. Perhaps it will help her to get well."

Several hours later Reiver gave Benjamin his letter and told him what he must do.

"Mama?" Benjamin said when he and his father went up to

Hannah's room and gathered around her rocking chair. "Uncle Samuel sent me a letter. Would you like me to read it to you?"

No response.

Reiver knelt by her side, stroked her limp hands, and stared into her blank, unseeing eyes. "It's a letter from Samuel, Hannah. Samuel. You remember him, don't you?"

A flicker of awareness shone deep in her eyes, but it disappeared before Reiver could dare hope.

He rose. "Benjamin, read the letter."

Benjamin sat cross-legged at his mother's feet and began reading, his young face bright and hopeful, his voice confident.

Dear Ben,

   I hope this letter finds you and the family in good health. Except for a bit of seasickness at the beginning of the voyage on the *Orion*, I am now as fit as ever.

He glanced up to see if his words moved this silent wraith that had once been his mother, and when he saw that they didn't, he continued reading about a storm at sea and the antics of the cook's pet monkey.

When Benjamin read the closing, Reiver watched Hannah carefully.

" 'Give my love to everyone,' " Benjamin said, " 'especially your father and mother.' " He placed the letter in Hannah's lap. "And look, Mama. Uncle Samuel drew a little picture of the cook's monkey. Isn't he a funny fellow?" His face shone expectantly.

Blink, look at the boy, do something! was Reiver's silent plea.

Benjamin tapped his mother's hand. "Isn't he?"

Reiver watched and waited, then placed comforting hands on his son's slumping shoulders. "Come, Ben. We've done all we can for her today."

Benjamin rose, his lower lip trembling with a manly effort to keep from crying in front of his father. They turned and left the room, neither of them seeing Hannah's face light up like the sun suddenly breaking through roiling dark clouds. But the determined clouds devoured the sun, relegating her once again to the oblivion of swirling snow.

• • •

The snow was going away.

Hannah tried to gather the drifts around her again, but to no avail. Bright pictures of people and scenes flashed through her mind, slowly at first, then faster and faster. A man with dark, curly hair . . . another man with sorrow in his eyes . . . a little boy seated at her feet, mouthing words she couldn't hear.

Then she could hear quite distinctly: "Uncle Samuel drew a little picture of the cook's monkey. Isn't he a funny fellow? Isn't he?"

The man who drew the funny monkey . . . Uncle Samuel . . . her Samuel. His features came into sharper focus, and Hannah saw dark, curly hair and ghostly pale eyes brimming with love and laughter. He had loved her once. He still loved her. Now Hannah remembered.

Then she heard the scream.

Something snapped. The snow disappeared. Hannah awoke to find herself shivering in her own bed, a softly burning oil lamp illuminating her own bedroom, with another scream shattering the night silence.

"Benjamin!"

Hannah tumbled out of bed, grabbed the lamp, and ran down the hall barefoot toward the boys' bedroom, unmindful of a door opening behind her and a man's voice obliterated by another scream.

She flung open the bedroom door at the far end of the hall. "Benjamin, what is it? Are you having a bad dream?"

By lamplight, she saw her two sons sitting up in bed and staring at her with wide, incredulous eyes, as if she were a stranger. She set down the lamp and went to the eldest, enfolding him in her arms.

"It's all right," she crooned, hugging his trembling body.

But Benjamin pulled away and studied her face, his nightmare forgotten. "Mama?"

When Davey flung himself out of bed and into Hannah's arms, she hugged him and nodded at Benjamin through her tears. "Yes, I'm your mama."

"Hannah?"

She turned her head to see Reiver in his nightshirt, standing in the doorway, disbelief written on his face. She sighed heavily and nodded, then hugged her clinging children once more before gently disengaging herself and turning to their father.

"What happened to me?" She clasped her arms and shivered. "I feel as though I've been asleep for a long time."

"You've been sick." He gently brushed a lock of hair away from her face.

"I still feel so tired."

He took her arm. "Then why don't you go back to bed, and we'll talk in the morning?" He looked over her shoulder at his sons, wide-awake now and bursting with questions. "You boys go back to sleep."

"But Papa—"

"I said, go back to sleep. I have to tend to your mama now, so whatever you want to say will have to wait until the morning."

Hannah kissed them both and wished them pleasant dreams.

Both boys went to bed and pulled the covers up to their chins, but their eyes remained riveted on their mother as she left with their father.

Once back in Hannah's room, Reiver helped her into bed, then smiled and turned.

"Reiver, please don't go."

He turned back and hesitated, remembering all too well her vituperative accusations before she withdrew into her mind. But judging by the pleading in her eyes, she didn't remember. "I'll stay with you for as long as you like." He blew out the lamp, climbed into bed beside her, and drew her into his arms to comfort himself as well.

She fell asleep with her head pillowed against his shoulder.

Hours later, in the gray light of dawn, Reiver awoke to the sound of muffled sobbing and Hannah no longer in his arms.

He felt the bed shudder. "Hannah, what's wrong?"

"I remember now . . . what you told me the doctor said."

"I'm sorry."

"I know that now. I've been so selfish. All I could think of was myself and my own pain, but now I see that it must have hurt you deeply as well."

He knew he should say that he was sorry she had lost the baby, but he couldn't. Not yet.

Hannah rolled over on her side to face him, and even in the weak light he could see her tears had stopped, though her cheeks were wet. "But even if I can't have another child, at least we have Benjamin and Davey."

Reiver squeezed his eyes shut and uttered a silent prayer of thanks. "Yes, at least we have the boys."

Hannah paused. "I frightened them, didn't I?"

"You frightened us all very badly."

"But I'm better now."

Reiver prayed she would stay that way.

Hannah awoke the following morning feeling as though she had awakened from a long, soul-deep sleep. She was alone and glad of it. She needed solitude to come to terms with what had happened to her.

Shivering, she sat up, hugged her knees beneath the thick covers, and looked around her bedchamber, savoring the reassuring familiarity of the chest at the foot of her bed, the washstand with its plain white pitcher and bowl, and the rocking chair keeping vigil by the frosty window.

Hannah took a deep shuddering breath. "This is the day the Lord hath made," she said aloud, in humble thanks that her sanity had been restored.

The bedchamber door opened slowly and Mrs. Hardy peered in. "You're awake."

Hannah smiled. "In more ways than one."

The housekeeper bustled in with a breakfast tray and set it on the bureau so she could lean over and hug Hannah. "Reiver told us what happened last night," she said gruffly, trying not to cry. "It's about time."

Hannah fought back tears of her own. "Thank you for taking such good care of me, Mrs. Hardy."

"And it's a lot of trouble you were, I'll have you know." She walked around the room opening curtains to let in the daylight, then set the breakfast tray on the bed. "Now you eat this while I get a fire going. I swear it's warmer outside than it is in here."

"What time is it?" Hannah asked, pouring herself a cup of hot chocolate to warm her shivering insides.

"Almost eleven o'clock," Mrs. Hardy replied from the fireplace, ignoring Hannah's gasp of shock. "The boys wanted to see you before they left for school, but Reiver told them you needed your rest and weren't to be disturbed."

She wished they had come to see her. She felt an overwhelming need to hold her precious children in her arms again and let them see for themselves that their mother was well.

The fire lit, Mrs. Hardy turned and walked back to the bed. She reached into her apron pocket and removed a piece of paper. "Benjamin wanted me to give you this. He said he didn't think you heard him when he read it to you."

Samuel's letter.

The toast turned to sawdust on Hannah's tongue, but she took the letter in trembling fingers and tucked it beneath the rim of her chocolate cup's saucer. "I'll read it after I finish breakfast."

Mrs. Hardy nodded her silver head. "I'll have Millicent bring up hot water so you can wash."

When the door closed behind Mrs. Hardy, Hannah ignored her cooling oatmeal and opened Samuel's letter with trembling hands. She read part of it through her tears, then set the rest aside unread. The Samuel she knew had not written this impersonal account of shipboard life and a storm at sea. The letter contained none of his passion, none of his humor. It was written by a stranger.

Hannah swallowed hard over the lump in her throat. What did she expect? Samuel couldn't tell her that he still loved her and missed her in a letter that was sure to be seen and scrutinized by everyone in the family, especially Reiver. Still, she wished he had said something to keep her hope alive that he would return one day.

She thought of the child that she had lost—the one she knew was Samuel's—and felt a chill down to the marrow of her bones. Samuel had left for California without even knowing about it. She remembered how solicitous he had been when she had miscarried those other times, and she knew no man alive could have stopped him from returning to her side, if only he had known of the hell she had been enduring.

She had lost so much and had never felt more empty.

Hannah downed the remainder of her cooling chocolate, then rose and dressed quickly. There was much she had to do if she wanted to keep the snows of madness from ever returning.

The moment she walked into the noisy mill, everyone stopped working and stared.

"Good morning," Hannah said with a bright smile. "Or should I say afternoon?"

She saw surprise registered on the workers' faces, followed by relief mixed with happiness that their employer's wife had finally recovered.

Hannah smiled and exchanged greetings with Constance and Mary, making her way back to the machine shop where she knew she'd find James and Reiver. The moment she walked through the door, Reiver raised his head and looked at her in surprise.

"Shouldn't you be resting?" he asked.

"I'm feeling much stronger this morning," she replied. "And I wanted to show the workers that I've recovered."

Reiver nodded. "A day didn't pass that someone didn't ask about you."

James, who had been bending over a collection of mysterious belts and gears, looked up and started to say something, but obviously couldn't find the right words. Finally he came over and kissed her cheek. "Good to see you up and around."

Touched, Hannah smiled. Then she turned to Reiver. "May I speak to you for a moment?"

His blue eyes turned wary, as if he expected her madness to return. "Will my office be private enough?"

She nodded and followed him out of the machine shop, down a long corridor, and into his office.

He closed the door behind them and turned to face her, frowning. "You still don't look well, Hannah. You should be home resting."

"I'm fine, and I'm sick unto death of resting." She knotted her fingers together for the courage to continue. "Reiver, I'd like to help you run the mill."

His eyes widened in surprise. "But you already do so much."

"Yes, I buy books for the library and visit the sick, but it's not enough."

Astonished, Reiver took a step back and stared at her as if she had gone truly mad. "You have my home to keep and my children to raise. Surely that should be sufficient."

She shook her head. "But it's not."

He ran his hand over his long, wide jaw in consternation. "You're a woman. Women don't run silk mills."

"I merely want to help. Surely there's something I could do."

"You do a great deal as it is by concerning yourself with our workers' welfare."

"But it's not enough." She read only exasperation and frustration in his face, not real understanding. Hannah swallowed hard and said quietly, "I've lost so much."

His eyes darkened with shared pain. "What would you like to do?"

"Perhaps I could keep the accounts. I used to keep them for my father—his patient accounts, that is, not his gambling debts. I could also do your commercial correspondence. That would allow you more time to devote to other aspects of Shaw Silks. I could even accompany you to the New York sales office now and then."

Something flickered deep in Reiver's eyes when she mentioned New York, but it passed so quickly Hannah thought she had imagined it.

"Doing the accounts and correspondence is time-consuming," he admitted. "I don't enjoy it."

"Then let me do them."

"All right. I'll turn over the accounts and correspondence to you. But if the extra work should prove too taxing for you . . ."

"Then I shall give it up."

He smiled. "Agreed."

When Hannah headed for the door, Reiver placed a restraining hand on her arm. "Wait."

She stopped and looked at him expectantly, noticing his remote expression.

His hand fell away. "Are you going to tell Samuel about the child?"

A searing pain shot through Hannah. "Those who know what happened assume the child was yours," she replied softly, staring at the floor. "I see no reason to tell Samuel anything."

"It's for the best."

For whom, she wondered bitterly as she turned and left him, Samuel or Reiver?

CHAPTER
❧ 12 ❧

"WE should wait for Reiver," Hannah said, shivering in the chilly machine shop. "He wouldn't want to miss this momentous occasion."

She watched James slip a spool of silk thread on the spindle of the new Singer sewing machine and guide it along a route of loops and holes that ended in the tip of a needle poised to strike. After years of trial and error, he had finally perfected a loom capable of doubling and twisting their silk to make it strong enough to survive the rigors of this mechanized seamstress. Today he was going to put his new thread to the test.

James swept his hair off his brow. "I thought he would be back from New York by now."

Hannah glanced at the door as if expecting Reiver to materialize at any moment. "He was supposed to be home this morning, but with this sleet falling, perhaps the train was delayed." She wondered why Reiver had even wanted to travel to New York in February, with 1855's unpredictable weather making travel perilous.

She returned her attention to the machine Reiver insisted would make Shaw Silks' fortune.

"I feel so sorry for poor Mr. Howe," she said, shaking her head. "To have Mr. Singer steal his invention like that." Although Elias Howe had invented the sewing machine some years ago, public apathy drove him to London in an attempt to garner financing. When he returned, cheated and penniless, he discovered that several others were producing their own sewing machines, including one Isaac Merrit Singer.

Red streaked James' thin cheeks. "It makes my blood boil whenever I think of it."

"At least the courts found in Howe's favor, so he'll get some money for his invention."

"As much as I hate to admit it, Singer did add some significant improvements." James pointed to the metal foot. "This holds the cloth in place, and this"—he indicated a pulley beneath the machine's base—"keeps the material moving along with every stitch. If you didn't have these innovations, you'd never get a straight stitch. The seamstress would have to struggle just to keep the cloth even."

Hannah sighed. "I know Reiver would say, 'What do we care who invented it as long as Shaw Silks profits?' Everyone will be buying our thread to use in their new sewing machine."

James nodded. "That's exactly what my brother would say."

The telltale creak of the door opening interrupted their discussion, and Hannah looked up expecting to see Reiver, but Benjamin and Davey appeared instead, their cheeks rosy from the wind and traces of cookie crumbs on Davey's chin. Benjamin as usual led the way and his brother followed resentfully. Both boys kept on their wool caps and scarves.

"Is the thread strong enough this time?" Benjamin demanded of his uncle James, his eyes glowing with the avidity of a true Shaw as they pored over the sewing machine. "Does it work?"

"We don't know yet," James replied. "We're waiting for your father before we test it."

"Of course it will work," Davey said, giving his brother a disdainful look as he moved closer to the machine. "Uncle James is clever with machines."

Hannah sighed, wondering when her two sons were going to outgrow their exasperating rivalry, with Benjamin fighting to lead and Davey resenting having to follow. Perhaps never. Perhaps they would always scrap like two dogs over a bone.

Benjamin fidgeted. "Mama, when will Papa arrive?"

Hannah said, "He should be home at—"

The familiar creak interrupted her, and all four turned to see Reiver blow into the room on a gust of wind, his long wool coat decorated with diamonds of frozen sleet and his prominent nose red from the cold.

"Have you tried it?" Reiver demanded, going right to the sewing machine and stamping his feet to warm himself.

"Hello, Reiver," Hannah said, trying to keep the annoyance from her voice. "I trust you had a profitable trip in spite of the weather?"

"Yes, yes, I did," he muttered, scanning the sewing machine. Finally he stepped back, noticing his wife and sons for the first time. He kissed Hannah on the cheek and plucked the wool caps from his sons' heads. "I trust you boys behaved yourself in my absence?"

"Yes, Papa," they said in unison.

The social niceties dispensed with, he whipped off his wet hat and coat, threw them aside, and looked at James. "So, have you tried it yet?" he demanded again. "Is the thread strong enough?"

"We were waiting for you," James said. "We knew you wouldn't want to miss the big moment."

"I would've had your hide if you started without me," Reiver said. He placed his hands on his hips. "Now, show us what our new thread can do."

Hannah took the boys out of James's way so they could observe. James sat down at the sewing machine, placed a length of thick homespun fabric in position, then set his feet on the treadle and pumped back and forth, back and forth.

The sewing machine hummed, whirred, and clacked faster and faster. Hannah didn't know where to look first, at the spool of thread whirling around on the spindle or the needle jabbing at the cloth moving beneath the metal foot. So she looked at her husband's face instead and held her breath.

Beads of sweat stood out on Reiver's furrowed brow. His blue gaze darted everywhere as he waited for the thread to snap, along with his hopes and dreams.

"It's holding!" he cried. "You've done it!"

James grinned and peddled faster in his own euphoria. A dark, even line of stitches appeared like magic in the cloth.

Hannah's hand flew to her mouth in amazement. "It would take me hours to sew that much!"

Benjamin added, "And the thread hasn't broken like all the others."

Davey piped up, "Uncle James is a genius!"

"That he is," Reiver agreed, his eyes gleaming with thoughts of a spool of Shaw thread on every sewing machine in America. "That he is."

Later that night, long after the sleet, the flow of hot apple brandy, and the ringing echo of triumphant laughter had all finally ceased, leaving the house hushed and its inhabitants sated with victory, Reiver lay alone in his bed and finally allowed himself to think of Cecelia. Without the mill's concerns and celebrations to keep her at bay, Cecelia filled him like water poured from a pitcher, an image so potent that he could smell the sweetness of her heliotrope perfume and feel the beguiling softness of her lips against his.

He rose and padded across the smooth, chilly floorboards to the east window, where he stared out into the soothing winter darkness and thought of their last momentous assignation.

He had been standing at a far different window just yesterday afternoon, looking down into the slushy, bustling New York street, counting the endless seconds until he and his mistress would be together again for the first time in three months. Just when he thought he would go mad, a hired carriage pulled up to the Union Square Hotel and a furtive veiled figure stepped out daintily onto the curb.

Soon there came an urgent knock on his door. Heart pounding, he drew her inside and shut out the rest of the world. The moment she flung back her veil and he saw her white, drawn face, he should have known something was wrong, he who prided himself on knowing her so well. But after all this time he was too eager to have her. Again and again.

After they both lay replete and exhausted, Cecelia raised herself on one elbow and looked down at him out of troubled brown eyes.

"What is it?" he asked, alert in spite of the luxurious lassitude.

Her lower lip trembled. "I'm with child."

He looked away. "Tuttle should be pleased."

"It's not Tuttle's."

Reiver's head snapped back and he stared at her.

"It can only be yours," she said.

His child . . . his and Cecelia's. For a moment he felt numb, followed by a painful rush of elation. He took her hand and kissed it in silent reverence.

"There's no mistake," she said quietly. "I haven't slept with Tuttle in over four months, and—"

"—and we were together just three months ago," he finished for her. "There can be no question that it's mine?"

"According to my own calculations and my doctor's, I've been in this condition for three months."

Reiver thought her breasts felt heavier and her belly appeared more rounded. Now he knew why. He leaned over and kissed one dusky nipple.

She closed her eyes and shivered. "I didn't mean for this to happen, but now that it has, what are we going to do?"

Reiver gathered her into his arms and placed her head against his shoulder. "What do you wish to do? If you don't want to bear it, there are doctors who—"

"Reiver Shaw, how can you think that I would ever even consider destroying your child?"

He lifted her chin and looked deeply into her eyes. "But how are you going to explain your condition to your husband? Even if he believes the child is his, there is bound to come the day when someone notices that it resembles a Shaw more than a Tuttle. We Shaws do breed true, you know. Then what will you do?"

She lifted one smooth white shoulder in a careless shrug. "I will decide when the time comes. All I know is that I want this child. Do you?"

"It's a part of you. How could I not want it?"

She smiled. "I knew you'd feel that way."

"But you cannot bury your head in the sand, Cecelia. Tuttle forgave you once. I doubt that even he would forgive you for trying to pass off another man's child as his."

She bowed her head. "I seduced him as soon as I learned of my condition. Though the child will be born prematurely, he will think it's his. At least for a while."

Reiver thought of Cecelia sharing intimacies with her husband and stiffened with white-hot jealousy. "You could always leave Amos. I could set you up in a little house of your own somewhere near Coldwater. We'd be able to see each other more frequently, and you'd want for nothing."

"If I left Amos, would you leave Hannah?" she asked, though she knew his answer.

"You know I can't."

She smiled wanly. "And I can't leave Tuttle. For all his faults, he is a decent man, and deserves my loyalty, if not my fidelity. Besides, I would never leave my children. No, my love, though my life here isn't perfect, it's endurable."

"As you wish."

"This is the way it must be, Reiver," she said gently. "We've always known we couldn't be together, that we have to grasp what happiness we can."

And they had.

Reiver kissed the top of her head and noticed several gleaming strands of silver standing out among the chestnut ringlets, and an unexpected fear gnawed at his gut. Cecelia was thirty-seven, surely too old to endure the rigors of pregnancy and childbirth.

She felt him tremble. "What is it?"

"I don't know if I want you to take the risk."

"Reiver, what are you saying?" She pulled away, eyes wild with alarm. "That you want me to—to kill your child?"

"It's you I'm worried about." He stroked her cheek to gentle her. "Childbed becomes even more dangerous as a woman grows older, and the thought of losing you . . ." He looked away.

Cecelia's desperate expression melted. "I want to bear your child, whatever the risk."

"But I'm a selfish man, and I'm not sure if I want you to."

"Please don't fight me about this." She placed a beseeching hand on his chest. "I see you so seldom. If I had your child, at least I could always have a part of you with me. And if the day ever comes when you grow tired of me . . ."

He turned and grasped her wrists. "Have I ever grown tired of you? I never will, so don't ever say that to me, even in jest."

To punish her, he deliberately aroused her again until she writhed and moaned beneath him. When he finished with her, he helped her dress, hooking her corset and buttoning her gown with the efficiency of long practice.

"When can I see you again?" he whispered, brushing her neck with his lips and making her tremble.

She ignored his kisses and smoothed her skirts. "It will be impossible for me to leave the house for social calls once my condition becomes apparent. Tuttle always becomes annoyingly solicitous at such times." She straightened her narrow lace collar. "So we won't be able to meet until after the baby is born."

Reiver frowned. "Six months? That's a lifetime."

She smiled and patted her abdomen. "But you'll be with me."

"It's not the same and you know it."

Cecelia gave him a mocking smile. "My bold, impatient lover . . . we shall both have to make sacrifices."

Reiver slipped his arm around her narrow waist and crushed her to him, his mouth seeking hers for one last, passionate kiss. Cecelia melted in his arms, and he fancied he could feel their child nestled in her womb.

When she drew away, her eyes sparkled with happiness. "Good-bye, my love. Until we meet again."

He grasped her hands and brought them to his lips. "Take care."

"I shall." She put on her bonnet, tied the broad satin ribbons beneath her chin, and drew the black veil over her face so she was hidden from him. Then she was gone.

He watched from the hotel window as she climbed into a carriage and drove away.

Now, standing at his bedchamber window and looking out into the black, moonless night, Reiver watched a shooting star streak across the heavens, then die, leaving only a memory of its brilliance.

Sick with dread and foreboding, he padded back to bed, wondering if he had seen Cecelia for the last time.

August found Hannah sitting in the study with tears coursing down her cheeks. Sniffling, she blotted her eyes with a handkerchief and blew her nose. Grief shook her shoulders and turned sniffles into sobs.

The study door opened and Reiver walked in, startling her, for she wasn't expecting him back from New York for another two days. He stopped and snapped, "Why are you crying?"

Then he turned gray. "Has something happened to one of the boys?"

Hannah shook her head, dried her eyes, and waved her book in the air. "It's *Uncle Tom's Cabin.* I've just finished the part where Simon Legree has poor Uncle Tom flogged to death." Fresh tears sprang to her eyes and she rose from her chair. "I can't believe that there are people in our own country who would be so cruel to other human beings."

"Well, there are," Reiver replied, loosening his cravat against the wilting August heat. "I've heard more and more talk that something's got to be done to free the slaves. And that means war."

Hannah stared at him, aghast. "War? With our own countrymen? Brother fighting against brother?"

For once Hannah was grateful that Samuel was far, far away.

He nodded absently and walked over to the window. For the first time Hannah noticed the dark circles under Reiver's red-rimmed eyes and deep grooves of strain bracketing his mouth.

She set down her book, poor Uncle Tom's painful demise forgotten. "Reiver?"

"Cecelia Tuttle is dead."

"I beg your pardon?"

"I said she's *dead*, damn you!"

The vehemence of his outburst made Hannah flinch and she turned away. The beautiful Cecelia, her rival, now dead . . . images flowed unbidden into Hannah's mind: Cecelia at the dinner party, vivacious and charming, Reiver lying on the hallway floor after Amos Tuttle had shot him, and poor Benjamin coming home crying from school in the shameful aftermath of his father's infidelity.

Seven years had passed since Reiver broke off his affair with her, and now she was dead.

Hannah turned back to her husband. "What happened?" she said gently. "Was she ill?"

"No. She died in childbirth."

"How horrible." Hannah shook her head. Though the woman had caused her much heartache, Hannah felt nothing but pity and sadness for her now. She knew how devastated she would be if Samuel died. "Why don't you sit down and I'll fetch you a glass of cold cider."

He nodded numbly and sat down.

When Hannah returned with a tankard of cider, she found Reiver cradling his head in his hands, his shoulders shaking with muted sobs. He raised his head to look at her. Reiver had never been good-looking, but now grief distorted his features into homeliness. He took the proffered cider with trembling hands and gulped it down without once pausing for breath.

He set the empty tankard down. "I loved her."

His careless words slit like a blade reopening an old wound. "Reiver, I'm sorry that Mrs. Tuttle is dead, but I think it's rather callous of you to make such an admission to your own wife! Let's leave her in the past where she belongs, shall we?"

"I can't."

Long-slumbering anger and resentment awoke deep in Hannah's breast. "If you have any consideration for my feelings, you will."

He shook his head. "You don't understand. There are . . . things about me and Cecelia that I must tell you."

"Well, I don't wish to know them." Her head held high, Hannah whirled on her heel and marched to the study door. Reiver's wail of anguish brought her up short.

"Please, Hannah! You must listen to me. I'm begging you."

She turned to stare at him in puzzlement. Reiver never begged; he commanded and expected to be obeyed. She hesitated. What could be the harm in listening to her husband ramble on about his late mistress? Surely she could put her own feelings aside to ease his pain.

She walked over to the chair opposite him and sat down.

He smiled wanly and rested his elbows on his knees. "Cecelia died giving birth to my child."

In spite of the sweltering heat, a bone-chilling coldness stole through Hannah. She rose calmly and stood behind her chair as if she needed a physical barrier between herself and her husband.

She grasped the back of the chair so hard, she thought her knuckles would pierce the skin. "*Your* child?"

His gaze slid to the carpet and he nodded.

"How do you know this child is yours?" she asked with a deceptive calmness. "For that to be true, you and Cecelia would still have to be—"

"Lovers."

And then Hannah understood all too well. "I see. So these trips you've been making to New York City all this time . . . they haven't been to visit the sales office. You've been meeting Cecelia secretly."

"They were to conduct business. But also to see her."

"And what of her husband? After all this time poor Mr. Tuttle never suspected anything?"

"Never. We were very careful."

A knot of bitter loathing uncurled in Hannah's belly. "You sanctimonious, hypocritical bastard! All the while you were condemning my love for Samuel, you were carrying on with your mistress!"

He stared at her, his cheeks flushed with a rare display of shame.

Knees wobbling, Hannah staggered over to the open window and breathed in great gulps of the tepid summer air to keep herself from collapsing.

Reiver rose. "Don't you see! I couldn't help myself! I've always loved her, and she's always loved me. I couldn't give her up. We had to be together."

Hannah whirled around, mimicking him savagely. "Don't you see? I couldn't help myself! I loved Samuel and he loved me. I couldn't give him up, either. I had to be with him, but you sent him away."

"I suppose I deserve that."

"I've heard quite enough." Hannah started to make good her escape, but Reiver blocked her path.

"You said you'd listen."

"What is there for me to hear? You've just told me that you've fathered an illegitimate child by your mistress. I'm sure I'll endure this scandal just as I endured the previous one."

"Please listen. The situation is much more complicated."

Hannah hesitated.

"While Cecelia lay dying of childbed fever she told Tuttle that the child was mine. You recall the telegram that arrived for me several days ago? It was from Tuttle, informing me that he wanted to see me; that's why I went to New York.

"I was reluctant to go at first. He had already shot me once, and I wasn't eager to repeat the experience."

"I can hardly blame him now, can you?" Hannah snapped.

Self-righteous anger flared briefly in Reiver's eyes, then died. "No, I suppose I can't. But when I got there, all I found was a broken man, grieving for his wife. He had the nurse show me my daughter."

Hannah's blood stopped in her veins. Cecelia had given Reiver a daughter.

Suddenly Reiver smiled, a great warmth and tenderness suffusing his sad expression. "She is so beautiful, Hannah, so perfect. She has the biggest blue eyes you ever saw. Right now she's as bald as an egg, but—"

Hannah drew back her arm and slapped him with all her strength. She watched with grim satisfaction as his head jerked to the side, his body recoiling from the blow.

"That's for Abigail."

Rage simmered Reiver's eyes to a dark blue as he recovered, cradling his stinging cheek in one hand, but he made no move to retaliate.

Hannah clutched at her skirts to keep from striking him again. "I don't want to hear one more word about your little bastard, do you hear me? *Not one word!* After the despicable way you treated your own daughter, never giving her one little crumb of affection . . ." She trembled. "I wish Amos Tuttle had killed you."

She made an attempt to brush past Reiver, but he caught her wrist. "Tuttle won't have anything to do with her." He took a deep breath. "She is my own flesh and blood, Hannah, and I want to raise her in this house, as a Shaw."

The cold, deadly calm returned, giving Hannah strength. "What you're saying is that you expect me to raise your bastard as if she were my own. Well, I will not!"

"Hannah," he murmured, his voice cajoling, "she is so tiny, so helpless. Once you see her, I know you'll fall in love with her. Surely you won't blame an innocent babe for its parents' sins."

"I had a daughter and she died. I will not raise your bastard to take her place."

"If I don't take her, Tuttle is threatening to send her to a foundling home."

"Then install a nurse in a little house somewhere and let her raise it."

"I don't want my daughter to be raised by strangers. I want her to know her father and her half-brothers, to never feel the scorn of illegitimacy."

"You should have thought of that before you resumed your . . . liaison with your mistress. Quite frankly I don't care what happens to her child."

His eyes narrowed and hardened into blue glass. "This is my house, and my word is law. If I wish to do this, you won't stop me, Hannah. I can make life deuced uncomfortable for you if you don't agree." He let his blatantly sexual gaze rake her up and down.

Hannah raised her chin a stubborn notch. "I swear to God that I'll go to Samuel and leave you with three children to raise."

Her threat took him aback for a moment, then he dismissed it with a wave of his hand. "You're bluffing. If you wouldn't leave the boys to run off with my brother, you won't leave them now."

"They were younger then. Now that they're old enough to understand . . ." She bared her teeth in a ghastly parody of a smile. "I wonder how long your own sons will hold their father in such high regard when they learn that he drove their mother away?"

The blood drained from Reiver's face, making the print of Hannah's hand stand out in bright crimson relief. "You wouldn't do that to your own children. You couldn't be so heartless."

"Don't test me, Reiver."

And without another word, she flew out of the study.

This time he knew better than to try to stop her.

She had to get away.

Hannah left the house and walked faster and faster. She resented the hot, placid day, with nary a breeze to stir the listless leaves. Her rage demanded a wild, howling storm with scudding black clouds that conquered the sun and a high wind to break the trees' backs.

She didn't stop until she reached Nate's tobacco field. Unmindful of the sun beating down on her bare head, Hannah sat on the stone wall and looked out over the tobacco plants. She cried herself dry, then wiped her wet cheeks with the back of her hand.

She remembered the day an eternity ago when Amos Tuttle had shot Reiver and Hannah had learned of her husband's infidelity. Humiliated and furious, her emotions in turmoil, she had come back to this field to decide her future. And that's where Samuel had found her.

If she closed her eyes, she could feel his arm tightening about her waist so he could lift her into the saddle, and the hardness of his body against her back. She had kissed him defiantly, and he had returned that kiss against his will. Hannah moistened her lips as if she could still taste him, but there was only the whisper of a memory.

She sighed. Dreams were all well and good, but she had to contend with the present.

"What am I going to do?"

She knew she couldn't stop Reiver. He wanted his child to be raised as a Shaw and he expected Hannah to comply with his wishes like a dutiful wife. But she couldn't, not after the way he had treated Abigail. And what about Benjamin and Davey? What would happen to them if this child replaced them in their father's affections?

Hannah rubbed her arms, feeling suddenly cold in spite of the heat. She frowned. There had to be something she could do to thwart Reiver. She rested her chin in her hand and stared at the horizon as if she could find the answer written there.

Half an hour later she smiled in triumph and slid off the stone wall. This time there was no Samuel riding down the road like a white knight to comfort her. She was alone, and she prayed for the courage to fight her husband.

Along the western horizon, black clouds gathered like a flock of crows. Perhaps Hannah would have her storm after all.

She found Reiver still in his study, seated at his desk and pressing the heels of his hands into his tired eyes. He looked up expectantly.

Hannah closed the door and faced him. "I will agree to raise your daughter—"

"Hannah, I don't know what to say." He sprang to his feet, his eager face alight with a mixture of relief and gratitude, and started toward her, his hands extended. "I knew you couldn't abandon a helpless infant."

She stepped back and raised her hand to ward him off. "I haven't finished." Reiver stopped, his expression darkening with suspicion. "As I started to say, I will agree to raise your daughter. But on two conditions."

"Hannah—"

"Two conditions, Reiver."

He paused, wary now. "What are they?"

"I want legal control of Shaw Silks."

Reiver burst out laughing. "Don't be absurd."

"Oh, I assure you I am quite serious. If I am to suffer the humiliation of raising your mistress's child, I expect you to pay a very heavy price. So I've decided that I want what you love best—your silk mill." Hannah strolled around the room. "I want sixty percent of your shares, and you may retain ten percent. So even with James's and the boys' shares, you will never gain control from me."

His face twisted with rage. "I worked my fingers to the bone to build this company from nothing, and I'll be damned if I'll let anyone take it away from me!"

"Oh, you would still run it, of course. But I would expect to be consulted on major decisions, and I would have the final say."

"Be reasonable. You know nothing about running a silk mill."

"That's not true. Who thought of giving our silks an Italian name? Who suggested that another person should know Giuseppe Torelli's dye formulas? And I've been keeping the accounts. One can learn much from accounts."

"Women don't run silk mills, damn it! They're supposed to raise their children and make a comfortable home for their husbands."

"Then I shall be the exception." And her first order of business would be to make sure that children never worked for Shaw Silks again.

He ran his hand through his hair in frustration. "Hannah, this is insane. I can't agree to it."

She shrugged. "Fine. Then I suggest you find a suitable foundling home for your little bastard."

"Don't call her that, damn you! She's still my daughter."

Hannah ran her fingertips over the back of the settee. "And my second condition is that no one can know she's your daughter. She'll be my niece, the child of one of my New York cousins who died in childbirth. I offered her a home out of the goodness of my heart. When she's old enough to understand, you may acknowledge her."

"You've thought of everything, haven't you?"

"Yes, I believe I have."

Reiver's lip curled in contempt. "You stupid, heartless bitch! You would ruin everything I've worked for, just to satisfy your own petty female hunger for vengeance."

Hannah arched her back like a cat ready to spit and claw. "This isn't about vengeance, but you're too bullheaded to see it. This is about protecting my sons' birthright. If I control this company, you'll never be able to give it away to your little bas—daughter."

"Is that what you're afraid of?" He looked genuinely shocked. "Benjamin and Davey are my sons. I would never cut them out of this company."

"I don't trust you anymore, so I've got to look out for my own welfare and that of my sons." She clutched the back of the settee. "You're an arrogant, selfish man, Reiver Shaw. You married me against my wishes, you never showed my daughter one crumb of affection, and you banished your own brother from his family to salvage your own pride while you continued to see your mistress."

Two spots of color stained his cheeks, but he made no retort.

"And now, in your supreme arrogance and insensitivity, you expect me to swallow my own pride and raise your mistress's child." She steeled herself for what she had to say next. "Perhaps if I thought it would make you love me, I wouldn't hesitate. But I've come to realize that you'll never love me, no matter what I do. You'll always love Cecelia first and foremost."

Hannah hesitated, giving him a moment to deny it, but he didn't. She continued, "So I expect to be repaid, and handsomely. I've named my price."

"And if I refuse to pay it?"

"You won't. You may be arrogant and selfish, but you do love your sons and you wouldn't want them to come to resent you as you resented your own father. You could send me away, but you would never separate your sons from their mother, even to give your daughter a home. You could also tell the boys of my affair with Samuel, but then I would go to him and you'd be left raising three children alone."

Hatred smoldered in his eyes. "I'll agree to your terms. But know this, Hannah. You'll control Shaw Silks, but you'll never control me."

He strode out of the study and slammed the door behind him.

Trembling, Hannah sank down into the sofa and clasped her cold, shaking hands in her lap.

Her husband had become her worst enemy.

CHAPTER
☙ 13 ❧

REIVER cursed himself for ever agreeing to Hannah's outrageous, unreasonable demands.

Seated beside his wife in a Hartford–New Haven railway car heading back from New York, he observed Hannah trying to resist the baby cradled in the wet nurse's arms, and failing.

"Do you think she's too warm?" Hannah asked Georgia Varner, the placid young farm girl they had hired, for Mrs. Hardy's advanced age and cantankerous, impatient nature made her unsuitable to care for a demanding infant.

Ginger-haired Georgia, who looked too delicate to lift heavy pails of milk and hoe rock-strewn fields, laid the backs of her fingers against the baby's forehead. "She doesn't seem warm at all, Mrs. Shaw."

Baby Elisabeth—named after Cecelia's mother—mewled and wrinkled her tiny face, causing Hannah's concerned gaze to lock on her with the possessiveness a tigress feels for her cub. "Perhaps she's hungry."

"I fed her before we left," Georgia said. "Would you like to hold her?"

Hannah stiffened. "I'll only disturb her. She seems quite content in your arms."

Reiver turned his attention to the lush Connecticut countryside rolling past the window and silently cursed himself again. He had known his wife's strong maternal instinct would prevail, and he should have insisted that she see the baby first. Then she would have agreed to anything.

Hannah had outsmarted him. Only when the ink was dry on

the papers that gave her legal control of Reiver's company did she agree to see Cecelia's child.

To Reiver's chagrin, the moment they arrived at Amos Tuttle's house and Hannah held Elisabeth in her arms for the first time, her coldness melted, though she feigned a certain reserve for his benefit. He could tell that this tiny scrap of humanity had moved Hannah and captured her heart. That pleased him.

Hannah said, "Do you think you'll like living in Connecticut, Georgia?"

"Yes, ma'am." Her warm hazel eyes never left the baby in her arms. "I wanted to get away from the farm real bad, especially after—" She blushed, obviously thinking of her own stillborn baby born out of wedlock and her own ensuing shame. "Now I have a chance to make a fresh start. I disgraced my family and they weren't about to let me forget it, especially my pa."

"Everyone makes mistakes," Hannah said gently. "Surely your father could forgive you for yours."

"No, ma'am, not him. I shamed him, and he was going to make me pay. That's why I ran away to the big city, to go into service and get away."

"Well, we're fortunate to have you," Reiver said. "I know you'll take good care of my—" He almost said "daughter," but stopped himself in time. "Elisabeth."

The placid Georgia ran one finger down the sleeping baby's cheek. "Don't you worry none, Mr. Shaw, I'll care for her as if she were my own."

Hannah smiled. "We're counting on that."

Georgia's face clouded. "I feel bad for your cousins, ma'am, perishing together in that fire and leaving this little angel all alone in the world. It's right charitable of you and Mr. Shaw to take her in."

"It's the least we could do," Hannah said. "Otherwise she would have been sent to a foundling home."

Georgia's eyes widened in indignation. "Surely not!"

Reiver addressed Hannah directly for the first time since they had boarded the train. "My softhearted wife couldn't bear to let that happen, could you, my dear?"

She met his gaze and held it. "Of course not. I'm sure little Elisabeth will repay us tenfold for our charity."

Reiver turned his attention back to the scenery. "We should be arriving in Hartford shortly."

A rapt, wide-eyed Davey peered into the cradle. "She looks all red and wrinkly," he said, "like a newborn piglet."

"All babies look like that, you fool," his brother scoffed. "But they grow out of it. Except for you."

Sensing tension in the room, Elisabeth screwed up her face and let out a lusty wail.

Hannah glared at them. "Now you've made the baby cry." She lifted Elisabeth onto her shoulder and the wailing ceased.

"I don't see why she has to come live with us," Davey grumbled. "She'll cry all the time and keep us up at night. And when she gets older, she'll want to tag along after us."

Benjamin turned pale. "I hadn't thought of that."

Hannah said, "By the time Elisabeth is old enough to tag along, you two will be grown men. You mustn't be so selfish. Elisabeth's parents are dead and she has nowhere else to go. Just because she's here doesn't mean that your father and I love you boys any less."

They exchanged sheepish looks.

She smiled. "Both of you are strong, so you must protect your little cousin, not be jealous of her."

Benjamin gave an indignant snort. "Mother, I am fourteen years old. I am not jealous of a baby."

Hannah suppressed a smile. "Why don't the two of you go to the kitchen to see if Mrs. Hardy has baked you anything—unless, of course, you're too old for cookies."

The two boys walked out of the nursery with as much adult aplomb as they could muster, leaving Hannah alone with Cecelia's daughter.

She rested her cheek against the downy head and breathed in the warm sweet scent of baby, fighting back tears as she thought of her own lost Abigail and the child she would never give Samuel.

Despite all her best attempts, she couldn't harden her heart against a helpless infant, even if she was a living, breathing reminder of her husband's infidelity. Yet Reiver knew her better than she knew herself; once she saw the baby and held her, she would love her as fiercely as she loved her own children.

Hannah would never let him know that.

Suddenly the nursery door opened. Reiver stood there, watching her with a strange expression that made her shiver. Ever since she had taken control of his company, he regarded her with barely disguised loathing.

"I'm surprised at you, Hannah," he said. "Such a display of warm maternal feeling for my mistress's daughter."

Hannah set the baby back down in her cradle and faced him. "I don't believe in blaming an innocent child for the sins of her father. I promised you that I'd raise your daughter as if she were my own, and I shall." She crossed her arms. "But never think that she will mean more to me than my own children. That would be a grave mistake."

"Oh, I never intend to underestimate you again, dear wife," he said coldly.

"See that you don't." She looked down at Elisabeth, now asleep. "You are right. Shaws do breed true. Elisabeth looks nothing like her mother. She has your hair, your eyes, and Samuel's chin." Hannah looked over at Reiver. "I'm surprised James and Mrs. Hardy didn't notice the resemblance right away."

"They will, in time." He walked over to the cradle and peered in. "You're wrong. She may have my hair and eyes, but she looks exactly like Cecelia. When she grows up, she'll be exactly like her mother."

Not if I can help it, Hannah thought.

Reiver straightened. "What happens now?"

She walked over to a window to put distance between them. "We go our separate ways. You will continue to run Shaw Silks without interference from me—unless, of course, I choose to interfere—while I raise the children."

He came to stand behind her and she used superhuman effort to keep from stepping away. She could feel the menacing warmth of his breath ruffling the fine hairs on the nape of her neck.

"I'm still a young, virile man," he said. "I won't live like a monk."

She stared down at the boys in the yard below, laughing and talking with Georgia. "Perhaps our new nurse would be willing to become your mistress, once Elisabeth is through nursing.

She's quite comely and sweet-tempered. All I ask is that you be discreet." She turned to face him. "But then, you always were."

Rage flared in Reiver's eyes. "That's low."

"I feel nothing for you, and after fifteen years of marriage, I can't pretend anymore. I'll raise your daughter, but I will not share your bed."

His hand shot out and he grasped her wrist. "I could take you whenever and wherever I wish."

Hannah forced herself to remain calm, though her heart was pounding. "Yes, you could. However, the mill would suffer."

He dropped her wrist as if it had turned white-hot and stepped back, letting his gaze rake her over. "You used to be attractive. You were kind, generous, and forgiving, all that a woman should be." He shook his head. "But you've become so twisted and bitter that I doubt if even Samuel would love you now."

"No matter what you say, Samuel has always loved me, and he always will." She raised her head proudly. "He taught me never to allow anyone to denigrate me."

"That's before you changed." His features turned bleak. "You know, since Cecelia died, you haven't once spared a thought for my suffering. The woman I loved died, Hannah, and I can't even wear black for her. Do you know what that has done to me?"

She reared back. "You'll get not one shred of sympathy from me, Reiver Shaw. You and that woman caused me nothing but humiliation and heartache."

"Why did I think you'd ever understand? You're nothing but a cold, heartless bitch."

"Whatever I am, you made me."

He glared at her, then whirled on his heel and stormed out, slamming the door behind him.

When Reiver's angry footsteps died away, Hannah let out the breath she had been holding, staggered over to a nearby chair, and sank down. She hugged herself to stop the violent shudders racking her body.

She must have been insane to take Reiver's mill away. She was no match for him. He was far too clever and ruthless, far too strong. He would win back his company and make her rue the day she was born.

Hannah took several deep breaths until the shaking stopped. She had to keep her wits about her. She had to think. She would have to be on her guard from now on because she was all alone, and could rely only on herself.

Reiver stood behind the new girl and stared over her shoulder while her nervous fingers sorted the latest shipment of cocoons.

He came around the table to stand before her. "What is your name?" She looked very young, all of fifteen, if that.

"G-Grace Alcorn, sir."

He should have known her name, for he had just hired her yesterday to replace Constance Ferry, but for the last two months, ever since signing over his mill to Hannah, Reiver couldn't concentrate on business matters.

"Well, Grace Alcorn," he said, "you'll have to move faster if you expect to remain at Shaw Silks."

Tears sprang to her fearful eyes. "P-please, Mr. Shaw, I need this job or m-my family will starve."

He picked up a broken cocoon and shook it right under her nose. "If you want to keep this job, then you'll have to remember that the object of sorting cocoons is to separate the perfect ones from the broken ones like this." His voice rose. "You do not put them in the same basket, do you understand me?"

Her lower lip trembled. "Y-yes, Mr. Shaw."

"See that you do, because I can't abide incompetence." Without another word, he whirled around, and when he caught several workers staring in shock, he glared back. "I pay you to work, not gawk, so get back to it!"

They averted their eyes and resumed working.

Reiver stormed out of the room before he fired every last one of them, and headed for the stables that had replaced the old barn. He saddled his horse and rode out of the yard at a canter, needing to get away before he exploded.

He didn't slow down until he reached Coldwater's wide, tree-lined main street. Roger Jones, the blacksmith who had once thrown Reiver's belligerent drunken father out of the local tavern, now smiled and nodded as he hammered a glowing horseshoe at his anvil. Bart Putnam, the livery-stable owner who had once refused Rummy Shaw's eldest son a job as a groom because he put on airs, waved and called out a friendly greeting. Old Granny Fricker, sweeping dried autumn leaves off her porch, beamed at him in approval instead of chasing and cursing the hungry boy trying to swipe a peach pie cooling on her windowsill.

The hard-won respect he now enjoyed couldn't compensate for the loss of his company.

Hannah had cut off his balls as surely as if she had used a knife.

It wasn't as though she had marched into the mill and announced that she would be giving the orders now. Just as she had promised, she kept their home and raised the children as she always had. She made no attempt to challenge Reiver's decisions or usurp his authority. Only their lawyers knew what she had done.

He couldn't deny that her outsmarting him still rankled like a boil on his backside. Even though no one could see it, Reiver knew it was there and felt it every time he moved.

He came to the end of Main Street and turned his horse northward. Adding to his frustration was the fact that he hadn't had a woman in two months. He had debated forcing himself on his wife, but thought better of it. Hannah had sworn the mill would suffer, and he couldn't risk calling her bluff. He would have to seek his pleasure elsewhere.

Reiver thought of Georgia, with her ginger hair and quivering breasts, and grinned. It would serve Hannah right if he availed himself of the nursemaid in his wife's own house. She pretended not to care, but he knew otherwise. Besides, Georgia was too sweet for his tastes, and he put the thought of seducing her right out of his mind.

There had to be some way to get his mill back. Some way . . .

"Something's troubling Reiver."

James watched Hannah carefully as she looked up from the accounts, but she revealed no emotion in her gaze or features. She had changed gradually over the years, from outgoing and as eager to please as a puppy to pensive and reserved. Not that he could blame her. Having a child die and losing her husband to another woman was enough to make any woman guard her heart. She was still pretty, though.

Hannah smiled and sat back in her chair. "There must be a great change in him for you to notice."

James blushed, set down his toolbox, and settled his lanky frame into the chair across from her desk. "I just keep the looms running and mind my own business. But even I can see that there's something wrong with my brother. You're his wife. Haven't you noticed?"

Hannah grew more guarded. "Reiver and I have never been as close as some married couples, and these days I find it even more difficult to gauge his moods."

"I'm sorry, Hannah. None of my business."

She shrugged off his sympathy with a brief wave of her hand. "What has he been doing to warrant your concern?"

James groped for the right words. He could describe the complex workings of a machine without hesitation, but people puzzled him.

"Just this morning," he began, "Reiver lost his temper with the new girl who sorts the cocoons. He hired her just yesterday, so he can't expect her to know what to do right away. When she mixed in some broken cocoons with the good ones, he flew into a rage. I could hear him shouting all the way down in the machine shop."

Hannah frowned. "What happened to Constance Ferry? She isn't working for us anymore?"

James shook his head. "She went to work in that new silk mill that just opened up in Rockville."

"Why did she leave Shaw Silks? Did she say?"

"They're paying her more money."

"That's a good reason. And Reiver didn't try to match it?"

James shrugged. "I don't know. I only take care of the looms." He hesitated. "I did hear some grumbling among the workers that Reiver cut their wages."

Hannah's blue eyes widened in astonishment. "If he did that, more of our workers are going to desert us for the Rockville mill."

"Perhaps," he agreed. "Something is wrong with my brother. Cutting wages and hollering at the girls . . . that's not like Reiver at all."

"You're right. I'll see if I can learn what's troubling him."

James took his toolbox, walked to the door, and turned. "Is Miss Varner up in the nursery?"

"I expect so. Why?"

His face grew hot. "She said Elisabeth's cradle has been squeaking. I thought I'd go up and fix it for her."

Hannah's guarded expression softened. "You may see Georgia anytime you want, James. You don't need to ask my permission."

He blushed again and left the study.

Hannah stared at the closed door and smiled to herself. So James was smitten with Georgia. Hannah had never seen the shy Shaw brother express interest in a woman before. He always seemed to prefer machines that, once he fixed them, stayed fixed.

She rose, went to the window, and stared out at nothing in particular. It was apparent to her why Reiver was on the rampage. He resented her outsmarting him. That delighted her. But his cutting the workers' wages angered her.

She needed to gather ammunition to use against him. Hannah closed her account books and went to fetch her cloak.

Upstairs, James stood before the closed nursery door. He swept his hair out of his eyes, moistened his dry lips, rubbed his spotless hands against his trousers, then hesitated. What would he say to her? "Miss Varner, I've come to fix the squeaky cradle." That sounded good. He mentally rehearsed it several times before knocking.

"Come in."

At the sound of her soft, sweet voice that reminded him of cooing doves, James felt his heart leap into his throat. He opened the door and hesitated in the doorway.

Georgia Varner sat in the same rocking chair that had soothed both James and his brothers when they were babies, feeding Elisabeth with a rapt serenity that touched James deeply. Autumn light, as thick and golden as honey, poured over her through the window, outlining her curling ginger hair with fire and turning her bare breast into smooth carved ivory. James wondered if it would feel warm and heavy to his touch. His groin tightened.

Georgia looked up and turned crimson. "Mr. Shaw . . ." She

took one end of her shawl and modestly covered herself. "I—I thought you were Mrs. Shaw or Mrs. Hardy."

"I had some free time and thought I'd fix the cradle."

"The cradle? What's wrong with it?"

"You said it squeaked."

She smiled, and it was as if the sun had just burst forth on a rainy day. "How kind of you to remember my mentioning it. Do come in."

James went over to the cradle, set down his toolbox, and looked over at Georgia. "Do you mind if I remove . . . what's inside?"

"The bedding? No, I don't mind at all." She offered Elisabeth her finger to grasp, and beamed in approval when the baby grabbed it.

James turned over the cradle and went to work. His attention may have been focused on the cradle, but he was all too aware of Georgia Varner seated not ten feet away. He heard the muffled sound of the rocker's runners going back and forth, back and forth on the bare floor, and the accompanying sigh of her long skirts. Out of the corner of his eye, he could see her stealing glances at him.

How he wished he could say something charming and clever like Samuel, but try as he might, his mind remained blank.

"Mrs. Shaw tells me that you can fix anything," Georgia said suddenly, startling him.

James ducked his head. "Everyone has something they're good at, and I'm good at fixing things."

"I think it takes real skill to find what's wrong with something and fix it."

Her praise made his cheeks grow warm. "Do you like living here?"

"I like it fine. Mr. and Mrs. Shaw have been kindness itself to me." She gave him a conspiratorial smile. "But that Mrs. Hardy . . ." She rolled her eyes. " 'Don't do this to the baby.' 'Don't do that to the baby.' "

James smiled. "She always was testy, and she's gotten worse with age. I think it's hard on her, not being able to see as well as she used to, and do all the things she once did when she was young."

"You're very compassionate, Mr. Shaw."

He glanced over at her. "How do you like taking care of the baby?"

"I couldn't love her any more than if she was my own."

The sudden watery tremor in her voice caused James to look over at her, and to his dismay, her hazel eyes were bright with tears. He gaped at her helplessly.

Georgia wiped her eyes with one corner of her shawl. "Do forgive me for blubbering, Mr. Shaw. But every time I think of my poor stillborn babe—she was a little girl, too, you know—I can't help myself."

Elisabeth, sensing her nurse's distress, spat out the nipple and let out a thin, high-pitched wail.

"Now I've upset this angel as well," Georgia muttered, rising. "Would you take her for a minute? That is, if you don't mind holding a baby."

"Mind? I like babies."

James rose, crossed the room, and took the crying baby from her. Her shawl fell away, but before he could steal a glance at Georgia's bare breast, she turned away, and when she turned back to take Elisabeth from him, her bodice was buttoned.

Georgia placed the baby against her right shoulder and rubbed her back, murmuring, "There, there," until the crying ceased.

James knew he should say something—do something—but what? He thought of Samuel again, and touched Georgia's shoulder shyly. "I can't claim to know how it feels to lose a child, but you have my deepest sympathies, Miss Varner."

She managed a tremulous smile. "You're very kind, Mr. Shaw. But I knew that the moment I laid eyes on you."

James stood there awkwardly, lost in the warmth of her hazel eyes. "I—I'd better see about fixing the cradle."

He worked in silence, save for Georgia humming a lullaby in her soft, sweet voice. When he was through, he rocked the cradle several times to test it, and replaced the bedding.

Georgia beamed at him. "You've fixed it." She carried the sleeping baby over. "Let's see how Elisabeth likes it, shall we?"

James stepped back, but Georgia was still too close to ignore, flooding his senses. She smelled fresh-scrubbed and milky, with a subtle spicy scent of her own that had nothing to do with soap or perfume. His fingers itched to let down her ginger tresses and discover for himself if her hair felt as soft and silky as it looked.

She set the baby in the cradle, straightened, and looked right at James. He hadn't noticed until now that her hazel eyes were deeply flecked with gold like dark pebbles strewn at the bottom of a clear, shallow brook. And her lips were curiously mismatched, the upper lip being much thinner than its full lower counterpart. He wondered how it would feel to kiss them.

James swallowed hard and stepped back out of danger.

Georgia smiled. "You're a godsend, Mr. Shaw. Now the squeak won't keep Elisabeth up when I rock her."

"If anything else needs fixing, Miss Varner, all you have to do is call on me."

"Oh, I will, Mr. Shaw, I surely will."

Later that evening, long after James returned to the homestead and the boys went to bed, Hannah gathered her courage and went to confront Reiver.

She found him in his dark, quiet study, sitting in his favorite chair by the light of the fire, with his legs stretched out on a footstool and a half-empty glass of apple brandy in his hand. Deep lines of weariness scored his cheeks, and his mouth drooped petulantly. Hannah refused to feel sorry for him.

"What do you want?" he snapped.

"I want to talk to you, but not in the dark." She went over to the desk and lit the oil lamp. Soft light flooded the room.

"And what do you wish to discuss, dear wife?"

Hannah went over to the fireplace and extended her hands to warm them, for a distinct chill filled the distance between them. "James is worried about you." When Reiver made no comment, she added, "He said you shouted at the cocoon sorter today."

"The girl is incompetent," he growled. "She's lucky that she still has a job."

Hannah's hands dropped to her sides. "It isn't like you to shout at your workers."

He glared at her. "And why is that, I wonder?"

"I have no idea."

"Oh, but you do." He rose and faced her, anger radiating from him in palpable waves. "I don't like working with my hands tied behind me, Hannah. It makes me irritable and I lose my temper."

She raised her brows in affronted innocence. "Have I once interfered in the running of the mill in the two months since you signed over your shares to me?" she couldn't resist reminding him. "I haven't. So if you're feeling constrained, it's by your own design."

"You don't understand. It's my mill. I want to control it."

"But you do."

He dragged his hands through his hair in frustration. "It's not enough, Hannah. I want my mill back. It's not . . . seemly for a woman to have such control over a man."

"Fine. If you want your mill back, send Elisabeth to a foundling home."

He stared at her as if she had suddenly grown two heads. "Your coldness appalls me."

She crossed her arms to keep them from shaking. "We made a bargain, Reiver, and I'm going to hold you to it."

"Hannah—"

"I didn't come here to discuss our bargain. I want to know why Constance Ferry left our employ?"

"She went to work at the Rockville mill."

"She must have had some reason for leaving, since she's been with Shaw Silks for over fifteen years."

Reiver poured himself another apple brandy. "She told me they agreed to pay her more money."

"And you didn't match their price?"

"Why should I?" He tossed off the brandy in one swallow. "Mill workers grow on trees. If one leaves, there are two to take her place."

Hannah clasped her hands together. "Is that why you've reduced everyone's wages?"

He grew very still. "Who told you that? James?"

"Constance herself. I went to see her today, and she told me everything. I was bound to find out sooner or later."

He returned to his chair. "So I reduced everyone's wages. What of it?"

"And what if all of your workers go over to the competition?"

"I'll merely train others to take their place."

Hannah walked over to the window and stared out into the darkness, listening to the whistling wind. "Most of these people have been with us for over ten years. I know each one of them by name, and I know their children's names. I've brought food and clothing to them when they've had a run of bad luck, and sent the doctor to them when they're ill. They're like family."

Reiver regarded her out of scornful eyes. "And just what is the moral of your touching little tale?"

She turned, her heart racing at the prospect of incurring his wrath, for she was still so new to defying him. "I don't think that you should cut the workers' wages. If anything, you should raise them to encourage them to stay."

"What!" Reiver swore and leaped to his feet. "Of all the stupid, harebrained . . . do you think money falls from the sky, woman?"

"Of course I don't," she replied coldly.

"Try very hard to understand this simple concept, Hannah. I am not in business to make our workers wealthy. I'm in business to make the Shaws wealthy."

"Don't speak to me as if I were some half-witted child. I'm not suggesting that we make our workers wealthy, merely that we offer them a decent standard of living and inspire loyalty. They're not our slaves."

He jammed his hands into his pockets. "I'm trying very hard not to lose my temper, but you make it damned difficult. You don't know anything about running the mill, Hannah. You think that just because you've gained legal control of my company you know how to run it. You don't, so stop trying to pretend that you do."

"If you'll stop insulting me long enough to listen to reason—"

"Reason won't make new looms to manufacture silk ribbons! That's why I've cut wages. Does that explanation satisfy you?"

"You want to make ribbons as well as thread?"

"Yes." He glanced at the ribbons trimming her dark blue dress. "As you know, ladies demand miles and miles of ribbon to trim their gowns and bonnets. We may not be able to compete with silk cloth from France and Italy, but we can certainly corner the market on ribbons."

Hannah contemplated his announcement in silence for a moment. "If you need these new looms, surely we can find the money somewhere else without having to reduce wages."

He nodded with exaggerated patience. "Yes, yes we could. We could pension off Mrs. Hardy so we don't have to feed and clothe her. Or perhaps we could sell your fine new carriage and horses. Or would you prefer that the boys go without shoes?" He walked toward her and stuck his face almost up to hers. "What I'm saying, my ignorant wife, is that for our workers to prosper, you'll have to beggar our family."

"I don't believe you. I want the workers' wages restored."

Reiver's complexion turned purple, and a vein throbbed on his forehead. He loomed over Hannah, threatening her with his physical presence. "Haven't you heard a word I've said?"

She stood her ground. "I will make economies elsewhere so you'll still be able to afford your ribbon looms."

"It won't work."

Hannah raised her chin and looked him straight in the eye. "As the controlling shareholder of Shaw Silks, I want you to reinstate those wages. If you don't, I'll see my lawyer in the morning."

For one heart-stopping moment, Hannah thought Reiver would strangle her. But he just shook his head in disgust and strode for the door, cursing her under his breath. When he reached it, he turned, his face livid in the lamplight.

"You may have your own way this time. But be forewarned, Hannah. I'll see you rot in hell before I let you destroy this family!"

He slammed the door behind him and Hannah was alone with the dying fire and the sighing wind.

She stood quiet and still for a moment, waiting for the anger and tension to dissipate. When the room settled and became friendly once again, she sat down before the dying fire, put her feet up on the ottoman, and massaged her aching forehead. She so detested these confrontations.

She soothed herself with dreams of Samuel. She saw herself riding into his mining camp somewhere in California while he sat sketching some breathtaking mountain panorama. She would call his name, and when he turned and saw who it was, he would stare in shock and disbelief. But only for a second. He would run to her and sweep her off her horse into his arms, and crush her to him, kissing her eyelids, her cheeks, her willing mouth.

She missed him so.

Feeling the familiar sting of tears, Hannah fumbled for a handkerchief. "He's not coming back. Why must you torture yourself?"

Because her dreams of Samuel were better than nothing at all.

CHAPTER
❧ 14 ❧

CHRISTMAS was just a week away, and in two weeks 1855 would finally draw to a close.

Hannah stood at the frost-rimmed parlor window, watching the neighborhood children pile on their wooden sleds and shoot down the long, snow-covered slope of Mulberry Hill, their shrill screams and laughter lingering in their wake.

Snowfall always made her melancholy, for when she watched the thick, white flakes wheeling down from the flat gray sky to blanket the earth, she thought of Samuel. And the child she had lost. At least now, five years since his banishment, she could think of them without crying.

He was still in California, according to his last letter to the boys, but that was over eight months ago. He had never discovered gold with the other forty-niners, but he wrote enthusiastically of his travels up and down the West Coast. He never mentioned a woman. That saddened Hannah, for she hated to think of him being as lonely as she was.

She moved away from the window and lit an oil lamp, for the parlor became shadowed and cheerless on such a gray afternoon in spite of the fragrant evergreen boughs decorating the mantel and the tall Christmas tree in one corner, a custom adopted from England's Queen Victoria. But while the light warmed the room, it did not warm Hannah's heart.

She sat near the fireplace and closed her eyes, picturing Samuel as vividly as if he had just walked in the door, his warmth, his conspiratorial smile, his pale eyes dark with longing for her. She remembered his gentle, exciting touch, and her eyes flew open at her body's flaring response. She shook her head. She mustn't torment herself this way.

Samuel was gone. He wasn't coming back. She was alone. Her eyes filled with tears.

"Mr. Shaw!"

James looked over his heavy armful of logs at the dainty feminine figure approaching him, and his chest constricted painfully. With her ginger hair and rust-colored cloak, Georgia reminded him of the last autumn leaf skittering defiantly across the snow.

He stopped at the homestead's backdoor and waited for her. "Yes, Miss Varner?"

"I don't mean to bother you," she said, her breath coming in clouds of white vapor, "but Mrs. Shaw said that you might be willing to hitch up the cutter and take me into town. I need a few things at the general store."

Alone with Georgia Varner in the cutter . . . he hadn't been alone with her since the day he had fixed the squeaky cradle. "I'd be happy to."

"You are too kind, Mr. Shaw."

Minutes later James handed Georgia into the cutter and climbed in after her. He unfolded the heavy rug that was always kept on the seat and spread it across their laps.

"This should keep us warm," Georgia said, settling herself so close that their thighs touched.

James felt dizzy at her nearness. He picked up the reins, clucked to Racer, and they rode out of the stable yard, the clopping hooves muffled by the snow. Passing the base of Mulberry Hill, they waved to the children sledding. All but Benjamin waved back. He just stood there at the foot of the hill, staring.

"I loved to go sledding when I was a little girl," Georgia said wistfully. "There are plenty of steep hills to slide down on my father's farm, but you had to watch out for the trees."

James sat in silence. By her sidelong glance he knew she expected him to say something, but his tongue stuck to the roof of his mouth again and he feared he would sound foolish. He didn't want Georgia Varner to think him a fool.

She said, "Did you like to go sledding when you were a boy, Mr. Shaw?"

"My family was very poor when I was little. They couldn't afford ice skates, or even a sled for us boys, so we could go skating when the Coldwater River froze over. We always had to borrow someone else's."

"That must have made you feel real bad."

He turned in his seat, stunned. "How did you know?"

She shrugged. "That's the way I would feel. I'm proud and I don't like people feeling sorry for me."

"Why would anyone feel sorry for you? You're so pretty." The words popped out before he could stop them.

She didn't embarrass him further by thanking him for the compliment. She said, "They all felt sorry for me because I had a babe and no husband."

James kept his eyes on the road ahead. "No one is perfect, Miss Varner. Anyone can succumb to temptation."

"Others aren't so charitable, Mr. Shaw." She clasped her mittened hands together atop the blanket. "I was young and foolish, and I made a terrible mistake, one I'll never make again. I trusted the wrong man, and he betrayed me."

"Then he wasn't worthy of you, Miss Varner."

"You really think so? That makes me feel so much better, Mr. Shaw."

They fell silent, and minutes later the cutter drove up to the general store. James helped Georgia down and waited while she went inside with the promise not to keep him waiting very long.

True to her word, she emerged from the store not ten minutes later.

Once James got her settled and was about to turn the cutter toward home, Georgia grasped his arm. "Do we have to go back right away?"

He looked at the overcast sky and the still-falling snow. "Where would we go in this weather?"

"Anywhere. Everywhere! I'd like you to take me on a drive around the town. I've been so busy with the baby that I haven't seen much of it, you know."

"But it's snowing."

Her hazel eyes twinkled mischievously. "Then let's be daring, shall we?"

James, who ran his life as predictably as one of his machines, suddenly craved the unexpected as much as he wanted to kiss the vivacious young woman by his side. "As you wish," he said, clucking to Racer and turning the cutter in the opposite direction.

They drove away from Coldwater. Houses grew farther and farther apart, and snow-covered trees met overhead. Soon the only sounds were the dull clopping of hooves, the jingling of the harness, and snow dropping softly from weighted branches. James and Georgia were alone.

To his bewilderment, she kept sticking out her tongue. "What are you doing?" he asked.

She laughed. "Catching snowflakes. Haven't you ever done that?"

"Not since I was a boy."

"Do it now."

He ducked his head. "I'm thirty-seven years old."

Georgia raised her brows in surprise. "You seem much younger, more my age."

He felt more her age these days. "I'm a grown man. I'd feel silly."

"Why? No one's looking. There's just you and me alone on this country road." She placed her hand on his arm. "Please, Mr. Shaw. Don't be an old sour pickle."

James glowered at her in mock annoyance. "An old sour pickle, am I?"

He did just as the bewitching Georgia bade him. Whenever a wet flake fell on James's tongue, Georgia would laugh with childlike glee. He found himself laughing, too.

And more than anything he wanted to kiss her. But would she object to being kissed by a man almost twenty years her senior? Would she think him too bold? After the craven way her seducer had treated her, she had every right to be suspicious of any man, no matter what his age. Still, if he didn't make his intentions clear, someone else might claim Georgia's heart.

What would Samuel do in my shoes, he thought?

James knew the answer without having to think twice. He pulled back on the reins and Racer stopped in the middle of the road.

Georgia's laughter died. "What's wrong?"

"Nothing," he said softly, staring at those beguiling mismatched lips. "I'd just like to kiss you."

Her eyes clouded, then her gaze fell to her mittened hands. "Oh, Mr. Shaw, you're placing me in an awkward position."

"How is that?"

"I'm afraid that if I let you kiss me, you'll think me a—a loose woman." She raised her chin proudly. "And I'm not. I may have made a mistake once, but that doesn't mean I'm loose."

Again, the spirit of Samuel came to his rescue. "I would never do what that other man did. I'm not like that."

She gave him a wistful smile. "Then you may kiss me."

He may have been a shy man, but he didn't need a second invitation. He wrapped the reins around the brake, and though his cheeks burned, he slipped one arm around Georgia's slender waist and cradled her cheek in his other hand. Then he closed his eyes and kissed her.

Breathless, Georgia pulled away first. "Oh, Mr. Shaw . . ."

"James."

"James, I don't think I've ever been kissed that way."

He thought of his teachers, the skillful ladies in the Hartford brothel Reiver took him to once "to make a man of you," and he said, "Neither have I."

When he felt Georgia cling to him and shiver, he said, "Cold?"

"No. If you wouldn't think me too forward, I would like you to kiss me again."

By the time James and Georgia returned to the house, neither one felt cold. Mulberry Hill was empty, only the cross-hatched runner streaks showing that any sledders had ever been there at all.

"Mama, may I speak to you for a moment?"

Hannah looked up from her account books to find Benjamin standing in the study doorway, his clothes neat and tidy, and she was struck with how much he had grown. Tall and lanky like his uncle James, with his father's light brown hair and blue eyes, Benjamin reminded Hannah more and more of her own father, with his finely chiseled good looks.

When did my baby turn into a young man? she asked herself, sentimental tears stinging her eyes.

She fought them back and closed her account books. "Of

course you may, Benjamin. Close the door and sit down." Since she sensed this was to be an adult conversation, Hannah indicated the chair opposite her desk. She waited until he sat down before she said, "Now, what do you wish to speak to me about?"

"Women," he said.

Hannah coughed to hide her rising panic. "What do you wish to know?" She would let him speak his mind before deciding to turn this discussion over to Reiver.

"How can I make them like me?"

Hannah felt a catch in her throat. It seemed only yesterday that females were nothing but an annoyance to Benjamin, worthy only of having their hair pulled.

She cleared her throat. "You must be honest."

He frowned. "Honest? In what way?"

"You shouldn't try to be something you're not to impress a young woman." Hannah searched for an example. "If you knew a certain young lady likes men who play the piano, would you pretend that you could play just to make her like you?"

Comprehension lit Benjamin's face. "Of course not. Since I can't play, I would only make a fool of myself."

"Exactly. You must also realize that not every young woman you like will like you back, no matter what you do."

His face fell.

"She may choose someone else, and there's nothing you can do about it. As hurtful and unfair as it may be, that's life."

"Did you and Father like each other when you first met?"

Hannah decided honesty was best. "At first we didn't know each other well enough to know that." Now for the loving lie. "But after we were married, we discovered that we liked each other very much."

He nodded. "Will a woman like me if I give her gifts?"

"Benjamin, you can't buy a woman's love. A woman who likes you just because you give her gifts is not the type of woman you want."

"I understand."

But there is so much that you don't, Hannah thought. She said gently, "Is there a particular young lady you fancy, Benjamin?"

"No, Mama," he said. "There is no one special. I was just curious, that's all."

"Well, if you have any other questions, I would suggest that you ask your father."

"Yes, Mama." Then he thanked her and left.

When she was alone, Hannah rose from her desk and paced the study. Could Georgia be the reason for all his questions? Every time Hannah looked up, there was Benjamin talking to Georgia, following Georgia, sitting at Georgia's feet and playing with Elisabeth. But Georgia had eyes only for James.

Hannah sighed. Benjamin had to learn the hard, cruel realities of love sooner or later. As his mother, Hannah wished he would never have to deal with such heartbreak at all.

The sumptuous Christmas dinner was over.

Reiver patted his full stomach and beamed at Benjamin. "Those were fine birds, son," he said, referring to the two wild turkeys that Benjamin had shot for their feast.

"Thank you, sir." At fourteen, Benjamin had outgrown calling his father Papa.

Davey glared at his brother. "You never would've bagged them if I hadn't pointed them out to you."

"You're just jealous," Benjamin retorted, not wanting his prowess with a rifle diminished in Georgia's eyes, "because you couldn't hit the side of a barn."

"Boys, please!" Hannah said, rising. "Let's have a little peace from the two of you on Christmas day."

"Yes, Mama," they replied.

"My turnips were cold," Mrs. Hardy grumbled. "And the baked onions had no flavor. Hannah, I told you that the cook should have added a pinch more sugar to them."

"She'll remember next time, Mrs. Hardy," Hannah said patiently. "Now, shall we all retire to the parlor and open our gifts?"

Georgia, who had dined with the family, rose and picked up the baby from her nearby basket, causing Mrs. Hardy to snap, "You shouldn't hold her all the time. You'll spoil her."

"This little angel? Nothing could spoil her."

Mrs. Hardy muttered under her breath that no one ever listened to her anymore and glowered at the young nursemaid.

They all filed out of the dining room. Hannah noticed how James lingered so that he could walk with Georgia, and she also saw the stricken look Benjamin was trying so manfully to hide.

To her surprise, Reiver joined her and placed his hand beneath her elbow. When she regarded him as if he had gone mad, he gave her an enigmatic smile and whispered, "It's Christmas day."

So, he had declared a truce for the holiday.

Once gathered in the parlor, with the crackling fire scenting the room with pungent wood smoke, everyone sat down while Reiver passed out the gifts. Each took turns opening one to the accompaniment of "oohs" and "aahs."

Hannah's thoughts were not on gifts this evening, but on her family, and on what the future held for them. Benjamin didn't trouble her, for he was a confident, charming young man whom everyone liked, just like her own father. Hannah was confident that he would outgrow his hopeless infatuation with Georgia. Davey, on the other hand, worried her. Though now eleven, he showed no signs of outgrowing his bitter envy of his older brother. Benjamin was better looking . . . Benjamin was their father's favorite . . . Benjamin was everyone's favorite.

Mrs. Hardy had aged much this year, growing frail and stooped, and Hannah feared her friend wouldn't be with them much longer. And as for herself and Reiver, the less said, the better.

Observing James seated beside Georgia, regarding her with such tenderness, Hannah felt renewed and hopeful. But baby Elisabeth brought her the most joy.

Reiver handed Georgia a small package. "I believe this is from Benjamin."

Georgia thanked him, her eyes sparkling. "Now, I wonder what this can be?" Inside was a tortoiseshell comb that Benjamin had bought from old Septimus Shively, the peddler. Georgia thanked him again.

Hannah wondered if she alone noticed her son's flush of pleasure and the mooncalf look he gave Georgia.

Reiver distributed another round of gifts and returned to Georgia. "I think this is a very special gift from James."

Hannah held her breath, hoping the girl would appreciate its special significance.

With flushed cheeks, Georgia tore off the paper and lifted the lid. "Ribbons!" she exclaimed, her eyes widening. "Ribbons to match my hair. Oh, thank you, James. This is the nicest present anyone has ever given me."

Benjamin flinched as if struck. How can she like plain old ribbons better than my comb? said his plaintive gaze.

"They're very special," James said, pushing his hair out of his eyes. "I had the man who mixes the dyes for our silks make up a special batch of that particular ginger color just for you."

Reiver added, "And that shade will never be sold to anyone else."

"My very own color? Just for me?" Her eyes became unnaturally bright. "I—I don't know what to say."

Judging by James's expression, Georgia's enthusiasm was reward enough, and when he opened her gift to him, a wool scarf that she had knitted herself, he looked as though she had given him a chestful of gold.

Finally, when all the gifts had been distributed, opened, and exclaimed over, Reiver stood up and removed a long, flat package from his coat pocket and faced Hannah. "Merry Christmas."

Hannah's face grew hot as she thanked him, conscious of all eyes on her. "Now what can this be?" she said, tearing the paper. "It's much to small to be a shawl or gloves."

Benjamin said, "You'll just have to open it and find out."

"It's very special," Davey added.

A special gift? From Reiver?

Hannah opened the box. Inside was the most exquisite necklace she had ever seen, perfectly matched opaque green stone beads supporting a carved dragon. "It—it's beautiful." She held it up for all to see and admire.

Reiver beamed. "It's genuine jade, from China, and hundreds of years old. I bought it from a China trader on his return trip."

"Humph," Mrs. Hardy grumbled. "Looks heathen to me."

Everyone ignored her.

"Let's see how it looks on you," Reiver said.

Hannah rose, handed him the necklace, and turned so he could fasten it around her neck. The jade felt curiously warm against the skin bared by her low-cut gown. She went to the mirror over the fireplace and stared at her elegant reflection.

Was it her imagination, or did the dragon writhe and stare back at her out of glowing eyes?

"The merchant who sold it to me said it once belonged to an empress," Reiver said, looking over her shoulder and meeting her gaze in the mirror. "I thought it fitting that you should have it."

What new ploy is this, Reiver Shaw? You've never given me anything this grand in all our years of marriage.

"It's lovely," she said, turning and kissing him on the cheek. "I shall treasure it."

By the time the clock on the mantel struck midnight, all that remained of Christmas day was a pile of torn wrapping paper scattered beneath the tree and the fire dying in the grate. Stifling yawns, everyone else had taken their treasures to their rooms and gone to bed. Only Hannah and Reiver remained to witness the holiday's demise.

Hannah turned from the window, where she stood staring at the clear starry night, and looked at Reiver seated in his favorite chair, watching the embers die.

She fingered her necklace. "Why did you give this to me?"

He looked up, his blue eyes surprised. "I wanted to give you something special, to thank you."

"Thank me? Forgive me if I seem incredulous, but ever since I gained control of your company, we have hardly been on the best of terms." She turned her attention back to the night sky. "I didn't expect you to give me anything for Christmas."

Reiver rose. "As much as it pains me to admit it, you were right about not cutting wages. Ever since I reinstated the workers' pay and rehired Constance Ferry from my competitor in Rockville, production has increased. No one is slacking off, and no one has left. If anything, more people than ever want to work for us."

He bowed gallantly. "You were right, and I was wrong." He straightened and smiled. "The necklace is my way of apologizing."

Hannah eyed him warily. "If you think I'll sign back control of the mill to you just because you've given me this necklace, you—"

"Lord, you are the suspicious one!" He laughed. "The necklace isn't a bribe. It's a token of my appreciation, nothing more."

"Forgive me once again if I seem suspicious of your motives, but you must admit that you haven't given me much cause to trust you lately."

He raised his hands in surrender. "This is Christmas—or what's left of it. I don't want to argue with you."

Hannah turned away from the window and went over to the tree. "James is quite taken with Georgia. I wonder if he'll ask her to marry him."

Reiver jammed his hands into his pockets. "It's the first time I've ever seen him interested in a woman. He's usually more comfortable consorting with his machines."

"He is thirty-seven. Maybe he wants to settle down before it's too late. After keeping company with machines all day, one would think he'd appreciate having a live woman to come home to." Hannah turned to look at him. "What do you think of having Georgia in the family?"

He shrugged. "What I think doesn't matter. If James loves her and wants to marry her, that's his choice."

Hannah looked surprised. "No objections to her past?"

He went over to the fireplace, took the poker, and jabbed at the dying embers. "I'm hardly in a position to judge anyone's morals, now, am I?"

"Decent of you to admit it," she muttered. Out of the corner of her eye, she thought she saw Reiver's hand tighten on the poker, but when he didn't raise it and come after her, she thought she must have imagined it.

She said, "You do know that Benjamin is infatuated with Georgia as well."

Reiver straightened and stared at her. "Our Benjamin?"

"Our Benjamin."

Reiver shook his head. "Well, I'll be . . ."

"You mean you haven't noticed the calf's eyes he makes every time she walks into a room?"

"I'm afraid I've had weightier matters on my mind."

Hannah massaged her temples. "I don't want to see him hurt. He may be fourteen years old, but he's still a baby in so many ways."

"Stop coddling him, Hannah. He's old enough to father a child."

She whirled on him. "Then you had better speak to him about a gentleman's responsibilities. One illegitimate child in this house is quite enough!"

Anger flashed in Reiver's eyes, then vanished. "Easy, Hannah," he said gently. "You're becoming distraught over nothing. I hardly think that Benjamin is going to seduce Georgia as if he were some English nobleman and she the upstairs maid." He smiled. "Anyone can see that Georgia is smitten with my brother. She will do nothing to encourage Benjamin, and this infatuation will die on the vine."

Hannah sighed. "You're right. The thought of Benjamin seducing Georgia is rather ludicrous."

"I will speak to him, though."

"I think that would be wise." She stifled a yawn. "It's time I retired." She wished him good night, gathered her skirts, and glided out of the parlor.

Once upstairs in her bedchamber, Hannah lit the lamp and turned down the coverlet, amazed that she and Reiver had actually just had a civil conversation.

She smiled cynically as she unhooked her jade necklace and put it away in the bureau drawer. Belonging to an empress indeed. As if Reiver would give a gift symbolizing power and strength to a wife whose iron will he despised. No, he was scheming to regain control of his mill, and she wondered what he would do next.

Once she had undressed and slipped into her nightgown, she hurried to bed and burrowed beneath the covers. In the darkness that hid her deep shame, she touched herself in every way that Samuel was wont to do, imagining him lying beside her, not thousands of miles and years away. But her body accepted the lie, just as she accepted her solitary release.

Downstairs, Reiver sipped his apple brandy, stared into the cold fireplace, and cursed himself for a fool.

He recalled the day Hannah had named her price for raising his mistress's child as her own, and what she had said: *Perhaps if I thought it would make you love me, I wouldn't hesitate. But I've come to realize that you'll never love me, no matter what I do.*

He remembered how she had paused hopefully, giving him the opportunity to deny it, but like a fool he hadn't.

Now he realized that she had handed him the key to her devotion on a silver platter, and he had knocked it aside.

Perhaps it was not too late. If only he could convince Hannah that he loved her, she would do anything for him.

Reiver set down his glass and steepled his fingers. He would have to proceed slowly and carefully.

His plotting done for the night, he rose and went upstairs to his own room.

Several days later Reiver took Benjamin hunting in the thick woods south of Coldwater, but shooting deer or pheasant was not uppermost in his mind.

Walking silently through the forest, his rifle cradled in the crook of his arm, scanning the pristine snow for tracks, Reiver was about to bring up the subject of women when his son startled him by asking, "Father, why did Mr. Tuttle shoot you?"

An unnatural, expectant hush fell over the woods, as if every squirrel, bird, and deer stopped, waited, and listened for Reiver's reply.

He took a deep breath and said, "He shot me because his wife and I were lovers." He looked at his son. "Do you know what that means?"

Benjamin gave him a scornful, curiously adult glance. "Of course I do, Father. I'm not a child. One . . . hears things from one's fellows."

Reiver nodded, then paused, wondering exactly what to say next. "Are you angry with me for what I did?"

"I'm more confused. You married Mama. Why should you"—he turned beet red—"want to—to fornicate with another woman?"

"Because I loved Cecelia—Mrs. Tuttle—long before I met your mama."

Benjamin scowled and reached beneath his brown wool cap to scratch his head. "Now I'm more confused than ever. If you loved another woman, why did you marry Mama?"

Following a winding stream deeper and deeper into the woods, Reiver explained how much he needed the Racebrook land for the mill, and how he had had to marry Hannah Whitby to get it.

He stopped and placed his free hand on Benjamin's shoulder. "So you see, son, love often has nothing to do with marriage. And I hope you won't be angry with me for loving another woman instead of your mother."

Conflicting loyalties warred on Benjamin's face. "You're my father." As if that absolved Reiver of any wrongdoing. "Mama must have been very hurt when she found out about you and Mrs. Tuttle."

"Not so much hurt as angry."

So angry that she had an affair with your uncle Samuel, Reiver thought. But he would never say that to Ben.

Reiver said, "She never would have known if Tuttle hadn't shot me. I was always discreet, as a gentleman should be in these matters. But she found out, and felt that I had betrayed her."

"Mrs. Tuttle is dead now, isn't she?"

"Yes," Reiver said over the lump that suddenly formed in his throat, "but I loved her and will always miss her."

Benjamin kicked at the snow and said nothing, though Reiver could tell he wanted to.

"Your mother has never understood me," he continued. "All she could think about was her own hurt. She couldn't see that I loved Mrs. Tuttle, and forgive me. But then, women are strange creatures, not like men at all."

This piqued Benjamin's interest. "In what way?"

Reiver crouched down to examine some fresh tracks in the snow. "They're delicate creatures of emotion. They're ruled by their feelings rather than their intellect, which is considerably less than ours. That makes it difficult to reason with them." He rose. "Other men understand why I had to be with Mrs. Tuttle, but women are much less tolerant."

"If Mr. Tuttle was so understanding, why did he try to kill you?"

"That's different. He saw that I was stealing his property. A man never lets another man take his property, son, whether it's his wife or his land. It's part of being a man. Remember that. And as much as getting shot hurt, I respected Tuttle for coming after me. I would have done the same in his situation."

They walked on, snow crunching underfoot and branches snagging their clothes. In the distance some small unseen animal went crashing through the underbrush.

Benjamin, taking advantage of this newfound camaraderie with his father, asked, "Did you fornicate with many women before you fell in love with Mrs. Tuttle?"

Reiver frowned at him in mock severity. "Where did you learn such language? I should wash out your mouth with soap."

Benjamin turned red. "The fellows."

"What I do with women is my own business. A gentleman never boasts of his conquests, especially to 'the fellows.' He must protect a woman's reputation whether she's well-bred or a servant, and he must never take advantage of the powerless and the weak. Do you understand?"

"Yes, Father." Benjamin took a deep breath and blurted out, "What do you think of Georgia?"

"I think she's very pretty and very sweet. But you're to leave her alone."

"Why?" Benjamin wailed.

"First of all, your uncle James wants her."

"But he's so—so old!"

Reiver suppressed a smile. "Perhaps Georgia sees him as mature and settled. Even if your uncle didn't want her, remember what I just said about never taking advantage of the powerless?" When Benjamin nodded reluctantly, Reiver added, "Georgia is a servant in my household. I'll not have a son of mine seducing servants."

"Yes, Father."

Reiver grasped his son's shoulder. "Don't be disappointed, son. I know you like her, but there will be many other women, believe me. You're handsome, smart, and the heir to Shaw Silks. Women are attracted to handsome, smart, wealthy men."

"She thinks I'm still a boy, not worth a second look."

"When you're older, I'll introduce you to a special lady friend of mine, and she'll teach you all that you need to know about that part of being a man, just like she taught me and your uncles."

Benjamin's face brightened. "I've heard the fellows talk about such women. They say that kind are quite"—his blue eyes twinkled expectantly—"disreputable."

Reiver thought of the Countess and her diverse collection of women and smiled. "They are most certainly that, but they can teach a young man much about women and the world."

"When will you take me to meet this lady friend of yours?"

"Not until you're sixteen."

Benjamin's face fell. "That's two years away!"

"You mustn't be impatient. And you must promise not to tell your mama. She wouldn't understand. Or Davey. He'd be jealous."

"It will be our secret, Father."

They walked on, and didn't return home until Benjamin had shot a doe.

CHAPTER
❧ 15 ❧

THE spring of 1856 found all of Coldwater talking about nothing but the evils of slavery, especially after abolitionists led by Connecticut native John Brown killed five proslavery settlers in Kansas. James Shaw, however, could think of nothing but Georgia Varner.

His obsession had only one cure.

So he waited for the perfect day, one warm, sunny morning in late May. Then he put on his Sunday best, hitched up Racer, and drove to the main house, where he found Georgia in the nursery, kneeling on the floor some distance away from Hannah, who was holding a standing baby Elisabeth around the waist.

Georgia extended her arms. "Come to me, Lizzie. Come to Georgia."

"Go to Georgia," Hannah whispered, letting go.

Elisabeth stood there teetering for a moment as if undecided whether to flop down or walk. Then she got a steely look of determination in her wide blue eyes, hurled herself toward Georgia, and wove across the floor like a drunken sailor.

"You did it!" Georgia cheered, her hazel eyes sparkling as she caught the laughing baby and lifted her triumphantly over her head.

Hannah sat there, beaming as proudly as if she were Elisabeth's real mother. When she noticed James standing in the doorway, she rose and dusted off her skirt. "You were just in time to see Lizzie take her first steps," she said. "We're quite proud of her."

"And so you should be," James said, entering the room, his eyes on Georgia.

Georgia's gaze took in his clean dress shirt with its high collar points, gold brocade waistcoat, and immaculate hands. "Why are you all dressed up?"

He swept his hair off his forehead. "I have something important to do today, and I'd like you to come with me." He glanced at Hannah. "That is, if you can spare her for a while."

Hannah took the baby. "Oh, I suppose I could watch Lizzie myself for the rest of the morning."

James extended his hand to Georgia and helped her to her feet.

"Let me get my bonnet and I'll be right with you," she said.

When Georgia left the room, James said to Hannah, "I've noticed that Ben's been cold toward me lately, and I can't understand why. Would you know?"

Hannah hoisted Lizzie into her arms. "He's sweet on Georgia, too, and sees you as his rival."

James rocked back on his heels in surprise. "Ben sweet on my Georgia?" Then he nodded ruefully. "The comb he gave her for Christmas . . . I should have realized . . . but I'm such a dunce when it comes to reading people."

"No, you're merely a man in love wearing blinders. Reiver spoke to him, and while he's heartbroken, he realizes that Georgia is already spoken for."

James hoped that after today Georgia would be more than spoken for.

When she appeared at the door in her new bonnet trimmed inside the brim with copper-colored ruching and a big satin bow tied under her chin, James found it difficult to breathe.

Georgia smiled at him. "Shall we go?"

He nodded and offered her his arm.

Once outside, Georgia said, "Now, what is this important something that you have to do?"

"You'll see." James handed her into the carriage and got in beside her. He drove in silence for ten minutes, skirting the town, then stopped and handed Georgia down.

"What a lovely spot," she said, looking around at the small, still pond surrounded by magnificent white birches and maples.

"I used to come here often as a boy," he explained, "when I needed solitude." He looked around. "It's so tranquil."

He took Georgia's hand and led her over to a collection of

boulders at the water's edge. One bore an indentation that created a natural seat. "I used to pretend that I was a king, and this was my throne." He ducked his head. "Since you're as beautiful as a queen, why don't you sit there today?"

Georgia sat down and giggled. "Queen Georgia of Coldwater . . . sounds rather grand for such a simple country girl, doesn't it?"

"You are a queen to me," James said gravely. He took her hand and fell down on one knee. "And I'd like to make you my wife, if you'll have me."

She stared at him, her eyes wide and bright. "Oh, James . . . I—I don't know what to say."

She's going to refuse me, he thought, panicking. She thinks I'm too old. "I—I realize that we haven't known each other for very long," he began, his tongue sticking to the roof of his mouth again, "but I do love you, Georgia, and I know I could make you happy, if—"

"Yes."

He blinked. "Yes?"

"Yes, I'll marry you, James."

"You will?" He jumped to his feet, his heart pounding out of control. Then he grasped a laughing, beaming Georgia around the waist and helped her down from the "throne," twirling her around before her feet could touch the ground.

Dizzy with happiness, he set her down and hugged her. "You have made me the happiest man in Coldwater!"

"And you have made me the happiest woman on the face of the earth." Georgia wrapped her arms around his neck, stood on tiptoes, and kissed him.

With those mismatched lips pressed delightfully against his, James wanted to kiss her deeply with his tongue, as the Countess's girls had taught him, but he restrained himself. There would be time enough for that and much more once they were wed.

He pulled away.

Georgia looked at him, her great hazel eyes hurt. "Don't you like my kisses, James?"

"I like them fine." He blushed. "Too well."

She smiled. "You're my betrothed now. You may kiss me as much as you like."

James stared at the tips of his shoes. "I fear that if I do that, I'll turn into the kind of man who shamed you."

Georgia's eyes filled with tears. "Oh, James, you could never be like him if you tried. Anything you did would never shame me."

"I still want to wait until we're married."

She smiled up at him. "Then we had better marry quickly, or I shall go out of my mind."

He drew her into his arms and tucked her head beneath his chin. "I'd like my brother Samuel to come to the wedding."

"Mrs. Shaw told me about him. He's the artist who did that beautiful picture of her and went to California."

"Now he's in Australia, according to the letter Benjamin received last month."

Georgia stood back and smiled. "Before we can invite your brother to our wedding, we have to tell the others. Perhaps we can make an announcement tonight at dinner."

James thought of Benjamin and shook his head. "I'd rather tell them personally, if you don't mind."

"Just as long as you tell them."

James grinned and kissed her again.

Benjamin took the news of his uncle's betrothal better than Hannah expected. When Reiver told him that evening before dinner, the stalwart Benjamin turned pale and his eyes grew unnaturally bright, then he pulled himself together and said that he wished James and Georgia every happiness.

He repeated his good wishes that evening at the dinner table, making Hannah glow with pride at her son's newfound maturity.

"When do you wish to marry?" Hannah asked them. "Fall is a beautiful time of year for a wedding."

James said, "We want to invite Samuel, so we'd wait until he could come home."

Hannah tensed, her eyes darting to the head of the table, where Reiver sat as still as stone.

"I wouldn't have my heart set on it," Reiver said.

Davey said, "I don't think Uncle Samuel is ever coming back."

"Why should he?" Mrs. Hardy muttered. "He's probably happier where he is."

Hannah took another sip of soup, her mind whirling. Samuel back in Coldwater . . .

Georgia said, "There must be some way we could tell him." She glanced at her fiancé. "James does have his heart set on his brother being here for our wedding."

"I could write him another letter," Benjamin suggested.

"No, I shall," Hannah said, avoiding looking at her husband. "But you two mustn't get your hopes up. Australia is a long journey to make just to come home for a wedding."

"Perhaps Uncle Samuel would come home for good," Davey suggested.

But Hannah knew Reiver would never allow that.

Later that evening, just as Hannah was about to go upstairs, Reiver stopped her in the downstairs hall.

He extended his hand. "Come for a walk with me. It's a beautiful moonlit night."

She eyed his hand warily before letting him tuck her own through the crook of his arm.

Outside, a huge full moon hanging low in the star-strewn sky almost rivaled the sun in brightness, though this light was cool and silvery. Hannah and Reiver needed no lamp to guide them as they strolled around Mulberry Hill, now carpeted with green spring grass instead of snow.

She waited until they were far enough away from the house to be overheard before saying, "Are you going to let Samuel come home for James's wedding?"

"Why not?" Reiver replied. "He's been gone for almost seven years." He looked at Hannah, his expression in shadow and therefore unreadable. "I'm assuming that you don't feel the same way about him."

"I don't." She looked away.

"I'm delighted to hear it. Otherwise, having him here would prove most awkward for all concerned."

They walked on in silence.

Suddenly Reiver stopped and turned to face Hannah, his blue eyes looking black in the moonlight. "Write to Samuel and invite him to James's wedding. Tell him that I want to let bygones be bygones between us, and that he's more than welcome to come back to Coldwater."

Hannah fought to keep her voice soft and level so it wouldn't carry. "Why don't you just let sleeping dogs lie?" When he raised his brows, she plunged on. "I have no more feelings for Samuel, but perhaps he still harbors deep feelings for me."

"As long as you don't reciprocate them, there should be no problem." He offered her his arm. "It's getting late. Shall we go back?"

Hannah placed her hand on his arm, and they strolled back to the house.

Once she was alone in her bedroom, she sat up in bed and hugged her knees. Why was Reiver suddenly championing Samuel's return? Hannah refused to believe that her proud husband was ready to forgive and forget.

Vivid memories she had suppressed for years assaulted her. Samuel's friendship during that lonely, confusing first year of her marriage, his many kindnesses to simple Abigail, that wild afternoon in his studio when he had burned away her feelings of worthlessness in a heated blaze of passion . . .

To have him back in Coldwater . . . how would she ever endure it?

She wrote to Samuel the following morning.

A few weeks later Hannah was filling in for an absent worker in the packing room when Reiver burst in, his face flushed with excitement.

"Hannah, let someone else do that," he said. "I've got to talk to you."

She looked up from her work. "There is no one else to do this. Bridget is sick, and this shipment has got to go out today."

"Then let it wait." He stood there, shifting his weight from one foot to the other impatiently.

Hannah rose and followed him outside into the warm June morning, matching his long, quick stride. "Now, what is it that you have to discuss with me?"

"Nate Fisher is selling the Bickford farm."

Hannah stopped and stared at Reiver, who kept on walking. When he realized that she wasn't following, he stopped and turned.

She asked, "Who told you this? And why is he selling? Uncle Ezra's grandfather established that farm. It's been in the family for over a century."

"Roger Jones told me when I went to have Racer shod this morning," Reiver replied. "He heard it from Nate himself just yesterday. Apparently Nate thinks there's no future in Coldwater, so he's selling out, packing up and taking his family out west."

She caught up to Reiver. "I can see that this news interests you. May I ask why?"

"Because I want to buy that farm."

Hannah's eyes widened in astonishment. "Buy it?" Before Reiver could say a word, she added, "Of course. To expand Shaw Silks further someday."

"You understand."

"Why are you so surprised? I doubt that you would want to make farmers out of Benjamin and Davey."

"Certainly not." He looked back at the mill, his eyes shining with pride. "All this will be theirs one day." He turned back to her. "So, do I have your permission to buy it?"

"You're actually asking my permission?"

"You do own controlling interest in the mill."

Hannah gathered her skirts and walked toward the house. "You surprise me. I had expected demands from you, not a request."

He shrugged. "What good will demanding do? We'll just start arguing, and I'm tired of fighting with you."

"Oh, I had thought you rather enjoyed our arguments."

He regarded her with a certain gravity. "You're wrong."

What sort of game is he playing now? Hannah wondered, walking the rest of the way back to the house in silence. It was so unlike Reiver to request anything of her. He usually ran the mill as he saw fit, trying to get away with as much as possible, then arguing with her when she stated any objections. It was as if he were finally acknowledging her control of his mill, and that made her suspect his motives all the more.

Once back in the house, Hannah got out the account books and did some quick calculations while Reiver waited. "If you want to buy the farm, we'll have to get a loan," she said.

"You'll agree to it?"

She nodded.

"Good. I'll visit some Hartford banks and see about it." He smiled ruefully. "All except Tuttle Senior's, of course."

"Quite prudent of you, under the circumstances." Hannah rose. "Now I shall get back to my packing."

Walking past Reiver, Hannah was surprised when he placed a restraining hand on her arm. He said, "Thank you for not fighting me on this, Hannah."

"I want what's best for Shaw Silks, too. If you think acquiring the Bickford farm will benefit us in the future, then go ahead."

"I will." He kissed her lightly on the cheek and left.

Back in the packing room, listening to the hum and clatter of the looms and feeling the floor vibrate beneath her feet, Hannah pondered the subtle change in her husband over the last few months. First he seemed willing to allow Samuel to come home. Now he had actually consulted her first before going ahead with a project for the mill.

That kiss on the cheek had been the biggest surprise of all, since their physical relationship had died long ago.

"We'll see, Reiver Shaw," she said aloud, stacking spools of thread in their boxes. "We'll see."

Reiver flung his silk top hat across the kitchen, his face flushed and his stocky form taut with rage. "None of the banks will lend me any money."

Hannah placed a loaf of freshly baked bread next to the smoked ham in the basket she intended to bring to poor sick Bridget's family. "That's surprising. How many banks did you go to?"

"Every one in Hartford." He raked his hand through his hair. "And they all turned me down. They're all cautious with this talk of a possible insurrection. If I manufactured armaments, like Colt or Smith and Wesson, they'd be happy to loan me as much money as I needed."

Hannah added a jar of blueberry preserves to the basket. "Well, I guess that puts an end to our buying Nate's farm."

Reiver paced the kitchen like a caged panther. "Something's not right. Shaw Silks is a solvent company with a bright future.

There's no reason any bank should turn us down for a loan. Unless . . ." He rubbed his chin.

Hannah looked up from her task. "Unless what?"

"Unless someone told them not to."

A summer breeze blew through the open kitchen window, carrying the sound of Georgia's laughter as she chased Elisabeth across the lawn.

Hannah stared at Reiver. "You think the banks are purposely refusing to do business with you? But why?"

A muscle twitched in his wide jaw. "Think, Hannah. Who has cause to hate me so much?"

"Amos Tuttle. But surely you don't think he would—"

"Use his influence to keep my company from succeeding? I wouldn't put anything past him." He went to the window and stared out, hands on hips. "Remember Tuttle Senior wrote off my first loan because I didn't press charges against his son for shooting me, but he didn't promise to give me another loan, either. And who knows? Perhaps he asked all of his banking cronies not to lend me money."

"I didn't think bankers allowed personal feelings to stand in the way of profit."

"Most of them don't, but I wouldn't trust Tuttle."

Hannah added some molasses cookies, then covered the basket with a clean linen cloth. "It's too bad Samuel isn't here. I'm sure he'd lend you the money from the sale of his lithographs, as he used to."

Reiver gave her an odd look. "But he's not, so we'll have to get the money by some other means."

Hannah settled the heavy basket into the crook of her arm. "I'm going to bring this over to Bridget's house. I shall be back shortly."

On the way to Bridget's, Hannah thought about Amos Tuttle being the cause of Reiver not getting a loan. On the way back from Bridget's, she came up with an idea that might make him change his mind.

A week later Hannah stood before the unimposing facade of the National City Bank and fought down the butterflies in her stomach.

When she had told Reiver she intended to go to New York

and speak to Amos Tuttle directly, he exploded. What could she possibly hope to accomplish? And what would Tuttle think if Reiver Shaw sent his wife to fight his battles for him?

Hannah remained adamant. Reiver finally agreed to let her try, but only if he accompanied her.

So here she was, standing in front of Tuttle's bank on a hot summer's day, with Reiver waiting in a carriage around the corner.

She went inside, and a clerk escorted her to Amos Tuttle's upstairs office. While waiting, she forced herself to remain composed and rehearsed what she planned to say.

"Mrs. Shaw?"

She looked up to see Amos Tuttle standing in the doorway.

Gone was the ebullient whey-faced young man Reiver delighted in disparaging. This Amos Tuttle was a gaunt, middle-aged man who looked twenty years older, with meticulously groomed thinning hair and a hard, weary face sculpted by suffering and disillusionment. He had the look of a man who was cared for solely by servants.

Hannah hesitated. Would he regard her as his enemy's wife and send her packing? To her relief, a flicker of something akin to sympathy flared deep within his eyes.

Betrayal forged an undeniable bond.

"Mr. Tuttle . . . thank you for agreeing to see me."

"Come in." He stepped aside so she could precede him, then he shut the door to his spacious, elegantly appointed office and offered her a seat in a plush leather chair. "I must confess that I'm surprised to see you here, Mrs. Shaw, and quite curious as to why you would seek me out, under the circumstances." He sat down behind his wide mahogany desk and leaned back in his chair.

Hannah took a deep breath. "I have come to ask a favor for my husband."

Tuttle's hard face turned so red, Hannah feared he would have an apoplectic fit. He jumped to his feet and glared down at her out of narrowed, outraged eyes. "Have you no pride, Mrs. Shaw? After the way your husband betrayed you, making you the laughingstock of Coldwater, you would lower yourself to come here and ask a favor of me for him?"

Though her cheeks burned at his insult, Hannah remained

calm. "Yes, I would, and you'll understand when I explain why."

"This should be interesting." He sat back down. "Proceed."

Hannah told him what had happened when Reiver went to the Hartford banks for a loan to buy the Bickford farm, and how he had been turned down repeatedly.

She faced Tuttle squarely. "We think that you are behind this ostracism, and that you have asked the other Hartford bankers to refuse to deal with the Shaws."

He burst out laughing, a thin, wheezing sound. "I've never heard anything so absurd in my life."

Yet Hannah detected a blatant falseness in his tone.

"Besides," he added, "even if it were true, you'd have a devil of a time proving it."

She rose. "I agree. But I'm sure you are behind this because it is exactly the sort of thing I would do if I were in your shoes."

"Would you, now?"

"Without hesitation." Hannah strolled over to a large window overlooking crowded Wall Street. "Do you know what my husband had to agree to before I would take Cecelia's daughter?"

"No, Mrs. Shaw, I don't," came his strained reply.

"My price was a controlling interest in Shaw Silks."

Tuttle's eyes bulged. "He gave it to you? Without a fight?"

"Yes, he did, but not without a fight. For all of Reiver Shaw's many faults, he loved Cecelia and he loves their daughter." She looked at him. "He chose his daughter over his silk mill. Now I legally control sixty percent of the company."

"I don't believe it. Shaw would never—"

"If you need proof, I'll give you the name of my lawyer and he will substantiate my claim. Reiver continues to run the mill, of course, and as a sop to his considerable pride, we let the rest of the world think that he still controls it. But he doesn't."

"You do surprise me, Mrs. Shaw. When I first met you at dinner that night, I thought you were a lovely and charming woman, eager to please her husband, but not particularly strong-willed. I never suspected you of being so—so—"

"Devious, Mr. Tuttle?"

He spread his hands in an apologetic gesture. "Clever is the word I would have used."

Hannah raised her chin. "You were not the only victim of Reiver's selfishness. I had to endure being the object of gossip, and my children the taunts of their school friends. I will never forgive my husband for subjecting my sons to that as long as I live."

She smiled. "But I digress. If you agree to speak to your fellow bankers in Hartford and persuade them not to ostracize Shaw Silks, both of us will benefit."

"I fail to see how I will benefit at all."

"If the company should fail, Reiver's dreams would be destroyed, true. But if Shaw Silks prospers, I will continue to control it." She raised her brows. "Wouldn't that be punishment enough for a proud man, to see his mill prosper and to know that it will never be his again?"

They locked gazes for what seemed like an eternity. Hannah held her breath and prayed.

"How do I know you won't return control of the company to your husband?"

"If I did that, I'd put myself in Reiver's power again. He could divorce me or take another mistress. Then where would I be?"

Tuttle nodded. "I take my hat off to you, Mrs. Shaw. You'd do a Borgia proud."

She was relieved he couldn't see her knees knocking beneath her long skirts. "It's a rather fitting revenge, don't you agree?"

"Most fitting. Why kill a man quickly when you can make him suffer and kill him slowly?"

"Exactly." Hannah paused. "So, you will talk to your Hartford banker friends?"

"I'll see what I can do."

She thanked him and turned to leave.

"Mrs. Shaw?"

She turned back. "Yes, Mr. Tuttle?"

His hard face twisted with pain. "How is Cecelia's daughter?"

"She is a sweet, happy little girl, as beautiful as her mother, and I love her and care for her as if she were my own."

Having told Tuttle what he yearned to know, Hannah left his office without a backward glance.

• • •

"Well, what did he say?"

Hannah seated herself across from Reiver in the carriage and settled her skirts about her. "Nate's farm is as good as ours."

Reiver let out a loud whoop of triumph that caused a passerby to stare through the carriage window. "So the bastard was behind it after all."

"He wouldn't admit it," Hannah said, "but I think he was."

Reiver grinned and shook his head as if he was unable to believe his good fortune. "What did you say to him that made him change his mind? I'm surprised he agreed to see you at all."

"I threw myself on his mercy, that's all. I told him that if Shaw Silks didn't get this loan, it would surely fail. And if that happened, my children—including Cecelia's daughter—and I would be destitute."

"You mean to tell me that he agreed to talk to the Hartford bankers because he felt sorry for you? That I find hard to swallow."

"Why? Amos Tuttle is a very compassionate man." And a hard and bitter one, thanks to you. "He couldn't bear to hurt a helpless woman and her children."

Before Hannah could blink, Reiver was at her side, holding her hand. "Thank you, Hannah. I'll remember what you did today as long as I live."

He brought her hand to his lips and kissed it.

Hannah recoiled at his touch. She drew away and fussed with her collar. "Shouldn't we be getting back to the train station?"

Reiver nodded and returned to his side of the carriage, signaling the driver to be off.

But he didn't stop staring at his wife.

CHAPTER
❧ 16 ❧

HANNAH thought it fitting that the Bickford farm now belonged to the Shaws, just retribution for all she had suffered at the hands of her own cold, uncaring relatives.

She stood beside the dry-stone wall bordering the tobacco field where she had once toiled, so stooped over that she thought she'd never straighten her spine again. The plants no longer shivered in the warm summer breeze, for they had all withered and died from Nate's neglect and been cut down to rows of ugly stubble. Someday houses for the Shaw workers would rise in their place.

"Hannah?"

She adjusted her parasol to block out the sun and kept staring out over the field, caught up in her own dreams.

Reiver came to her side. "Are you looking over my latest acquisition?"

"I was reminiscing."

Reiver placed one foot on the stone wall and leaned on his knee. "This is the place we first met. Do you remember?"

"Of course. I almost collapsed because of the heat, and you insisted on taking me back to the house."

"Isn't it amazing how one incident can change a person's entire life?"

Hannah absently shooed away a horsefly. "Yes. If my parents' carriage hadn't skidded that winter night, I'd be still living in Boston right now, no doubt married to a doctor, like my father."

Reiver removed his foot from the wall and sat down facing

her. "Do you think your life would have been better if you hadn't come to Coldwater?"

She refused to spare him. "In many ways, yes."

He winced. "Candid, as always. Granted, our life together has been far from perfect, but it hasn't been all bad, has it?"

"No," she agreed. "You gave me Benjamin and Davey." And Samuel, by not loving me.

Reiver smiled slowly. "They've grown into fine young men any parent would be proud of."

"Yes, but I wish Davey weren't so envious of Benjamin."

"A little competition between brothers is to be expected. I wouldn't have them any other way."

Hannah frowned. "You're uncharacteristically sentimental today."

He shrugged. "I've been examining my life, too. I'm forty-three years old. The best years of my life are almost over. When you're young, you think you'll live forever." He looked out over the field. "Where does the time go?"

She regarded him closely, and for the first time she saw the subtle signs of aging. While Reiver's stocky physique was still as hard and sleek as it had been in his twenties, new lines scored his face, and his thick light brown hair revealed strands of silver.

She knew she should offer him some reassuring platitude, but she couldn't. "It's too hot out here. I'm going back to the house." And she turned to go.

"Wait." Reiver slid off the stone wall and walked over to her, his blue eyes beseeching. "It's time we put the past behind us, Hannah. I want us to start fresh." He looked back at the field. "We can pretend it's the summer of 1840 again and I've just rescued you from heat prostration."

"You ask the impossible of me."

"I've forgiven you for Samuel. Why can't you forgive me for Cecelia?"

"Because my affair with Samuel didn't hurt you as much as your affair with Cecelia hurt me."

His gaze slid to the ground. "I'm sorry I could never love you as you wanted to be loved, but I loved Cecelia long before I met you. I won't insult your intelligence by saying that I never did."

He sighed. "Now she's dead, and no matter how much I want it, she's never coming back."

Hannah flinched, surprised at how his love for Cecelia could still wound her.

The most she could offer him in the way of comfort was to say, "You have Elisabeth. Part of Cecelia still lives in your daughter."

"That is of some comfort to me, but I need more."

Hannah raised her brows.

Reiver grasped her free hand and stared deeply into her eyes. "I want peace between us, Hannah. I don't want us to spend what's left of our lives alone, two strangers living in the same house."

"By 'peace,' I'm assuming you wish to avail yourself of your husbandly rights?"

He grinned, his eyes sparkling as they roved over her appreciatively. "You're still a beautiful woman, Hannah. Of course I'd want to share your bed."

Now that Cecelia wasn't here.

"We don't love each other, and I doubt if we ever will." She drew her hand away. "I won't sleep with a man I don't love."

The light died in his eyes. "We can learn to love each other."

"But I don't have to."

And Reiver knew why.

Hannah adjusted her parasol and started back to the house. She fully expected him to explode and rail at her, but to her surprise, a subdued Reiver fell into step beside her, his hands clasped behind his back.

"I've been a fool. I've had a treasure under my nose all this time, and I've thrown it away."

Hannah stopped and faced him. "What nonsense is this?"

"I suppose I can't blame you for being so suspicious of my motives, but this time I am sincere." He bowed his head. "You've stood by me, Hannah. You've borne my sons and raised them into fine young men. You even adopted my illegitimate daughter." He looked beyond her. "I can't even fault you for the way you've run the mill."

"Coming from you, that is a high compliment."

"All I want is a second chance."

She resumed walking. "I'll have to think about it."

"You're the kind of woman who needs a man," he said, his voice low and seductive.

She shivered as if he had physically caressed her. "I have my children and the mill. Why should I need a man?"

Reiver smiled slowly, his gaze languid. "Don't you remember what it felt like when I kissed your neck and licked your breasts?"

Cheeks flaming, Hannah stopped and glared at him. "That will be quite enough!"

He just smiled. "Do you remember how you'd guide my hand to where you wanted me to touch you, and—"

She drew back her hand, but before she could slap him, Reiver caught it and pressed her wrist against his lips.

Hannah yanked her hand away. "Don't you dare touch me again!"

His eyes held a mocking twinkle. "But I like touching you. Your skin is as soft as Shaw silk."

"Why don't you go to a whorehouse and leave me alone? I'm sure they'd welcome your patronage."

Reiver laughed, for he had been doing just that. "I had forgotten what a little Puritan you can be." Then he raised his hands in surrender. "I'm sorry if I offended your great sense of propriety with my bawdy talk. I shan't do it again unless you give me your permission."

"That will never happen."

Reiver increased his stride. "Don't be too sure," he called back over his shoulder, and disappeared down the path.

By the time Hannah got back to the house, her head was pounding and she felt jittery, so she went upstairs to lie down.

"All this talk of making peace . . ." she muttered to herself as she unbuttoned her dress. "This is just a plan to get the mill back."

Reiver's words echoed through her mind: *I've been a fool. I've had a treasure under my nose all this time, and I've thrown it away.* Hannah shook her head. Did he really think she was so—so gullible as to believe such sentimental twaddle?

She stripped down to her chemise and pantalets and was heading for her bed when she caught a glimpse of her reflection in the mirror. She stopped and stared, wondering if Samuel would still find her desirable.

Even though she was a thirty-four-year-old matron, her body was still supple and slender, though her breasts were fuller—hardly a flaw in any man's estimation. Hannah thought the tiny lines radiating from the corners of her eyes added character and maturity to her face. Not one strand of silver marred her hair.

You're still a beautiful woman, Hannah, Reiver had said. *Of course I'd want to share your bed.*

Hannah sat down on the edge of the bed Reiver wanted to share and placed her aching head in her hands. Uncertainty niggled at her. What if her husband really had changed? What if he finally desired her as a woman? Shouldn't she give him a second chance?

"Don't fool yourself, Hannah," she said aloud, lying down. "That conniver will do anything to get the mill back. Even pretend that he loves you."

As she dozed off she dreamed of a man making love to her again, but it was Samuel's gentle hands caressing her, not Reiver's.

"When are you going to surrender?"

Hannah surveyed the dining room, ravaged from the crush of Shaw Silks employees and their families who had been invited to the main house to partake of refreshments and welcome in the first day of 1857. "I wasn't aware that we were at war."

Reiver leaned against the mantel and smiled slowly. "You know we are." He saluted her with a raised glass of claret. "You've been able to resist me so far, but I will win you in the end."

Hannah pretended to examine the glass punch cups for chips, but inside she felt the tense foreboding of a wild animal who hears the hunter's footsteps drawing inexorably closer.

Reiver had been stalking her. There was no other word to describe his calculated pursuit.

She gathered her skirts and headed down the hallway. Reiver followed, ever the hunter.

"That shade of green is very becoming on you," he said. "It's too bad it's imported French silk and not our own."

"I thought the color complemented my jade pendant," she

said, absently fingering the dragon. This past Christmas Reiver had given her matching teardrop-shaped jade ear bobs, another extravagant gift.

Hannah went to the front door and peered out through the sidelights. "Where is Mercy? She's supposed to clean up tonight."

Reiver stood too closely beside her. "It's New Year's Day. Give her a little time." He paused. "Why are you so skittish tonight, Hannah? Am I making you nervous?"

She turned, her taut nerves finally snapping. "I'm tired of your badgering!"

He raised his brows in affronted innocence. "Badgering? I think of it as courting my own wife."

"I don't wish to be courted! I want to be left alone."

"I don't believe that for a minute," he said, his voice soft and low. "Every woman wants to be wooed with soulful looks and sweet compliments."

"It's too late for soulful looks and sweet compliments," she replied, trying to keep the bitterness out of her voice and failing. "The time to woo me was when we were first married. I would have appreciated it then."

"Don't be such a crosspatch, Hannah. This is a new year, a time to look forward, not back to the past."

I mustn't let him wear me down, she told herself. I must resist him. I must.

Yet as loath as she was to admit it, when Reiver exerted himself, he could be damn near irresistible. Tonight, with the severe black of his frock coat accentuating his fair coloring and that sensual, teasing gleam in his blue eyes, he looked dangerously attractive.

Like a true predator, he sensed her thoughts changing direction and her weakening resolve. "What's 1857 going to hold for us, Hannah? Is it going to be another year filled with the same bitterness and blame, or are we going to write a new chapter in our lives?"

She stepped away from the door and ran her hands up and down her arms as if to warm them.

"Cold?" he asked. Before she could reply, he set down his wineglass, grasped her hands, and warmed them with his own, his compelling blue gaze trapping hers.

Standing there mesmerized, Hannah thought of the coming year, another year spent alone in her cold, empty bed, another year of barricading her emotions behind a wall of hard resolve, and she wavered. What could be the harm in accepting what Reiver offered?

Don't be a fool! a little voice inside her cried. He only wants his mill back.

Reiver's mouth hovered perilously close to hers. All Hannah had to do was close her eyes and surrender.

The thought was like a dash of cold water in her face. She pulled her hands away. "I think I hear Mercy now," she said. "If you'll excuse me . . ."

She left Reiver kissing air.

"Just you wait, Hannah," he said to himself as his furious eyes followed her retreating form. "I'll have you before the spring buds start to bloom."

Yet by the time spring came, Reiver still hadn't won his wife.

Hannah and Georgia sat in the private display room of Miss Zenobia Zola's Hartford dress shop, sipping tea and admiring bolt after bolt of colorful Italian and French silk brought out for their inspection. Although Hannah had been feeling out of sorts all morning, she had promised Georgia a visit to the dressmaker and didn't want to back out at the last minute, especially since James wanted his bride-to-be to have an extensive wardrobe befitting her new status.

Hannah fingered a soft blue slubbed silk enviously. "I long for the day I'll wear a gown made from Shaw Silks."

"Why can't we make cloth now?" Georgia asked, holding up a length of flattering forest green jacquard against her and admiring the effect in the long pier glass.

"The tariffs on imported silk are too low," Hannah explained. "If Congress would raise them, we'd be able to compete."

Georgia sighed. "It's all too complicated for me to understand. I just like wearing silk."

Hannah smiled in spite of the persistent sore throat that was spoiling her afternoon.

"What do you think?" Georgia held up the forest-green silk, then a dark brown one.

Hannah assessed one, then the other. "Both accentuate your

coloring, but the dark brown is much too drab. I think James would prefer to see you in something more colorful, like the green."

Georgia's face lit up with childlike delight. "I think so, too." Then she frowned at Hannah. "Why does your voice sound funny?"

Hannah dismissed her sore throat with a wave of her hand. "It's nothing."

Georgia looked guilty. "Why did you agree to come with me if you're sick? I could have waited."

Hannah smiled. "I'm not sick. I merely have a slight sore throat. And you need a little time away from Elisabeth. She's a darling little girl, but she's been running you ragged."

"I don't mind."

Miss Zola entered the room carrying a contraption that caught her customers' attention immediately.

Georgia said, "Is that one of the new hoops that all the ladies are wearing?"

"*Oui*, mademoiselle," Miss Zola said. "By wearing one of these beneath your skirts, not only do you give them a graceful bell shape that the gentlemen admire, but you also don't have to wear several layers of heavy crinoline."

She lifted her own skirt to demonstrate the advantages of the new collapsible hoop that resembled a bird cage. While Georgia exclaimed over the ingenious new invention, Hannah felt herself growing uncomfortably hot.

She fanned herself with her handkerchief. The weather was so unseasonably warm for late April.

Georgia looked at Hannah. "Do you think we should get one?"

"Of course." Hannah dabbed at her sweating brow with her handkerchief. "We may live in a small town, but that's no reason for us to be unfashionable."

"You must be careful when you sit down," Miss Zola warned them, "or the hoop will fly up in your face and display your unmentionables for the world to see." She placed her hand on her cheek in an attitude of dismay. "Most embarrassing, no?"

Georgia giggled.

"And," the dressmaker went on, "you must be careful going through doors. If your skirt is too wide, you may become stuck, and the gentlemen will have to push you through. Most embarrassing, no?"

Georgia squinted at Hannah. "Are you sure you're all right? Your face is so flushed."

"I'm fine. Now, shall we order some dresses and be on our way?"

By the time they finished at Miss Zola's, Hannah was racked with chills that grew worse all the way back to Coldwater. By the time the carriage pulled up to their front door, she was so dizzy she could barely stand and had to rely on Georgia to help her.

The minute they stepped into the hallway, Georgia called out, "Someone help us. Please!"

Mrs. Hardy, who had been dozing in the parlor, scowled at them. "Quiet down, will you? It's too noisy in here."

Georgia glared back at her. "You selfish old lady! Can't you see that Hannah's ill?"

Mrs. Hardy hoisted herself out of her chair, her wrinkled face furious. "Selfish, am I? See here, you snippy little upstart, I—" She stopped abruptly when she saw Hannah swaying on her feet. "Let's get her upstairs."

With Georgia on one side and Mrs. Hardy on the other, they managed to navigate the stairs and get Hannah into her bedroom, where she sank down on the edge of the bed.

"I—I feel so weak," Hannah murmured.

"You go for Reiver," Mrs. Hardy said to Georgia. "I'll undress her and get her into bed."

"Don't worry, Hannah," Georgia said, flying out the door in a flutter of ribbons. "You're going to be all right."

That evening the family gathered in the parlor to await old Dr. Bradley's verdict.

Reiver stood at the window with his hands clasped behind his back, staring out of glazed, unseeing eyes into the darkness. James sat with Georgia on the settee, stroking her hand, while the boys sprawled on the floor. Mrs. Hardy occupied the wing chair by the fire, knotting her fingers together in her lap. No one said a word, but the silence stretched as taut as a wire.

Finally Benjamin said, "Father, is Mama going to die?"

"Of course not, you idiot!" Davey snapped, punching his brother's shoulder.

Georgia burst into tears, and James drew her into his arms, murmuring reassurances. Mrs. Hardy just stared into the cold fireplace, her rheumy silver eyes misty.

Benjamin took a retaliatory swipe at his brother, causing Reiver to whirl around and growl, "Now stop it, both of you, before I box your ears. Damn it, your mother's sick, and the last thing any of us need is the two of you fighting!"

Both boys muttered their apologies and sat there in subdued silence.

They all sprang to attention at the sound of footsteps in the hallway. Dr. Bradley appeared in the doorway, his face grave.

Reiver went to him at once. "How is she?"

The doctor surveyed the room. "Not well, I'm afraid. She has a high fever and an infection in her lungs. Perhaps with diligent nursing, she will recover, but to be honest with you all, I don't hold much hope. I've seen several cases of this fever in Coldwater, and only one patient survived." He paused. "I'm sorry."

Georgia sprang to her feet, dabbing her eyes furiously. "Hannah won't die if I have anything to do with it. I want to nurse her."

Dr. Bradley said, "Mrs. Shaw can only have one nurse. And I must warn you that you run the risk of getting sick, too."

James took Georgia's hand, his eyes pleading with her not to make such a sacrifice.

"I have to," she said to him. "Hannah saved me when I had no place to go. It's the least I can do."

"I'll nurse her," Mrs. Hardy said from the depths of her chair. "You may be a fresh little upstart, but you're too young to die. I'm old and they'll be stitching mourning samplers in my memory soon enough. It doesn't make any difference to me."

"Neither of you will." Reiver rolled up his shirt sleeves. "She's my wife. I'll nurse her."

Benjamin sprang to his feet. "No, Father! What if you catch the fever, too?"

Dr. Bradley said, "The boy has a point, Mr. Shaw. You have your family to consider. We wouldn't want to lose both of you."

Reiver placed his hand on Benjamin's shoulder. "This is

something I have to do, son." He smiled. "Don't worry. I'll be fine." Then he turned to the doctor. "Now, what do I have to do?"

"First we have to cut her hair so it won't sap her strength. . . ."

Reiver bathed Hannah's flushed face and neck with cool water to try to bring down the fever that was devouring her. With her shorn hair, she looked as young and vulnerable as a baby.

Restless, she tossed her head, her clutching fingers trying to push away the mound of quilts piled on top of her. Reiver patiently drew her hands away and covered her again. Dr. Bradley had said they might burn the fever out of her if they kept her hot enough.

Fighting fire with fire, Reiver thought, wringing out the compress in a basin of cold water.

The sound of her labored breathing sent shivers down his spine. Every breath was a struggle for her, ending in an ominous rattle.

On this second full day of his vigil, Reiver himself felt drained and exhausted. When Hannah grew still, he dozed on a feather bed on the floor near her bed, but most of the time he did what he could to make her comfortable and waited for her to die.

Hannah dead . . . Reiver rubbed his stubble-roughened jaw. She had been a part of his life for seventeen years, sharing his bed, bearing and raising his sons. If she died, he would feel as if he had lost an arm or a leg. He would miss her and grieve for her.

Yet if she died, he would regain control of Shaw Silks.

And he did want his mill back, but did he want it at the price of Hannah's life?

He shook his head. "You unprincipled bastard." But he had always known that about himself.

Reiver placed his hand against her forehead. Her flesh felt as though it were on fire. The doctor said that if her fever didn't break soon and kept on rising, convulsions and death would certainly follow.

It wouldn't be long now.

Hannah moaned, mumbling something unintelligible.

Reiver put his ear closer to her parched lips.

"Samuel . . . come to me. I need you now. Where are you? So alone . . . alone." Her voice faded away into a whisper and ended in a choking cough.

A bitter smile twisted Reiver's mouth. On her deathbed all Hannah could think of was her lover.

A soft knock sent Reiver to the door. When he opened it just a crack, he found Georgia standing there as he knew he would, her tearstained face exhausted and bleak with worry.

"How is she?" she whispered.

"Not good," he whispered back. "The fever just keeps going higher." He looked back at the bed where Hannah lay tossing and turning. "She was delirious a minute ago, talking to herself."

"Poor Hannah." She sniffed into her handkerchief.

"How are the boys faring?"

"They're trying to be brave, but I can tell they've been crying, especially Davey."

Reiver shook his head in sympathy for his poor sons, then asked, "What time is it?"

"Almost two o'clock in the morning."

The Grim Reaper's favorite calling hour.

"I'd better get back to her," Reiver said, closing the door when Georgia went away.

No sooner did Reiver return to his chair than Hannah became agitated again, thrashing about with extraordinary force, flailing her arms as if fighting off death. Her breathing came faster and faster.

Reiver watched her, waiting for the end.

Without warning, Hannah sat bolt upright. Her eyes flew open, and she stared into the far corner of her bedroom at something only she could see.

"Mama?" she cried, and fell limp and lifeless against the pillows.

She was dead. The mill was his.

Reiver placed his head in his hands and closed his eyes. They flew open when he heard his dead wife sigh.

He placed his hand against her cheek, and the flesh felt cool to his touch, not the deep cold of death. The fever had peaked and broken, and now she slept.

He rose, relief and guilt flooding through him in equal measure, and staggered to the door. Flinging it open, he yelled, "Everyone! Come quickly! The fever's broken!"

Hannah would live after all.

Hannah sat up in bed and stared at her reflection in the hand mirror. She fingered her shorn locks and made a face of distaste.

"I look like a little boy," she said to Georgia.

"But a very pretty little boy," Georgia replied, taking away the lunch tray.

Hannah set down the mirror. "I'm just glad to be alive. I shouldn't care what I look like."

Georgia grinned. "All women care what they look like." Then her smile died. "You gave us all quite a scare."

"I think Benjamin and Davey most of all. They come to visit me every day, and sit so quietly like perfect little gentlemen. They don't even argue." Her eyes twinkled. "Imagine that!"

"The thought of losing their mama really put the fear of the Lord into them." Georgia headed for the door. "Well, enough of my chatter. I should leave you alone so you can get some rest. It's only been two weeks since your fever broke."

Hannah sighed. "I feel like it's been an eternity."

She lay back against the pillows. She knew she had come within a hairsbreadth of dying. In her delirium, she had seen her life unfold before her as if she were watching it from a great distance, one last look, she supposed, before bidding it farewell. She had even imagined that her mother was with her in the bedroom, as warm and loving as she remembered, coddled in a serene golden light. Reiver had said that she had called out for her mother just before her fever peaked.

Most surprising in her whole ordeal was the fact that Reiver had risked his own life to nurse her. Perhaps he felt something for her after all.

She dozed, and when she awoke, she found Reiver standing in the doorway.

He said, "I hope I didn't wake you."

"No, I was just dozing. I'm really quite tired of lying in bed all day. I want to be up and about."

"Well, today's your lucky day." He reached for her dressing

gown, which was draped over a chair. "Put this on and come with me."

Bursting with curiosity, Hannah put on her dressing gown, took Reiver's proffered arm, and let him escort her downstairs.

When she realized he was leading her toward the front door, she balked. "I can't go outside like this!"

"But I have a surprise for you."

Reiver flung open the front door. When Hannah stepped out onto the porch, she gasped in surprise, for everyone who worked for Shaw Silks stood there clapping.

Maria Torelli, Giuseppe the dye master's youngest daughter, dressed in her Sunday best, stepped forward with a large bouquet of wildflowers and, with a shy smile and a curtsy, presented them to Hannah.

Tears filled her eyes. "I—I don't know what to say. Thank you all so much."

Constance Ferry, who had returned to the company after Hannah had persuaded her husband to reinstate the wage cuts years ago, stepped forward. "I know I speak for everyone when I say that we were all praying for your recovery, Mrs. Shaw. Thank God our prayers were answered."

Hannah thanked them again, and the workers turned and headed back to the mill.

Back in the house, Hannah smiled at Reiver. "How sweet of them to do this."

"They all think the world of you," he replied. "James told me that while you were sick, the minute he walked into the mill in the morning, all the workers gathered around him and asked for you. And when they learned you were going to get well, they hugged each other and cried. Even some of the men."

Hannah stopped at the foot of the stairs. "That's because we don't exploit them. If you treat people fairly, you'll win their loyalty."

Reiver smiled wryly. "So you've always told me."

Once Hannah was back in bed, Reiver walked over to the window, his features somber. "Will you give me another chance now, Hannah?"

She ran her hand over the coverlet. "Reiver—"

"When you were dying, the thought occurred to me that if

you did die, the mill would be mine again." He studied her. "I can see that I've shocked you. I shocked myself by even thinking it." He walked over to the foot of her bed and stood there, his emotions baldly written on his face. "I know I haven't been a good husband to you, Hannah, but I didn't want you to die. I realized how empty my life would be without you, and it terrified me.

"I've done everything I can to win your trust, but—" He shrugged helplessly.

Little by little she felt the wall surrounding her begin to crumble. She had no illusions about Reiver. She could never surrender to him completely, but perhaps she could learn to get along with him and make something meaningful of the rest of their lives.

She slipped out of bed and walked over to him. "If you're willing to try again, so am I."

A huge grin split his face. "Hannah, I—"

"But I have to go slowly."

He knew what that entailed. "All I ask is another chance."

"Then you shall have it."

She hoped she wouldn't live to regret it.

"We can't wait any longer," James announced to the family members who were seated at the dining-room table.

Hannah said, "Can't wait for what?"

He brushed his hair out of his eyes and glanced at Georgia, sitting beside him. "We can't wait for Samuel to come home before we get married."

"The summer's almost over," Georgia said. "Before we know it, winter will be here." She made a face. "We don't want to get married in the winter."

When James asked if anyone had received a letter from Samuel, Hannah shook her head. "It's been a year since I invited him to your wedding."

Reiver looked around the table, his expression grave. "I think we all have to consider the fact that Samuel may be dead."

Hannah felt the blood drain from her face and she suddenly lost her appetite. He couldn't be dead. Not Samuel.

"If he were alive," Reiver continued, "I'm sure he would have responded to an invitation to his brother's wedding."

James reached for Georgia's hand and squeezed it. "That's what we thought."

Davey looked glum. "I always liked Uncle Samuel. He used to draw me pictures."

"I wish he had never gone away," Benjamin said.

"I warned him not to," Mrs. Hardy muttered, "but no, he wouldn't listen to me."

Hannah looked at James and Georgia. "Why don't the two of you go ahead with your wedding plans? Set a date and make the arrangements. Then if Samuel does return, he'll find he has a new sister-in-law."

Reiver said, "Since we're talking about weddings, this is as good a time as any. James and Georgia, Hannah and I would like to give you the Bickford house as a wedding present. Not the farm itself, of course," he added with a laugh. "I'm no fool. But if you want the house, it's yours."

Georgia's face glowed. "Oh, James, a house of our own to fill with babies."

James turned pink with pleasure. "We wouldn't have to live in the homestead." He rose and kissed Hannah on the cheek. "We'd be glad to accept the Bickford house."

Later, Hannah slipped out of the house into the warm August night and let the moonlight guide her path down Mulberry Hill. When she reached the homestead, she stopped but did not go inside. She folded her arms and stared up at the dark topmost windows, where Samuel's studio used to be.

She sensed rather than heard someone approach, but she didn't turn around.

"Georgia's looking for you," Reiver said. "It's time to tuck Elisabeth into bed. She's asking for her aunt Hannah."

"I can't believe he's gone," she said. "I want to mourn him, but I can't."

"I know. At least if we knew what happened to him . . ." His voice trailed off.

Hannah turned. "Is there some way we can find out?"

Reiver's wide jaw hardened. "I think we should let it go for both our sakes, don't you?"

She stepped back a pace and stared at him in shock. "Don't you want to know what happened to your own brother, Reiver?"

He shrugged. "Australia is at the end of the world. It would take too much time and money that could be better spent on the mill. Even then we still might not know. Surely you can see that."

Hannah bowed her head. "You're right."

He drew her hand through the crook of his arm. "Come back to the house. Elisabeth is waiting."

But Hannah couldn't stop thinking of Samuel.

Hannah lay the small bouquet of late yellow roses on Abigail's grave, then bowed her head in silent prayer that ended with a promise never to forget. A film of tears blurred her vision, so she didn't get a good look at the man standing at the edge of the cemetery, watching her.

When she blinked, he vanished.

Hannah shivered, but more with excitement than uneasiness. The man had been standing near a tall weeping willow tree, half-concealed by long green fronds that swept the ground, and too far away for her to get a good look at him. Still, he seemed so familiar.

"It was just a passerby, that's all," she told herself, striding through the cemetery's shifting, dappled light. Yet she found herself looking for him, unable to shake the feeling that he wanted her to follow him. She walked faster.

The homestead loomed ahead, quiet and empty. Or was it? Hannah walked around the building and stopped when she saw the open back door.

"Georgia?" she called, peering inside. "James?"

No answer. Just faint, echoing footsteps.

Heart pounding, Hannah rushed upstairs to what used to be Samuel's studio. The door creaked when she pushed it open. She wasn't alone.

He was standing in the middle of the room, his back toward her, but she knew who he was. Hannah held her breath, not daring to move for fear that she was dreaming.

Then he turned and she saw that he was real. Her hand flew to her mouth in shock.

"Hello, Hannah," Samuel said.

CHAPTER
❧ 17 ❧

AT least she thought the man standing there was Samuel.

His height hadn't changed, or his physique, though he looked much thinner. His hair, as dark and curling as she remembered, now fell to his collar, and two wide swaths of gray flared out from his temples. A gray-flecked beard concealed half of his handsome countenance. The ghostly pale blue eyes that Hannah remembered always brimming with laughter and understanding, now seemed curiously devoid of their former fire.

Uncertainty filled her. "Samuel?"

He didn't move. "Hannah . . . it's been a long time."

The voice, that unmistakable voice that had murmured such sweet endearments to her and sent her spirits soaring, sounded flat and weary.

"Eight years," she said.

"What happened to my studio?"

"Reiver turned it into a storeroom."

Hannah stood there, suddenly awkward and unsure. What should she do next? She wanted to fling herself across the dusty room into his arms, to feel the welcome hardness of his body against hers, to drown helplessly in his love again. Yet he made no sign that he would welcome her embrace, no tentative step toward her, no outstretched arms to enfold her.

Then she saw why.

She had noticed that Samuel held his right arm close to his body as an injured bird would protect a broken wing. Puzzled, she stared at it. Then she saw that the cuff of his coat sleeve had been shortened to just above the wrist, turned up, and sewn shut.

Samuel had no right hand.

The blood drained from Hannah's face as she stared goggle-eyed at where Samuel's hand used to be. The hand with its delicate touch that had evoked such pleasure, the hand capable of depicting such beauty in his paintings and engravings . . .

Because she knew he would disdain her pity most of all, Hannah tried to remain composed and unaffected, but the shock overwhelmed her. When the studio tilted ominously to one side and she swayed along with it, she gasped for breath and leaned heavily against the door to keep from fainting.

Samuel crossed the room slowly, his footsteps sending dust motes spiraling into the hot, stale air. When he reached her side, he made no attempt to touch her, just stared out of empty eyes. "I don't want pity," he said, each word clipped and strained, "yours most of all."

But he did need her strength. She took another deep breath to banish the light-headedness and moved away from the door. "You'll get no pity from me, Samuel Shaw." She stood on tiptoes and kissed him on the cheek. "Welcome home."

His eyes held hers defiantly. "Aren't you going to ask me what happened to my hand?"

"Not unless you wish to tell me."

He spoke as if he were repeating an uninteresting story he had told a hundred times before. "I lost it in a mining accident in Australia. There was a cave-in, and a ton of rock crushed my hand. The doctors had to cut it off."

Hannah cried inside when she thought of the pain he must have endured, and the horror when he realized that he would never paint again. She let out the breath she had been holding. "I—I don't know what to say. 'I'm sorry' seems so inadequate, but I am sorry this happened to you, of all people. And it's sympathy, not pity," she added hastily when she saw him stiffen.

"You always did know just what to say to make a person feel better."

"I'm just glad you're home."

He smiled wryly. "I don't think Reiver will be overjoyed to see me."

"Reiver's changed," Hannah said. "That's why he agreed to invite you to James and Georgia's wedding."

Samuel rocked back on his heels. "My baby brother is getting married?"

"Didn't you know? We sent a letter to Australia inviting you to the wedding."

He shook his head. "I never received it. Of course, I've been traveling around so much, it's no wonder." He smiled. "James getting married after all these years . . . I still can't believe he worked up enough nerve to court someone."

Puzzled, Hannah said, "If you're not here because of the wedding, why did you return?"

Dared she hope his love for her had drawn him back?

"Isn't it obvious?" He held up his right arm. "I'm a cripple now. I can't earn a living. What else is there for me to do except slink back to my family like a whipped dog with my tail between my legs and throw myself at their mercy?"

Hannah reared back, eyes flashing with anger. "For someone who doesn't want pity, you're certainly adept at pitying yourself, Samuel Shaw! This is your family. You will always have a place here, no matter what your circumstances." Her voice softened. "No one will think of you as a whipped dog or a charity case."

He turned away. "Forgive me for the outburst. Self-pity and bitterness aren't attractive traits, and I try not to indulge in them too often."

"No one could blame you if you did." She placed a hand on his shoulder. "In spite of what happened in the past, Reiver is your brother and he cares about you. He won't turn you away." I will see to that.

Samuel said, "Will you tell him that I'm here, and prepare everyone for how I've . . . changed? That's why I came up here first."

"I'll tell him," Hannah said. "But we've all changed. You should be prepared for a few shocks of your own."

She turned and left the studio.

As she hurried across the lawn to the mill, Hannah's thoughts skittered through her mind with dizzying speed. She felt as though her world had suddenly turned upside down. Her former lover had become a cold, withdrawn stranger.

She blinked, forcing back helpless tears. She could certainly understand why. How could an artist like Samuel endure life knowing he would never paint or engrave lithographs again? How could he avoid not turning bitter?

She quickened her step. He was home now. His family would shelter and succor him, and Hannah would make him whole again.

She found Reiver, James, and Benjamin together in the machine shop.

Benjamin looked at her oddly. "Mother, what's wrong? You look as though you've seen a ghost."

"I have." Hannah paused to catch her breath. "Samuel is here."

"Uncle Samuel?" Benjamin's face lit up with anticipation and he looked past his mother's shoulder at the door.

Reiver's brows rose in surprise. "Samuel? When did he arrive?"

"And where in the hell is he?" James added, putting down the broken gear he had been repairing.

Hannah raised her hands to silence them. "He's in the homestead, but before you all go charging off to see him, there's something you've got to know."

Three faces stared at her expectantly.

Hannah knotted her long fingers together. "Samuel had an accident in Australia." Her voice broke. "He lost his right hand."

The three men looked as though they had been struck by lightning.

Reiver stepped forward, his face a mask of stunned disbelief. "Are you saying . . .?"

"Are you deaf?" Hannah snapped, her self-control slipping. "The doctors amputated his hand."

"Poor Uncle Samuel," Benjamin said, shaking his head.

"You musn't say that to him," Hannah said. "The last thing your uncle needs is our pity." She looked from Reiver to James. "That's why I came ahead, to prepare you for the shock."

Reiver nodded absently. "James, why don't you go back to the house and tell the others? I'll go to see Sam."

Hannah joined Reiver, matching his long stride as he hurried out of the mill. "Are you going to let him stay?" she asked.

"Of course," he replied. "He's my brother. He may stay as

long as he likes." He looked at her askance. "Did you think I would turn him away? I told you I was willing to forget the past."

Hannah made no comment, for she had wondered what Reiver would do. She said, "He's changed a great deal in other ways, so try not to look shocked."

Even though Hannah had warned him, Reiver couldn't believe the change in his brother when they came face-to-face in the homestead's parlor a few minutes later.

Gone was the charming, outgoing Samuel with the sparkling eyes and contagious zest for life that drew people to him; in his place was a hollow man, all shadows and silences.

Reiver went to him without hesitation and hugged him. "Welcome back."

When they drew away, both men had tears in their eyes.

"I know we didn't part under the best of terms," Samuel began.

"That's all in the past." To his surprise, Reiver found that he meant it. "Let's forget it, shall we?"

"I didn't have anywhere else to go." Samuel swallowed hard. "I don't know how I'll be able to earn my keep now, but—"

"Don't talk nonsense. You've bailed us out more times than I can count." In his daydreams Reiver once thought he'd relish seeing his brother humbled someday, but never like this. "We owe you."

Hannah said, "Once James is married, he and Georgia will be moving out, so you may have the homestead all to yourself."

Samuel thanked them, then added, "I'd like to see the others. Is Mrs. Hardy . . .?"

"Still alive?" Hannah said. "Yes, and as sharp-tongued as ever. Benjamin and Davey have grown into fine young men you won't recognize, and we have several new additions to the family?"

"You've had more children?"

Reiver's gaze flew to Hannah. He held his breath as a flicker of pain crossed her face, but it vanished the moment she smiled. "Not exactly, but you'll see."

Walking up to the main house, Reiver watched Hannah and Samuel together for any sign that their mutual passion had flared anew, but he sensed nothing except an exaggerated politeness that affects people after long absences.

Hannah chatted easily, telling Samuel that later she wanted to hear all about his travels in California and Australia. He said he was amazed at how much Coldwater had grown in his absence. And the mill, he added, stopping to look. So Reiver told him how they had acquired the Bickford farm and planned to expand the mill even further one day.

When they arrived at the main house, Reiver saw Samuel stiffen, as though girding himself for battle, before going inside.

They entered the parlor, where everyone had gathered to welcome Samuel home. Judging by the bleak, stricken expressions, Hannah could see that her family hadn't had enough time to absorb the shock.

Please don't let anyone say something hurtful, she said to herself.

James greeted his brother first, hugging him as Reiver had done. Then he proudly introduced Georgia, who managed to keep her curious gaze focused on Samuel's face.

When Samuel greeted her with a curt, unsmiling nod and a simple "hello," Georgia looked disappointed, as if she had been expecting quite a different reaction from a man of his reputed charm.

She smiled. "It's a pleasure to meet you at long last, Samuel. We were hoping you'd be home in time for our wedding."

"I'm looking forward to it," Samuel said. Then he noticed his two nephews. "Benjamin? Davey?"

They stepped forward, suddenly shy.

Samuel shook his head. "I can't believe how you've grown."

"I am almost sixteen, Uncle Samuel," Benjamin said, extending his right hand. When he realized his mistake, he turned bright red with embarrassment, muttered, "Sorry," and stuck out his left instead.

Samuel's expression tightened, but he took the boy's proferred hand.

Davey shook hands reluctantly and mumbled some unintelligible greeting before stepping back. Hannah made a mental note to have a talk with him later.

"And here is the newest addition to our family," Hannah

said, trying to salvage the situation. Crossing the parlor to where Elisabeth sat quietly on the floor, playing with her rag doll and observing the proceedings out of solemn blue eyes, Hannah picked her up and brought her over to Samuel. "This is Elisabeth, the daughter of a cousin of mine who died. Reiver and I adopted her."

The moment Samuel looked at the child, an odd expression flickered across his face.

He knows, Hannah thought in dismay.

He recovered himself and chucked Elisabeth under the chin. "Hello, little Elisabeth. Aren't you the pretty one?"

Elisabeth flashed him a coquettish smile, then buried her face in Hannah's shoulder. Hannah shook her head. "She's such a flirt."

"That's right," came a cantankerous voice from the wing chair by the fireplace, "just ignore your Mrs. Hardy because she's old and half-blind and feebleminded."

Samuel went right to her and kissed her on the wrinkled cheek. He managed a teasing smile, giving everyone a fleeting glimpse of the old Samuel. "You, feebleminded? I'd sooner believe the moon is made of stale bread."

Rheumy silver eyes stared at his missing hand. "Lost your hand, did you? That was damn careless! But you're still the handsomest devil I've ever seen, Samuel Shaw, and as long as you've still got a good stiff cock on you . . ." The old lady gave Samuel a ribald wink.

Everyone in the room froze in embarrassment. Someone gasped. But Samuel leaned over and whispered something in Mrs. Hardy's ear that caused her to let out a deep whoop of laughter and slap her thigh.

The danger averted, Hannah relaxed.

"Samuel, I'm sure you're tired after your long trip," she said. "Why don't we get you settled in the homestead? There will be plenty of time to talk with everyone later."

"Whatever you say."

Samuel stared at the supper tray that Hannah had sent over to spare him the ordeal of dinner conversation tonight. He almost wept when he saw that she had cut up his roast into bite-size pieces.

Leave it to Hannah.

When he had seen her at the cemetery, laying roses on Abigail's grave, he wanted to put his head in her lap and sob like a baby. He fought down the impulse, for self-pity was the refuge of cowards.

Alone in his old bedchamber, he expertly flicked open the napkin, spread it on his lap, then sampled the tender roast. He was used to the pitying stares and whispers now, and could even tolerate painful, blunt questions without lashing out in bitterness. But there were times. . . .

He rose and looked out the window at the main house bathed in late-summer twilight. He felt safe and secure at last, like a wounded bear finding the familiarity and comfort of its den.

On the endless voyage home Samuel had wondered how Reiver would react to his return. He had prepared himself to swallow his pride and beg for forgiveness. He had forgotten that no matter how much he and Reiver fought and sometimes hated each other through the years, during times of adversity they always stood shoulder to shoulder to protect each other.

Samuel returned to his supper and resumed eating, but the food had lost its flavor. Just seeing Hannah again released a flood of emotion he thought had long since died in the rugged goldfields of California and the vast Australian wilderness.

What had been between them could never be again.

Late that night, after everyone else had exhausted the topic of Samuel's return and gone to bed, Hannah sat in the quiet parlor, staring into space and sipping her second glass of sherry.

Reiver watched her from the doorway. "You'd better be careful, or you'll wind up like my father."

"I still can't believe it."

He sat down beside her on the settee. "About Samuel?"

Hannah nodded. "It's so sad. My heart just goes out to him."

"I can't get over the change in him. Did you notice the way he hung back when he came into the parlor?"

"He wasn't sure how everyone would react to him, and he was afraid."

"He shouldn't feel that way. We're his family."

Tears stung her eyes. She had noticed that when Samuel was introduced to Georgia, instead of smiling and charming her as he did most women, he had withdrawn even further. Since he had lost his hand, was he afraid that women wouldn't find him attractive? The company of women had once been as vital to Samuel as his engraving.

Reiver passed a weary hand over his eyes. "Of all the calamities that fate could send his way, for him to lose his hand . . ."

Hannah's gaze focused on her portrait that Samuel had engraved that first year of her marriage. "He'll never be able to make a sketch or an engraving again. Drawing isn't just something he did, it was what he was."

Reiver fell silent.

Hannah sipped her sherry. "How would you feel if someone came along and took Shaw Silks away from you?"

He gave her a wry glance. "Someone did."

She colored as his barb hit home. "It's not the same at all. I may control the company, but I've never taken away your life's work, have I?"

"No," he agreed. "You've been most reasonable about that."

"Thank you again for letting Samuel stay. I know he's your brother and you felt obligated to let him return, but it was still very generous of you."

Reiver brushed a speck of lint from his trousers. "My generosity does have its bounds."

Hannah grew very quiet and waited.

A muscle twitched in her husband's tense jaw. "You and my brother will not resume your . . . liaison under any circumstances. The both of you may have made a fool of me once, but I'll not tolerate it again." He paused. "Do we understand each other, Hannah?"

She caught the underlying note of pain in his voice, and it surprised her. She set down her glass and placed her hand on his. "That happened a long time ago. The . . . passion that Samuel and I felt for each other is gone." She wondered if she was trying to convince Reiver or herself. "We won't be running off together."

She recalled the day Samuel suggested they run away to Europe, and she remembered a remark Reiver had once made about how a single incident can change someone's life forever. She couldn't help the guilty feeling that if she had run away with Samuel, he wouldn't have gone to Australia and lost his hand.

"There's nothing stopping you now," Reiver said softly. "The boys are grown up enough to understand such things and would survive. I have no hold over you."

"You're forgetting Elisabeth. I could never leave her. She's as much my daughter as Abigail was." Again, an innocent child bound her with loving chains.

Hannah downed the rest of her sherry and smiled slowly at Reiver. "And I would never give up my control of Shaw Silks."

He raised his brows. "Not even for love?"

"Not even for love." To her surprise, she meant it. She must be growing cynical in her old age.

Reiver laced his fingers behind his neck, leaned back, and closed his eyes. "Neither did I."

She knew he was referring to Cecelia. "Did you ever regret it?"

He regarded her from beneath half-open eyes. "No, I can't say that I have. As much as I loved Cecelia, Shaw Silks has always been my passion, and I make no apologies for that." But the pain in his voice belied his words.

"At first I wanted her because she symbolized all of my aspirations. She came from a family of wealth and privilege, and she was so beautiful. No one jeered at her father for being the town drunk. No one threw mud at her for being the town drunk's child. I felt that if I could win her, I would add one more accomplishment to what I hoped would be a long list."

"That sounds rather cold and heartless, treating Cecelia as if she were some prize to be won," Hannah said.

"It was. Until I fell in love with her. I would have married her once the mill was established." He shrugged. "But fate has a way of ruining our plans, doesn't it?"

And here we are, taking what we were given and making the best of it, Hannah thought.

She didn't know why, but tonight, sitting here with Reiver and talking about their lost dreams, she felt the old resentments and antagonisms fade. If their loves were lost to them forever, why couldn't she and Reiver offer each other a little comfort, at least for tonight?

"Reiver?"

When he turned his head, she leaned over and kissed him on the mouth. At first his lips were stiff and unresponsive, but when Hannah didn't pull away, they softened and parted. One strong arm slipped around her waist and drew her to him.

Reiver ended the kiss. "Shall we go to bed?"

Hannah looked into his eyes. "Yes."

"Are you sure?"

In response, she rose and extended her hand.

The following morning Samuel rose late and dressed himself without too much difficulty, though cravats and ties were beyond his capabilities these days.

When he walked downstairs, the tantalizing aroma of coffee teased his nostrils, and he knew that Hannah had breakfast waiting for him in the dining room.

"Good morning," she said, smiling brightly. The table was set for two. "Did you sleep well?"

He suppressed a yawn. "After some of the places I've slept, sleeping in that old bed was like sleeping on a cloud."

He noticed that no matter what the fashion, Hannah still wore her thick, glossy hair parted in the middle, swept over her ears, and arranged in a heavy chignon at the nape of her neck, the neck he always kissed before unpinning her hair and letting it cascade down her bare back. . . .

"Breakfast is ready, so why don't you sit down?" She sailed off toward the kitchen, calling over her shoulder, "There's bacon and eggs, and muffins." When she returned, she carried two plates.

"You shouldn't have gone to all this trouble," he said, sitting down.

"It's no trouble at all." She set a heaping plate in front of him and poured the coffee.

Samuel ate slowly, trying to find a way to tell her that her presence was too painful to endure and he would rather she left.

"Where is James?" he asked.

"He is either at the mill, as usual, or spending time with Georgia." Hannah sipped her coffee. "What do you think of your future sister-in-law?"

Privately Samuel thought Georgia Varner pretty and utterly

charming, but lacking the complexity and depth he preferred in a woman. "She is rather young, isn't she?"

"Georgia's just as old as I was when I married Reiver. But she's good for James. She adds a certain lightheartedness to his life and keeps him from turning into a bobbin."

That coaxed a small smile out of Samuel. He continued eating, and an awkward silence ensued. He could tell that Hannah expected certain responses from him, yet he didn't know how to broach what he needed to tell her.

Finally she set down her cup and folded her arms on the table. "Why are you so nervous around me? You're acting as though we're strangers who had just been introduced."

He looked up. "We are. It's been eight years since we've seen each other, Hannah. You said it yourself. We've both changed."

"We used to be lovers. We should at least be able to talk to each other freely, without this—this tension between us."

His appetite gone, he pushed his plate away and rose, drawing his right arm against his side protectively. "I'm sorry. It's just that Reiver has forgiven me and taken me back into the family fold. I can't betray his trust."

Comprehension dawned on Hannah's face. "You think that my presence will make you do something to betray that trust?"

Samuel looked at her. "Oh, yes."

Hannah rose, her expression soft with understanding. "I'm flattered that you still find me capable of inspiring such thoughts, but you needn't fear. I have no intention of trying to seduce you. If you're going to stay here, it's impossible for us to avoid each other, and I wouldn't want to. Before you were my lover, you were my very dear friend, and now that we're not lovers, I hope we can still be friends."

Having had you as a lover, how can I ever settle for friendship? he wondered. He knew he had to, for he had no other place to go.

He nodded. "I would like that."

"Good, because we have to talk."

After breakfast, Hannah had the groom hitch up Racer and she took Samuel for a drive around Coldwater. She pointed out all the changes as she drove down Main Street. She nodded at people she knew, but did not stop, even when they stared at the strange bearded man seated stiffly at her side, for she refused to satisfy their curiosity at Samuel's expense. Word would get around soon enough that Samuel Shaw had returned to Coldwater a broken man.

When she reached a hill overlooking the town, she turned the carriage onto a side road and stopped.

Samuel looked out over the buildings clustered between the green oaks and maples. "The town certainly has grown."

Hannah wrapped the reins around the brake and turned sideways to face him. "Yesterday, in the parlor when you saw Elisabeth . . . you knew right away that she's Reiver's daughter."

"She looks exactly like him," he replied. "Why did you claim that she's some dead cousin's daughter?"

"Because she's Cecelia Tuttle's daughter, too."

His pale eyes widened in astonishment. "Reiver and Cecelia?"

While Samuel listened, Hannah told him all about Reiver's trips to New York City for trysts with Cecelia under the guise of mill business, and how she had died giving birth to Reiver's child.

"Just before Cecelia died, she told her husband that the baby was Reiver's. Tuttle threatened to send her to a foundling home if Reiver didn't take her."

Samuel looked aghast. "He brought his mistress's child here and expected you to raise it as your own? And you agreed to it? That's noble and very generous."

"Hardly that, because I demanded a high price in return. I wanted controlling shares in his company." She paused. "And he gave them to me."

He stared at her in stunned disbelief. "You've been running Shaw Silks?"

"Reiver does, but I have the final say. I am not a figurehead."

Samuel leaned back in his seat, balancing himself with his left hand. "Well done, Hannah."

"No one else knows about Elisabeth's true parentage," she said. "If they've guessed, they've prudently kept it to themselves."

"Your secret is safe with me."

"I knew it would be."

"And the mill?"

"To the world, Reiver still runs it." Hannah's brow furrowed. "I know it was petty and vengeful, but I had to do it for Benjamin and Davey. I was afraid that Reiver might leave everything to his illegitimate daughter, and I couldn't have that. Not after the way he treated Abigail." Her eyes filled with tears.

"Your children always were the guiding force in your life."

She thought of what Reiver had said last night about nothing keeping her here if she chose to leave with Samuel. "They still are."

He glanced at her. "You have changed. You're much stronger than you used to be."

"Amos Tuttle once called me devious."

"Devious? You're the most honest woman I know."

Then Hannah told him how she had helped Reiver to acquire the Bickford farm.

"So Shaw Silks has become your passion as well."

"You sound disappointed."

"Not disappointed, envious." He stared at the horizon. "Everyone has a purpose in life except me." Then he shook his head. "There I go again, feeling sorry for myself."

"You needn't. Shaw Silks will become a part of your life as well."

Hannah would see to that.

CHAPTER
❧ 18 ❧

MONDAY, September 21, 1857, was the perfect day for James and Georgia's wedding.

Hannah stood off to the happy bride's left as her attendant and listened to the half-deaf Reverend Crane shout out the marriage ceremony as if everyone else couldn't hear.

How different this wedding is from mine so long ago, she thought.

Today over one hundred friends, relatives, and workers crowded the small church, most filling the pews to overflowing and the rest packed together in the back. Unlike Hannah's wedding, this bride and groom wanted to marry each other.

Hannah's eyes filled with sentimental tears when Georgia said her vows so enthusiastically, her words rang like the joyous pealing of wedding bells. She smiled when James brushed his hair out of his eyes before placing the wedding band on his bride's finger.

May you always be as happy as you are today, Hannah thought.

Then the groom kissed his bride and they walked down the aisle as husband and wife, out into the late-afternoon sunshine that was pouring its own blessing down on them.

Hannah circulated among the guests on the lawn surrounding the main house, complimenting the women on their finery and being complimented in turn on her elegant blue silk gown trimmed with flounces and narrow satin ribbons.

Mostly she kept an eye on Samuel.

From across the lawn she watched him as he sipped a cup of

punch and appeared deep in serious conversation with the overseer of the new Hartford ribbon factory. Samuel avoided women, though one or two cast come-hither looks in his direction. He ignored them.

Hannah drifted over to the group of men gathered around Reiver.

". . . and have you been satisfied with Chinese silk?" one of them asked.

Reiver shook his head. "Not at all. The raw silk I've been getting has been so inferior that it makes me wish we could breed silkworms in this country."

Burrows the paper mill owner laughed. "We all know what happened when you tried that!"

The rest of the men joined in the laughter.

Reiver continued with, "I've heard talk that next year we'll be signing a commercial treaty with Japan to open their port of Yokohama to foreign trade."

Another man said, "Why Yokohama?"

"Geographically it's the nearest Japanese port to the United States," Reiver replied, "and it's accessible to their big silk-producing districts. Right now producing silkworm eggs and selling them abroad is most profitable to the Japanese. I think if they turn from egg production to producing raw silk, we will have a whole new source, higher in quality than the Chinese can produce." He paused. "In fact I'm considering traveling to Japan to meet with their silk merchants myself."

Hannah started. Reiver traveling to Japan?

Burrows glanced at Hannah and noticed her stunned expression. "I think you'd better tell your wife your plans, Shaw."

"Please do," Hannah said. "I'd be interested to hear them."

Reiver just grinned disarmingly. "I've put off telling you because you'd try to talk me out of it." He looked around at his cronies. "Hannah can't bear to be without me."

"A devoted wife."

"Worth her weight in gold."

"Wish my wife would miss me as much."

Hannah shut her ivory fan with an annoyed snap. "If my husband's absence benefited Shaw Silks, he could stay in Japan for as long as he liked." She turned and glided off in an angry hiss of silk.

So Reiver planned to go to Japan. She wondered if he was going to wait until he booked passage before telling her.

Hannah had scant time to reflect on Reiver's latest plan. She was in the middle of a wedding reception and her concern for her guests' enjoyment of the festivities had to take precedence.

As she approached the refreshment table her worst nightmare came true. She overheard a woman say, "What a shame that Samuel lost his hand."

"I was so shocked when I saw him," said another.

The speaker was none other than Patience Broome, the woman Reiver had once told Hannah Samuel loved. Now a plump matron, Patience piled her plate with sandwiches as heedlessly as she spoke.

"I always thought him so handsome," Patience said, her voice carrying, "but what good is a handsome man if he's a cripple?"

Standing on the other side of the table was none other than Samuel. Judging by his stricken expression, he had heard every word. Drawing his right arm close to his body, he turned and walked away.

Seething, Hannah wanted to pull out every bouncing ringlet on Patience's golden head. Instead she waited until the tactless bitch had a cup of punch in her hand, then she purposely swung around, her elbow jabbing Patience in the ribs.

"Oh, how clumsy of me!" she exclaimed as punch splashed a wide brown swath down the front of Patience's dress.

"My dress!" Patience wailed, dropping her plate. "It's ruined!" She had seen what Hannah had done, but dared not accuse her hostess of bumping her purposely.

"I'm so sorry," Hannah said, trying not to gloat. "I will, of course, pay for a new one. Just have your dressmaker send me the original bill."

Her satisfaction was worth every penny.

Hannah counted the minutes until the reception would finally end and she could go find Samuel.

She found him in the homestead, sitting alone in the parlor with only shadows and silence for company.

Hannah maneuvered her wide skirts through the door. "It's so dark in here. May I light a lamp?"

"If you wish."

"I brought you a piece of wedding cake, since you weren't there when the happy couple cut it." She set the plate down so she could light the lamp. Its warm glow revealed Samuel sitting in a chair with his elbows propped on its arms and his long legs stretched out before him, crossed at the ankles.

Seeing him there with his proud head bowed and his shoulders slumped, Hannah felt a fierce, overpowering urge to protect him. She wanted to build a wall around him and keep the rest of the world at bay, but as she reminded herself, he was most adept at doing that without her help.

He smiled wryly. "You needn't come hunting me down to soothe my hurts."

She gathered her skirts and settled herself in the chair across from him. "Not all women are as cruel and thoughtless as Patience Broome, you know."

"I used to think I knew women." Samuel rubbed his forehead. "But after the accident I discovered that I didn't know them at all."

"How do you mean?"

"As long as I was attentive, whole, and gainfully employed, I was worthy of their attention, but once I lost my hand, they avoided me as if I were a leper."

"Samuel Shaw, do I detect a faint note of self-pity in your voice?" When he colored, she added, "I thought you told me that you never indulge in it."

"I am merely offering a more realistic assessment of your fair sex."

Hannah raised her brows. "And are you including me in that assessment?"

"You're the exception." He stared into the cold, empty fireplace. "I've always held you in the highest esteem."

"I should hope so. We were once lovers."

As always, any mention of their former relationship caused Samuel to withdraw from her, becoming as unreachable as the stars. She wondered why.

"Surely on your travels you met some admirable women."

Samuel's shifting moods flitted across his features. "Yes, I did. One was a prospector's young widow searching for gold. She always wore men's trousers and her late husband's shirts.

Another was a dance-hall girl offering her favors to as many men as she could to save enough money to return east. They both offered me comfort when I needed it most. And in Australia, I was going to marry a lady rancher descended from English convicts."

Hannah's eyes widened in surprise even as an unexpected knot of jealousy tightened deep inside her. "Why didn't you tell us?"

"After I lost my hand, she called off the wedding. She said she was sorry, but without a hand, I couldn't help her work the ranch. She gave me enough money to return home and sent me on my way."

"Of all the cruel, insensitive—"

"You needn't be indignant on my behalf. She was a practical woman and I don't blame her for bowing out."

"I'm afraid I couldn't be as charitable."

A bittersweet smile touched his mouth. "Ah, but you were very much alike. You both put duty before personal desire."

Stung by his mild reproof, Hannah became reflective. Samuel was right. She always had followed the dictates of duty and family obligations, but they had served her well. Benjamin and Davey were fine, upstanding young men, and she now enjoyed the unexpected satisfaction and heady power of controlling Shaw Silks.

Suddenly Samuel's company weighed her down with melancholy. Hannah rose. "I have to get back to the house to supervise the cleaning up."

He rose. "You needn't worry about me, Hannah. It takes more than a cutting remark to defeat me."

You are still so fragile, she thought, no matter what you may think.

She smiled and wished him good night.

Walking up Mulberry Hill on her way back to the main house, Hannah saw Davey's heavyset figure hurrying toward her, his round face flushed with indignation.

Hannah groaned inside, for she recognized his determined expression all too well. Davey's private scales of justice were out of balance again, tilted in Benjamin's favor, and he was seeking to right them with a vengeance. "What is it?" she asked.

Huffing and puffing, Davey paused to catch his breath. "Mama, Father has taken Ben into Hartford, and he wouldn't take me with them."

"Hartford? At this hour? It's almost dark." The sun had set long ago, leaving only the lingering September twilight. "Did he say where they were going, or why?"

"No, Mama, they wouldn't tell me, and Ben goes around acting like he knows something I don't. Did Father say anything to you?"

"No, he didn't. I assumed that your uncle's wedding and reception would be enough excitement for one day." Evidently not.

Davey thrust out his lower lip. "Why does Father always leave me out?"

"Don't sulk. It's an unattractive trait in a young man."

"He doesn't love me as much as he loves Ben, does he?"

"David Shaw, that will be quite enough!"

"Why? I'm his son, too."

"Your father loves you both equally, and I'll not hear another word about it." Hannah placed her hand on her son's shoulder. "I don't know where they've gone, but I'll find out once they return."

Back at the house, Hannah sat in the parlor and waited. And waited. The room grew dark as the hours slipped by, but she didn't bother to light a lamp. She dozed fitfully, sitting up in her chair.

She awoke at the sound of the front door slowly opening.

She listened. She heard soft, deliberate footsteps, followed by lowered voices and an emphatic "Sssh!" Hannah rose, lit a lamp, and walked into the hall.

Reiver and Benjamin froze when they saw her.

Hannah folded her arms. "Where have you two been?"

Reiver exchanged a guilty look with his son. "Hartford."

"And you couldn't take Davey with you?"

"Not this time." Reiver looked pointedly at Benjamin and grinned.

By lamplight, Hannah noticed the disarray in both Reiver's and Benjamin's clothing, as if trousers had been hastily pulled on and cravats clumsily tied. She smelled faint traces of alcohol on Reiver, but Benjamin reeked of a woman's cloying perfume.

Hannah stared at her son, rage and reproach in her eyes. He looked away. She turned her attention to Reiver. "You've taken my son to a whorehouse!"

Her sixteen-year-old son had lain with a whore.

Hannah's hand trembled so violently that she had to set down the lamp on a nearby table. "Benjamin, go to your room. I have to speak with your father in private."

Emboldened by his rite of passage, Benjamin said, "I'm going to stay. This concerns me as well."

"Do as I say!"

He lowered his head in a defiant gesture reminiscent of his father. "I am not a child. You can't order me to my room as if I were five years old."

"Do as your mother says," Reiver said calmly.

"But, Father—"

"Leave us. It's late and it would be better for all concerned if you went to your room."

Hannah suddenly felt helpless. They were allied against her, two reasonable men against a hysterical female who didn't understand their masculine natures.

Benjamin glared at Hannah as if she had stripped him of his newly won manhood, but obeyed his father and went upstairs. Hannah took the lamp and headed for the study. She would have Reiver's head for this, so help her God.

Inside the study, Hannah set down the lamp so hard, the flame jumped and flickered. She whirled around to face Reiver when she heard the door shut. "You depraved bastard, taking a boy to a whorehouse!"

Reiver raised his hands. "Calm down."

Hannah backed against the desk, her fingers gripping the edge as if it were Reiver's throat. "Calm down? I could kill you."

"It wouldn't be the first time." He eyed her warily. "Benjamin is not a boy. He's sixteen years old, the same age I was when I had my first . . . experience with a woman."

"Why was it even necessary?"

"It's part of becoming a man."

"Part of becoming a whoremaster, you mean."

Reiver turned red with anger. "I don't expect you to understand, but this is a part of any young man's education. He should be as skilled in the bedchamber as he is in business."

"You've ruined him."

"On the contrary. I've made a man of him. I know you're determined to protect him, to keep him an innocent boy forever, Hannah, but whether you will admit it or not, he is a young man, and it's time you started treating him as such."

She stepped away from the desk and clenched her hands into fists. "I do not regard him as a child, but neither do I think he's ready to go fornicating his way through the bedchambers of Connecticut!"

"You have so little faith in him."

Shaking, Hannah headed for the door. "When some poor girl appears on a doorstep with Benjamin's illegitimate child, don't expect me to raise this one."

Reiver caught her arm as she passed. "Right or wrong, it's done, Hannah. Accept it. Otherwise you will drive your son away."

Hannah jerked herself free. "I won't forget this." She stormed out of the study, slamming the door behind her.

Hannah's wrath lingered as if it were a palpable presence, causing Reiver to sigh and shake his head. Women . . . they just didn't understand men and their needs. He poured himself a glass of apple brandy and stretched out in his favorite chair.

If Hannah hadn't been waiting up for them, she never would have known what he and Benjamin did tonight. He supposed Davey tattled on them. There were times when he honestly disliked his younger son, with his exasperating demands for absolute fairness and equal attention. As Reiver had discovered long ago, no parent ever loved all his children equally, and he couldn't help loving Benjamin best. Davey was too much Hannah's son.

He smiled. Benjamin, on the other hand, was exactly like his father. Tonight, when Reiver had introduced him to the Countess and her beautiful women, Benjamin had approached them with the reverence and curiosity of an acolyte eager to be initiated into a secret and mysterious ceremony.

Later, after Reiver had attended to his own pleasure, a smiling Countess informed him that his son had been an apt pupil. Just like his father.

Reiver finished his brandy, rose, and extinguished the lamp. He wished he could say something to appease Hannah, but she was too angry and upset to listen to reason.

Perhaps she would listen tomorrow.

Hannah slept fitfully that night and awoke before dawn. A heavy gray fog pressed against her bedchamber window, mirroring the despair she felt smothering her.

She dressed quickly. No one else stirred at this hour, not even the maid firing up the kitchen stove. She wondered how Reiver and Benjamin could sleep so soundly after their night of debauchery.

Hannah pulled on her shawl and went outside. She ignored the wet grass dampening her slippers and trailing hem as she hurried down Mulberry Hill. The homestead suddenly loomed out of the blurry mists like a ghost on some godforsaken English moor. A light shining in an upstairs window distracted her, but only momentarily. Hannah kept on walking and didn't slow down until she came to the path that ran through the woods.

She hadn't gone twenty feet when she heard footsteps behind her.

"Hannah, wait!"

She turned to find Samuel coming down the path. His tousled hair and absence of a jacket told her that he had left the homestead in pursuit of her.

His eyes, as ghostly as the fog, regarded her with concern. "What are you doing out here at this hour?"

Hannah burst into tears.

Samuel moved toward her, his arms extended. Then he remembered Reiver and stopped short, his arms falling helplessly to his sides. "Why are you crying?"

Hannah took several deep, shuddering breaths to compose herself. "Reiver took Benjamin to a whorehouse last night."

Hannah told him how they had gone off to Hartford after James's wedding and their condition when they came sneaking in at one o'clock in the morning.

"It was disgusting." She dabbed at her eyes with her hand-kerchief. "There was my baby reeking of some whore's perfume and Reiver looking as if he had done something to be proud about. Samuel, if I had had a gun, I swear I would have shot him."

Samuel placed an awkward hand on her arm. "I don't think Reiver intended for you to find out."

"How could I not find out!" she wailed. "The Benjamin who walked through that front door had changed so much, I'd have to be blind not to realize that something catastrophic had happened." She leaned back against a nearby tree, letting the rough, damp bark bite into her spine. "It was just too soon for him to lose his innocence. Too soon!"

Samuel broke off a twig from a nearby tree and twirled it. "When I turned sixteen, Reiver did the same with me, and later, James as well. You could say that it's a tradition with the Shaw men."

"Don't you dare defend him, Samuel Shaw!"

"Benjamin isn't a little boy anymore, he's a young man, and there's nothing a young man hates more than being treated like a child by his parents."

"He's grown away from me. I could see it in his eyes last night, this smug, superior air that dismissed me as nothing more than a mettlesome woman to be humored and ignored."

"Hannah," he said gently, "do you remember your reaction when you first saw the portrait I did of you?"

She fell silent, thinking back. "Yes."

"Well, you're seeing in Benjamin what I saw in you, the same sensual awakening." He shrugged helplessly. "It's not disgusting. It's part of becoming a man or a woman."

She rested her head against the tree trunk and listened to the calming sound of water dripping off nearby branches. She looked at Samuel standing in the middle of the path. In an un-guarded moment desire warred with restraint on his perfect features.

Hannah stepped away from the tree toward him. "God, how I've missed you!"

He stepped back a pace. "Hannah, don't."

Distraught and emotional from the events of the previous night, she reached for him. "I need you."

He caught one of her wrists, but his strength was no match for Hannah's determination. She slid her free arm around his waist and drew him toward her with a contented sigh.

He stood stiff and unresponsive. "Hannah, you're not being fair to me. This is wrong."

"Hold me, Samuel. Just hold me. There can't be anything wrong with that." She rested her head on his chest, listening to his strong, steady heartbeat. "I don't care if it's right or wrong. When I lost your child, I thought I'd—" She stopped, appalled.

The fog thickened around them until the woods disappeared. All Hannah saw was Samuel's bloodless, anguished face staring down at her. His lips moved, but he spoke not a sound.

"Forgive me," she said, stepping away. "I vowed never to tell you."

"A child?" His voice trembled. "You were going to have my child?"

"It could have been Reiver's, but I wanted it to be yours." She pulled her shawl more tightly about her. "It happened not long after Reiver banished you." Her eyes filled with tears at the memory. "The very day I learned I was with child, I lost it." A child's existence reduced to blood on the snow. "So cruel, so unfair . . . I didn't even have time to love it. Then when I learned that I couldn't have any more . . ." She raised her head. "So you see, you're not the only one who is crippled."

Samuel cradled her cheek in his hand, and she shivered at his touch. "Hannah, I'm so, so sorry," he whispered. "Dear God, why didn't you write and tell me? I would have come back."

"What good would it have done?"

"You wouldn't have had to face such pain alone."

She tasted tears on her lips. "I've grown used to it."

That undid him. He stepped toward her, his right arm sliding around her waist and holding her as tightly as if he still had a hand. His pale eyes searched her face as Hannah entwined her arms around his neck and her fingers in his soft, silky hair.

"So beautiful," he murmured, just before devouring her mouth with his own.

Hannah's kiss flooded his parched soul like a sweet spring rain, and her eager body pressed along the length of his kindled the dormant fire within him. He had been too long without her. He wanted to sheathe himself in her and love her, love her, love her.

Hannah took his face in her hands and showered his cheeks, his eyelids, his forehead with kisses, branding him as her own. "I love you. I've always loved you. I thought I'd die when Reiver sent you away."

He silenced her by kissing her again, but her insistent fingers kept running over his chest, sliding down his ribs, seeking his belt buckle.

Reiver's face flashing in Samuel's mind's eye forced him to fling himself away from Hannah just in time.

"We can't." Panting, he put his hand against a nearby tree to support the weight that his shaking knees could not.

She stared at him out of soulful eyes, hugging herself. "I—I thought you wanted me."

"I do, but I can't betray my brother, not while I'm living here on his charity."

Hannah's eyes burned with anger. "Your staying here does not depend on Reiver's benevolence. I want you here, and as far as I'm concerned, you may stay here for as long as you like. So you needn't fear that Reiver will cast you out if you displease him."

"I'm grateful."

"I don't want gratitude or humility. I want to see you proud and whole again."

He looked down at his missing hand. "That might present something of a problem."

"I meant whole of spirit." When he said nothing, she stepped away from him and looked around. "It's nearly dawn and the fog is lifting. I suppose I had better get back."

Samuel fell in step beside her. "What are you going to do about Ben?"

Hannah sighed. "Apologize for treating him like a child."

When she returned to the main house, she found Benjamin eating breakfast alone at the kitchen table. Hannah poured herself a cup of coffee and joined him.

He regarded her sullenly while she explained why she had been so upset with him last night, but when she admitted that she had been wrong to treat him as a child, his surliness vanished and he became the son she remembered, even rising to kiss her on the cheek.

Before he left for the mill, he kissed Hannah on the cheek once more, and she knew that her son had truly become a man.

Hannah stood in the same parlor that she had dusted, swept, and polished for Aunt Naomi and smiled in satisfaction. "I hardly recognize the place, Georgia."

With the addition of wallpaper in tiny red roses, framed lithographs of seasonal New England scenes, and multicolored braided rugs scattered on the floor, the Bickford house now revealed a welcoming warmth that had been sorely lacking when Hannah lived there.

Georgia set down her tray. "This place was such a pigsty! Black fingermarks on all the walls, grease building up inside the stove, dirt ground into the floorboards . . . my Ma would've died of shame to keep her house that way."

Hannah took the cup of tea Georgia proffered in a practiced, ladylike manner. "Knowing Nate as I do, I'm not surprised his wife was just as slovenly."

Georgia looked around, beaming with pride. "Well, Georgia Shaw is the mistress here now, and she's going to see that it stays a real home for my husband and babies."

Hannah said, "And where is your husband? I checked the mill, but he wasn't there, and I have to ask him if he'll help me with a special project."

Georgia blushed prettily. "Ever since we got married, James hasn't been going in as early as he used to."

Hannah smiled. "Why should he, now that he has . . . more interesting things to do at home?"

Georgia giggled. "It's nine o'clock, so he should be dressed by now. Shall I get him for you?"

"No need, my love," came James's voice from the doorway. He greeted Hannah, brushed his hair out of his eyes, and crossed the parlor to kiss his blushing wife on the cheek.

Hannah said, "Before you go to the mill, I'd like to speak to you about a project."

James poured himself a cup of tea and raised his brows. "What kind of project?"

"I want you to make something very special for me, something I suspect will be very difficult to construct."

"James can build anything," Georgia said.

James sat down and turned to Hannah. "Tell me what you want me to make, and I'll tell you if I can."

Hannah leaned forward and described what she wanted. When she finished, she sat back and waited for their reactions.

"Oh, Hannah," Georgia said, "that would be wonderful."

Hannah looked at James, still sitting there silently. "Can it be done?"

His brow furrowed in concentration, and Hannah could almost hear his mental wheels turning as he considered all possibilities. Finally he smiled. "I think so. At least I'll try my best to see what I can fashion."

"I can't ask for more than that." Hannah rose. "Don't either of you tell anyone about this, especially Reiver. I want it to be a secret in case it doesn't work."

"We won't tell a living soul," Georgia said, rising.

James rose also. "I'll find a way to work on it without anyone else knowing."

Hannah stared over James's shoulder. "Will it work?"

He shrugged. "The only way we'll know that is to try it."

She shivered, more from her own nervousness than from the draft of cold November air swirling around her skirts. Now that the project was completed, second thoughts plagued Hannah. What if it didn't work? What if it caused irreparable damage?

Hannah knotted her long fingers together and stared at the creation of wood and straps on James's workbench. "I don't think this was such a good idea. Perhaps we ought to throw it away and forget about it."

"Don't worry," James said. "Even if it doesn't work, he'll be touched by the sentiment behind it." He grinned. "Besides, this is my masterpiece! I've put too much blood and sweat into it to discard it now."

Hannah took several gulps of refreshing air. "You're right.

I'm being silly." She took another breath. "Well, it's Judgment Day. Shall we go?"

James nodded, and together they left the Bickford barn, where they had been conspiring in secret for almost two months. The overcast sky with its threat of snow mirrored Hannah's feeling of foreboding.

When they arrived at the homestead, James said, "Hannah, you look as though you're going to a hanging."

"I am . . . my own!" She couldn't stop shaking. "He's going to hate me for this."

"If anything, he'll be moved by your concern for his feelings."

They went inside without knocking. "Samuel?" Hannah called.

He appeared a minute later, a book tucked under his arm. His gaze went to the package James held. "What's this? An early Christmas present?"

Hannah nodded. "In a way."

He smiled. "Come, don't keep me in suspense."

James offered his brother the package, but Hannah stayed his hand. "Samuel, before you open it, I have to say that I hope you won't be offended when you see what it is."

"Now I am intrigued. Give it over, baby brother."

When he saw the contents, he turned so ashen, Hannah thought he would faint.

"It's an artificial hand," she said, her voice shaking. "James made it out of wood and leather so you could strap it on your arm and fit it with a glove. It—it's not as good as a real one, of course, but I thought . . ." She stared at him helplessly.

He looked at the wooden hand with its fingers flexed in a natural resting position and a hollowed-out cup to anchor the stump. Then he took his time examining the straps. His eyes revealed not a thought. A mask held more expression than his features. He didn't smile or register any enthusiasm or gratitude for what they had done.

He loathes it, Hannah thought, and he loathes me even more for thinking he would accept this.

Samuel looked from Hannah to James and back to Hannah. "I—I don't know what to say."

James said, "Why don't you let me show you how it works?"

When Samuel started to remove his coat, James raised his brows. "You intend to undress in front of Hannah?"

She looked away. How was James to know that she had seen Samuel in far less?

Samuel said, "Of course not. Let's go into another room." And he walked out with James following.

Hannah waited. And waited.

After what seemed like hours they returned. Hannah's gaze went straight to Samuel's face, searching for any sign of resentment or reproach.

"What do you think?" he asked.

He held his right arm close to his body as before, but instead of his coat sleeve being sewn shut, it came down naturally to the end of his wrist. With the wooden hand covered by a black leather glove, no casual observer could tell that Samuel's hand was missing.

Hannah managed a tentative smile. "Now it doesn't call attention to your—your—"

"Infirmity," he finished for her.

An awkward silence ensued. Finally James slapped his brother on the back. "I've got to get back to the mill or Reiver will think I've left town." After accepting Samuel's thanks, he left Hannah alone with him.

Hannah crossed her arms to hide her nervousness. "I—I know it's a poor substitute, but I—oh, Samuel, I didn't mean to embarrass or insult you." She shrugged helplessly. "Say something, please!"

"I'm speechless." Now he radiated such warmth that Hannah felt as though she were standing before a roaring fire on a cold winter's day. "Just when I think I've seen the pinnacle of human kindness, you do something like this."

He took her hand and pressed his warm lips into her palm, causing her to tremble. When he released her, his eyes sparkled with gratitude. "I don't have enough words to thank you properly."

"I just want you to be whole again."

Samuel watched her walk back up Mulberry Hill, her skirts billowing in the brisk November wind. Her gesture had touched him more than he could show. When he thought of Hannah planning this and enlisting James's help, and the two of them working all these weeks in secret . . .

He wished he had Hannah's courage and her boundless optimism. He wished he could be whole again for her, but he couldn't. He didn't know if he even had the energy to try.

CHAPTER
❦ 19 ❦

IN late March of 1858, Reiver came to a decision that he dreaded telling Hannah.

That afternoon he found her in the study, seated at the desk with her pen in hand, answering a pile of business correspondence. When she didn't acknowledge his presence, he said, "Would you stop writing for a moment? I have to talk to you."

Hannah set aside her pen and folded her hands on her desk. "You have my undivided attention."

Reiver sat down across from her. "I'm going to Yokohama. And I'm taking Benjamin with me."

After eighteen years of marriage, he knew how to read her. By the way her eyes darkened and narrowed, he could tell she was not pleased. The slight tightening of her lips indicated resistance and a possible battle. Reiver was prepared.

Hannah sat back in her chair. His decision didn't come as a complete surprise. She had overheard him discussing the matter with several of his cronies at James's wedding reception last year. Since he hadn't mentioned it afterward, she thought he had discounted the idea.

"Do you really think such a voyage will benefit Shaw Silks?" she asked.

"Immeasurably. You know how I've been displeased with the inferior quality of Chinese silks for years. Japanese silk has the potential of being the highest quality, and now that they're receptive to trade with the United States, this is the perfect time to establish a business relationship with them."

"Why do you have to be the one to go?"

Reiver raised his brows in surprise. "I should think you'd welcome the opportunity to be rid of me for a while."

Hannah looked chagrined. "I merely meant that you are forty-six years old and this is a long, arduous voyage better undertaken by a younger man."

Reiver slapped his flat stomach. "I'll have you know I'm still capable of doing the work of a man half my age. Besides, who else would I send? James is to be a father soon, and Samuel doesn't know enough about the business. My new overseer is still too green." He shook his head. "No, Hannah, the only two people qualified enough to go are me and you."

She gave him a level look. "I have no intention of going to Japan. Not with Elisabeth to look after."

"Somehow I don't think the Japanese would deal with a woman, anyway, so you're spared."

"What if there is a war? What happens if you're cut off and can't return to Connecticut?"

"I plan to be back before that happens."

Hannah rose in an agitated rustle of taffeta. "Why must Benjamin go with you? He's—"

"Too young? Hannah, we've been through this before. Shaw Silks will belong to Ben and Davey someday. Davey is still too young to learn about the company, but Ben isn't. By going to Japan, he'll meet the people he'll be dealing with in the future. He'll be an invaluable asset."

She went over to the window, parted the curtains, and looked out. "Intellectually I know you're right, but in my mother's heart, I don't want him to go."

Reiver crossed the room and placed his hands on her shoulders. "I know, Hannah," he said gently. "You worry needlessly. He's my son, too, and I promise to take good care of him."

She turned. "But to not see my son for such a long time . . ."

"You'll have Davey and Elisabeth. And Georgia's new baby. And you can run the mill without my interference."

Hannah smiled dryly. "That is certainly the best inducement. Are you sure you can trust me with your precious mill?"

"Yes, I can. You haven't let me down yet."

It was the highest compliment he could give her, and she knew it.

Hannah looked away. "Are you sure you can trust me with Samuel?"

"I trust the both of you," he replied without hesitation. Samuel posed no threat to him. He had returned to Coldwater in little pieces, and even with Hannah's clever gift of an artificial hand to keep people from noticing quite so readily and staring, Samuel still wasn't the man he once was. As much as he claimed to want to earn his keep, the most he accomplished was to spend his days in the homestead, hiding from the world. He wouldn't betray Reiver again.

Yet even if Samuel and Hannah did become lovers again, Reiver considered it a risk well worth taking. He wanted to go to Japan more than he wanted to police Hannah and Samuel.

"How long will you be gone?" Hannah asked.

"One or two years. Maybe more."

"That is such a long time. So much can happen while you're away. Mrs. Hardy isn't in the best of health."

"That tough old bird will outlive us all."

"What if something happens to you or Benjamin? Storms at sea, shipwrecks, unfriendly natives could befall you."

Reiver smiled gently. "All of life is a risk, Hannah. You know that."

"And what of Davey? He'll see this trip as another example of you favoring Benjamin over him."

Reiver scowled in annoyance. "Damn it, Hannah! I can't stop doing things with Benjamin just because Davey gets jealous. Ben's the eldest, and his age confers certain privileges. Davey will just have to understand that."

"I wonder if he ever will." Then she said, "How does Benjamin feel about making this trip with you?"

"He wants to go as badly as I do."

Father and favorite son conquering the world together, Hannah thought.

Having exhausted all her objections, she sighed. "If you feel this trip is necessary for the future of Shaw Silks, you and Benjamin may go with my blessing."

Reiver's eyes sparkled with an enthusiasm that Hannah hadn't seen since he first started raising silkworms. "We're embarking on a new age, Hannah, and Shaw Silks is going to be in the forefront."

But her main concern was for the son she wouldn't see for two or more years.

Every member of the Shaw family crowded the Hartford train station platform to see Reiver and Benjamin off one month later, even a stooped, cantankerous Mrs. Hardy and a glowing Georgia trying to hide her condition beneath a loose-waisted gown.

After the public farewells to their workers and private farewells to each other, there wasn't much to do at the train station except shake hands, wave handkerchiefs, and call a tearful, "Good-bye! Godspeed!" as the train pulled out of the depot.

Hannah watched the train through her tears and prayed that Reiver and Benjamin would return safely to her. By the time she and the others boarded a train to take them back to Coldwater, she was forming plans of her own.

She felt as though she had been handed the keys to the kingdom, and she intended to open the doors wide.

She started with Davey.

Once they arrived home, she gave him several hours to sulk about his brother's good fortune and wallow in self-pity, then she went up to his room, where she found him stuffing himself with molasses cookies.

Hannah gave him an icy, disapproving stare. "David, I would like to see you in the study in five minutes. Brush those crumbs off your chin and make yourself presentable."

She ignored his stunned expression and left.

Five minutes later Davey appeared at the study door, his hair combed and no sign of cookie crumbs decorating his chin.

"Mama, why are you acting like Papa?" he asked.

She indicated the chair opposite her desk. "Because while Papa is away, I am the head of the Shaw family. I've decided that it's time you grew up and assumed your rightful place as a future heir to Shaw Silks."

Davey looked puzzled. He obviously relished the idea of being treated as his older brother's equal, but as for the rest of it . . .

Hannah said, "You will start by assisting Mr. Torelli in the dyeing shed."

Davey wrinkled his nose. "It's so damp and smelly in there."

"David, not everything in life is pleasant or fair, and it's time you learned that lesson. If you want to help your brother run Shaw Silks someday, you have to know everything about the company. And the only way you'll learn that is by working."

"But, Mama—"

"You will start tomorrow at six in the morning."

"But, Mama, that is too early."

"That's the time the mill opens, and that is when you'll begin work as well." Hannah turned her attention back to the papers on her desk, dismissing him.

Davey left the study.

Next Hannah summoned Samuel.

We're alone, Hannah thought the moment he walked through the door. *Reiver is on his way to Japan and will be gone for a long, long time.*

All she had to do was look into Samuel's pale, ghostly eyes and feel her body respond to know that she still loved and desired him. She wanted to run her fingers through the silver at his temples and feel the heavy heat of his mouth on hers again. She wanted him to touch her breasts and bare them. . . .

"You wanted to see me?"

Hannah snapped out of her erotic reverie.

Samuel walked over to the side table half a room away, as if purposely trying to put physical distance between himself and Hannah. He kept his right arm close to his side, a sure sign of his nervousness.

"Do I make you uneasy?" Hannah said.

"Not you." He gave her an anguished glance. "It's the temptation of seeing you day after day and knowing I can't have you."

So he still felt it, too.

"If he were so concerned about us becoming lovers again, he wouldn't have gone to Japan," Hannah said. "Quite frankly I don't think he cares."

"He trusts us, Hannah."

She sighed wearily. "I didn't ask you here to discuss Reiver and trust. I need you to help me with a matter of great importance to the company."

Samuel raised one brow. "Me?"

Hannah placed her hand on a thick sheaf of papers. "For years Reiver and the other silk manufacturers in this country have been trying to persuade Congress to increase the tariff on imported silks to help our domestic silk industry. It hasn't been successful."

"What can I do?"

"I'd like you to study these documents and papers and go to Washington to make another appeal for increased tariffs."

Samuel's eyes widened. "I don't know anything about tariffs."

"You can learn." When Samuel appeared reluctant, Hannah said gently, "Ever since you returned, you've said you wanted something productive to do. I think this would be perfect. After all, you lost a hand, not your mental faculties, and I desperately need someone to do this."

"What about James?"

"He's an inventor." She sat back in her chair. "And can't you just see me—a woman—storming the hallowed halls of Congress, trying to persuade stodgy old senators and representatives to establish such a tariff? They'd laugh me off Capitol Hill."

A rare hint of amusement lit Samuel's eyes. "I can see your point."

"You're a Shaw. They will listen to you."

"You really have this much faith in me?"

"Of course, otherwise I wouldn't have asked you."

He rose and reached for the papers. "I'll study these and see what I can do."

Hannah stood as well, damning them both for their politeness. "Let me know when you're ready to go to Washington."

Samuel smiled and left.

Hannah leaned back in her chair. Two years . . . how was she ever going to avoid temptation for two years? Samuel had sensed it as well when he was here, the currents still running as strong as ever between them. He tried to conceal it with a veneer of politeness, but Hannah saw through his ruse right away.

She rose. Both of them would just have to keep busy.

A man needed responsibility to achieve his full potential, Hannah decided. She was pleased with what it had done for

Davey during that difficult summer of 1858, when not a letter arrived from Reiver or Benjamin enroute to Japan, and Georgia almost died giving birth to twin boys.

During those bleak, frustrating days one of Hannah's consolations was watching the transformation in her younger son from an overfed, petulant child to a diligent, hardworking young man. On this tranquil night in late September she would learn if responsibility had transformed Samuel as well.

Hannah sat in the parlor and listened to a soft breeze sighing through the maples. She cast a worried look at Mrs. Hardy in the wing chair by the fire, a throw warming her. The old housekeeper had grown even more frail over the summer, her wrinkled skin turning as opaque as parchment and her thin shoulders becoming even more stooped. Her tongue, however, had not mellowed with age.

"When's he coming?" she muttered from the depths of her chair. "I can't wait up all night."

Hannah glanced at the tall-case clock. "It's nine o'clock now. He should be home soon. Perhaps the train from Washington was delayed."

Two weeks ago Samuel had left for Washington to try to convince Congress to increase the tariff. He was due back tonight, when Hannah would learn of his success or failure in person, rather than by telegram.

"Then he should have taken an earlier train," Mrs. Hardy said.

To distract her, Hannah asked the old lady if she wanted a cup of tea or an extra throw.

"Tea keeps me up at night." The rheumy silver eyes sparkled with youthful mischief. "I could go for a nip of Reiver's imported sherry, though."

Hannah smiled. "So could I." She poured two glasses and gave one to Mrs. Hardy.

The old lady slurped it greedily. "I never could understand why Reiver even touched this stuff after what demon rum did to his father."

Hannah shrugged. "Perhaps he drank now and then to prove to himself that he could without turning into a drunkard."

Mrs. Hardy nodded her silver head. "That sounds like

Reiver." She cocked one brow at Hannah. "You must be mighty lonely without him around."

Actually Hannah didn't miss him at all.

"I don't have time to be lonely. Running the mill is very time-consuming, even though I have plenty of help. And there's always the family to keep me company."

"Especially Samuel," Mrs. Hardy said, taking another swig of sherry. "Couldn't resist that charmer, could you?"

Hannah felt a chill race down her spine. "You knew we loved each other, didn't you?"

"I may be half-blind, but I'm not stupid. Of course I knew. I never told anyone, though, and never will, even on my death-bed, which won't be long in coming."

That reality saddened Hannah, but she said, "Before he left, Reiver said you'd outlive us all, so let's not hear any talk of dying, Mrs. Hardy."

The silver eyes twinkled. "You'll miss me when I'm gone." The laughter in her eyes faded. "If you go on working as hard as you have these past months, you're the one who won't be around for long."

Hannah sipped her sherry. "I must admit that running the mill is more tiring than I expected."

"That's because it's men's work." Mrs. Hardy drained her glass. "I can't keep my eyes open another second. Tell Samuel he didn't get here in time, so he missed seeing me."

"I will." Hannah helped the frail old lady upstairs to bed, then returned to the parlor to keep her vigil.

She went to the front door to peer out the sidelights and see if anyone was walking down the drive. All she saw were the tall maple trees silhouetted against the blue-black twilight sky.

Just as she was turning away, movement caught her eye. She turned back to see a familiar figure separate from the shadows and walk down the drive.

Samuel.

Hannah opened the door and went out on the porch. "Welcome home."

In the fast-fading light she couldn't discern Samuel's features well enough to tell if his mission had met with success or failure. When he stepped into the light coming from the hallway, Hannah knew.

"No higher tariff this year," Samuel said, setting his valise down in the hall.

Hannah studied him carefully. While deep shadows underscored his eyes, they flashed with determination rather than defeat, and he held himself straight and tall, like a warrior awaiting another skirmish.

Hannah smiled and helped him with his coat. "Come have a glass of sherry and tell me all about it."

Samuel sat down in the wing chair vacated by Mrs. Hardy and rubbed his eyes. "Everyone's too preoccupied with the possibility of the slave states seceding to concern themselves with the silk manufacturers."

Hannah poured him a sherry and refilled her own glass. "Was it a good fight?"

Samuel grinned, a flash of white teeth. "A very good fight."

She handed him his sherry, sat down across from him, and listened while he spoke of Washington. He told of the tense, divisive mood in the capital between representatives of the industrialized North and the agricultural South, of the long, frustrating days and evenings meeting with congressmen on both sides to try to convince them that supporting such a higher tariff would benefit everyone.

Samuel leaned back in his chair. "I think the only way we'll get legislation passed is if the South secedes and we go to war."

Hannah shuddered. "I wouldn't want to see that happen, even if it means that Shaw Silks has to manufacture only thread and ribbons forever."

"Don't let Reiver hear you say that."

Hannah smiled dryly. "He wouldn't mind a war if it meant Shaw Silks would prosper." She added, "As long as Benjamin and Davey didn't have to fight in it, of course."

Samuel shook his head. "I can't believe the change in Davey since he's been working in the mill." He stared into the cold fireplace. "Or the change in myself since you involved me with this tariff legislation." He looked at her, his gaze bright and warm. "Don't think I don't realize what you've been doing."

Hannah sensed his mood shift at once. Gone was the wounded, withdrawn Samuel, always keeping Hannah at a distance, treading softly lest he anger his brother. The man sitting across from her was infinitely more dangerous.

She widened her eyes innocently. "What have I been doing?"

"Giving me back my self-respect." Samuel rose, set his glass on the mantel, and leaned against it. "When I lost my hand, I wanted to die. I considered killing myself, but when I thought of never seeing you again, I couldn't go through with it. I felt worse than useless, especially when I returned to Coldwater."

"You shouldn't feel that way. This is your home."

He bowed his head. "But most of all, I regretted letting Reiver banish me to California. I should have stayed with you, Hannah."

She rose and went to him, just stopping short of flinging herself into his arms. "Once Reiver discovered us, there was nothing else either of us could have done. I couldn't leave my children, and if we tried to see each other secretly, Reiver would have harmed you."

"I still have so many regrets."

"Don't, Samuel. At the time we weren't fated to be together."

He grew very still, his body taut. "And now?"

Hannah's heart stopped. She couldn't breathe. His words hung between them as solid and tempting as Eve's apple in the Garden of Eden.

She reached for him, helpless to stop herself. Samuel's arms encircled her and his mouth possessed hers with such sweet ferocity that Hannah couldn't think a coherent thought. Oddly enough, when his hand found her breast, her conscience awoke with a shriek.

Hannah pulled away, panting hard.

Samuel stared at her. "What's wrong? I thought you wanted—"

"We mustn't!"

He ran his hand through his hair in frustration. "Reiver's in Japan. We have nothing to fear."

"But I am afraid." She clasped her hands in front of her. "I'm afraid that if I start loving you, I won't be able to stop."

He smiled gently. "And that would be so bad?"

"It would be heaven . . . until Reiver returns. Then what? We'll have to stop loving each other? Pretend that we were never lovers?" She shook her head vehemently. "I couldn't bear it."

"So we shouldn't even start?"

"We shouldn't start what we can't finish. It will just be too painful."

He fell silent. "Do you remember what I once told you about living for the moment?"

"You said that we should because it might never come again."

His pale eyes grew wistful. "Well, I would rather be your lover for two years than never at all."

"All I would do is live in dread of the day I would have to give you up again."

Samuel took a step toward her, an expression of desperate appeal written on his face. "Hannah, I love you. I don't know if I can be so close to you day after day without going mad if I can't have you."

"As much as I love you, I can't resume our affair knowing it will have to end." Tears filled her eyes. "We have no future together, Samuel. We have to accept it."

"I can't accept it, not when I've found you again." Furious, he strode out of the parlor, grabbed his coat, and stormed out the front door, letting it slam behind him with a bang.

Hannah was just about to go after him when a terrified wail resounded through the downstairs.

"I'm coming, Lizzie." Hannah turned and went upstairs to banish the child's nightmare.

In late April of 1859, almost one year to the day that Reiver and Benjamin left for Japan, Martha Hardy died in her sleep.

Hannah stood weeping behind her black veil in the cemetery, clutching Elisabeth's hand as mourners threw a handful of earth onto the pine box before leaving.

"Reiver said she would outlive us all," she said to James, standing on her left.

He touched her elbow. "She was seventy-seven years old. She lived a good long life."

Three-year-old Elisabeth looked up at Hannah out of wide, somber eyes so reminiscent of her father. "Is Mrs. Hardy in heaven, Aunt Hannah?"

"Yes, Lizzie." Sharp tongue and all.

Hannah smiled at the thought of Mrs. Hardy confronting Saint Peter. "There must be some mistake, you old fool," she would say. "I must belong in the other place." But he'd let her in, anyway.

Davey swiped at his eyes with the back of his hand when he thought no one was looking. Hannah wondered if he was thinking of all the times Mrs. Hardy smuggled him cookies.

As the family walked from the cemetery back to the main house, where funeral meats awaited the mourners, Georgia said to Hannah, "How are you going to tell Reiver?"

"I can't. I don't know where he'll be, and letters take so long to arrive that we can never be sure if they reach him." The last letter she had received from him at Christmas was from California, though he was sure to be in the Hawaiian Islands or even Hong Kong by this time. "I suppose he'll just have to wait until he's home to learn that Mrs. Hardy is no longer with us."

At the mention of Reiver, Samuel's back stiffened as he walked ahead of Hannah. She knew his expression would be dark and fierce, for ever since Hannah had rejected him the night he had returned from Washington, he seethed with a frustration that often manifested itself in a Mrs. Hardy–type cantankerousness.

When the mourners returned to the main house, with its somber black funeral wreath on the door and sepulchral silence inside, Samuel drank only one glass of sherry, then excused himself to leave on business for Shaw Silks in New York City. He told James to say good-bye to Hannah for him.

He was never absent from Hannah's thoughts.

She spent a sleepless night, wandering restlessly from the window facing the homestead to her bed, where she tossed and turned. The following morning she told Davey and Georgia that she had to go away for a few days on business and scandalized her son by traveling alone on the next train bound for New York City.

Hannah endured curious and disapproving stares in the plush lobby of the Union Square Hotel for three hours before she saw a tired-looking Samuel walk through the door.

She rose. He saw her at once and stopped, a look of disbelief on his face.

He walked up to her. "What are you doing here?"

"I came to see you."

"I just called on the sales office, and they're doing—"

"I don't care about the sales office." She took a step closer. "I'm here to see you."

Suspicion darkened the depths of his pale eyes. "I thought we've said all we had to say to each other."

Hannah glanced around the crowded lobby and lowered her voice so they wouldn't be overheard. "Is there somewhere we can go that's more private?"

"Only my room."

"That will be perfect, for a variety of reasons."

Samuel's mouth tightened. "Don't toy with me, Hannah."

"I wouldn't think of it. Now, shall we pretend we're husband and wife so the management doesn't think I'm a woman of easy virtue soliciting its patrons?"

Samuel didn't smile, just extended his arm to her and took her valise.

Once upstairs in his room, he closed the door and turned to face her. "Now, why are you really here?"

She clasped her hands tightly in front of her. "Do you know what I thought about yesterday when we buried Mrs. Hardy? Abigail and the child I lost that I believed was yours." Her voice quavered. "I had them for such a short time, and then they were gone, lost to me forever."

"Hannah, don't inflict such pain on yourself. Please."

She made a dismissive motion with her hand. "No, I have to say this no matter how much it hurts. Back at the house after the burial, I thought about how we've been so estranged these last few months. I lost you when Reiver sent you away, and you almost died in that mining disaster. Miraculously, you were returned to me." She shrugged helplessly, her eyes filling with tears. "Now I have the chance to love you again, and I'm just throwing it away."

Samuel stood very still. "You said you couldn't bear the thought of giving me up when Reiver returns."

"I still can't, but now I'm ready to live for the moment, because I don't know when it will ever come again. That is, if you'll still have me after the way I've treated you."

"Oh, Hannah . . ." Samuel extended his arms to her.

This time she went to him without reservations, and when

Samuel kissed her, she thought not of endings or consequences, but a perfect moment not bounded by past or future.

When they parted, Samuel stroked her cheek. "Are you sure? We'll be betraying Reiver."

Hannah sighed. "Reiver has always loved someone or something more than I, and he always will. First Cecelia, then the company. I'm tired of always being second best." She took his hand. "I may have the boys and control of Shaw Silks, but I feel so empty inside."

Samuel hugged her. "I've felt that way ever since that day I left you."

"Then let's fill those empty spaces.

"My beloved Samuel." Hannah took his face in her hands and stared deeply into his pale eyes that were igniting passion. She drew his head down toward her waiting mouth, and when their lips met, her spirit soared like a caged bird finally set free, and she welcomed his tender possession of her mouth. Behind her closed lids, tears stung her eyes at the sweet, familiar taste of him and the years of heartbreak and separation retreated to the past, where they belonged.

When they parted, breathless and trembling, Hannah said shyly, "I hope my body doesn't repulse you." How to explain to him that her breasts lacked their youthful high carriage and her waist would never measure nineteen inches again, even with the tightest lacing? "I'm no longer a lissome girl, you know."

"Need I remind you that I'm no longer a young man? And I don't have a hand, but I can still love you."

Samuel's reassurances notwithstanding, Hannah still felt awkward as he unbuttoned her bodice dexterously, his eyes following every square inch of exposed flesh. When he finished, he stepped back, and a blushing Hannah stripped down to her chemise and pantalets.

She risked a quick look at Samuel as she stepped out of the tangle of black silk on the floor, and caught her breath when she saw the look of raw yearning twist his handsome face.

"Your turn," she whispered, her trembling hands helping him remove his frock coat, shirt, and trousers, leaving only his drawers. Hannah swallowed hard, for her fingers itched to touch his chest and shoulders, to feel the heat and smoothness of his skin and the hardness of muscle and bone beneath it, to inhale his masculine scent, but she held herself back. Patience. She didn't want to rush this after waiting so long.

Samuel whispered, "May I see you? I've waited an eternity. . . ."

Hannah pulled down her chemise straps and bared her breasts, fearing the worst. She had worried needlessly. The look in Samuel's ghostly pale eyes told her quite plainly that to him, no matter what toll time took upon her, she would always remain twenty-six.

He cupped her heavy, warm flesh, catching the dusky nipple between his fingers and arousing it until Hannah became dizzy with the pleasure unfurling within her. She groaned and swayed, grabbing Samuel's shoulders to keep herself from falling. "Samuel!"

"Do you like this?" he asked, his voice hot and ragged. His eyes never leaving her face, he performed the same erotic magic on her other breast.

"Yes, oh, yes. Please, more." Forbidden pleasure, white-hot and exquisite, seared through her like a jagged lightning bolt, tingling her whole body right down to the ends of her fingertips and toes.

"As you wish." He grinned wickedly and lowered his head to draw his tongue across one nipple, then the other, back and forth, tasting her until Hannah thought she would expire right there.

In loving retaliation, she ran her hand down his chest in a light, teasing caress and came to rest between his legs. Samuel straightened and sucked in his breath with a startled hiss. "Wanton."

Hannah's eyes sparkled mischievously. "Mrs. Hardy was right. All you need is a good stiff—"

"Hannah Shaw, such bawdy language from a lady!" But Samuel was laughing even as he admonished her. Then he sobered. "I think it's time you removed my drawers."

"If I can," she retorted. "They're very tight."

Samuel chuckled at that, slipping his arm around her waist and drawing her to him for another long, leisurely kiss. "We'll manage," he said against her mouth.

When Samuel finally stood naked before her, Hannah touched him, needing to prove to herself that she still had the

power to arouse him. Samuel closed his eyes, shuddered, and
groaned, moving against her hand.

He entwined his fingers in her hair. "If you keep this up, my
love, I won't be much good to either of us."

Hannah brushed her lips lightly against his mouth. "Then
let's make up for lost time, shall we?"

Lying in each other's arms, they loved each other slowly, as
if every touch, every sensation, had to be savored and stored
away like some precious memento.

"I missed you so much," Hannah whispered, her eyes filling
with tears.

Samuel brushed a lock of hair away from her face. "There
have been so many times over the years that I missed you so
much, I just wanted to die."

"I'm glad you didn't."

When he parted her thighs and entered her welcoming
warmth, Hannah felt as though a missing part of herself had finally been returned. Moving in love's ageless dance with Samuel, she let their passion sweep her to the heights, where she
shouted his name in exultation, and made a vow that someday
they would be together forever.

When they returned to Coldwater, they remained secret lovers, sharing trysts whenever they could, though Hannah
dreaded the day Reiver would return.

As the months flew by with no word from Reiver or Benjamin, Hannah feared that her husband and son would never return, especially after the abolitionist John Brown was hanged
for the massacre at Harpers Ferry in December, 1859 and talk of
secession swept through the land like a raging fever. A year
later, when South Carolina seceded from the Union and Reiver
and Benjamin still hadn't returned, Hannah wondered if she
would ever see her husband and son again.

CHAPTER
❧ 20 ❧

ON April 16, 1861, Reiver and Benjamin returned home after a three-year absence.

Hannah stood on the platform in the Hartford train station with the other Shaws, her heart relieved that her son and husband had arrived in New York City unscathed in spite of the long siege of Fort Sumter. Insurrection or not, they were safe. That's all that mattered.

But every beginning heralded an ending.

Hannah exchanged soulful looks with Samuel. We've lived for the moment, his seemed to say, and now our moments together are over. They had both become resigned to the hopelessness of their love and stopped dreaming of ever being together.

"Isn't that their train?" Davey asked, his voice devoid of enthusiasm, for he had thrived without the competition of his older brother and wasn't looking forward to resuming his place in Benjamin's shadow.

"Right on time," James said, brushing his graying hair out of his eyes and yearning to be back home with Georgia and their third child, a new baby girl to civilize their boisterous twin boys.

The train slowed and finally stopped in a loud *swoosh* of steam and an earsplitting screech of wheels. Doors swung open and passengers poured out onto the platform. Hannah craned her neck, searching the crowd of unfamiliar faces for the two she knew best.

"Mother!"

The familiar voice didn't match the tall, lanky young man

hurrying toward her, but when Hannah saw the near image of her father's face smiling back at her, she recognized her older son. Enfolding him in her arms, she hugged him as fiercely as when he was a little boy.

He stiffened. "Mother, please. You're embarrassing me."

She stepped back, eyes wet with tears of joy. "You'll have to forgive your sentimental old mother, but it's been such a long time since—" Hannah's eyes widened in shock when she saw the fine angry red scar running along his cheekbone. "Benjamin Shaw! What happened to your face?"

He touched the scar with obvious pride. "Oh, that . . . it's nothing. Father and I walked right into the middle of a Chinese war." Before Hannah could comment or swoon, Benjamin moved away to greet his uncles and brother.

Hannah came face-to-face with Reiver.

While his light brown hair was beginning to recede and deeper lines scored the corners of his eyes and mouth, Reiver hadn't changed that much since the day she bade him farewell. She wondered if he remained unchanged inside as well.

His keen blue eyes inspected her quickly. "There's something different about you."

"I'm three years older." Then she hugged him as she would a friend after a long absence. "Welcome back. I'm glad you brought my son home in one piece."

Reiver grinned and looked ten years younger than his forty-eight years. "We did have some close calls, but we survived." Then he left her to greet his brothers, hugging them both and pounding them on the back.

When he saw Davey, he stopped and shook his head in wonder. "I left a boy and return to find a young man."

Davey, who had never quite forgiven his father for leaving him at home while taking Benjamin, stood there awkwardly. "I'm sixteen now, and I've been working in the mill."

"And doing an excellent job," Hannah added.

Reiver looked around. "Where's Elisabeth?" He already knew about Mrs. Hardy's death from one of the few letters he had managed to intercept in his travels around the Orient.

"Elisabeth wanted to welcome her uncle Reiver home, but she's at home with the sniffles and I didn't think it prudent to let her make the trip."

Reiver looked around at his assembled family. "Ben and I have so much to tell you."

"And we have much to tell you," Hannah said. "But why don't we wait until we're home?"

Reiver's eyes glowed with expectation. "Until we're home."

". . . and if Captain Lawson hadn't taught me how to fight with a saber," Benjamin told his enthralled audience, "I wouldn't have stood a chance against those heathen Chinese."

Hannah glanced at the tall-case clock, unable to believe that it was already one o'clock in the morning. Ever since Reiver and Ben came home, the family had been sitting in the parlor, spellbound by their tales of adventure. Storms off the Strait of Magellan vied with the Chinese Opium War for sheer hair-raising excitement, though Hannah would have preferred hearing about Japanese silk rather than her son's many brushes with death.

Finally she said, "It's late, everyone. Perhaps we should all get to bed."

Stifling yawns of weariness rather than boredom, everyone rose and, after saying good night, drifted off one by one until only Hannah and Reiver remained to share an uneasy silence.

Will he ask me if I've been unfaithful? Hannah wondered. She and Samuel had already decided to deny it.

"There's so much we have to say to each other," Reiver said, his blue eyes unreadable.

Will he expect to share my bed? "The mill has been very profitable, as you'll see from the account books. Samuel has been to Washington several times to plead our case for a higher import tariff, and Davey has taken to the business like a duck to water."

"Yes, I noticed how eager he was to impress me with everything he's learned."

"We'll have to be very careful how we treat the boys," Hannah said. "Davey's carved out a niche for himself since Benjamin left, and any hint of favoritism could prove disastrous."

Reiver, ever Ben's champion, surprised Hannah by agreeing.

Then he said, "Lizzie is quite the little beauty. I'm surprised she remembered me, since she was so young when I left."

"I talked about you and Ben every day to her so she wouldn't forget you, and showed her tintypes of her 'Uncle Reiver' and 'Cousin Ben.' "

"That was awfully decent of you." He hesitated. "Tonight, when you brought her downstairs for a few minutes, I could see that she's become very attached to you."

"Why wouldn't she? I am the only mother she has ever known."

A wistful expression touched Reiver's face. "I think Cecelia would be happy to know that her daughter is well taken care of."

"Lizzie is everything Abigail couldn't be," Hannah said softly.

Reiver stared down at his hands and said nothing. Even after all these years he still couldn't bring himself to talk about Abigail, because he had never loved her.

As they resumed conversing about their family and the mill, Hannah realized that after twenty-one years of marriage, they had finally become comfortable with each other, fitting easily like well-worn shoes. Time had leached out the pain of old wounds.

Finally Hannah rose. "I've got to go to bed before I fall asleep on my feet."

"It's been an exhausting day." Reiver stood, his expression inscrutable as he waited for her to join him.

He took a lamp and they walked upstairs together. When they got to Hannah's room, she stopped at the door. Was he expecting her to invite him to share her bed? Would he insist?

Reiver kissed her good night, turned, and walked to his old room without a backward glance.

Hannah expelled a small sigh of relief and entered her room to sleep alone.

Reiver rose late the following morning, dressed quickly, and went to the mill. Walking down Mulberry Hill, he breathed deeply of the fresh spring air, grateful to feel solid Yankee soil beneath his feet once again and to hear English spoken.

For the past three years, while seeing many startling and

wondrous sights on his travels, he had thought of nothing else
but regaining control of his company.

He had made that devil's bargain with Hannah for Lizzie's
sake because he had no other choice, but now that his daughter
was older, there had to be some way he could force Hannah to
relinquish the company.

His task would not be easy. He could see that his wife had
grown to relish the power that almost none of her sex attained,
and she would hate to relinquish it. But there was a way. He had
to exploit her weakness.

And that weakness was Samuel.

Georgia and Hannah sat beneath the shade of the tallest oak
tree one hot July morning, enjoying a brief visit before Hannah
left to call on the mother of a Shaw employee who had answered President Lincoln's call to enlist in the Union Army and
had been killed in the Battle of Bull Run on July 21. He was
only seventeen.

Georgia's eyes filled with tears. "I didn't know Artemus, but
James said he was a hard worker and wanted to help end slavery."

"He was very idealistic. He took *Uncle Tom's Cabin* out of
the mill library several times."

Georgia shuddered. "It makes the war seem close, doesn't
it?"

Hannah looked out over the idyllic landscape of cloudless
blue summer sky, lush green trees, and the stagecoach kicking
up clouds of dust on Hartford Road and found it difficult to
imagine that elsewhere in her own country there were battle-
fields strewn with wounded and dying young men like
Artemus.

She smiled sadly at the waste. "Let's be thankful that Ben
and Davey are home where they belong, and the twins are too
young to go to war."

Georgia blushed. "Speaking of the twins . . . soon they and
Victoria will have a new little brother or sister."

Hannah's eyes widened in surprise. So soon? "Why, that's
wonderful! You'll be filling the Bickford house with all those
babies you and James want."

Georgia, whose confinements never lasted longer than eight

hours, glowed with vitality and anticipation. "I love the feeling of having a baby growing inside me. I'm going to have a dozen, if I can."

Hannah thought of the children she could never have and felt a twinge of jealousy, but it passed quickly. "You're fortunate."

Yes, Hannah thought as she excused herself and left for her condolence call, wars might rage, but life went on. As long as Confederate soldiers didn't storm Mulberry Hill and women kept buying thread and ribbons, she and her family would remain untouched by the horror.

When Hannah returned to the house, she found Reiver waiting for her in the study.

"Where have you been?" he asked, his voice edged with impatience.

"I called on Artemus's mother."

Reiver shook his head. "Damn fool boy, running off to join the army like that."

Hannah dabbed her damp brow with her handkerchief. "I felt so sorry for his mother. It's tragic to lose a child at any age, but more so when they've been with you awhile."

His fingers drummed the desk nervously. "There's something important I'd like to discuss with you."

Hannah sat down on the settee and arranged her hoop skirt carefully. "You sound so serious. What is it?"

"I want my mill back."

She raised her brows in surprise. "Why should I give it to you? We made a bargain, remember?"

He leaned back against the edge of his desk and crossed his arms. "We struck that devil's bargain years ago. Circumstances have changed, and I want to renegotiate."

"I don't see how anything has changed."

"The boys are grown, and Lizzie is no longer a baby."

"I wanted controlling interest in the mill in exchange for caring for your illegitimate child. Are you telling me that you don't want me to care for Lizzie now?"

"Oh, no. Lizzie is much too attached to her aunt Hannah to separate the two of you."

Hannah laughed incredulously. "You still want me to raise

her, but you also want the mill back. I'm sorry, but I will not agree to that."

"If you agree to my terms, I'll give you your freedom."

Hannah froze, unable to believe her ears. "My freedom?"

He nodded. "If you return all of my shares, I'll give you a divorce. You will be free to marry Samuel."

"Why should I want to marry him? I told you that our feelings for each other died long ago. There's nothing between us now."

"You may deny it all you like, but I doubt that you and he have been able to keep your hands off each other for the last three years."

When Hannah opened her mouth to protest, he held up his hand to silence her. "I honestly don't care. I just want the mill back. Since my brother is incapacitated, I'll also give you a ten-percent interest in the company to support you both very comfortably for the rest of your lives. You may live in the homestead. All I ask is that you keep Lizzie with you."

She stared at him as if he were deranged. "Why the sudden turnabout? You were so adamant that Cecelia's daughter be raised as a Shaw. You even sacrificed your mill for her. Now you don't care?"

"At the time, I had no other choice. Now that she's older, she'll be fine if you agree to take her."

Hannah shook her head. "I don't know. . . ."

Reiver stepped away from the desk, his expression imploring. "This is best for all concerned. You and Samuel would be together without any interference from me, and I'd get Shaw Silks back."

"What of my involvement in the company? Will you expect me to give it all up?"

Reiver's gaze slid away. "I suppose you could still do the accounts if you wanted to, and call on the workers when they're sick, but as I would now have controlling interest, I would make the major decisions."

Would he reduce the workers' wages again? she wondered. Would he callously replace anyone dissatisfied with the new lower wages? Would he realize her dream of eventually providing their employees with inexpensive housing? Knowing Reiver as she did, Hannah doubted it.

His expression hardened. "Why are you hesitating, Hannah? I'm offering to give you everything you've ever wanted."

But now Shaw Silks means as much to me as Samuel does, and I don't know if I can give it up, she thought. "I'll have to consider your offer," she said, gathering her skirts to leave.

Reiver's hand shot out and caught her wrist. "Shaw Silks belongs to me. I built it up from nothing, and I will have it back. Don't cross me on this, Hannah, or you'll live to regret it."

She shivered at the calculating menace in his voice. "I said, I will consider your offer." She jerked her arm free and swept out of the study.

Once outside, she headed down Mulberry Hill toward the homestead.

Hannah found Samuel sitting at the dining-room table with his shirt sleeves rolled up and papers strewn about him.

He looked up, his pale eyes warming at the sight of her. Then he frowned when he examined her expression more closely. "What's wrong?"

Hannah smiled dryly. "What could possibly be wrong? Reiver has just offered to give me everything I've ever wanted." At Samuel's puzzled look, Hannah proceeded to enlighten him.

When she finished, Samuel said, "What did you tell him?"

"I told him I'd think about it." The minute the words were out of her mouth, Hannah realized her mistake. She shot Samuel a look of alarm, dreading to see the betrayal on his face.

"If I were a younger man, I'd be furious with you for not jumping at the chance to spend the rest of your life with me." He sighed dismally and ran his hand through his hair. "But I realize there are more important matters at stake than my own selfish concerns."

Hannah went to him and touched her hand to his grizzled beard. "You know I'd like nothing better than to do just that. But this doesn't involve just you and me. There is Lizzie to consider, and the welfare of the workers."

"Reiver has always treated them like family."

"Not always. He cut their wages once, and if I hadn't insisted that he reinstate them, he would've just replaced anyone who left. Unlike many factory owners, I've also refused to hire children. Who knows what Reiver plans to do in that regard?"

Hannah paced once around the dining room and stopped. "This may sound unfeminine of me, but I enjoy controlling Shaw Silks, and I think I've done a damn fine job. When nothing else in my life was going right, it provided a great source of comfort and satisfaction."

Samuel rose and went to her. "Do what you think is best."

She clenched her fists in frustration. "It's not that simple. Reiver has threatened that I'll live to regret it if I don't do as he wishes."

He drew her into his arms and held her. "I won't let him hurt you."

Hannah pulled away. "I'm not worried for myself. You live here on Reiver's bounty. What if he decides to cast you out again? I can't let him do that."

He looked chagrined. "I'll have you know I'm not quite the charity case everyone thinks me to be just because I've got this." He held up his wooden hand. "I'll have you know that several congressmen were quite impressed with me when I went to Washington."

Hannah smiled. "How could they not be?" Her smile faded. "But there's Lizzie. What if Reiver remarries and takes her away from me? She may be Cecelia's daughter, but I love her as if she were my own, and it would break my heart to give her up." She shook her head in disgust. "I thought Reiver loved his daughter better than his mill, but I was wrong. Shaw Silks will always be first in his heart."

Samuel stood there in silence. "So what will you do?"

"I'll ask Reiver to give me until Christmas to decide. Hopefully by that time I'll know what to do."

The second Sunday in November dawned bitter cold and so still, not a bare branch shivered. After church services Benjamin reported that he had heard the Coldwater River was frozen solid and perfect for an ice-skating party.

With predictions of a long war and the North now blockading the South's ports, both Hannah and Reiver agreed that a skating party would lift the family's spirits. So Hannah bundled up Lizzie and invited Samuel and James to come along.

When they arrived at the river, they discovered that the cove was already crowded with skaters of all ages and sizes gliding around and around.

Hannah sat on an overturned log and put on her skates, casting a worried look at the river running past the cove. "Benjamin," she said, "the river isn't frozen. That's open water out there."

He gave her a supercilious look. "The river may not be frozen, Mother, but the cove is. Look at everyone skating. It's perfectly safe."

She was not reassured. "Stay away from the edge of the ice. It isn't safe."

"Yes, Mother," he replied in a bored, placating tone before skating off.

Hannah watched him in growing annoyance. Ever since returning from the Orient, Benjamin had been acting like a spoiled brat, disrespectful to his mother and condescending to everyone else. He was turning into a most unpleasant young man.

"Aunt Hannah," Lizzie said, "will you skate with me?"

"Just let me get your skates on, and we can take a turn around the ice."

Once Lizzie's skates were laced tight, Hannah took her hand, and they started off slowly, going around and around. Hannah smiled at people she knew, always keeping her eyes on her sons, who seemed intent on proving who could skate the fastest.

After several turns around the cove, Lizzie announced that she was tired, so Hannah returned to the log at the edge of the ice to catch her breath and watch the skaters.

"Look!" Lizzie said, pointing to a thick log half-submerged in the water and frozen in the ice. "Davey's going to jump."

Hannah held her breath as her younger son skated in long, swinging strides toward the fallen log, gaining momentum with every second. Then he leaned forward, drew up his legs and jumped, sailing over it with inches to spare. Miraculously he landed without mishap and skated on to loud applause from the onlookers.

Reiver skated over to Hannah. "Enjoying the contest?"

She shook her head. "One of them is bound to fall and crack his head open."

"Spoken like a true mother hen." He looked down at her. "Perhaps we'd better take a turn around the ice before people start to talk."

"But people are talking now," Lizzie piped up, frankly puzzled.

"Yes, honey, they certainly are." Hannah looked up at Reiver, surprised that he would even ask her to skate with him. He had not been pleased with having to wait until Christmas to learn of her decision, and relations between them had been as cold as this day in November.

"Someone has to watch Lizzie," she said.

Reiver hailed Benjamin skating past. "Son, watch your cousin while your mother and I go skating."

"Father, I am not a nursemaid."

Reiver's wide jaw clenched. "You are while your mother and I are skating. Now do as you're told."

Benjamin muttered something under his breath, then extended his mittened hand to Lizzie, and off they went. Hannah joined hands with Reiver, and they skated off in tandem.

"At least pretend that you're enjoying this," he said through clenched teeth.

"I'm not, so why should I?" she replied.

As they rounded the cove and came back Hannah noticed that Benjamin and Lizzie were too far away, out near the edge of the open water.

"Reiver," she said in alarm, "Ben has taken Lizzie too near the river. It's dangerous. Let's call them back."

He dismissed her fears with an irritated, "Ben won't let anything happen to Lizzie. She's safe with him."

"I'm worried. I want to call them back."

Reiver tightened his grip on her hands so she couldn't pull away. "You've always wanted to keep those children wrapped in cotton batting. Now stop worrying."

As they started to take another turn around the ice, Hannah glanced back around her shoulder to check on Benjamin and Lizzie. Without warning, the ice gave way with a sickening crack.

Ben and Lizzie dropped into the water and disappeared.

Hannah screamed and pulled out of Reiver's grasp. "Dear God, they've fallen in!"

"Stay back!" Reiver cried, and before Hannah could blink, he was skating toward the broken ice and open water.

A collective gasp of shock rippled through the skaters, and everyone stopped. Several men went flying past Hannah, who stood there as if her skates were frozen to the ice. Then a grim-faced Samuel was beside her, gripping her hand.

When Hannah saw Reiver's intention, she screamed his name and lunged forward, but Samuel restrained her. Together they watched in horror as Reiver dived into the black, freezing water to save his children.

Hannah stood there, her hand pressed to her mouth to keep from screaming. She saw three dark heads bobbing like balls in the water, and two men stretched out on the ice to distribute their weight evenly and keep from crashing through themselves, their arms extended. One of them was James.

Please God, let them be safe, Hannah prayed. I'll do anything you ask. Anything.

One of the men caught someone and pulled him onto the ice, which was cracking ominously under the additional weight.

"Benjamin!" Hannah cried. "Dear God, he's safe!"

One of the skaters rushed out with a lap rug and wrapped it around the drenched, shivering Benjamin, leading him back to safety. Though she wanted to go to her son, Hannah couldn't tear her eyes away from the life-and-death drama unfolding on the edge of the ice. Lizzie and Reiver were still in the water, and it looked as though Reiver was keeping her afloat.

Suddenly both men grabbed another bobbing figure and hauled it out of an icy grave. Another rescuer wrapped little Lizzie in a blanket and carried her over to Hannah.

"Lizzie, dear God, oh, my baby . . ." The child was soaked and shuddering, her lips tinged with blue and teeth chattering, but her dazed eyes were half-open and she was alive. Tears streaming down her cheeks, Hannah kissed her on the forehead. "We've got to get her warm before she freezes to death."

Then Hannah looked for Reiver, but he was nowhere to be found.

She searched the place where the men had rescued Benjamin and Lizzie, waiting for the third survivor. All she saw was

James and the other man making their way slowly back over the ice.

One look at Samuel's stricken face and she knew.

"No!" she screamed.

Shivering James, his clothes wet and half-frozen, and cheeks stained with tears, stood before her. "I'm sorry, Hannah," he said through chattering teeth. His voice broke. "I almost had him, but he was in the water too long and he just gave out. He couldn't reach me before—before the current took him." He broke down sobbing.

Later, when they were all back safe and warm at the main house, Hannah asked James if Reiver had uttered any last words before the current took him.

Still dazed, he replied, "Just one word. Cecelia."

Hannah just smiled through her tears, for Reiver had finally set her free.

Rummy Shaw's eldest son departed this earth in a style more befitting a king than the son of a no-account drunkard. Those same citizens of Coldwater who had jeered at the father came to pay their respects to his son, along with dignitaries from Hartford and New York.

If anyone heard Reiver Shaw's widow's amused bubble of ironic laughter behind her thick mourning veil, they attributed it to hysteria and bowed their heads in prayer.

"Benjamin, it wasn't your fault."

A week after Reiver's lavish funeral, a black-clad Hannah stood in the parlor trying to console her son. Benjamin sat slumped on the settee, as gray-faced and red-eyed as Hannah's doctor father whenever he lost a patient.

"It is my fault," Ben moaned, holding his head in his hands. "I shouldn't have skated out so far with Lizzie. She could have drowned like Abigail, and Father is dead!"

Standing by the warm fireplace, Hannah shivered. How could she have forgotten that Abigail had died because her brothers were watching a rabbit hole instead of her? Now Ben blamed his father's death on his carelessness.

Hannah walked over to the settee and stared down at him sternly. "Now, you listen to me, Benjamin Shaw. You were only a little boy when Abigail died, and you were not responsible. And as for last Sunday, several of the men at the pond said that the spot you were skating on should have held. Anyone could have fallen in."

Fresh tears streamed down his face. "Why did Father have to try to save us? Why didn't he let somebody younger and stronger—"

"Son, listen to me." Hannah knelt down and grasped his hands. "Your father tried to save you and your cousin—"

"You don't have to lie anymore, Mother." Ben pulled his hands away and leaned back. "I know Lizzie's my half-sister. While Father and I were in Japan, he told me that she is his daughter."

What else did he tell you? Hannah wondered as she rose. That Samuel and I were lovers? That I took Shaw Silks in exchange for raising his daughter?

"We can discuss that later," she said. "What I've got to make you understand is that in spite of his faults, your father loved his family very much. He could no more stand by helplessly than he could stop loving you.

"Son, I don't know why the Good Lord chose to take your father from us. As painful as it is, we have to accept it because nothing is going to bring him back to us."

Ben flung himself off the settee. "I'll never accept it! Never!" Before Hannah could stop him, he stormed out of the parlor and out the front door, letting in a blast of frigid air before slamming the door behind him.

Alone in the silence, Hannah rubbed her aching forehead.

"Mama?"

She turned to see Davey standing in the parlor entrance, looking somber and haggard in his mourning clothes. "Are you all right?" he asked. "Can I get you anything? A glass of sherry or a cup of tea?"

She smiled wanly and extended her hand to her younger son, who had surprised her with his strength and compassion during this sad time. "I'm fine, really, and I've had enough tea to last me a lifetime." She looked at the front door. "I'm afraid Ben has been taking your father's death especially hard."

Davey shrugged. "I'm not surprised. He and Papa were always close."

"Your father loved you, David," Hannah said. "You mustn't think that he didn't."

"I just wish he had told me."

Hannah hugged her son, also wishing he were a little boy again. She indicated that he should join her on the settee. "Your father was a complex, difficult man. There were times when I loved him, and times I hated him."

Davey raised his brows. "You hated Father?"

"Sometimes. Do you think me terrible for saying it?"

"No. There were times when I hated him, too." He grinned. "And Ben." Then he became serious. "Perhaps I should go after him and see if I can help."

"No, I think he needs to be alone."

But Hannah needed company.

Samuel's papers cluttered the homestead's dining-room table, but he was not there working on them.

"Samuel?" Hannah called from the foot of the stairs.

"I'm up here," a faint voice called back, "in the studio."

Hannah found him standing before the window that looked toward the main house, the weak winter light playing up the bleakness in his pale eyes.

"I can't believe he's gone," he said, not looking at her.

"Neither can I." Hannah rubbed her arms. "Isn't it ironic that Reiver died the same way as Abigail?"

He stared straight ahead. "The daughter he could never love."

"I like to think that he redeemed himself by saving Lizzie."

"Perhaps that's why he went in after her."

"He had to. She was his daughter."

Samuel turned. "And how are you, Hannah? With the funeral, and people surrounding you every waking minute, I haven't had a chance to be alone with you."

Hannah crossed her arms. "I'm still numb inside from the shock. Reiver and I may have had a stormy marriage, but now that he's dead, I find that I miss him." She smiled wanly. "Odd, isn't it?"

"No, not at all." Samuel stood there quietly for a moment. "Reiver's death is going to cause so much change in your life."

"It's still too soon for me to even think about it."

His pale eyes regarded her somberly. "Do you know what my first thought was this morning? That now you and I are finally free to be together. Then this terrible feeling of guilt overpowered me, and I wept for my brother."

Hannah went to him and placed a hand on his shoulder. "I've had the same thoughts, but it's still too soon. We have to finish grieving for Reiver before we can start thinking about spending the rest of our lives together."

Samuel hugged her. "You're right." Then he extended his arm and escorted her out of the studio. "I think the time is right for me to go to Washington and make another bid for a higher tariff."

The mill . . . how it eased her pain and fortified her.

"But there's a war going on."

Samuel's eyes shone. "Exactly. The government needs money desperately to pay for it. Well, we manufacturers are going to tell the government that we can't afford to pay unless we receive protection from foreign competition in the form of war duties."

The mill is getting into his blood, too, Hannah thought.

When they reached the dining room, Samuel searched through his papers. "You've heard of the Cobden Treaty?"

"That was the treaty enacted last year allowing French silks to be sold in England duty-free."

He nodded. "Mark my words, that treaty sounded the death knell for the English silk industry, but it's only going to help us." Samuel stuck his hand in his pocket. "You're going to see an influx of skilled English weavers into this country, and when those English manufacturers fail, don't be surprised to see their machinery on the market."

Hannah caught his excitement. "We would be able to buy ready-made looms to make silk cloth and jacquards."

"For a very low price."

"When do you leave for Washington?"

"Tomorrow." Samuel hesitated. "I feel odd going so soon after Reiver's death. It seems disrespectful somehow."

Hannah shook her head. "Reiver wanted this tariff as much as you do. You must go."

● ● ●

Two weeks after Samuel's departure, Hannah was in the study doing accounts when Benjamin appeared in the doorway.

"Mother, I have to speak with you." With his head lowered belligerently in imitation of his father, Benjamin strode into the study, closed the door behind him, and stood facing Hannah with his hands clasped behind his back.

Hannah put down her pen. "What is it?"

"I want you to give me the controlling interest in Shaw Silks."

Dumbfounded, Hannah stared at him.

Benjamin's blue eyes flashed with anger. "Father told me how you tricked him out of the company."

Hannah tried to maintain her composure, but she couldn't control her trembling hands. "I did not trick your father out of anything. We made a bargain fair and square."

"You call that a bargain, Mother? That was no bargain. You swindled him!"

Shaking with fury, Hannah rose. "Don't you ever raise your voice to me, Benjamin Shaw! Your father had an illegitimate daughter by his longtime mistress, and then he expected me to raise that child as if she were my own."

"Any man would. She was his daughter. A good wife would have done anything to please her husband without asking anything in return."

"You know nothing about it, so don't presume to judge me."

Benjamin placed his hands on the desk and leaned forward. "All I know is that Father was stunned you could take advantage of his weakness to gain control of his company. His company, Mother!"

"And what about me? Did your father concern himself with how I would feel, forced to raise his mistress's child?"

He stood back and dismissed her with, "You love Lizzie, so why would it matter?"

Hannah took several deep breaths. "It's pointless arguing with you, Benjamin, since you've already taken your father's side and refuse to consider my point of view."

"Father would have wanted me to have the company. I'm his eldest son, and he taught me a great deal about silk manufacturing when we went to the Orient together."

"You're still very young."

"I'm twenty!"

"Your father was twenty-five when he started the company."

Ben glared at her. "You're a woman. Women don't run silk mills."

"Well, this woman does, and quite capably despite the handicaps of my sex." Which were mostly ignorant men.

He clenched his hands into fists. "I want my birthright, Mother. Are you going to give it to me, or not?"

"No. You're too young and you don't know enough about this company to do your father's memory justice."

"Then I'm enlisting in the army."

Hannah's heart gave a sickening lurch, and she stared at him, stunned. "The army?"

"If you're going to cheat me out of what's rightfully mine, I may as well seek a military career."

Hannah thought of poor Artemus blown to pieces by cannon fire at Bull Run, and her blood ran cold, but when she saw her son's sly, expectant look, she realized he was probably bluffing. "Do what you must, Benjamin," she said.

He glared at her before turning on his heel and storming out of the study, leaving Hannah staring at the open door.

Later, when her thoughts returned to some semblance of order, Hannah realized that Benjamin hadn't said anything about her affair with his uncle Samuel. If he had known, he certainly would have thrown it in her face.

Reiver must never have told him.

Blackmail. Hannah's son was blackmailing her. If she didn't agree to turn over controlling interest in the company to him, he would enlist in the army and risk death.

Several days after Benjamin delivered his ultimatum, Hannah bundled herself up and walked over to the mill, where she stood until her feet were so cold, she thought she might get frostbite.

He was her son. She had a mother's responsibility to keep him safe. And why shouldn't he have his birthright? Reiver intended for his sons to have Shaw Silks one day.

Yet the company was part of Hannah, too. She had made it what it was today just as much as Reiver had. People depended on her for their livelihoods and she had a responsibility to pro-

vide them with decent working and living conditions. Why
should she turn it over to Benjamin just because he wanted it,
like some toy he insisted on having?

Hannah prayed Benjamin's childish threat was nothing more
than a bluff to pressure her. If it wasn't, she would lose her son
forever.

Two days later Hannah made her decision.

She couldn't risk losing Benjamin. Despite her reservations
she would agree to turn over controlling interest in Shaw
Silks.

She was leaving the study to find him when the front door
suddenly opened, and Samuel walked in.

Just one look at his face told Hannah all she needed to know.
Grinning, she ran down the hallway into his open arms. "We
won!"

He swung her around and around. "We got it." He set her
down. "Do you know what this means, Hannah? We can make
silk cloth to rival the best of France and Italy. We can make
American silk manufacturers the envy of the world!"

Hannah hugged him again. "Congratulations, Sam. This is
wonderful news."

It didn't make her decision any easier.

After Samuel left, Hannah called Benjamin into the study.

"Well, Mother?" he demanded, flopping down on the settee
with studied insolence. "Are you going to choose the mill, or
me?"

Hannah folded her hands on her desk. "Before we discuss my
decision, there's something else I have to tell you." And she
told Benjamin all about his uncle's efforts to have the import
duty raised. "Do you know the ramifications of this legislation?"

Benjamin shrugged, his boredom evident. "We'll make more
money."

Hannah rose. "Yes, we'll make more money, but you don't
know how, do you? Or why? Your father would have known,
and so do I." She smiled sadly. "I must admit that in a moment
of weakness, I considered giving in to your demands, but I decided against it. You're too inexperienced."

He turned livid, his scar standing out in an angry slash across his cheek, and he jumped to his feet. "You selfish—"

"Bitch?" his mother finished for him. Hannah raised her head proudly. "Yes, Benjamin, this time I am going to be a selfish bitch. I'm going to do what I want, not what someone else expects me to do. I married your father because my uncle wanted me to, but I am going to keep control of Shaw Silks because I want to. I know I can make it the success Reiver dreamed of."

"Fine," he snapped, "keep your precious company. I'm leaving tomorrow to enlist, and when I die, it will be your fault!"

"If you want to be childish, then I can't stop you. There will always be a place for you here, if you should ever decide to come back."

"I won't."

"Godspeed, then. Be careful." *And always remember that I love you no matter how much you hurt me.*

He left without a backward glance.

Hannah stood at the study window, watching Benjamin shake hands with Davey before boarding the stagecoach.

"You did the right thing," Samuel said, wrapping his arms around her and drawing her close. "Turning the mill over to Ben would have been disastrous."

Hannah nestled against him and tried to keep from crying. "In my mind I know that to be true, but in my mother's heart . . ."

"He's a grown man, Hannah, and he's been acting worse than a two-year-old. He had no right to blackmail you. Besides, he chose to go. He could have stayed."

"Still, I feel as though I'm sending him to his death."

"No, you've made a man of him in ways that matter." He turned her around to face him. "Hannah, you have a responsibility to your workers, too. With someone as inexperienced as Ben running the company, what would their futures be?"

She sighed. "You're right."

"And you know he wouldn't take your advice if you tried to help him."

"I'm sure he wouldn't. He'd be just as bullheaded as his father and want to do things his way whether they were right or not."

Samuel traced the curve of her jaw with his finger. "Now that you're a widow, and your children—with the exception of Lizzie—no longer need you, will you finally marry me?"

"Yes, Samuel Shaw, I'll finally marry you."

Her eyes filled with tears, but this time they were tears of joy.

EPILOGUE

THEY had dubbed Coldwater "Silk Town."

I never dreamed I'd live to see it, Hannah thought, leaning heavily on her silver-headed cane and surveying her kingdom from the top of Mulberry Hill.

She never thought she'd live to see the turn of the century, either, but here she was, an old lady of seventy-eight getting ready to attend the wedding of Lizzie's youngest daughter on June 7, 1900.

Her eyes misted over with pride as she counted eleven long red brick buildings housing Shaw Silks. These days they didn't make thread or ribbon but elaborate silk jacquards and velvets that surpassed any in the world. Not only did Shaw Silks have a sales office in New York City, but also in Chicago, to keep up with all their orders.

Hannah walked slowly across the crest of Mulberry Hill. Passersby tipped their hats and nodded respectfully at the familiar figure always dressed in pale blue Shaw silk, with her serene wrinkled face and snow-white hair always arranged in a chignon at the nape of her neck.

She stopped to talk to several of the workers' children who were playing in the front yard of the house their parents owned thanks to low mortgages funded by their employer. Throughout the years, when many factory owners throughout New England were exploiting their workers for their own gain, Hannah held fast to her belief that workers should be well paid and treated decently, even if it kept their employer from becoming too rich. As a result, though the workers came from Ireland, England,

Scandinavia, and Poland now, generation after generation went to work for Shaw Silks.

Feeling too tired too quickly, Hannah said good-bye to the children and made her way back to Mulberry Hill. Now five mansions surrounded by great oaks lined its crest, two of them designed by the famous architect Stanford White, a close friend of Davey, who was now president of the company his father founded. Benjamin, who had survived the Civil War intact to become the family's lawyer, lived in one of them with his wife and four of his six children. James had given up the Bickford farm and moved into one of the mansions when his beloved Georgia died of tuberculosis. He had never fixed another loom again and died in his sleep a year ago, clutching a faded lock of his wife's ginger hair. All of his ten children were scattered across the United States as if they found the close Shaw family ties their parents' treasured unbearably stifling.

Hannah stopped at the main house and looked down toward the homestead. She watched as a man came out and sauntered off toward the mill, his carriage and stride so familiar to her. For a moment she thought it was Samuel coming for her at long last, and her heart sang with happiness. Then she realized that it couldn't be: her beloved husband had died in her arms of a heart attack fifteen years ago.

"But it won't be long now, my love," she said to herself. "Be patient."

"Aunt Hannah?"

She turned her tired old bones slowly to see Lizzie coming toward her, the morning sun glistening on her thick, chestnut hair, and for a moment Hannah sensed Cecelia's presence so profoundly, it took her breath away. Years ago, when Hannah had finally told Lizzie the truth of her parentage, she feared the girl would feel so betrayed that she would leave the Shaw fold for good. But she didn't, to Hannah's everlasting joy.

Lizzie drew Hannah's thin, freckled arm through her own and held it securely. "My Hannah Elisabeth is getting ready to leave for the church. She wanted to make sure you came with us."

"Humph. I don't know if I trust the groom's newfangled motorcar. A horse and carriage were good enough for me." Was it her imagination, or was she beginning to sound as cantankerous as Mrs. Hardy?

Hannah looked back toward the homestead. The man was gone.

Soon she would be gone, too, but Shaw Silks would remain.

Hannah had succeeded and made a fortune. Now everyone in Coldwater said, "What else could you expect of Reiver Shaw's wife?"